Highest Praise for Candice Fox and Her Archer and Bennett Thrillers

HADES

WINNER OF THE NED KELLY AWARD
FOR BEST FIRST FICTION

"Horrors abound in Australian author Fox's first novel, a gritty police procedural set in Sydney. In this twisted noir world, love goes as wrong as it can go. Readers will look forward to the sequel set in this not-for-the-squeamish nightmare world Down Under."
—*Publishers Weekly*

"The comparisons to Jeff Lindsay's 'Dexter' series will be unavoidable, but this fast-paced first novel, with its unusual protagonists and dark, disturbing scenes, stands on its own. Readers will anticipate eagerly the planned sequel."
—*Library Journal*

"Compelling . . . Candice Fox makes a strong debut with the first thriller in a series about a serial killer. Exploring the concept of whether killing for justice could ever be rationalized, *Hades* is a chilling read."
—*Sydney Morning Herald*

ALSO BY CANDICE FOX

Hades

Eden

FALL

AN ARCHER AND BENNETT THRILLER

CANDICE FOX

PINNACLE BOOKS
Kensington Publishing Corp.
www.kensingtonbooks.com

PINNACLE BOOKS are published by

Kensington Publishing Corp.
119 West 40th Street
New York, NY 10018

All Kensington titles, imprints, and distributed lines are available at special quantity discounts for bulk purchases for sales promotions, premiums, fund-raising, educational, or institutional use. Special book excerpts or customized printings can also be created to fit specific needs. For details, write or phone the office of the Kensington sales manager: Kensington Publishing Corp., 119 West 40th Street, New York, NY 10018, attn: Sales Department; phone 1-800-221-2647.

ISBN-13: 978-0-7860-3998-2
ISBN-10: 0-7860-3998-1

First printing: September 2017

10 9 8 7 6 5 4 3 2 1

Printed in the United States of America

First electronic edition: September 2017

ISBN-13: 978-0-7860-4065-0
ISBN-10: 0-7860-4065-3

For Danny, Adam, and Jess

Before the blood, before the screaming, the only sound that reached the parking lot of the Black Mutt Inn was the murmur of the jukebox inside. It was set on autoplay, tumbling out the cheerful lineup of greatest hits, but there were none of the sing-alongs of usual pubs, no thrusting of glasses, no stomping of heels on the reeking carpet. The jukebox played in the stale emptiness of the building, and by the time the music reached the parking lot it was no more than a ghoulish moan. It was windy out there, and the stars were gone.

The Black Mutt Inn attracted bad men and had been doing so for as long as anyone could remember. Nightly, a bone was broken on its shadowy back porch over some insult, or a promise was made beneath the moth-crowded lamps for some violence that would come on another night. Sometimes a plot was hatched; the corners of the bar's undecorated interior were good for whispering, and the walls seemed to grow poisonous ideas like vines, spreading and creeping around minds and down necks and along legs, to the rotting floorboards.

On this night, Sunny Burke and Clara McKinnie entered the Black Mutt with their laptops and bags of chili jerky and bright suntanned smiles. The man behind the counter said nothing, saw nothing—he just served the drinks.

Sunny and Clara walked to the counter and set up shop under the mirrors. Against the wall, three men sat whispering. At the pool tables, another two stood looking through the shadows at the two travelers fresh from Byron, stamped with its optimism and cheap weed stink. Clara ordered a champagne and orange juice, and downed it quickly. Sunny sat nursing a James Squire.

Into the dim halo of light stepped a man from the pool tables.

"G'day, mate," the man said, thumping Sunny between the shoulder blades. The man was tall and square and roped with veins, and the two hands hanging from his extra-long arms looked all-encompassing. Sunny looked up, appreciated the density of the man's beard, and smiled.

"Hey."

"Just down from Byron, are we?"

"We've been there a week," Clara said, beaming.

"I can see." The man brushed the backs of his fingers against the top of Clara's shoulder, a brief brotherly pat. "Sun's had its way with you, beauty!"

"We're just on our way back to the Big Smoke," Sunny said.

"If you ask me, you've just come *from* the big smoke," the stranger jibed and nudged Sunny in the ribs, hard. "Tell me you've got some grass for sale. Please, tell me!"

Sunny laughed. "Sure, mate." He glanced at the other figure in the shadows, the man by the table leaning on his cue. "No problem."

The stranger threw out a hand and Sunny gripped it, felt its calluses against his palm. "No probs, no probs. How much are you after?"

"Aw, we'll do all that later. Hamish is the name, mate. Can I invite you to a game?"

"Yeah! Shit, yeah. This is Clara. I'm Sunny."

"Me mate over there's Braaaadley, but don't you worry 'bout him. He don't talk much. Plays a rubbish game of pool, too, don't you, Brad? Aye? Wake up, shithead!" the man squawked back toward the pool table, but roused nothing in his partner. "Excuse me, miss, but me old Bradley's prone to leaning on that pool cue till he drifts off and no amount of slapping can get him back, if you know what I mean."

"Right," she laughed.

They racked the balls while Clara and the silent one watched, now and then letting their eyes drift to each other, the hairy man in the dark struggling beneath the weight of his frown, the young woman swinging her hips, holding on to the cue. She finished the champagne and wanted another, but the men were talking and laughing and making friends, and Sunny had always had trouble making friends, so she didn't interrupt.

"How about a little wager, just to make things interesting?" Hamish asked.

"Yeah, sure." Sunny puffed out his chest, ignored a warning look from Clara. "Where do you . . . ? I mean. What do you usually . . . ?"

"Five bucks?"

Sunny laughed. "Sure, mate, sounds great."

They played. Clara was the most excitable of them all, howling when she sunk the white ball, cheering when Sunny scored. There was plenty of kissing, rubbing of backsides. The men in the booths watched them. The happy group at the table were cut off from the rest of the world by the cone of light that fell upon them.

"Very good, young sir," Hamish said, offering his big hard hand again. "How about another?"

"Twenty bucks this time," Sunny said. "You can pay me in labor, if you like. The van needs a wash."

"Sunny!" Clara gasped.

"Listen to this guy, would you?" Hamish laughed, squeezed the young woman on the shoulder, and made Clara's face burn red. "What a cocky little shit. You're lucky you're so goddamn beautiful, Sunny, me old mate. No one's gonna knock that gorgeous block off no matter whatcha say."

They laughed and played again. Hamish was hard on Bradley. The balls cracked and crashed and rolled into the pockets. Clara was good. Her daddy had taught her the game young, bent over the felt, his hips pinning her against the side of the table. But she knew when to sacrifice a shot so that she didn't lean over too far and give Bradley a view of her breasts, her ass. The man looked at her funny.

"One more?" Sunny said. The bar was empty now but for the bartender, who was motionless in the shadows. Sunny won, and won again.

"One more, little matey, and then it's off to bed with you. What say you we make it interesting, eh? Everything you've won, you give me the chance to win it back. We go even. I lose, you take the notes right outta my hand, no hard feelings."

"Mate," Sunny drawled, "you win this and I'll give you double what you owe me."

"Sunny!"

"Oh ho! Just listen to this guy!" Hamish laughed.

"Sunny, no!"

"Cla." The boy drew her close. "They haven't won a game all night. It's fine. I'm just having a laugh."

"Sunny—"

"Just shut up, would you?" Sunny snapped. "I'm only having a bit of fucking fun."

Clara watched the men shake hands, rack the balls. Hamish leaned down, took aim, and began sinking balls.

The table was empty of Hamish's balls in less than two minutes. Then he sunk the eight ball in a single shot. Sunny never got a turn.

"Mate," Hamish said when it was done, straightening and leaning on his cue, the smile and the charm and the humor forgotten. "Seems you owe me quite a bit of cash."

In the parking lot, Bradley walked behind them, keeping watch now and then toward the Black Mutt, although no such careful eye was needed. A hidden hole drilled straight to hell warmed the air as it breezed across the asphalt and ruffled Clara's thick, dark curls. Hamish's hand on the back of her neck was like a steel clamp. They approached the Volkswagen van, the only vehicle in the lot, parked out in the middle of a huge barren wasteland so that the young couple would be safe from whatever might be lurking in the towering wall of dark woods around the bar when they returned. Clara put her hands out to stop Hamish from slamming her into the side of the van, and turned. Bradley had let a steel pipe slide down from where it was hidden high up inside his sleeve.

"Give me an inventory," Hamish said.

"There's the CD player, some cash, and Clara has some jewelry," Sunny was saying, fumbling with his keys. "There's the hash, too. You can take it. Please, please, I'm asking you now not to hurt us."

"You go ahead and ask whatever you like, you snotty-nosed little prick," Hamish said. "You bring out whatever you can from in there and we'll see if it's enough. If it's not, I'll decide if anyone gets hurt."

"Take 'em up to the ATM," Bradley grunted. Clara jolted at the sound of the silent man's voice. She turned and found him staring at her, eyes pinpoints of light in the dark.

"Sunny," Clara croaked, tried to ease words from her swollen throat. "Sunny. Sunny!"

"Shut up, and hurry," Hamish snarled.

"I'm going. Please. Please!" Sunny was pleading with anyone now. Clara heard the pleas continuing inside the van, heard the rattling of boxes and drawers. As soon as the boy was out of sight, she felt the man with the concrete hands slip his fingers beneath her skirt. Hamish smiled at her with his big cracked teeth and pressed her against the van.

"All this excitement getting you wet, is it, baby?"

"Sunny! God! Please!"

"Your pretty boyfriend better come up with something very special, very soon, babycakes, or I'm afraid you're footing the bill."

"How about this?" Sunny said as he emerged from the van, hands full, thrusting the items at Hamish. "Will this do?"

The knife made Hamish stiffen, made his eyes widen as they dropped to the items in Sunny's hands, which all fell away and clattered to the ground, revealing the leather handle they concealed, the leather handle attached to the long hunting blade that was now buried deep in Hamish's belly. Sunny, as always, didn't give the man a chance to appreciate the surprise of the attack but pulled the knife out of his stomach and plunged it in again, pushed it upward into the tenderness of Hamish's diaphragm and felt the familiar clench of shocked muscles.

Clara slid away as the young man went for a third blow, took her own knife, the one she kept flush against her body between her breasts, and went for Bradley. The hairy man backed away, but Clara's aim was immaculate. She set her feet, pulled back, breathed, swung, and let go. The knife embedded in Bradley's back with a *thunk* between the shoulder blades. The man fell and rolled like roadkill on the tarmac.

She went to the silent man and pulled out the knife, wiping it on the hem of her soft white skirt. Bradley was still alive, and she was happy, because it would be a long time until she was finished with him. Clara liked to play, and though it wasn't Sunny's thing, she thought maybe because they were on holiday he would indulge her just once with some games. She turned. Bradley was still gurgling against the asphalt under his cheek.

"Baby." She turned on her sweet voice for her killer partner. "What if we took this one home and—"

A whistle, and a *shlunk*.

At first it seemed to Clara that Sunny had tripped, until she felt the wet spray of his blood on her face. She tried to process the noise she'd heard, but none of it made sense. She crawled, shaking, and with her hands tried to piece back together the split halves of her boyfriend's skull, grabbed at the bits of brain and meat sprayed across the asphalt around him. She knelt in the blood, both his and Hamish's, little whimpers coming out of her like coughs. Hamish was sitting up beside the van, his hands still gripping at the knife wounds in his belly.

A whistle, and a *shlunk*, and the top of his head came off. He slid to the ground.

Clara looked around at the tree line behind her, a hundred yards or so away, and then at the trees in front, the same distance, dark as ink and depthless. The silence rung. Under its terrifying weight she crawled, tried to get to her feet, heading toward the bar. Another whistle, another *shlunk*, and her foot was gone. Clara fell on her face and gripped at the stump of her leg. She didn't scream or cry out, because there was only terror in her, and terror made no sound.

Clara lay and breathed, breathed, and after some time began crawling again. She heard the sound of uneven footsteps, punctuated by a metallic *clop*, and looked up to see a figure coming toward her, barely distinguishable against the dark of the trees. The sounds kept coming out of her, the shuddering breaths through her lips. The metallic clopping kept coming, and as the woman emerged into the light from the van, Clara could see she was leaning on an enormous rifle, using the gun like a crutch.

The woman stepped between the bodies of the men, and Clara lay in the blood and looked up at her. She thought, even as shock began to take her, about the woman's black hair, how it seemed to steal some blue out of the night and hold it, like the shimmer woven through the feather of a crow. The woman with the gun bent down used the enormous weapon to lower herself into a crouch, and Clara wondered what wounds gave the other killer such trouble.

Eden looked at the trees, the bar, the girl on the ground.

"Just when you think you're the deadliest fish in the water," Eden said to the girl.

Clara gasped. Her fingers fumbled at the wet stump where her foot had been. Eden sighed.

"I admire the game," Eden said. "I really do. It's clever. Two naïve travelers just waiting to be picked on. You flounder around like you're drowning in your own idiocy, and you see which predators come to investigate. Who could resist you? You're adorable. You lure them out into the deep, dark waters and then you surge up from below. Pull them down."

Clara fell back against the asphalt, her mouth sucking at the cold night air.

"If I were well, this would have been more personal," Eden said, her leather-gloved hand gripping the rifle tight. "But I haven't been at my best lately, so I'm afraid there's no time for play."

Clara couldn't force words up through the whimpers. They came out of her like hiccups. The woman with the long dark hair rose up, pushing the rifle into the ground. When she'd risen fully, she actioned the great thing with effort, hands once strong betraying her as the bullet slid into the chamber.

"I'm the only shark in this tank," Eden said.

The last gunshot could be heard inside the Black Mutt Inn. But no one listened to it.

The Victims of Crime support group of Surry Hills meets every fortnight. The only reason I started going was because my old friend from North Sydney Homicide, Anthony Charters, goes there. If I hadn't had a friend there, I'd have never bowed to my girlfriend Imogen's demands that I get counseling for the "stuff that had been going on with me" the last few months.

That vague collection of terms, the "stuff" and its propensity to "go on with me," had come between the beautiful psychologist and me in our first few weeks of dating, when she realized she'd never seen me sober. She said she couldn't imagine me "relaxed." Privately, I argued I was a lot more relaxed a person than Imogen herself. Imogen takes an hour and a half to get ready in the morning, and the first time I farted near her, she just about called the police. That, ladies and gentlemen, is not "relaxed."

But, you know. You don't tell them these things. They don't listen.

Imogen liked me, but I was an unpredictable, volatile, and difficult-to-manage boyfriend. She couldn't count on me to turn up on time, say appropriate things when I met her friends, drive her places without her having to worry that I was about to career the car into the nearest telephone pole. She couldn't be sure when I ducked out of the cinema that I wasn't going to down six painkillers in the glorious solitude of the men's-room stall, or that I wasn't going to lose myself in thought and just wander off, turn up back at her apartment at midnight drunk and stinking. I was a bad beau, but I had potential, so she didn't give up on me.

Imogen took me on, and Imogen started nagging me to get help. So, I started trudging, with all the huffing melancholy of a teenager at church, to a basement room of the Surry Hills police station every Sunday to sit under the fluorescent lights and listen to tales of horror and fear. It made Imogen happy. It made Anthony happy. I considered it my community service.

Somewhere, sometime, somebody set up a support group in a particular way and now all support groups are set up like that, whether you're trying to get over being sexually assaulted in a public toilet or you're addicted to crack. You've got the gray plastic folding table pushed against one wall, the veneer pulling away from the corners and the top stained by coffee cups set down, midconversation, to indicate concern. You've got the two large steel urns full of boiling water for coffee and tea. If you go anywhere near them, even to fill your name in on the sign-in sheet, they will burn some part of you. There's no avoiding the coffee-urn burn. To this you add a collection of uncomfortable plastic folding chairs forming a circle just tight enough to inspire that quiet kind of social terror triggered by things like accidental knee-touching, airborne germs, unavoidable eye contact . . . and *voilà*! You've got a support group.

There were fifteen chairs set out tonight on the industrial gray carpet. Anthony was sitting in one when I arrived. I responded to his presence with a wave of paralyzing nausea. Getting over a painkiller-and-alcohol addiction makes you respond to everything with nausea. You get nausea in the middle of sex. It lasts for months.

I'd worked with the bald-headed, cleft-chinned Detective Charters and his partner for about two weeks after my former partner committed suicide and the bigwigs were trying to find me someone else as a playmate. I'd have liked to have stayed with him. He was inspiring; somehow still enthusiastic about justice and the rule of law and collaring crooks like it was a calling, even though his own seventeen-year-old son was in prison for five years for accidentally leaving a mate with brain damage from a one-punch hit at a New Year's Eve party. If Anthony could keep on keeping on after everything that had happened to him, maybe I could get over all the women I'd failed in my life.

Anthony had been powerless to save his own son. And yet here he was, smiling at me as I came to sit by his side. Maybe being powerless was okay.

When I'd asked him, Anthony had put his unshakable spirit down to the support groups. He attended one for drug addiction, one for victims of crime, and one for anxiety. I thought I'd give it a whirl. It would shut Imogen up.

"Francis," he said. I cradled my coffee and licked my scalded pinkie.

"Anthony."

"How's the come-down?"

"I think I'm past the shakes." I held out my hand for him to see, flat in the air before us. My thumb was twitching. "I'd still murder you for a Scotch, though, old mate."

"I reckon Scotch might be on your trigger-words list, mate."

"Probably. It's a big list."

Some recovery groups don't let you say particular words, "trigger words," because the level of addiction some people are getting over is so great that even the sound of the name of their drug can send them into a relapse spiral. Even if you're not an addict, but you're in a support group parallel to addiction groups, like Victims of Crime, or After Domestic Violence, or Incest Survivors, you have to acknowledge that some members of the group might also be enrolled in addiction groups, so, for their benefit, you don't say the words.

The first step of Drug Recovery Group is that you do not talk about Drugs at Recovery Group.

It sounded like bullshit to me. I wasn't sure all the tiptoeing around helped anyone. I'd tested my trigger-happiness, said "oxycodone" loud and slow alone in my car, like a little kid whispering the S-word at the back of class. I had not gone and started popping pills. But I was a rule-follower by nature, so I didn't say "oxycodone" in or anywhere near the meetings I attended. I didn't say "Scotch," or "bourbon," or "cocaine," or "ecstasy," or "Valium"—all guilty pleasures of mine at some time over the previous months. I'd mentioned that I had a variety of "drugs of choice" at my first meeting when I introduced myself, but I hadn't shared anything since.

In fact, I hadn't said anything else. Imogen had told me to "go" to the meetings. She hadn't told me to "participate."

People stopped milling around the treacherous urns

when the facilitator, a hard-edged little blonde named Megan, came into the room with her large folder of notes and handouts. I had about twenty-five of her photocopied handouts in the bottom of my car, boot-printed and crumpled, hidden in a forest of take-out containers and paper bags. The handout titles peered at me from beneath old newspapers and cardboard boxes. *Six Ways to Beat Negative Thoughts. How to Tell Your Friends You're in Danger of Self-Harm. When "No" Means "No."* Sometime after the first meeting, I'd lost my eight-step grief diary. I hadn't even put my name on it.

Diaries are for little girls.

When Megan was in place, the people around me joined in the opening mantra in a badly timed monotone reminiscent of the obligatory "good morning" we used to give our teacher in my primary school.

"I am on my way to a place beyond vengeance, a place beyond anger, a place beyond fear. I am on my way to a place of healing, and I take a new step every day."

I didn't recite the Victims of Crime mantra. It was way too cuddly for me.

"We've got a couple of new members with us tonight," Megan told the group, as Justin, the group kiss-ass, brought her a paper cup of green tea. Justin had been gay-bashed to within an inch of his life on Mardi Gras night when he was twenty-one. Victims of Crime was his life. "This is Aamir and Reema."

The Muslim couple next to me nodded. Reema was looking deep into her empty paper cup as if she'd found a window out of the room. I was jealous. She ad-

justed the shoulders of her dress, and her husband sat
forward in his seat, a big man, his hands clasped between his knees.

"Hi, Aamir," everyone said. "Hi, Reema."

"Now you don't *have* to share," Megan assured
them. "No one has to share in these groups. Sometimes
it can be healing just to listen to the stories from those
around us and to recognize that the trauma we have experienced in the wake of serious crime is not unique,
and neither is the journey to wellness."

"We don't mind sharing," Aamir said. I could see
the anger, tight in his shoulders and jaw. You get to
know the look of a man on the edge of punching someone when you're a young cop wandering between
groups of the homeless in the Cross, Blacktown, or
Parramatta. Bopping around the clubs on George
Street while groups of men hoot and holler at ladies in
cars. It becomes like a flag.

"Well, good," Megan smiled, "that's great. Like I
said—there's no pressure. Some of our members have
never shared." She glanced at me. I felt nauseous.
"This is a supportive environment where we have in
place attendee-centric mechanisms—"

"I'll share." Aamir stood up and moved to the center
of the group. No one bothered telling the big man that
standing wasn't part of the group dynamic—that in
fact it intimidated some of the rape survivors. He
rubbed his hands up and down the front of his polo
shirt, restless, leaving light sweat stains. "I'll start by
asking if anyone here in the group knows me. If you
know my wife."

It was great. I hadn't felt anything but nausea and

boredom in the group in all the sessions I'd attended, so this was a novel start to the night. The group members looked at each other. Looked at Aamir.

"No? You don't know me? You've never seen me before?" Aamir's stark black eyebrows were high on his sweating brow. He did a little half-turn, as though someone might recognize his back, the little tendrils of black hair curling on the nape of his thick neck. His wife wiped her face with her hand. No one spoke. Anthony examined the man's face.

"I don't think they underst—" Megan chanced.

"My son Ehan was abducted one hundred and forty-one days ago," Aamir said. He returned to his chair and sat down. "One hundred and forty-one days ago, two men in a blue car took my eight-year-old son from a bus stop on Prairie Vale Road, Wetherill Park. He has not been seen since."

He paused. We all waited.

"You don't know me, or my wife, because there has been little to no coverage of this abduction in the media. We've had *one* nationally televised press conference and *one* newspaper feature article. That's it."

Aamir was a lion wrapped in a man. The woman across the circle from him, who'd been in a bank holdup and now suffered panic attacks, was cowering in her seat, pulling at her ponytail. Megan opened her mouth to offer something, but Aamir raged on.

"If Ehan was a little blond-haired white boy named Ian and we lived in Potts Point, we'd be all over the national news."

"Oh, um." Megan looked at me for help. I said nothing as Aamir went on.

"We'd have a two-hundred-thousand-dollar reward

and Dick Smith flying a fucking banner from a fucking blimp somewhere. But we've had nothing. Two days the phone rang off the hook, and then silence. I forget sometimes that he's gone. Every night at eight o'clock, no matter where I am, no matter what I'm doing, I think, 'It's Ehan's bedtime. I have to go say good night.'"

Megan widened her eyes at me.

"What are you looking at me for?" I said. The sickness swirled in me.

"Oh! I wasn't!" Megan snapped her head back to Aamir. "I wasn't. Sorry, Frank, I was just thinking and you were in my line of sight and—"

"Are you a journalist?" Aamir turned on me. I didn't know how I'd been brought into the exchange until Megan buried her face in her notebook.

"No." I looked at Aamir. "I'm not a journalist. My girlfriend was murdered. I'm the only other person in the group who's here for murder-victim support. That's why she's staring at me. She wants me to say something hopeful to you."

"Our son wasn't murdered," Reema said.

"Well, Megan sure seems to think he was."

"I never said that!" Megan gasped.

"Your girlfriend was murdered." Aamir hovered, legs bent, inches from me. His huge black eyes were locked on mine. He knew his son was dead. And he was angry.

"She was murdered. Yes," I said.

"What was her name?"

"Martina."

"And what happened after she was murdered?" Aamir asked.

"What do you mean?"

"What happened?" he insisted. "What happened then?"

"Nothing," I shrugged. Everyone was looking at me. I licked my lips. "She was murdered. She's gone. There's nothing . . . *afterward,* if that's what you mean."

Aamir watched me. We could have been the only people in the room.

"Nothing happens afterward," I said. "There's no . . . resolution. You go to work. You come home. You come to these groups and you," I gestured to the coffee machine, "you drink coffee. You say the mantra. There's no *afterward.*"

Everyone looked at Megan to deny or confirm my assessment. She opened her folder, shuffled the papers, and collected her thoughts. One of the urns started reboiling itself in the taut seconds of silence. I heard the spitting of its droplets on the plastic table top.

"Let's look at some handouts," Megan said.

Anthony was waiting for me by the vending machine after the meeting. We walked up the stairs and onto the street.

"That was a bit harsh," he said.

"What?"

"The whole 'there's no afterward' thing."

"Reality is often harsh," I said. We paused to watch Aamir and Reema walking to their car. The big angry man glanced back at me as he opened the passenger-side door for his wife, and his expression was unreadable. The rage was gone, replaced by something else. His shoulders were inches lower. I didn't know what had taken over the boiling-hot fury that I'd seen in the meeting room, but whatever it was, it was cold.

"Do you really believe that?" Anthony asked me. "That it means nothing?"

"Yes," I said, "I do. You don't get over it. You don't realize the mystical fucking meaning in it. You don't accept that it, like everything, *happens for a reason.* Come on, Tone," I scoffed at him. He exhaled smoke from his cigarette.

"Every night at eight o'clock that guy tries to say good night to his dead kid." I nodded at Aamir's car as it pulled into the street. "And he'll be doing it until the day he dies."

She always felt better when night was falling. The darkness folded over her like a blanket, protective. Light had never been a friend to Tara. It seemed to fall on all of her at once, to wriggle into her creases and folds and dance around her curves, to expose her every surface. There had always been plenty of surface to Tara. She'd never been able to keep track of all there was of her. Joanie was always handy to point out to her the parts she'd forgotten, those bulges and bubbles and handles of flesh that slipped and slid from under hems and over belts.

Pull your shirt down, Tara. Pull your pants up, Tara. Pull your sleeves down, Tara. Jesus. Everyone can see you.

Everyone can see you.

She'd sit at the dinner table and Joanie would grab and pinch and twist a slab of flesh she didn't know was exposed, a roll above her jeans or the tender white flesh of the backs of her arms. You couldn't cover Tara with a tent, Joanie said. She could feed an African village. Getting downstairs to dinner became a journey she couldn't make, so she began to take her meals up in her attic bedroom, staring at the park, the runners going round and round between the trees. Sometimes getting from the bed to the computer was too much. Tara lay between the sheets and dreamed about African people cutting her up and sharing her, carving down her thighs in neat slices like a Christmas ham, until there was only bone—gorgeous, strong, light bone. Bone that shone, redemptive and clean.

The girls at school had giggled at her bulges, the blue bruises that peppered them. Though decades had passed, their voices still bumped and butted around the attic room, floating red balloons of hatred.

Why do you call your mum "Joanie," Tara? Doesn't she love you?

Tonight Tara stood by the windows looking over the park and watched the night falling, the bats rising, and remembered her mother. Tara could still hear her voice sometimes, her footsteps in the hall as she readied herself for some party or dinner or charity function, as she pulled on her silk-lined coat and checked herself in the hall mirror. Joanie, with her elegant ash-blond hair falling in filigree curls.

In time, all the light of the warm day dissipated, replaced by a wonderful darkness. Tara watched the runners in Centennial Park recede into shadows, only blinking lights indicating their jolting journeys as they continued round and round, as the hours rolled away.

Tara hugged herself in the window, let her fingers wander over the new landscape of her body. Bumps and ridges and flaps of flesh as hard as stone, lines of scars running up her arms where the fatty flesh had been sucked dry, cut, pulled taut, stapled. Bones poked through the mess at her hips and ribs and collarbones.

Her face was a mystery. She hadn't looked at herself since waking from the coma six months ago. She'd spent the first month in the hospital in silence. Neurologists came and confirmed that she could, indeed, understand them. Then a nurse had emerged from the fog and told her what she'd done to herself. Tara had made the first sounds since waking. To her it had been laughter, but to the nurse it had sounded like snarls.

I stood in the kitchen of my house in Paddington and looked at the burnt walls, the fingers of blackness reaching up the bricks to the charred roof beams. The tiles had fallen and disappeared, revealing blue sky and orange leaves. I smiled. The oven had been cleared away, the cupboards stripped off, and the sink unscrewed and discarded, leaving black eyeholes in the wall. The flames had warped the floorboards leading down to the bathroom and tiny courtyard. I folded my arms and looked at it all, smelled the plastic taint of melted things.

As first houses go, I'm well aware that they're traditionally purchased by much younger people than me, and in much better condition than this one. The row house on William Street had been a write-off from the start, advertised for developers who might be tempted to knock it over, put in a flashy deli, and be done with it. The kitchen was a bombed-out shell, the backyard was a wreck, and the upper floor wasn't safe for human habitation—the elderly owner had let the place go for decades, and the floorboards had taken it the worst.

By order of the Sydney city council, I wasn't even supposed to be sleeping in the building, and I was supposed to be wearing protective gear while inside. But I'd ignored that. My home base was the front bedroom, where I'd dragged a mattress and a few laundry baskets of clothes, my phone, and some snack food. The bathroom still worked. I still had the apartment in

Kensington, and there was always Imogen's place. But for a couple of nights a week I had been sleeping in my new house, just so I could drift off listening to the creaking and cracking of the building, city ambulances racing for St. Vincent's, drunks singing as they wandered home. Rats scuttling somewhere close by. It was dingy, but I owned it. I'd committed to something. That was big for me.

Committing to things. Listening to my girlfriend. Getting off the drugs and the booze. Yes, I was going somewhere, even if it wasn't some mystical place beyond anger that couldn't possibly exist. I believed what I'd said to Aamir. There is no "after murder." There is no reasoning, bargaining, or manipulating with murder. When someone close to you has been slain, something enters your life that will always be there, a little black blur at the corner of your vision that you learn to ignore as naturally as you do your own nose. Stained as you are, you have to go on and learn to see again. Build things. Change things. Own things. Martina wasn't coming back. It was time to return to life.

As I was standing in the sunshine from the informal skylight, I heard the front door open and close, and then Eden's uneven gait on the unpolished boards. She was walking with a single aluminum crutch with an arm cuff and a handle, having worked her way down from two of them. I'd seen her at the station gym a couple of days earlier trotting awkwardly on the tread-mill, somewhere between a jog and a walk, now and then reaching for the console to steady herself. The problem was her core strength, I thought, but I wasn't sure. A pair of serial killers had slit her open from sternum to navel, on their way to cutting her right in half. She'd lost most of the hearing in her left ear from having a gun fired in her face, and her nose wasn't straight anymore. But despite all her new little imperfections, to look at her now, it was hard to imagine how close she'd come to dying in my arms.

"Oh look, it's the invalid," I said. Eden had to be the world's most beautiful cripple, but I knew that underneath her whippet-lean frame and deep gothic eyes hid a creature that could hardly be described in terms of beauty. I had no doubt, standing in her presence, that though Eden couldn't run yet, was easily wearied, and had lost some of the sharpness of her dry wit, there was a very dark power residing in her still. She was as much a threat to me as she was to the killers, rapists, and evildoers she spent her nights hunting. She came up beside me and took in the black walls, raised her head and looked at a pigeon as it landed on the edge of the roof hole.

"Why didn't you just tell Hades to keep the money?" she asked, sighing. "He'd have been smarter with it."

Eden's father, Hades Archer, ex–criminal overlord and World's Cleverest Body Disposal Expert, had given me a hundred thousand dollars to find out what had happened to the love of his life. Sunday White had gone missing before I was born, and Hades had hired me as much to get one of her relatives off his back as to know himself what had become of the lost young woman. I'd put the cash together with my inheritance and bought the row house on William Street. Eden shifted papers around on the floor with one of her fine leather boots.

"I can't believe you, of all people, fail to see the potential in this place. Things of beauty are made of forgotten places like this, Eden." I started mapping the kitchen with my hands. "Stove there, stainless steel counters here, big kitchen island with one of those cutting-board tops. You know the ones? Drawers underneath. Rip all this out and put a big window in. Fucking brilliant."

"Stainless steel is so 1990."

"Marble, then. Wine rack over here."

"You're a recovering alcoholic."

"My cooking wine, Eden."

"Who do you think's going to do all this?" She squinted at me.

"Me."

"You can't change a lightbulb without adult supervision."

"You, then. Come help me. You're handy."

"No."

"You're just jealous." I shook my head. "There's no need to be cranky, Eden. You can come visit my brilliant new house whenever you want. Take photos of yourself in it to show your friends."

The pigeon sitting on one of the roof beams ruffled its feathers and crapped on my floor. We both looked up at it.

"We'll have dinner parties," I said.

"Look at you. Less than a year ago, your plates were getting dusty from disuse and the local Indian take-out guy had invited you to his wedding. Now you're planning soirees."

"I like the word *soiree*."

"It's a commitment, I guess, even if it is a shit hole," she sighed. "That's a big deal. Congratulations."

"I've been a big deal for a while now, Eden. You just haven't noticed."

"You could go on a commitment streak—marry that mindquack and have freckly children with abandonment issues."

"Let's not get ahead of ourselves."

As though she'd heard herself being spoken about, my girlfriend, Imogen, opened the front door and clopped into the hall in her second-favorite lavender velvet heels, her upturned nose wrinkled at the smell. She had an Ikea bag in each hand. What a sweetheart.

"Sorry, Frank, I didn't realize you had company," she said. "How are you, Eden?"

"Dr. Stone," Eden said. The tone had no warmth in it, I noted, and then reminded myself that, like an old gas heater, Eden took hours just to get to room temperature. Still, something passed between them. Eden's eyes fell to my missing kitchen cupboards and Imogen's stayed on Eden, searching, almost, for something.

I coughed, because I'm like most men—completely ignorant of women and their looks and tones and inferences and what they mean. The two could have been about to launch into a midair Kung Fu battle or hurl each other onto the ground in a passionate embrace. I didn't know. Imogen excused herself to wash her hands.

Eden stood playing with a live wire hanging from the ceiling, twisting the plastic casing around her finger.

"What's wrong with you?" I jutted my chin at her. "Someone asks how you are, you don't say their name and qualification."

"Oh, I'm sorry. Should I have responded with a list of neurotic compulsions I may or may not exhibit?"

"You've been colder since Rye Farm, Eden. Weirder, if that's possible."

"I did my mandatory counseling." She shrugged. "I don't need to be shrinked in my free time. If Imogen wants to shrink someone, she's got more than enough mental dysfunction going on here without starting on me." She gestured at me with an open hand.

"She's not shrinking you. She's my girlfriend. She's saying hello."

"Shrinks never stop shrinking. They shrink all day long until everyone around them is shrunk."

"You don't like her," I concluded.

"She's a *shrink.*"

"Stop saying shrink!"

"While you're here, Eden," Imogen said, emerging from the stairs, flicking water off her fingers (I had no hand towels), "I've been telling Frank for a while now that it'd be nice if the three of us got together for dinner sometime, maybe? I'm sure he hasn't passed this on to you. I thought it'd be nice to get to know you a bit. You know. Because Frank and I . . . Now that we're . . ."

"Fucking?" Eden said. I threw my head back and laughed at the ceiling. The pigeon flew away.

"In a *relationship*," Imogen said and sighed.

Eden's phone buzzed and she took it out of her pocket. Looked at it, slid it back in.

"We need to go, Frank," she said. "Now."

"All weeknights are fine with me." Imogen followed us to the door. I grabbed my jacket from the edge of the mattress in the front room and turned to hear Eden's response, but she was already heading through the front gate. I kissed Imogen before running out the door.

Ruben was pretty sure he'd gotten the cushiest job in Sydney. He'd been caretaking the three-story monster of a house on the edge of Centennial Park for three weeks, and he hadn't once seen the owner, or anyone associated with the building. He'd been translating job advertisements from the *Telegraph* using his phone, while sitting at the arrivals terminal at Sydney airport waiting for his bus. He had begun with the briefest ad: *Cleaner wanted, twice weekly*. He'd emailed the agency responsible for filling the job. The agency had explained that he was to let himself in, make sure the place was dust-, insect-, and mold-free, and leave.

He'd been in the country ten minutes, and already he had a job—great pay, zero human interaction, and self-directed. Too good to be true.

The only catch was that Ruben wasn't the best cleaner on earth. He'd never gotten over his teenage habit of shedding clothes and letting them drop wherever they fell, which had bothered a lot of travelers in the dozens of hostels he'd stayed in across Europe, down through Asia, and along the coast of Australia. He also loved tissues, gum, elastic bands—he'd use them and fling them, telling himself he'd pick them up later. He was a flicker of toothpaste onto clean mirrors and a leaver of stubble in sinks. Getting a job as a caretaker was a bit of a stretch for Ruben, but he was up for the challenge.

He was mailed a key and emailed a map to the

house on Lang Road, across the street from Centennial Park. He was to go through the house from top to bottom and alleviate the damages of misuse. Fight back the dust. Fluff the pillows. Spray bleach on the creeping mold. The emails, which he translated, didn't mention anyone living in the house. Nor did they mention when the occupants would return.

He'd spent the first day showing himself around, gathering the things he'd need for the job from the places where they were hidden all over the gigantic house. There were cleaning products in the kitchen, but everything was dust- and mold-covered, and he'd need a new vacuum. Ruben guessed his being hired was a reluctant measure from someone who didn't want the house to fall into disrepair. He'd arrived at the very moment dampness and mold threatened to cause permanent structural damage—the precise moment when vermin had begun to colonize the bottom floor, but hadn't begun to destroy it.

The overgrown back garden was a haven for spiders, who made their homes in the corners of every downstairs window. But the front garden, which might attract the scrutiny of passersby, was manicured. The house was dark and creaked a lot, and Ruben caught himself having to play music all day long to avoid getting the creeps. He kept out of the many bathrooms as much as he could. Horror-film ghosts always appeared in the bathroom mirrors first.

It took him until the very end of the first day to realize that there was someone in the attic. He'd ignored the creaking of floorboards that followed him everywhere, but as he rose through the levels of the house toward the attic, he heard a television playing. At first he thought it must be outside, next door perhaps, but when he stopped to listen he realized it was upstairs. Not only was the television playing—something was being played *on it*, an advertisement run through in full and then rewound to certain spots, played, then played again. Over and over, the words and the theme music repeated behind the door. He shook the dust from the covers in the rooms below, translating the words in his poorly remembered English.

"My ten-week program gives you everything you need to escape the *you* that you've become and find the person you should be. Take up the challenge today! It's easy!"

The words began over and over, halted, clipped, then stopped.

". . . escape the *you* that you've become . . ."

". . . escape . . . you . . ."

". . . find the person you should be . . ."

". . . find the person . . ."

"It's easy!"

Between the splintered phrases, silence stretched. Ruben listened for a voice, a movement, anything to indicate that a person was playing the advertisement. There was nothing. It was as though whoever was up there was a ghost.

I didn't get to the crime scene straight away. I was following Eden up the gentle green slope toward the tree under which the body had been found when I spotted little Amy Hooku standing nearby with her arms folded, staring at the grass in that girl-lost way she sometimes got about her.

Amy was barely seventeen years old and not afraid to show it, in a blazing-red top covered in dancing pandas, heavy black jeans, and silver Doc Martens sprayed with glitter. The extreme buzz cut of bleached-blond prickles jarred against her Vietnamese features. Complicated electronic gear hung all around her like vines on a small, thin tree—huge headphones at her neck, things clipped to her belt, two phones bulging in her back pockets—one personal, one police equipment. She was the only teenager in the country with a standard-issue cop phone, and it was only because she'd earned it. I came up behind her, grabbed the back of her skinny neck, and shoved her head toward the ground.

"I've got her. Backup! I need backup! I've caught Sydney's Greatest Liar."

"Get your hands off me, asshole."

She tried to swing at me and I grabbed her wrist, put a leg into the back of her knee. I let her hang helpless for a second. Her face was all teenage exhaustion at my incredible lameness. The crowd at the edge of the police tape gave us confused looks, the wild-faced white guy manhandling the stringy Asian girl.

"What is *wrong* with you?"

"I'm excited to see you. You must have grown a foot and a half." I pulled her up and grinned at her, punched her in her hard shoulder. She had grown taller but had not filled out at all, a miniature replica of the tall, lanky, and incredibly beautiful Asian woman I knew she would grow into. Her parents had been stunning—he a broad-shouldered football type, and his wife one of those bony models who always seem to have a golden glow. I knew Mrs. Hooku from the autopsy photos and the *60 Minutes* special on the murders. I'd seen Amy's father around the North Sydney Metro office, a quiet, shadowy figure who walked too fast.

"What are you doing here, Hooky Bird?"

"I'm on my way to class. Saw Simmons." She nodded toward another officer we both knew, a bald crime scene photographer from North Sydney Metro. "Knew it must be a good one."

Amy "Hooky" Hooku was a genius, but I tried not to think about that. Beyond the punk-Japanese-rocker, angry Hello-Kitty thing she had going on, she possessed a rare kind of superintelligence that had seen her drop out of high school like it was child's play and sail into top university courses in computer science with an engineering major. At *seventeen*. I'd met her in North Sydney Metro when I was there working in Asian Gangs. My work had been mainly chasing down big drug crime families warring over territory. They'd brought me in to consult on the Hooku family murders under the misconception that I could speak Vietnamese.

I'd been the one to sit Amy down in the principal's

office at her school a year and a bit earlier and tell her that her younger sister had murdered her parents that morning. It had been a violent bloodbath that Amy herself had only escaped because she'd spent the night at a friend's house and gone straight to school the next day.

I was a poor choice for this role. I was just about as alien to an Asian teenage girl as a person could be. But with counselors running late and the principal blubbering like a lunatic in the hall, it was down to me to tell Amy what had happened. Somehow, together, we'd worked through it.

I guess that from this time, together in the principal's office, I'd somehow managed to be separated from the rest of the world in Amy's mind. So Amy treated me like a human being and, however begrudgingly, put up with my childish bullshit, my roughhousing and my teasing, whenever I saw her. From what I heard from other people, though, she was difficult to get to know. Pulled the "Me no speak Engrish" act whenever she was approached by strangers. All that was crap, of course. She'd grown up in Wollstonecraft. When she couldn't back out of interaction by playing the voiceless migrant, she could be aggressive, or so the rumors went.

After her family had been killed, the North Sydney bigwigs had approved her for a few low-profile administrative jobs here and there to give her something to do while she hung around the station. She was a presence there after the murders, in the same clothes for weeks, sitting in the waiting rooms staring at the crims, or, if she could manage it, creeping into her dad's office to sit in his big leather chair.

People understood her obsession with the office—her dad had been rooted to that chair in his glass cubicle, a silent figure tapping away at the computer, chasing down Internet frauds, as rigid as a tree. I didn't know him but I'd been aware of him, the way someone will be aware of a chair or a desk without taking notice until it disappears or is moved. Detective Hooku didn't move, though, until he disappeared, and all that remained of him was in that office. The office smelled like his cologne. It was covered in his used coffee cups. The laptop screen was marked with his prints.

Amy wanted to be close to her dead dad, so she kept sneaking into the headquarters.

They'd chase her out, the other cops, but she'd get back in through fire-escape doors. Once they had front- and back-door staff on the lookout for her, she climbed in through a tiny window in the men's room. After a while, the North Sydney superintendent let her file incident reports as part of unofficial "work experience," quietly, trying to avoid the scandal of a kid having access to sensitive criminal information. I avoided Amy as much as I could in those days, though I wasn't around the station a lot. I felt uncomfortable around her. I'd seen her family's crime scene and didn't know how to not think about that when I spoke to her.

Amy thrived in admin, but she was hard to entertain. She started messing around with the station computers, installing new programs, making things easier, better, fixing bugs none of us dinosaurs had any idea about. When the Major Crimes Unit assembled a task force to combat online grooming of teenagers for underage sex, Amy was right there while our out-of-touch middle-aged divorcees pretended to be young girls and boys in online chat rooms and failed dismally.

Amy knew all the slang, the symbols. The cyber-crime section of the Major Crimes Unit started allowing Amy to be in the same room as the online chat sessions, consulting verbally only. Then they let her sit in one of the chairs near the screen, still only verbally interacting with the pervs, her words and advice translated through the police officer at the screen. Then, when one of the officers got up to get a coffee one day, Amy slid into the driver's seat and controlled the conversations with the online pedophiles, "supervised stringently" by cybercrime officers.

Amy's "work experience" had become work. Had the papers got wind of what she was doing, the kinds of people she was talking to, there would have been a national scandal. Somehow, the news never got out. It was because Amy was good. No one wanted to lose her.

She baited the chatters, reeled them in, and landed three major rock spiders in her first week on the job— one of them a cop at another station. She was a ruthless fisher, a convincing liar. She could be a sexually confused, bi-curious fourteen-year-old boy in one chat window, and a nerdy, love-starved twelve-year-old girl in another. Her words were full of the misguided romantic fantàsies so many normal young people her age brought to the online hunting grounds.

She was fast, and she was convincing. She made up names, family members, school grades, hobbies for her aliases. She could remember that the thirteen-year-old girl she was playing named Alice from Redfern had a cat named Stanley that'd been hit by a car and

sprained its left back leg, while at the same time remembering that the eleven-year-old girl she was playing named Jessica from Mosman didn't have pets
because she had allergies. She had photographs for
these people—multiple ones. I had no idea how she
did it. Amy could lie like some of the worst so-
ciopaths I'd ever met. She was a trapper of bad men.

"So, what's the story?" I motioned toward the
crowd under the tree.

"Looks like a jogger copped it. Bashed, I think."

"That's no good."

"Nope."

"How's your aunt?"

"Oh Jesus. How's *your* aunt?"

"All right, all right." I raised my hands in surrender.
Amy had a real aversion to being treated like a child,
even though she was one. She let me get away with it
most of the time, but when other people tried to mother
her, she snapped. You couldn't ask her how she was
doing at school or if she was seeing anybody or whether
she was eating right. I wondered sometimes if she did
eat right. She was all bones and sharp edges.

"What's your partner up to?" she asked.

"You know Eden?"

"No. But I guessed she's your partner."

"How?"

"She's giving you the stink eye."

I looked over and saw Eden at the edge of the hud-
dle, her eyebrows raised at me. I nudged Hooky off
balance and ruffled her spikes.

"See you round, punk."

"Yeah," she said.

Things were not good over by the tree. The victim

had been a beautiful woman, I think. Long, muscular legs in torn purple nylon tights, matching top, one sleeve of a green jacket hanging from the left arm. No shoes. Sporty socks. Eden held the tarpaulin up for me and I peered in. The onlookers shuffled to get a glimpse. The blue light falling through the tarp onto the mashed face turned the bloody meat it had become purple, as if she were wearing some melted Halloween mask. I looked for eye sockets but found none.

"Someone's angry," I said.

"Mmm hmm," Eden agreed.

An angry perp, someone capable of this kind of brutality, is usually known to the victim. Pretty difficult to get this aggressive, this violent, with a stranger. Facial injuries, in particular, are usually personal. The positioning of her body, lying on her back, hidden from view of the road—was the killer ashamed of his act? It was a bit confusing on that score.

According to the textbook, a victim positioned on her back and uncovered suggested a willingness for the body to be found. Usually if a killer is ashamed of what they've done, they curl the body on its side, suggesting peacefulness, sleep. Or they turn her over, hide her face and injuries in the grass. On the back, faceup, is probably how the victim fell out of the guy's arms, carried fireman-style and then flopped down, arms out.

So the guy wasn't displaying any shame in the positioning of the body, in particular. But leaving the victim off behind the bushes . . . that was strange. In the right circumstances, it could have been days before one of the joggers pumping along the road at the bottom of the hill smelled her, before someone let their dog off the leash and the beast came up here. A mixed display. Not ashamed, but not exhibitionist, either. There was . . . an uncertainty about it.

This was a first kill.

Eden looked around at the paperbarks ringing us, pale and spotted trunks that had stood watch over the girl's final seconds. Or had they? There was no indication that the brutality we were seeing had occurred here. No blood-spatter. But she looked like a Centennial Park jogger. I'd been one myself once. Centennial Park is a great starting ground for weight-losers rather than serious runners—it's mostly flat, and the familiarity of landmarks as you make your way helps you keep control of the panic that you'll never make it to the end. The main obstacles are old people, dogs, and kids on scooters. I shifted the girl's shoulder up a fraction and looked at the lividity, the dark purple on her back and hips where the blood had pooled.

If the runner was picked up *from* here, but she wasn't *killed* here, why was she brought *back* here? Why risk returning a victim to the place where you abducted her? Was the location important to the killer? Maybe she wasn't taken far. Maybe the whole thing had happened in the park. I looked toward the road, at the cars parked under the trees.

"Let's set up a tent before we move her. I want to catch any fibers."

Eden directed a tech near us to bring in a tent so that we could examine the body without onlookers gawking at us. I instructed another to go down and get a video of all the cars in the immediate vicinity, note down the license plate numbers.

I heard a noise and reached under the tarp and unclipped a mobile phone from the girl's waist. Wires ran up through her shirt, under her bra, to her collar. I pulled the earphones clear and looked at the screen. Her running music was still playing: "Hazard" by Richard Marx. Ominous. I scrolled through the songs and found the girl had a weird compilation going. Plenty of eighties love ballads and murder songs. Depressed taste. A recent break-up? Was she pounding the pavement to lose the weight gained during a now-dead relationship?

I sat back on my haunches and realized it was the first personal thing I knew about the girl. Her music taste. More personal details would follow, and they would all be sad to learn. Sometimes the stupidity of it hit me, right in the middle of the job. Everything she had been, whoever she was going to be—it was all over now.

"Hey, dickhead," Hooky called. I looked over at her. She was standing closer but still away from the center of the crime scene, not wanting to contaminate it with her DNA. It's easy to leave pieces of yourself at a crime scene just by standing there—flaking skin and dropping hairs—like a tree shedding its winter leaves.

"Did she have an app going?" Hooky asked.

I looked at her blankly. Hooky beckoned me and I approached with the phone. She tugged another pair of gloves out of my back pocket and handed them to me. I put them on and let her direct me around the phone. There would be no handling evidence for her.

"There are programs you can download on your phone for running," Hooky said. "They play your music, track your progress, time you, and mark your distance and elevation."

She gave me a bunch of quick directions for the

phone. I stopped the music, then brought up a screen full of numbers and images.

"How the hell do they do that?"

"GPS." She rolled her eyes. Eden approached us, looked over my shoulder. Hooky made me bring up a green and gray map crisscrossed with colorful lines and numbers in flashing bubbles.

"See here?" Hooky pointed with her pinkie finger. "She did two laps of the park. Then she went off track . . . through the bushes over there, Queens Park Road. There was a pause of . . . three minutes. Then we're onto a road. Her pulse goes up from 180 to 210 beats per minute."

"This thing can do *heartbeats?*" I looked at Eden. She was deadpan. I guessed this kind of technology had been around for a while. I felt old.

"Then she's off again." Hooky frowned at the phone. "She speeds up to forty . . . then sixty kilometers an hour. Either the bitch was running like the Terminator or she's been put in a car."

"Fuck me!" I said. "We can follow this right to the crime scene!"

Hooky tugged my arm back down so she could see the phone. "Yup. Looks like the killer drove her out to . . . Mangrove Road, Ashfield. Stopped for fifteen minutes. Then drove her back here."

I pressed the bubble on Mangrove Road, not sure what would happen. A window opened, marked with a small red X.

Heart rate error. Connection lost.

"We're going to need a secondary team to follow us, and a third to check out the pick-up point by Queens Park Road." Eden turned, walking toward the car. She beckoned for the head crime scene tech and gave him instructions as she hobbled down the slope, her aluminum crutch making holes in the wet grass. "Frank, give me that phone. We need to get screenshots of the map and send them to headquarters."

I glanced back at Hooky as I ran toward the car. She was smiling at the top of the hill.

Eden gets this look about her when she's on the hunt. Pointed. Cold. I like to try to keep things light and casual, especially when I'm sitting in the car as a passenger with no effect on how fast we go or what route we take. If I can't keep a lid on my excitement, I chew my nails, my knuckles, my collar. My stomach churns.

Since her run-in with a killer, Eden's pointed look has developed a deadly edge. She drives like she's handling a getaway car, sailing through gaps she has no cause to be confident about. I hang on to the seat belt and try to remember if you're supposed to go stiff or limp in a crash. We headed across the city toward Ashfield, people leaping from crossings and holding their children as the sirens announced our passing. The radio was playing, and as news broke on the hour, Eden glanced at it.

". . . the remains of at least four people in a burnt-out van outside the Black Mutt Inn near Suffolk Park, just south of tourist hot spot Byron Bay. It is believed at least some of the victims suffered gunshot wounds. Police are asking . . ."

Eden switched the radio off.

"Ashfield," I said, glancing at the phone, trying to avoid making myself sick. "Why Ashfield?"

"I don't know," Eden said.

"Bit of a horrible name for a place. Ashfield."

"You should pen a stern letter to the mayor."

"Maybe I will. The bus!"

"I can see the fucking bus, Frank." Eden swerved.

"Jesus Christ, we're both gonna die."

"Would you shut up?"

"Would you look at the road?"

We blasted through a massive intersection, a half a second's worth of gap between us and a moving van passing in front of our hood. Silence lingered in the car. It's always very present between us, the fact that Eden could at any time, and rightfully so, decide that killing me is the best thing for her future. As far as I could tell, it was only me and her father who knew what she really was, what she had done. People wonder, I'm sure—our colleagues, our clients, some of the journalists who have covered her career. They wonder about that hard look, about her incredible instinct for catching killers. She's a natural chaser, hunter, and fighter. Once Eden killed someone to save my life. But I didn't feel any safer. I couldn't afford to.

Arriving at the scene was anticlimactic. In an alley between two warehouses in Ashfield's industrial wasteland, the path the murdered girl had taken came to a point. Sandy black earth and bricks that hadn't seen sunlight in years. Eden parked and we walked into the alley, looked ahead to the wire fencing at the end, the dead grass. There were a couple of boot prints beside a pair of tire tracks. The tracks showed the vehicle had come into the dead end, where the driver exited, walked around the vehicle, got in the back, exited again, and got in the front. The GPS showed the van was stationary here for a mere fifteen minutes. Fifteen minutes to leave the victim totally unrecognizable.

Eden and I waited for the crime scene techs. There were plenty of cigarette butts and bits of paper around for collecting, but we collected none. I was still and silent because I wanted to be sad at the sight of the footprints, the reading on the phone in my hand. The heartbeat rose. Then the heartbeat was lost. It was a lonely place to die.

"Kill van," Eden said. Her arms were folded across her chest, her eyes squinting in the dim light, studying the footprints. "It's a good move. Mobile, so you can grab and go at any time. Easy to acquire. Don't need to clean it. Just light it up and leave it. Ted Bundy had one for a while."

She took her jacket off, crouched low with difficulty to look at the tire prints. I felt a little ill and went back to the car to wait.

Hades Archer had started to feel things were too quiet around the house, when he noticed the men gathered at the bottom of the hill. He'd been told men his age became restless toward their twilight years, sought the company of people who didn't want to hear their stories or drink their coffee. Men his age became a burden on people when they got bored—so the trick, it seemed, was not to get bored. Always have something brewing. A project. A purpose.

The average man took up golf in his retirement years. But Hades had never been close to average.

He'd kept this restlessness at bay by focusing on his work. His legitimate work, mostly. Waste rates in the city were always increasing, which meant he was constantly facing the challenge of finding space in his landfill for nonrecyclable garbage. He spent months considering which technology upgrades he could get government funding for, how to make use of the nonrecyclables, whether there were charities that could benefit from some of the items he couldn't find buyers for—the thousands and thousands of bags of clothes, the old but still operational appliances, the building materials.

He considered which landfill plots to turn over, knowing it took six or seven months for the bodies he hid beneath the layers of waste to degrade to the point that they wouldn't be decipherable amongst the sludge and decay when the ground was dug up and the plot relined for fresh garbage. He had to remember where he'd buried people, when, and what their body type and fat content had been. He wasn't dumb enough to write this down anywhere, so it was a mental game. A memory puzzle. He'd heard men his age were advised to play them to keep the brain ticking.

Hades would stand on the doorstep of his little shack on the hill and look out over the fields, the trucks in the distance spewing their black smoke into the air, and try to remember where he had buried this person or that person, how deep. Ah yes, over there, by the fence behind the car shed, he'd buried the skinny rapist Denny "the Preacher" Mills. East of the sorting center, he'd planted Sharon the Black Widow. And just last week, in the north quadrant, he'd sunk some junky punk whose name he'd never learned. He'd felt a twinge in his back as he loaded the boy's body onto the front of the backhoe. It would be about six months before Hades could use that spot again, until the earth and the garbage that decomposed onto it in layers would do its work on the corpse. Then, he'd dig down with another, when the ground was ready to receive another soul.

In a way, what Hades did was a lot like gardening. He'd heard gardening was good for retirees.

That evening, as the old man watched the sun falling behind the round, gray mountains of trash in the distance, a certain pulling in his chest told him that, for all his activities, his gardening and his memory games, there was still something lacking in his life. There was only so much organizing a man could do before there was nothing left to arrange. He had his nightly meals cooked up and frozen—hearty containers of lamb stew and shepherd's pie and soy chicken stir-fry in the dozens. He was well into his next artistic project—a mighty wolf he planned to assemble out of hundreds of black discarded Singer sewing machines. Lots of welding work, time-consuming and dangerous. But when he'd done his work for the day, there was an unsettling stillness left behind. A lack of purpose. It was then that Hades let his eyes wander from the horizon and spied the men gathered down the hill beside the last truck to come in.

One of the men turned away from the gathering and walked past him as Hades reached the bottom of the hill. Hades was surprised to see the grimy character had tears in his eyes. His fluorescent orange vest was spattered with all manner of muck—garbage juice, ink, paint, grease. Hades said nothing as the young man passed. You didn't acknowledge a man in his weak moments. Hades edged his way into the gathering.

All heads were bowed. At first Hades thought the object of their attention was a young kangaroo—the dog had the bony, elongated figure of a joey. But the color was wrong, and so was the size. The animal was the sunburnt caramel of ice-cream topping, and milk-chested, a mixed-breed thing with a long snout and a pink nose. It was far too thin for how long it was. In fact, the thing was starved beyond anything Hades had ever seen, and he'd seen the dingoes that frequented the dump get down to bones and leather during the wintertime, when the seagulls went back to the shores and wild cats were hard to come by.

The dog's lips were puckered inward, and its hips were a collection of intricate spikes and ridges pushing up against skin. It was lying lifeless, white eyes bugging from its skull. An open garbage bag lay beside it, spewing its contents onto the ground.

A second man in the gathering walked away.

"There's got to be something in here," one of the men said. Hades looked up and saw him rummaging through a garbage bag identical to the one the dog had been pulled from. "There'll be a bill with an address. A piece of paper. Something."

The men rifled through the bags. Three of them remained, staring down at the dog.

"You do it," one of them said to another.

"I can't fucking do it."

Hades bent, heard his knees pop and crack as he lowered himself beside the animal. To his surprise, the chain of furry bone links jutting from the dog's hindquarters quivered, then wagged. Hades put his hand on the animal's cheek, smoothed its hairless leather ear back over its bony head. The dog was colder than a live animal should have been. Its tail continued wagging.

"Someone's gotta do it," the man above Hades said. "We can't just leave it like this. It's cruel."

"Here. Here. Look. An address. I've got a fucking address. Let's go. Let's get the fucking pricks!"

"It might recover," Hades said, more to himself than to the men around him. "You never know."

Hades eased his big hands under the dog's hips and shoulders, gathered the thing into his arms. It weighed less than a child might. The dog was long, its narrow legs dangling over his arm, its head lolling. Hades looked at the faces of his workers as he got to his feet, and then he labored up the hill toward his shack.

* * *

That night, Hades sat on the floor of his tiny kitchen, his favorite things that had come from the dump adorning the walls all around him. Taxidermied birds and framed dried flowers. Ten pocket watches he'd collected over the years hanging from their chains in one corner, polished, renewed, and ticking with life again, their engraved tributes shining in the light of several mismatched lamps. *To Sam, On Your Graduation.*

The dog lay in Hades's arms in a bundle of blankets and looked at all the things above him, not having expected, Hades imagined, to see anything again after the inside of the garbage bag.

Plenty of things had come good for Hades out of the bottom of garbage bags over the years. The secret, he'd always believed, was seeing the potential when all was lost. Potential was a sly thing. It hid in the darkest of places. When the dog had wagged its tail at the center of the gathering of men at the bottom of the hill, Hades had seen that potential. He'd smiled to himself. Now, he held the dog to his chest, looked at his watch, and decided it could have more water. He took the plastic syringe he'd dug out of his medicine cabinet, filled it with water from the glass sitting on the linoleum beside him, and squirted a little on the dog's hairy lips. The beast awakened from its half-delirium and lapped.

It would be a long night, but Hades had nothing better to do.

Imogen Stone liked money, and she liked murder, and there was nothing wrong with that. If she'd been able to pass the exams for the police academy, she'd have been a homicide detective like her boyfriend, the Murder Police Poster Boy, Detective Frank Bennett. But she'd been young all those times she applied, and once the stain of her late-teenage "narcissistic tendencies" and "lack of life experience" had been recognized in the personality test, they stayed with her through her subsequent applications. She'd outperformed on the aptitude tests, but this couldn't overcome what the psychological report called her "grandiose sense of self." It was ridiculous.

At the time, eighteen years old and quick to anger, she hadn't known what these terms meant. So, she started researching how they were applied in psychology, and then worked toward disguising the traits in herself, so that never again would they stand in the way of what she wanted. She became more reserved. More studied. She cultivated "shy" and "sweet." She played down the "overconfidence" she'd displayed in the academy interviews. She got so good at understanding her own psychological dysfunctions that she fell in love with the science of it.

Being a cop psychologist was as close as she could get to that old dream of being a crime fighter, of rubbing shoulders with dangerous people, both in and out of the job, and she'd whizzed through the interviews for that role. But sitting there day after day in her leather armchair under the city windows, putting the pieces of broken cops back together, had done nothing to moderate her narcissism.

Imogen loved herself.

It was impossible not to. Imogen had taken her one and only failure in life and turned it into a thriving success. Sydney's boys in blue looked to her as their savior. They itched for her wisdom. It was Imogen they thought of deep in the night when sleep evaded them, sitting in the icy light of the bathroom, more comfortable among the razors and scissors than they were in their own beds next to their wives. It was Imogen they called. The first time she'd counseled one of the old boys who'd rejected her application as a young woman, she'd known what power was. Sitting there listening to him cry, she'd burned with hateful pleasure.

And then her first murder case. The missing Cherry boy.

George Cherry, eight, had gone missing on a walk home from school in the shark-infested waters between the classroom and home, where the number of kids getting into cars and walking hand-in-hand with adults masks the hunt of society's nastiest. At first, it was assumed the boy's estranged father had him. The critical first hours focused on the wrong man. Hours in the interrogation tank. More hours upturning the family home. Panic after the first lead failed; scrambling, stupid moves; roughing up of the town's resident kiddie fiddlers; and the cultivation of myths in the media. More interviews. More rummaging through drawers and leading dogs around tiny yards. Little George Cherry tumbled through the cracks. But he landed in the minds of his three pursuing detectives, and they never forgot him, no matter how hard they tried. Imogen had been counseling the detectives for four years before her curiosity piqued. She went online on a sheer whim, and the first thing her eyes beheld on FindGeorgie.com was blazing red lettering announcing a $200,000 reward.

Imogen had taken on the case. And Imogen didn't lose.

She also didn't follow the rules. She didn't fill in reports. She didn't respect privacy. Imogen was all about winning, and in some dark corner of her mind she knew this was because all her life she'd been terrified of ending up like her father, a thirty-year veteran of the same security firm. A pencil-thin, hopeless man, the butt of his friends' jokes.

Imogen was her own crime-fighting superhero. She didn't mind bending the law to get what she wanted, and that was what made Imogen so good at the armchair detective game. Dr. Stone put herself on the Cherry boy case, and eight months later was leading a squad down an embankment on the Murray River to the child's bones. She didn't let them mention her name in the paper. That would have been narcissistic. Grandiose.

Imogen had found something better than public recognition. She'd found murder money.

After the first case, she was hooked. She'd begun hunting the Internet for cold cases she could solve, or at least contribute to, gaining a tasty share of the reward money. Sometimes it required her to do some unethical things. She'd wandered around in police archives files she had no business viewing. Now and then she'd probed her clients for details on their cases, making them reveal things that wouldn't be therapeutic in their revealing. She'd cultivated a network of administrative assistants, lab technicians, and interns who now and then slipped her the information she needed. It wasn't ethical—but it wasn't hurting anybody. She told herself that all good cops bent the rules.

Imogen was far more powerful as an armchair detective than she might ever have been as a cop. Sometimes she pitied people like Frank, with his constant phone calls about reports, warrants, codes, legislation, crime-scene handling, and the endless, endless discussion of contamination. Contamination of crime scenes. Contamination of impartiality. Contamination of witnesses. Frank's work in homicide had turned him into a physical and metaphorical germophobe. He wrapped the tasteless chicken-and-mayo sandwiches he took to work as if they were radioactive. He wouldn't talk about anything related to his cases, wouldn't give her those tasty little tidbits she needed in order to fuel the hungry, voyeuristic thing inside her. Not until she begged him, anyway.

Imogen was no germophobe. She got as dirty as she could in her perfect hobby. She loved the feel of grit beneath her nails from digging and digging for truth, like a happy little mole.

After the Cherry boy, there'd been a few other half- and quarter-reward jobs, but nothing that had excited her like seeing the forensics team break earth for the first time at the boy's grave, the dig site marked out according to her direction. She solved the mystery. She caught the bad guy. She hadn't felt that same exhilaration since. But now, sitting outside Sue Harold's old house, Imogen believed she could feel that rush again.

She folded the map and looked at the dusty windows of the little hovel outside Scone, a nowhere place dotted with centers where everyone knew everyone, punctuating miles and miles in which no one knew anyone at all. The house had been difficult to find, but now that she had found it, Imogen wasn't leaving until she was certain the woman calling herself Eden's biological grandmother was revealed as a fraud. One at a time, Imogen would check off all of Frank's partner's lies, revealing her for what she was: the missing Tanner girl.

By the time she dropped this on the homicide department, there would be no keeping Imogen's name out of the papers. Eden Archer would be her greatest catch.

By the time Eden arrived that night at Pearl Massage in Vaucluse, she'd reverted back to using both of her aluminum crutches. It had been months since the mistakes of her last case left Eden physically ruined, a wreck of her once fit, strong self, but she was slowly mending. The day had been nothing but waiting, but it had weighed on her shoulders so heavily that she now walked bent at the torso, her neck twisted slightly to the side. Her eye socket throbbed.

She and Frank had stood by the secondary crime scene for four hours while tire tracks and footprints were cast, photographed, and collected. Details about the girl at the park flooded through her and Frank's cell phones as morticians, photographers, beat cops, and secondary detectives phoned in. They sat side by side, making notes in their own notebooks, pointing with their pens when something relevant came up, long lists emerging between them. Ivana Roth. Twenty-three. Flight attendant. Strangulation. Blunt force. Single. No bad relationships. No kids. Apartment. No indications of SA.

No indications of sexual assault. Eden had paused at that one, tapped the paper a few times with her pen. She'd waved at Frank, the phone hot and wet with sweat in her fingers, and underlined the words. He'd frowned, but no time had presented itself throughout the day to discuss what that meant.

Eden thumped into the brightly lit salon and re-

ceived silent glances from three of the nail artists
grinding at the fingernails of their middle-aged clients.
Merri came out from the back room and smiled at her,
all dazzling white teeth. She was a short woman, Vietnamese. The hard, high shoulder pads of her black jacket
made her look like a tiny war general, a Napoleon with
painted eyebrows far too long and square to appear even
close to real. Merri was a brutal woman. Her words to
the young nail girls were short, sharp, and loud. One of
the girls flew from her client, dropped her tools on the
white towel on the table, and began making Eden an
herbal tea.

"Dar-leeng," Merri said, taking Eden's arm in her
cold, hard hands. "You need help. You come. You
come now."

"I do. Thanks."

Eden followed the little woman into the candlelit
back room. She stripped to her underpants in the warm
glow, breathed deep the lavender incense choking the
oxygen out of the room. She lay on the towels and
sighed, trying to control the twitches that always began
when she knew she was about to be touched, the quiv-
ering in her calves, the chemical desire to flee. Merri
gathered Eden's long black hair, rolled it, tucked it into
a towel. Merri was a small woman, but she was strong.
It had taken Eden a long time to find someone who
would push her hard enough to find relief. She needed
to go well beyond the pain barrier of normal clients.
Far enough that the pain canceled out the worry and
confusion over Ivana Roth, the image of her ruined
face on the grass.

"Today, afterwards, we talk, dar-leeng," Merri said,
positioning Eden's feet at the end of the table.

Eden lifted her head from the towel. "About what?"

"Not now. We talk after. We fix you first."

"No, tell me. What are we talking about?"

"You quiet," Merri said and forced her knuckle into Eden's sole. Eden felt the heavy air rush into her, let it ease out as she relaxed back onto the table. It was never long enough. She needed to focus on every second.

Afterward, Eden lay in a half sleep, listening to the meditation album playing on the old CD player in the corner, the bird sounds and rolling waves, the gentle pipe music. The extraordinary pain Merri had forced on her had receded into an intoxicating warmth, a pleasurable ache in her muscles. She turned her head and found the masseuse sitting on a plastic chair beside her, pouring her second cup of tea. Eden propped herself up, took the china cup and sipped from it, felt the steam on her upper lip.

"Someone come here for you," Merri said, holding her own teacup. Eden felt like she was pulling herself out of a drunken stupor, though it had been years since she was drunk. She lay and looked at Merri, let the tea rest in her hand on the top of the counter. The older woman seemed worried. Eden closed her eyes.

"What do you mean?"

"Someone come *here*, for *you*," Merri said. "They want give me money for photo of you."

Eden pushed herself up, her body becoming colder in the warmth of the room. Merri stood, and the two women stared at each other.

"A woman," Merri said.

"You're . . . you're not making any sense."

"She come here, a lady. Pretty lady. She has picture of you." Merri illustrated with her hands, held up an imaginary photograph. "She tell me, 'Get picture of Eden Archer. I give you five thousand dollars. I give you five thousand—one picture.'"

Eden felt her heartbeat quickening. She felt it all over her body, her fingers pulsing as though being squeezed by invisible hands.

"When was this? What kind of picture did this woman want?"

"She want picture of this," Merri said. The little woman reached out and touched Eden on the bright pink birthmark beside her left breast. Eden lifted her arm and looked at the mark, at Merri's white fingers pressed into the colored flesh. She felt her stomach plummet. All the muscles in her back tensed, tugging her straightened spine crooked once more in a spasm of terror.

"Get me my phone," Eden said. "Now."

In the first few hours, the detectives didn't know much more about Ivana Roth that could help the case. The autopsy would go ahead overnight, and I could view her in the morning. There were no leads in the family—no one was acting weird, they were all horrified, and the mother was in a valium-induced coma. Ivana had been a mild-mannered, hardworking girl who was popular. She liked to party but wasn't a tweaker. We had plenty of friends and ex-boyfriends to sort through for potential suspects. Everything was fine at her job. Her colleagues were all your garden-variety flight attendant types—clean, neatly dressed people with lots of Tupperware.

I wasn't enthusiastic about following leads among Ivana's friends. If the attacker knew her, it seemed risky to grab her off the side of the Centennial Park jogging track in front of dozens of potential witnesses. He'd have had a much easier time grabbing her in her apartment, or at her car, or in a million other less populated places. My guess was that the attacker didn't know her, that she'd been a random pick. But then again, that didn't fit with the brutality, the obvious fury in the modus operandi. Who gets that angry at a perfect stranger? I sat on the kitchen floor and looked at the black bricks.

Imogen walked in at nine carrying take-out containers. The smell of curry preceded her. I tried to shake away the cerebral impulses that started zapping at the sight of her, those mental flashes that put my girlfriend and the murdered girl together and transposed the images before my eyes, my police brain trying to terrify me.

"It's my baby!"

"Hi, baby." She looked around, looked at me, looked at the three empty beers by my hand. Her pretty upper lip curled. "You know you're filthy, right?"

"Give me a kiss."

"No." She stepped around the pile of dust I'd swept from the floor and pulled a plastic step ladder from the wall, brushed it off before sitting on it. "You're drinking again?"

"They're virgins."

"Still."

"I know," I sighed. "I'll start again tomorrow."

"We should really go to my place. Get you a shower."

"I thought women liked men who worked," I said. I flexed my biceps. She missed it.

"Women like men who can afford other men to work for them."

I pointed at the ceiling. She looked up at the newly patched roof.

"Impressed?"

She said nothing. A call came in through my ears and I answered it with the button on the cord at my chest.

"Frank Bennett."

"What's up, dickhead?"

"Well, well! What's up, Hooky baby?"

"I called to see what's happening with that girl," Hooky said. "The park girl."

"Piqued your curiosity, has it?" I laughed. Imogen was watching me. I made an apologetic motion and got up, heard both my knees crack. I moved down the hall.

"I like to keep abreast of things," Hooky said. I could hear a train in the background. "North Sydney's not letting me have any fun while my exams are on. My life has become very pedestrian very quickly."

I walked out the front of my house and told Hooky what I knew so far about Ivana Roth's murder. It was a cool night, but nice. Watching a possum clamber along the gutter above the second-floor windows of my property and slip through the broken front window into the empty upstairs bedroom, I updated Hooky on everything I had. I heard a rustle and saw Imogen standing in the doorway. With an apologetic wave, I finished up with Amy, grabbed Imogen, and kissed her as I walked inside.

"Who was that?"

"Girl who works for my old station," I said, half dreaming at the sound of my feet on my own floorboards.

"*Woman* who works for your old station," Imogen corrected.

"No, actually." I laughed. "Girl. She's seventeen. Does some consulting work for us." I could hear the possum on the upstairs floor. I banged on the wall and listened to it scurry in terror. Imogen followed me back into the kitchen, where I retrieved the curry containers and snuck a forkful of Massaman from one. "We can go to your place now, if you like. I'm done here."

"Great." She slapped my butt when I bent down to get my backpack. She stood in the doorway as I gathered up bits and pieces I needed, mostly paperwork.

"What's a seventeen-year-old girl doing calling a middle-aged man on his cell phone?" she said. The words tumbled out of her fast, as though she'd spent the last couple of minutes holding them back, trying to talk herself out of them.

"Huh?"

"It's just a little bit slutty, isn't it?"

The thought of Hooky being anything close to warranting that term "slut" was absurd. I thought of her as something like an oddball little sister, or a niece—a little bird I'd seen take a big hit once, but who I was now happy to see flying again.

"She was just calling for an update on the case."

"Uh huh." Imogen folded her arms. "You called her 'baby.'"

"Holy crap! You're jealous. This is hilarious."

"Is it?"

"I've always called her 'baby.' It's not baby like . . . *baby*. Amy *is* a baby. She's like . . . a little girl."

"You call me baby."

"Ah. Well? I use the term with a different intention." This conversation was getting weird.

"Uh huh," Imogen said again.

Once again, I felt the sting of being unable to understand the ways of women, their secret codes and inferences. I didn't even have a basic grasp of what was being said here, what I'd done wrong.

"Baby," I said, reaching for Imogen, "don't be silly."

"Come on." She jerked her head toward the front door. "Let's go. It smells in here."

Tara remembered. The memories came as tides, slowly rising, hitting their peak, and when they did she would sit on the bed and indulge them, because she'd never had the strength to fight.

When she was at her most vulnerable, the memories were from when she was young—a Tara just starting to adapt to her pudginess, a Tara just beginning to assume her role as class reject. A short Tara, wide and soft, fleshy like a piglet, her little belly swelling and stretching the front of her sports polo as she panted. Cross Country day. The smell of freshly cut grass. The dread of the barbecue smoke in the school playground, the creamy fluorescent zinc being smeared on noses as the countdown to the afternoon session began. Tara the fat child, rotating through as many excuses to Mrs. Emmonds as she could muster, trying to find what would make the woman ignore her mother's threats. *My child will participate.* Tara heard the warning every year from the cordless phone in the kitchen, Joanie stabbing the countertop with a finger as house staff swirled and ebbed around her, preparing lunch. *Don't take any of her shit.*

Tara tucked herself into the dark corner of moldy bricks where the kindergarten building met the sports shed and listened to the big kids unloading the plastic markers and streamers with Mr. Tolson. Tara held her belly. She was just learning to swallow the crying.

She'd always been a crier before, but she was beginning to relish the hard, hot lump in her throat, the power she exerted in keeping it down, keeping the tears at bay. Tara didn't have power over many things. But she was beginning to learn, at eight, that she could control her own emotions. She could bring on or suppress rage like it was connected to a switch. She could make herself shake and sweat with fury, or make herself cold and fatigued with calm.

As the day wound down toward the big race, Tara watched the other girls weaving ribbons into their hair and painting zinc-cream dots on their cheeks. She went into the girls' bathroom and did the same, working the cream into her round face.

At the starting line, no one noticed her. She kept to the back, the horizon ahead dominated by the shoulders of the enormous year-six boys. Peter Anderson was wearing an Indian chief's ceremonial headdress, his freckled cheeks lined with zinc. The colorful tails of the feathers fluttered in the wind. The boy started a chant for Stuart House, and it grew so loud that it almost drowned out the crack of the starting gun.

Tara moved with the jostling bodies, and then she was on her own. Girls she remembered cowering in the playground on their first days in kindergarten rushed past her. She'd tried to befriend them once, and for a few days had held a posse of younger children as friends. But as they passed now, they seemed not to recognize her. Their class clans had fused together and shut Tara out. By the time she rounded the first-quarter marker, Peter Anderson was rushing past her, his huge legs striking out, hitting the grass with thuds. Boys from

Flinders and Cook houses followed, grabbing at the feathers. They were still chanting their house songs. Tara could hardly breathe.

Run, run, boys and girls,
Try to get away.
We won't stop, can't stop,
Gonna make you pay!

For the next quarter, she waited for the bigger boys to lap her again. When they did they came in silence, the game on now, the homestretch in sight. Tara struggled through the brush at the bottom of the school, followed the rustling pink streamers over rocky ground, her thick ankles twisting as she ran over sharp stones in the clay. Small helpless sounds came out of her. In the rocking, bouncing world, she spotted Mr. Lillington standing among the trees, a carpentry magazine in his hands, his heavy brow furrowed. He heard Tara bumbling along well before he saw her. Tara hung her head as he watched her approach.

"Hey," the man said, jutting his chin. "Harper. Harper. Down there and around to the right."

Tara wheezed, looked, and tried to control her whimpering. Sweat rolled down her calves. The teacher pointed, raised his furry brows.

"Down *there*, girl," he said.

He said "girl" the way Joanie said "stupid." When Tara looked, she saw the trail leading off toward the quadrangle. A shortcut. The woodshop teacher watched her go, his lined face softened by pity.

She heard other children laughing as she cut away. Tara only wanted it to be over. She emerged at the edge of the field as Peter Anderson sailed through the finish-line ribbon, his arms outstretched and shirt gone. Girls visiting from the high school pelted his hard, pale body with water bombs. Tara clambered up the rise and headed for the lines of teachers and parents waiting just past the finish line.

Her mother would be there among the crowd somewhere. Tara sucked in air and forced herself on. She was so slow she could measure individual expressions as she passed, heard snippets of words from the parents.

Whose kid is that? Harper. Harper girl . . . chubby little . . . rolls . . . Kid's gonna have herself a heart attack . . .

"She's snorting like a piggy," a girl at the edge of the crowd said, pointing at Tara. "Piggy, piggy, piggy!"

Tara felt sweat in her eyes. She pounded toward the finish line. A crowd of her classmates was waiting for her there, stretching their thin, strong limbs, zinc rubbed from noses and dribbling from wet chins. She could smell the barbecue.

Tubs of quartered oranges. Tara headed up the straight-away, and it was Craig Dune who threw the first slice.

"The food's up here, fatty boom-ba! Run run run!"

Tara felt an orange slice bump against her chest. Then another. A rain of them, boys and girls from older grades she didn't know hurling the slices at her legs, her face. Teachers shouting, reaching for little wrists. She caught a rind in the eye and slid in the wet grass. Fell hard on her side before the finish line. She could see the balloons, the girl with the broken leg and the timer, sitting on the stool.

Joanie was in the crowd, her arms folded, eyes on

the horizon. Tara scrambled to her feet and pushed through the adults, the forest of hips and stomachs, until she reached her. Her mother stood beside a woman who might have been her twin, both women caramel goddesses wrapped in fine gray silk. Joanie's ringlets were pulled tight in a ponytail over her shoulder, the curls cascading down her chest.

"Mum," Tara gasped through tears. "Mum."

"Is this your little one?" The woman beside Joanie looked down at Tara with a mixture of concern and humor, her crooked smile faltering when she noted the orange juice dripping from the girl's hair.

"Mum," Tara pleaded, tugging at Joanie's elbow.

"No, mine is out there." Joanie shrugged Tara's hand away, pointing toward the curve in the track.

"Mum—"

"Go find your mother," Joanie said, pushing Tara away. She turned her hip, blocking the child from the woman beside her. "Jeez. Weird kid. Anyway, so you were saying?"

Tara waited, but her mother didn't turn back around. In time, Tara walked through the crowds toward the school.

They try to tell you that you've got observers at the autopsy because they need experience for their forensic medicine degrees, but . . . I don't know. Even though I've had many young watchers hanging over my shoulder at autopsies through the years, I just can't get used to the idea that studying to be a ghoul is so popular. When we arrived to view the autopsy on Ivana Roth, two young men were already there, fumbling with their notebooks, surgical masks pulled tight like the shoelaces of kids on their first day of school. I gave them a fiery look as I waited for the tech to set up. I'm convinced a certain percentage of these students have just been too curious about murder corpses to stay away.

Beyond the glass, someone from Ivana's family was watching. An older brother, it looked like. I've only seen the parents attend once. I don't know why family attend at all. It's pretty grim.

Eden was unusually fazed by the whole situation. She was restless, sighing, looking at her watch. She'd ditched the crutch for the morning, but I expected her to be back to it by midday. Leaning against the table, with her ponytail pulling up the corners of her eyes and her blouse pressed to within an inch of its life, she might have been the old Eden again, the one I knew before her brush with death. Except that she was chewing a thumbnail. Her eyes were hard. I nudged her in the side and she jumped.

"What's wrong with you?"

"Too much coffee." She stretched her neck so that it cracked on either side. I knew that was a lie but I didn't push it. Eden could have snorted coffee like cocaine and not gotten the jitters. She absorbed chemicals like a sponge. I'd never seen her so much as tipsy.

"You've got to come to dinner with Imogen."

"No," she said.

"What makes you think you can put her off forever? She gets what she wants. She'll start turning up at your house."

"I would strongly suggest she doesn't do that." Eden looked into my eyes. I felt a cold splinter in my chest, sweat prickle at the back of my neck. I cleared my throat, tried to focus on the technician laying out his tools like a slow, methodical sadist. The brother behind the glass was watching the ceiling, fighting tears.

"What's your beef with Imogen?"

"I think you can do better."

I scoffed.

"Imogen is—"

"Imogen's an *owner*, Frank," Eden said. "She's going to own you and train you like a pup until you either bend to her command or snap her hand off one day, and it's probably going to be the latter before the former."

That hurt. She was referring to the time I'd hit my first wife in a drug-fueled brawl at our cheap rental house in the western suburbs. It was more than a decade ago, but Eden was never going to forget it.

"And when you do snap at her," she said, "then she's *really* going to own you."

"This conversation is getting far too deep," I said.

"Come to dinner. Please. I'm asking you nicely. Stave off your jealousy of Imogen for an hour or so."

"What could Imogen possibly have that I would want?"

I tapped my chest and gave her a happy wink.

"One of these days you're going to wake up to yourself."

"Hopefully not," I said.

I jostled her in the ribs again with my elbow and she jumped, swiping at me. I reached out and grabbed at her ribs, and heard a crackling sound under the fabric that was familiar to me.

"What is that?"

"Get your fucking mitts off me."

"Is that a tattoo?"

I was certain I'd heard the crackling of sticky tape and the squish of damp plastic wrap, the kind of dressing applied to a freshly inked tattoo. I'd stopped counting how many tats I had myself. I was most proud of the gigantic traditional-style eagle, wings spread, that dominated my chest. My first. It was tough to go big on your first ink, and that's basically all the image stood for—my young, stupid toughness.

"Do not touch me, Frank. Ever."

"We're about to get going here, people," the head technician said. He lifted the sheet from Ivana's body and pulled it down her naked figure. I looked up and saw that her brother was gone.

Ruben tried not to snoop, but he couldn't help himself. Something was very wrong in the house by the park. The path he took vacuuming from the ground floor kitchen to the stairs outside the attic room was like a morbid tour of the moment things went wrong, the last days of joy before the hellish fall.

The wrongness of it all had struck him as he entered the bedroom on that first day, fluffed the pillows, and shook the dust off the bedcovers. The bedroom belonged to a man and a woman. History books on his side of the bed, business-management books on hers. Ruben's written-English comprehension was terrible, but he'd flicked through the pages, found a shopping list bookmark in one. Then he'd spied the man's heavy Omega watch sitting by the lamp. He'd glanced behind him at the door. Felt a tingle in his palms. Why had the master of the house left his watch there? It was obviously his daily watch. No case or box. Why wasn't he wearing it when he left? Why hadn't he tucked it away, knowing that a foreign student with no paperwork and barely enough cash to make rent would be walking around the house?

There was more strangeness. The watch and the history books on the man's side of the bed were far dustier than those on the woman's side. The pages were yellowed from the sun. So they had lain untouched longer. Wherever he'd gone, she'd left his things just as they were. There was something sad about it.

When Ruben entered the downstairs living room, he'd found an empty wine bottle and a packet of sleeping pills on the little table beside the couch. There were three pills missing. On the floor was an empty sterile-needle packet. It was stamped *Prince of Wales Hospital*. The needle package, the wine bottle, and the pill packet were covered in dust. Whatever had happened here, the evidence had remained exactly as it had fallen.

Ruben had stood in the doorway, feeling cold all over. According to the advertisement he had answered, the family that owned the house had gone away to set up a business abroad. He'd heard a creak in the floorboards above him and had gone back to vacuuming. On his way out, he had ducked through the couple's bedroom to look at the master bathroom. All the toiletries were still there, the toothbrushes leaning, waiting, in their ceramic stands.

I was the first to arrive at dinner, so I kept busy by flipping through my notes on Ivana Roth's autopsy, my notepad on the empty plate in front of me. It was busy at Malabar South Indian Cuisine, on Darlinghurst Road, though it was a Wednesday. Groups stood outside the windows smoking and jostling in the growing cold, leaping forward when their numbers were called and darting away into the night, plastic bags trailing steam.

I tried to keep my mind on the job, but at the table next to me a strange kind of group had gathered. I couldn't keep my eyes off them. The woman attracted my attention first. I'm a red-blooded Australian male, so I notice women. This one was very eye-catching, and not in the traditional way.

She looked apocalypse-ready. She was muscled all over, the way survivors are muscled—a woman whose body was prepared both for running and fighting, for climbing and hiding and sliding down hills. She was more than "sporty." She looked dangerous. Three huge guys sat at the table with her, talking in low voices, passing bits of paper around and signing things. As the woman turned her ponytailed head and showed me her sharp profile, I watched all the muscles in her neck move, some loosening, some tightening, the wires and chains of a great machine working. Everything was skintight and rock-hard. It was exciting and kind of scary. I'm not sure it was my thing.

Get your mind back on the job, Frank.

We knew plenty about Ivana Roth from her body. There are no secrets when you're dead. The autopsy told us she'd been exercising for some time, lifting weights as well as doing cardio, and she liked upper-body exercises. Her triceps were well defined, and she had strong hands, sporting the nice little calluses you get on the upper pad of your palm from not bothering with gym gloves. She wasn't pregnant, a smoker, or a big drinker. She'd had braces once. She suffered mild psoriasis on her elbows. I tried to take note of all these little bits and then forget them. I didn't like knowing the victim too well.

Ivana Roth had been dragged somewhere, knocked about a little on the journey. She'd had her wrists taped—probably right up until she was dumped. She'd put up a fight but not much of one; there'd been no scratching or biting, which indicated to me that she'd probably been drugged. How do you drug someone while they're jogging around a public path in view of hundreds of witnesses?

Her water might have been spiked before or during the run. That wasn't the likeliest option, but it was possible. If the killer was someone she knew, he would have had to get hold of her water bottle before taking her. But if he knew her, why bother letting her go out for the run in the first place? If it was someone she didn't know, he would have had to somehow access the bottle she brought with her on the run—which might have occurred, if she'd stopped and put it down. A bit of a gamble, though, following a runner around waiting for her to put her water bottle down. What if she never stopped for a break during the run? What if she stopped, but she didn't let the bottle out of her sight?

Ivana Roth's autopsy had revealed a strange injury to the back of her left thigh, right below her buttock, bruised like a track mark and still open when she died. I didn't like the idea that there might be a killer out there with a tranquilizer gun putting down runners, but I couldn't think of another explanation. I had to wait until midnight for the toxicology report, but I was pretty sure it would back me up. Someone had hunted Ivana like an animal. Tracked her, caught her, and packed her into a van.

My phone vibrated in my pocket, a text. Imogen saying she was late, probably. She was the only person who texted me. When I opened it up, however, there was a message from Hooky. I felt my nose wrinkle involuntarily, Imogen in my ear like she was sitting beside me.

What's a seventeen-year-old girl doing texting a middle-aged man? Slut. Slut. Slut.

The text read: Tranquilizer gun, right?

I smiled and texted back: You're in pedos, girl. Not homicide.

She texted back before I had time to put the phone away: I want in!

When I looked up, Eden was settling into a chair beside me. She poured herself a glass of water, glanced toward the door without saying hello.

"You didn't change?" I frowned.

"Don't start."

"You attended an autopsy in that outfit, Eden. You think you could have slapped on a different shirt to come to dinner?"

"You're Murder Police, Frank, not Fashion Police."

"Imogen's going to come through that door in a second, desperately overdressed." I pointed toward the front of the restaurant. "It's going to be awkward."

"Frank," Eden smiled at me, patting my hand, "Imogen's always desperately overdressed."

We engaged in a long, uncomfortable silence, looking at the tablecloth. Imogen walked through the door, offering no relief at all in her foxy orange dress and little pearl earrings, and the pride of her collection—the eight-hundred-dollar Jimmy Choo shoes. She only wore orange when she really meant it; I understood it was a dangerous color to attempt. As she approached the table, I saw her face harden. When had I begun to sweat over what women were wearing? Imogen bent to kiss me and clouded me with Chanel.

"Eden, thanks so much for coming." She grinned and kissed Eden on the cheek. Eden hadn't seen the gesture coming and stiffened as though electrified. My phone flashed on the table, another text from Hooky. I tucked it away and Imogen gave me a look—the look a woman gives you when she's cataloging something in her mind, putting something away to burn you about later.

"Shall we order?" Eden asked.

"Imogen just sat down."

"I know what I want." Eden jutted her chin at the nearest waiter. He came to the table and Imogen scrambled for her menu.

"We'll order wine now." I kicked Eden under the table. "The Malbec, please."

The waiter retreated and Eden looked satisfied. She

picked up her knife and turned it on its point on the table.

"Well, what a crazy week," Imogen said brightly. "First that Byron Bay thing and now this."

"What Byron Bay thing?" I asked.

"Two hitchhikers and a couple of scumbags from some backwater hole behind Byron," Imogen said. "Police found them all stuffed into a burnt-out van. Can't seem to figure out who was going to kill whom. It's all over the news."

"Eh! How weird," I said.

"Do we have to talk shop at the table?" Eden snapped.

"Tough week, Eden?" Imogen smiled.

"I'm fine."

"Oh, I just mean—"

"She's not counseling you, Eden," I said. "She's just asking how you are."

"They never stop, Frank." Eden raised her eyebrows at me.

"Who never stops?" Imogen frowned.

"Let's order." I waved for the waiter.

Eden appeared to have a bit on her mind, which was unusual. She was pretty good at compartmentalizing, dropping the job when she couldn't do anything with it, picking it back up again when she could. She kept looking off toward the front doors, letting Imogen and me talk. She hardly ate, though what she'd ordered was by far the best choice on the table. She waved at me as I asked her if I could finish it. Imogen didn't seem to get the hang of Eden's closed personality. Kept plugging her with personal questions and getting nothing in return, though she spent plenty of time offering up examples from her own personal life as encouragement—stupid ex-boyfriends and her annoying sister and a nightmare boss who had come down on her too hard.

"Are you dating right now, Eden?"

"No."

"Single for a while?"

"Yes."

"I work with this guy named Nick who I think would be just perfect for you." Imogen glanced at me. "He's an anxiety specialist. I met him for the first time when . . ."

Now it was my turn to drift off. I like to tune out when Imogen talks about other men, in case I catch tales about guys with better jobs, bigger dicks, houses without possums in their upper floors. When I drifted back in, it was because Eden was kicking me under the table.

"What does it matter what my parents do?"

"Oh, I don't know. It doesn't *matter*, that's not what I mean." Imogen laughed uncomfortably. "It's just . . . I don't know. My dad inspired me to do what I do. He was a very clever man, but he never really fulfilled his potential. When I decided I wanted to be a psychologist . . . Maybe your father . . ."

I got out my phone, glanced at the time.

"We're going to have to wrap this up, ladies. I've got calls to make tonight." I put my arms around both of them. "Not that I'd rather be anywhere but sandwiched between you two gorgeous creatures."

Eden peeled my hand off her and got up, rifled

through her wallet with the hard-edged face of a john looking for money to pay a prostitute.

When I got back from the bathroom, Imogen was still sitting at the table, staring at the lone fork left over from the swift clearing the waiters had done. There's something sad about a freshly cleared restaurant table. The stains of a party attended, enjoyed, finished. Imogen didn't look sad, though, she looked cold. I sat down and went to grab my phone from where it sat in front of her, but her hand was over it before I could.

"What the fuck is this?" she asked. She pushed the button at the bottom of the phone and the screen lit up, flashing a preview of a message from Hooky. *Hook me up!*

"She's talking about the Roth case. The jogger. She wants some part in it, I don't know. She's hungry."

Imogen stared at me.

"What?"

No response.

I opened the message stream and showed her.

"See?"

"Why isn't she texting Eden?"

"She doesn't know Eden."

"Why isn't she texting Command?"

"She doesn't know anyone in Command." I laughed. "Jesus, they wouldn't want her kept in the loop anyway. It's not her case."

"So, you'd be doing her a favor." Imogen licked her painted lips. "You and some hungry little girl texting back and forth, doing each other favors."

"Fuck *me*, Imogen! This thing you've got going with Hooky is just . . . it's madness. She's a child. She's texting me in a wholly and completely work-related capacity. That's it."

"Oh, I'm sure."

"Babe, I don't know why I'm sitting here defending myself. I don't have to explain this to you. It's nothing, and I'm telling you it's nothing, and you're ignoring me. What you're insinuating is sick. She's seventeen years old."

"I'm not insinuating that you're trying to interact inappropriately with a seventeen-year-old, Frank. Open your ears. I'm insinuating that a seventeen-year-old is trying to interact inappropriately with you."

"And that I'm doing nothing about it."

"I'm trying to help you realize what's going on, so that you *can* do something about it."

"Well thank you, Imogen. Thank you very much. You're such a giving person."

"Fuck you."

"You don't know this girl. Her sister bludgeoned her own parents to death. She sprayed their brains all over their pretty pink bedroom."

"That's terrible."

"You're right. In fact, you have no fucking idea how terrible it was," I said.

"I'm sure it was the kind of terrible life event that might reorient a person's whole perception of the world. Of people. Of relationships. Of appropriateness."

"Oh Lord," I sighed. "Stop."

My face felt hot. I sipped the water nearest to me, tried to back down from the angry stairs I was slowly climbing.

"I mean, what are you doing going through my phone in the first place?"

You'll either bend to her command or snap her hand off one day . . .

"Why shouldn't I? Going through your phone shouldn't worry you, Frank, because you should have nothing on there that you wouldn't be happy for me to see."

Imogen threw her phone onto the table so that it bounced on the cloth. People turned in their chairs.

"You want to see my phone?" she snarled. "Go ahead!"

"I don't want to examine your phone, Imogen. I'm not that fucking needy."

And then when you do snap at her, she's really going to own you.

Imogen looked at me, broken. Then she got up and left. I tried to chase her, but she slipped through tiny gaps between the chairs of other patrons I just couldn't fit through. She was gone before I could see which way she went.

Here's the problem. A lot of people watch crime shows. There's an element of crime to most good television dramas. Not only are they rigidly formulaic, but they're fast. In minutes one to three, you get the crime. Minutes four to five, you get the detectives being called onto the job. Their shock and horror and heartfelt pledge to catch the guy (alongside some hints at their intoxicating hidden lust for each other). After that, you get a parade of standard possible suspects— cheerful big-city doormen, menacing drug dealers, the local cat lady, a cherry-cheeked schoolteacher. One of the detectives gets a seemingly innocuous phone call or public tip or something, remembers another apparently innocuous piece of information from the very beginning of the episode, and whammo! They nail the victim's boss, mother, boyfriend. The local sandwich shop guy. It's that easy.

People are used to crimes being solved before it's time for bed. In almost every scene, something is being done to solve the crime. Samples are being taken. Perps are being hassled or chased through rainy alleyways. No one eats or sleeps. They don't take bathroom or smoking breaks. They don't call their girlfriends and apologize for calling them "needy" (even though they clearly were being just that and possibly worse), or have make-up sex. They certainly don't stand around near the body talking, with their hands in their pockets.

Unfortunately, that's precisely what Eden and I were doing when they found the second girl in the Domain parklands, sitting upright against a tree near a bike rack in full view of the first person to ride past. The victim's jacket was over her head. From a distance, an onlooker might have thought she was chilling out after a long run. The jacket, however, was hiding grievous facial injuries, including a missing eye. The way her legs were stretched out, feet together, didn't suggest trauma. Whoever the finder had been must have gotten a nasty surprise once they pulled the hood back. The crime scene techs had erected a tent around the victim, but Eden and I had taken a quick peek and stepped out to confer, to let the five people inside do their thing. There was no phone this time, but earbuds had been left behind to indicate that there had been one at some point. A good crowd of morning joggers and a few members of the press gathered around the police tape, staring at us.

"Jacket over the head," Eden said. "Some shame still there, but we're growing out of it."

"A confused kind of display," I said. "Wants the body to be found, now. Clearly. But the killer's not particularly happy for everyone to know what's been done to the face."

"I don't think she can help what she does to their faces. I think that's the pure rage part. I think she just goes at the face before she knows what she's done."

"She?" I frowned.

"I'd say it's a woman." Eden looked at the crowd. "Wouldn't you?"

"Statistical probability would suggest otherwise," I said. "But I'll hear your theory."

"Clothes on this one aren't in disarray, the way they would be if they were removed and then put back on. I'm betting the rape kit will confirm no sexual assault once again. And then there's the facial injury. That's very feminine to me. Men go for the hair, the breasts, the wrists. They're objects for men. This . . ." she gestured to the tent, "this was personal."

"But we know it's *not* personal. We've pretty much ruled out anyone in Ivana Roth's life, and now—"

"Maybe it's personal by proxy," Eden said. She took a pack of cigarettes from her back pocket and slid one out, put it between her lips, patted her pockets for her lighter. "She can't get at the person she's imagining her victims to be. They might be beyond her reach somehow. So, she plays the fantasy out on random women. Once the face is messed up, she can picture the victim to be whoever she's *imagining* she's killing. It's pure Bundy."

Some bystanders at the tape near us bristled with excitement at the mention of Bundy's name. We took a step away from them and turned our backs.

"That's the second time you've brought up the old Bundy case," I said. "But you might be right."

It's always difficult to bring Ted Bundy into discussions about current cases. The "poster boy" of serial killing is a perfect model to use to teach young homicide detectives about serial murder, so Bundy is drilled into you from the second you transfer up from patrol. Bundy was responsible for the deaths of at least thirty-six young women in the midseventies, school girls as young as twelve to college students on the brink of starting their professional lives. He had a "type": women or girls with long dark hair parted in the middle, clever and beautiful girls who showed academic promise—girls who he lured into his tan Volkswagen Bug (and later kill van) with his charm and good looks.

It was never revealed why Bundy was so taken by girls with long dark hair parted in the middle, but some speculate that he was trying to symbolically kill an ex-girlfriend, Stephanie Brooks, who had humiliated him by rejecting him as a young man. Bundy was driven to murder Stephanie "by proxy," to rape and mutilate and bludgeon and strangle women who looked like her. Psychological understanding of serial murder was just kicking off around the time that Bundy was arrested, so he was the perfect model to use to test theories about killers.

I wasn't sure we had a "Bundy" killer on our hands here—there had been plenty of times in my career as a homicide detective that I'd heard the term mentioned. It was thrown around whenever violent crimes showed any kind of pattern. We were on our second victim. I thought it was too early to bring out Ted.

Eden waved at me for my lighter.

"What are you doing?" I lit her cigarette. "You don't smoke."

"I'd argue to the contrary." She eased smoke through her teeth.

"You're acting weird. The tattoo . . ."

"I got a tattoo, Frank. Big whoop. The press are over there if you want to make an announcement."

"This thing with Imogen."

"I don't have a thing with Imogen."

"It's just not like you to let someone piss you off like that."

"She doesn't piss me off." Eden gave one of her old

half grins, showed me a canine. "I just think she's a loser. I've got bigger fish in my life."

"Who?" I asked. "Is someone bothering you?"

"No."

"Well, I'm here if you need me."

"I neither need nor want you." She finished her cigarette and threw it on the ground, pushed it into the wet grass.

"Hey!" someone shouted from the crowd. Eden and I turned. It was hard to know who'd spoken at first among all the faces, the eyes examining us. A couple of people turned toward a man in his thirties in a full running skinsuit—black Lycra, slippery-looking, like a seal. He had a belt strapped to his waist with tiny bottles of water on it, a set of keys, and some kind of step-tracker device.

"Yes?"

"What the fuck are you two doing?" He put his gloved hands out. "You going to catch this guy, or what?"

"Excuse me?" I looked around, tried to determine if I knew the man. Eden was playing with her phone.

"I asked if you two are going to catch this guy," the man said, folding his arms. "You're standing there soaking up the morning like you're at a fucking picnic. People are scared out here, mate."

I laughed. I guess I was surprised and outraged and didn't know what else to do. I checked again to see if Eden was getting this, but she just looked bored. She'd taken my lighter out of my hand and used it to light another cigarette. The man in the seal suit pointed at her first cigarette on the ground.

"You're contaminating the crime scene."

Crime-show fan.

"The crime scene's in *there*, you idiot." I jerked a thumb toward the tent. "Who the fuck are you?"

A couple of the press cameras had turned toward us. I heard clicks, realized my jaw was out and my shoulders were up. Eden waved her cigarette in my face and brought me back around to her.

"I'm going to get onto the CCTV and get the tech-heads after that phone. If you're done cavorting with the locals, you can join me."

I glanced at her, but my mind was elsewhere—I'd spotted something odd over the shoulder of the dickhead at the edge of the police tape. It took me a few seconds to put together what I was seeing. A camera crew and a reporter were taping an interview with a woman just beyond the back of the crowd. I recognized the sharp ponytail, the muscled profile. It was the apocalyptic woman I'd seen at Malabar Indian. The fight with Imogen came to mind and my stomach flipped.

I ducked under the tape and worked my way through the crowd, stood behind the cameraman, and watched the woman giving the interview. She was wearing full running gear—the same kind of bodysuit the dickhead was wearing, but without, somehow, managing to look like a seal. She looked ready to rappel down into a bank vault and steal a diamond. There was no belt, no nylon cap. She thumbed the straps of a high-tech little camel pack with a water hose. There wasn't a bead of sweat on her. She was wearing thick bronze makeup and dark gold eyeliner. I couldn't decide if she was going to a charity ball or setting out to run to Parramatta.

"We need to recognize the message behind these killings," the woman said, swishing her ponytail. "And that is that strong, athletic, assertive women taking charge of their own health and well-being are threatening the dominant masculine archetype that's so much a part of Australian history."

"The what?" I looked at the cameraman. He was focused on the machine in his hands.

"Both these women were runners," the woman continued. "They were both targeted on their daily run, while they were out trying to better themselves, better their health and their lives. They were taking time for themselves. They were being self-*ish*, which is a misunderstood and demonized word applied by ignorant people to the women they want to be served by. I think we need to take the message that guy is giving us— that these women need to be punished for their self-empowerment, for their rejection of the simpering, weak, subordinate female mold—and we need to stick it where the sun don't shine."

"Who *is* that?" I asked the cameraman. The microphone guy emerged from behind him, leaning back as he lifted the furry mic hovering above the journalist's head.

"That's Caroline Eckhart."

"Who?"

"Caroline Eckhart." He went back to his mic with a shake of his head.

"So what you're saying is that these killings are a feminist issue," the journalist said.

"Oh yes. There's a deep misogyny at work here, one that all Australians need to recognize, not just those horrified by these brutal murders. Domestic violence is a frightening epidemic in this country, and whoever this man is, he's—"

"Who said the killer is a man?" I scoffed. Several people turned to look at me—the crew, the journalist herself—everyone but Caroline; she was on a rant, and nothing was stopping her. Her eyes were on the skyline, the glass windows of distant downtown. "What the hell is going on here?"

"Mate, you're messing up my sound bite" the mic guy snapped at me. I felt Eden's hand on my shoulder. She was pulling me toward the tent.

"Stop wasting time."

"Who is this chick?" I yelled as Eden tugged me away. "Woman, you have no idea what you're talking about!"

The crowd at the tape turned to look at me, almost all of them with hateful glares.

Hooky was haunted. But she didn't mind. To be haunted was never to be alone. From the moment they had come and taken her from her classroom to the principal's office, sat her down, and told her that her parents were dead, she had almost never been without their presence, or the presence of something she believed had been them. They hung on her, weighing heavy and hard in her chest like a rock on a chain. She became a kind of mouthpiece for them. A puppet. She became the advocate of angry ghosts.

In the beginning it had made her silent, drew her back from the cuddling and the crying and the sweets that had come when her parents had died, the inevitable flooding of love. She felt choked, suffocated by the smells that erupted all around her—flowers, fresh and then rotting and then dead in brown water, food, cakes, pickled things. It had made her explosive with those who tried to help her: her teacher; her friends. The awkward, scruffy-haired cop named Frank who didn't know how to be around her, who couldn't decide if he should treat her as a victim, a child, a woman, a survivor, an oppressed ethnic minority, or a toxic entity.

The hurt in her chest receded around him for some reason, the way it did when she managed to fight her way into her father's office, into his hard leather chair, the only place where she could get the true smell of him, the feel of him, onto her skin. That haunting hurt had pulled her there, and she hadn't known why, until she overheard the three officers at the computers arguing about who had blown their cover in the teen chat room, who didn't know what about teen language, whether Miley Cyrus was still cool or not, what "LOL" meant and when to use it. She'd felt tugged forward on that chain again. When she'd begun lying online, she'd felt in control for the first time since the deaths. She felt all right with being haunted.

In the early days, wandering aimlessly through Chinatown toward Paddy's Markets, cast out of the North Sydney Metro offices and put on a train back to her aunt's, she'd felt the twisted justice pulse within her. An elderly woman stopped at the McDonald's attached to the entertainment center, shook out a leopard-print umbrella, and set the pretty item on the bricks outside the store before going in and joining the queue. Hooky had been watching with her hands in her pockets, coming up the street behind a group of girls about her age, when she saw one of the girls—a lean creature with pink streaks in her hair—dart out and snatch up the umbrella and continue walking, her pace never slowing, the theft so seamless and natural it seemed almost expected.

Hooky had followed the girl into the public bathrooms inside the Market City shopping center, waited for her to emerge from the stall, and punched her, just once, square in the nose. The blow had crushed the hard, narrow bones there and launched a rush of blood down the front of the girl's sparkly top. Hooky had turned and left. Returning the umbrella to the old woman hadn't even crossed her mind. She didn't know if what she'd done had been justified, had been "right." She didn't know if justice was a real thing, anyway. All she knew was that the burning in her chest was eased.

Sometimes, Hooky felt compelled to cheat people, to make them believe things about her that were not true. She told herself sometimes that she did these things to hone her skills for her online games with the perverted souls who lurked there, the men who wanted to be daddies pushed too far by teasing stepdaughters, the women who wanted to teach boys how to make love. But she was also aware that she cheated and lied just because it was fun. She would strike up a conversation on a bus with an older man and build a Hooky that was not real, a twenty-one-year-old Hooky with a boyfriend named Ted who worked in graphic design, a Hooky who lived in a trashy little apartment in Erskineville and who couldn't get enough of this vegan café there. Hooky wasn't vegan. She'd only been to Erskineville once. The lies weren't even extravagant. But the way the older man nodded, accepted, didn't question— that was what thrilled Hooky. No one questioned her. People trusted. Hooky could be anyone she wanted.

Hooky bought costumes for her fantasy lives. Money wasn't a problem. Her parents, ever practical, had left their daughters everything and not bothered with conditions. She'd made the necessary arrangements to see her sister's share of the inheritance ordered over to her through Victims of Crime, to continue her parents' investments, to take over their stock portfolio, and to sign her name on the deed to their home. Hooky had sold the house in which they'd been killed for a quarter of what it was worth, just weeks after the murders faded from the headlines.

Snappy suits and ragged jeans and an old, stained chef's uniform. Silk-lined party dresses and demure librarian dresses, ankle-length and olive green. Sometimes Hooky trawled the nightclubs, made men buy her drinks, played the naïve Japanese tourist dumped by her friends, curious and a little frightened by white guys and their loudness. Japanese, Vietnamese, Chinese, these guys didn't know the difference, and didn't care, as long as she played to their expectations—was cowed and grateful and a little surprised by her own passion after a couple of vodkas. Naughty Oriental girl. Sometimes she'd indulge the fantasies of older businessmen, sometimes women, sitting at the bar at the Union Hotel with her expensive heels hanging off her toes, writing gibberish on napkins as she listened to a call from some director in the US who didn't exist. She never went home with them. That was the cheat. That was the point of it all. It was all lies. When their backs were turned, she vaporized.

Hooky knew, deep down, that she was in training for something, that the thing inside her wasn't only pulling her through these little fantasies but was also growing, escalating, becoming hungrier. She was evolving into a skilled con woman. Soon, cheating people with her chimera games wouldn't be enough. She'd begin robbing them. She'd begin hurting them, making them cry—emptying bank accounts and ruining lives, maybe. It was something she could see looming on the horizon like a wave, but there was no running to the shore before it crashed over her. Her legs were stuck, sinking, being drawn out from beneath her.

Maybe one day she would start killing them, luring them to their deaths. The thought that there was a killer inside her terrified her. Was that inside her, the way it had been in her sister, a killer genome cooking up chemicals in her brain, building a desire to inflict pain? Would the ghosts that had once been her parents haunt her so long that only blood would satisfy them?

Hooky was getting her morning fix of chameleon games when the woman came to the Sydney Metro police station counter and rapped on the surface. Hooky leaned back in her chair and saw glossy painted nails, acrylics, and then went back to her conversation with Badteacher69, her fingers darting over the keys. It wasn't Hooky's job to serve the counter. When the woman tapped again and called out a friendly hello, Hooky looked around and saw no one in the service area. She unhooked her headphones and went to the counter. The woman was small and blond and pretty, with a blunt-cut strawberry fringe sitting neatly on a freckled, uncreased brow. She glanced over Hooky's outfit, and the younger girl straightened her camouflage-pattern tank top, pulled up her baggy black pants full of items she'd never carry in a handbag.

"Can I help you?"

"I'm looking for Detective Frank Bennett," the woman said. "I'm his girlfriend, Imogen."

"Oh." Hooky laughed. The woman was so small and neat and stylish—hardly Frank's type. Hooky had never considered what Frank's type might be, but this woman looked like something best handled with care. She thought of Frank's big callused hands, the way he knocked things and crushed things, as if every room was slightly too small for him, like everything was too delicate. "Oh, right."

"I've brought him lunch," Imogen said, setting a

plastic Tupperware container on the counter. Hooky took the container, tried to determine what its contents might be. She saw raw carrot. Tried not to smile.

"Well, Frank's out, Imogen. So . . ."

"When will he be back?"

"There's no telling," Hooky said. She felt her eyebrows dart together. "Like, he could be anywhere."

Hooky knew her tone was patronizing, but couldn't help it. It was just the funniest thing she'd seen in a long time, some wifely figure right out of Pleasantville with her perky heels and her gold bracelets, dropping off lunch for her Frankie-bear. Hooky had once seen Frank eat a muffin with the paper still attached to it. Her amusement really had nothing to do with the woman before her at all, but Hooky watched as a coldness came over her face.

"So you're Hooker, are you?"

"Hooky," she said.

"Right." Imogen's features reassembled into the smile. "I get it now."

"He's spoken about me?"

"Yeah, some." Imogen smirked, looked at Hooky's shirt again. "I feel so stupid."

"Why?"

"Oh, I was worried. It's silly. I didn't realize you really are just a child."

Hooky's face darkened. Imogen turned, and Hooky watched her breeze through the automatic doors into the street.

Eden was on the edge. At first, when Merri had told her of the woman trying to get a picture of her birthmark, Eden had been able to control her inner "flight" reflex, that whispering voice that made her want to drop everything and run, as she had imagined doing so many times. Hades had always made sure she had a plan in place. Money, a bag, a new identity. Going to ground, being reborn as someone new—these things didn't concern Eden. Usually.

She'd been undercover enough times to know how to shed herself. Eden herself was a construction, after all—a mask she had been wearing since the morning she and Eric had become Hades's children, since they had adopted their new names, settled into their new life with the Lord of the Underworld playing Daddy. Eden wondered, sometimes, what sort of girl she might have been if the girl she had once been, Morgan Tanner, hadn't had to be snuffed out, just as effectively as Eden would have to be, perhaps. Who was Morgan Tanner? Who would be born when Eden Archer was dead? Eden wandered, up the hill toward the shack at the center of the Utulla Landfill, toward the warm golden lights of her home.

Whenever she visited now, something was changed, moved slightly, and upgraded to allow for Hades's slow decline—the back that wouldn't hold now under the weight of certain tools, the knees that cracked down steps. Everything was closer to the little house to eliminate the need to walk over uneven ground for long distances, the letterbox shifted up toward the front door, the bench where he liked to sit and watch the workers now beside the steps, under the awning.

Hades insisted on living by himself, beyond the reach of anyone who might change a lightbulb for him, who might lift a heavy pot from inside the oven. But there she went again—dreaming of lives that were not real. Hades was not a vulnerable old man. His hands were worn, but hard. His mind was dark, but quick. He was going to die one of these days as lethal and as malignant as he always had been. There would be no spoon-feeding in a nursing home, no adult diapers. He would meet a bloody end with one of his clients, or he would push the man into it—an end in war was Hades's only end.

Eden did not find Hades in the house. She walked over the hill toward the work shed, looking up as she passed beneath huge structures lining what had once been a rocky stone path but was now a set of immaculate steps cut into the hillside and laid with terra-cotta tiles to save the old man's ankles. A giant grizzly bear made from hundreds of bottles towered over her, the glass warped and melted together, the chest of the beast pocked and holed with open glass mouths strapped down with hunks of wire against a rib cage of old wood. A mouth roared at the sky, the innards of the skull pipes and tubes welded and tied together, the gaping eyes microwave doors, tilted, sad, one burnt through from an inner explosion.

Across from the bear, a lion was frozen midpounce, the claws reaching over Eden's head, polished brass parts from a series of ancient machines—clocks and printing presses, the dozens of typewriters chucked into the dump each month. Down the lion's back, a rippling curve, thousands of typewriter keys spelled gibberish, the letters glimmering, black and white and yellowed with age. She went down toward the work shed and stepped through the open door, nothing stopping some stranger from wandering in here and seeing him at his dark work, as always. Hades had never been one to hide.

He was bent over a workbench. A body lay on the table before him, the thick head turned away. An old handsaw rocked in Hades's fist, back and forth, and Eden walked around the table in time to see the corpse's left leg crack off at the knee, flopping wetly to the table.

"What seems to be the problem, officer?" Hades said. He put down the saw and wiped his hands on the cloth apron he would later burn, smearing black blood down his chest like war paint. Hades had always liked getting bloody. He didn't wear gloves or a mask. Blood droplets had spattered his left cheek. Eden took out a handkerchief, sighed, and swiped at her father's temple.

"What is this? You said you were done."

"I am done."

"Well, who's dropped this on you, then?"

"Oh, that idiot. Jesse Jeep. It was a favor returned. That's it, now. I really am done."

"Uh huh." Eden glanced into a huge duffel bag lined with black garbage bags sitting behind the table. "And *you've* got to do his chop work?"

"The chop work was sort of half done." Hades shrugged one shoulder. "Arms, at least. You know these kids, Eden. They have no stomach."

Eden rolled up her sleeves. Hades handed her a long-toothed hacksaw and she set it to the man's right knee. She was about to begin cutting when she noticed a basket on the other side of Hades's feet, overflowing with old blankets.

"What is that?" As she spoke, the creature in the basket awakened. A pink nose on a caramel snout emerged from the blankets, snuffled the air, and sunk away again.

"Is that a roo?"

"No. It's a dog."

"You got a dog?"

"I don't go out and *get* things, Eden." Hades smiled a little. "You know that."

For a while, they sawed the body apart in silence, Hades stopping now and then to sip from a blood-covered mug. Eden stood to the side so that the spray of fluids from the backward motion of the saw didn't stain her trousers. As she was laying the leg in the duffel bag, she paused.

"Hades, there's another leg in here."

"What?"

"You heard me."

"I just put a leg in there."

"Yeah," Eden said, holding up the leg she'd cut by the calf. "So there's two in the bag and one in my hand."

Hades put his saw down and limped over. He looked into the bag, then at the leg in Eden's hand.

"That's a tricky sort of business," Hades sniffed.

"Someone's mixed up the distribution. Looks like a woman's. Calf is shaved."

"That's two grand right there, that extra leg." Hades pointed to the bag with a stubby finger. "The price I gave was for one body. One. Not a body and a . . . a tenth."

"You better call him up."

"Oh, I will," Hades muttered as he set the saw to the corpse's throat, took a handful of hair, and swung the blade. "The cheek of these young people. The absolute cheek."

"Could have been an honest mistake."

"These young pricks."

"Hades, I want to talk about my parents."

He stopped sawing. Leaned on the head on the table, his palm mashing the face into the bruised wood.

"I'm almost certain I've told you everything I know over the years, girl."

"No one ever knew?" Eden shifted the leg in her hands, looked down at the toes against her forearm. The nails were sharp. Yellow. "Even Maggie . . . ? You never told her where we came from?"

"All I told Maggie was that if anyone ever came asking, her daughter had dropped two brats off on me, just before she necked herself. Eden, a girl, and Eric, a boy. Daughter'd only been dead a week at that time, so Maggie welcomed the money. It was a simple lie. Two grandchildren she never saw, given back to their deadbeat dad. Didn't know nothing about 'em, didn't know where they were."

"What if someone approached Maggie?" Eden said. "What if someone asked to see pictures of the children?"

"Maybe there never were none. Jesus. I don't know. It's been, what . . . twenty years?"

"There was a Western Australian kid that went missing. Bainbridge. Ten years ago. You seen the news?"

"Redheaded kid. I saw it. Didn't know the name."

"The Stronghearts Foundation has been running with it. The anniversary. They've been getting the government behind all these old cases."

"So?"

"People don't forget, Hades. Not ten years later, not twenty years later. They're still writing books about Mr. Cruel. That's twenty-six years ago, the first one."

"And?"

"I looked at our case. Eric's and mine. They're bumping the reward money up by a hundred thousand dollars. The Stronghearts Foundation has recommended the government increase the reward money on a bunch of old cases to get them solved. Us, the Evans girl, the Beaumont children. The redheaded kid, Bainbridge. There's a big push right now."

"The reward money has always been big, Eden."

"Maybe it'll be big enough now for someone to act on a hunch they've had. Maybe someone's decided to just . . . go for it. I don't know."

"Eden."

"Maggie. You gave her our birth certificates, didn't you?" Eden chewed her nails. "Some . . . school records?"

"I made it real, Eden. I've done it before." Hades adjusted the grip on his saw. "You're not the first human beings I've reinvented. Reinventing people is a bit of a talent of mine. I've never failed."

"What if you failed this time?"

"Eden."

"What if someone found out we weren't real? What if someone connected us to the Tanners?"

Hades put down his saw. He walked forward and took the leg from Eden's hand, dropped it into the bag.

"My fucking birthmark was in the paper."

Hades cocked his head.

"This." Eden touched her side. "It was in all the news reports at the time we went missing. My only unique, distinguishing feature. Twenty years ago, it was all over the news. And now thousands of people must have seen it on the front page of the fucking *Herald* when Frank carried me out of that farm."

"You look at the case files for your parents' murders, Eden, and it'll say bikers," Hades said. "It's stamped unsolved, but there's a good four or five leads that all end with bikers. Some pieces-of-shit skinheads in the Dugart gang or someone or other found out about your father's windfall and blasted the two of them, came up empty-handed. Botch job. Sold you or buried you or . . . something. No one asks these questions, Eden, not anymore. No one's going to come after you because of a birthmark. The lead officer on your case is dead. He'd be the only person on earth who would remember something as tiny as that."

"I think you're wrong. Someone is looking for us."

"You're being paranoid." Hades tucked a strip of her dark hair behind her ear, remembered how hard it was for her to accept the touch of another human being, and stopped. "There have been times, over the years, that you've—"

"Someone visited Maggie. Asked her about her grandkids."

Hades's jaw twitched.

"I feel it," Eden said. "Someone knows."

Hades paused, looked at his work on the table, one of many ended lives he had hidden over the years. Since he retired, his life had been all about hiding things, burying things, making things clean. Tying up loose ends and folding down corners, making murder not only clean and neat but easy, economical. Out in his dumping grounds, only the souls of those buried there remained. The leachate acid that built up between the layers of landfill dissolved rapists, murderers, con victims, and gamblers who'd pushed the grace of their bookies too far. Sometimes Hades heard screams in the night, but there was no telling if these were from those lost and frightened out there in the dark, in the ground, or if they were echoes of his own past, memories of people who'd deserved his wrath, and people who hadn't. He reached out and took his daughter's hand, squeezed the fingers, stained them with blood, just as he had done the night she came to him, a child newly orphaned, a problem he had to fix. He had stained her. He had made her the monster she was.

"We'll bury it," Hades said. "That's what we do."

"I think something terrible happened at my house," Ruben said. Phillipe sat beside him in the back row of the small bare classroom, texting his new Australian girlfriend, a tall, leggy blonde who'd come to the hostel to complain about the music. Ruben looked at the posters on the classroom walls. *"G'day, mate!"* cried a cartoon kangaroo. Ruben hadn't heard anyone say "G'day" since he arrived in Australia, nor had he seen a single kangaroo.

"Something terrible like what?" Phillipe asked in Italian.

Ruben told him about the watch by the bed, the inconsistent amounts of dust on the books. He told him about the pill packet on the living room floor, the footsteps in the attic bedroom that was always locked, the television that played the same phrases over and over.

Reach out and take what you've always wanted.

You deserve it. You deserve it. You deserve it.

Phillipe brushed him off.

"Why don't you just go up there? Just knock and say hello?"

"The house is a nightmare."

"Come work with me, then." Phillipe put down his phone. "I can get you a job at the Argyle. It's pumpin' there, brother. The chicks, oh. The chicks." He smiled at the ceiling.

"What time did you finish up last night?"

"Three."

"That's why I don't come work with you." Ruben tapped his friend's chest.

"Are you guys listening back there?" the teacher called.

"Yes," the boys answered in English. They opened their notebooks in unison with the rest of the class. Ruben spread a stack of old newspapers before him.

"What are these?" Phillipe asked.

"The translation assignment, idiot. You had to bring something in."

"Oh, shit!"

"Yeah, I brought extra for you. You'd forget your own mother."

"What are these? They're so old."

"They're not that old. They've just been lying in the sun. I found them at the house, in one of the bedrooms. You're going to help me figure out what they say."

"You're like Scooby-Doo," Phillipe sniggered. "Solving mysteries. Getting to the bottom of things."

"Shut up and translate." Ruben shoved the dictionary into his chest. "I don't want to hear any more of your shit."

"Are you guys working back there?"

"Yes," they answered.

A feeling much like defeat takes me whenever I open a package from Ikea. I would have been very good as a Neanderthal—rolling rocks together and covering them with lumps of wood. But when it comes to tiny screws and pieces of plastic and stickers and things that you pop out of perforated sheets, I'm incapable.

I stared at the instructions for my new kitchen for a while and decided I'd figure everything out when I'd gotten all the pieces out of their boxes and onto the floor. Bad idea. I sat in the middle of my mess and opened fake beer and went to the instructions again. The cartoon handyman with his oversize Allen wrench was grinning at his construction like a fool.

It was midnight. I couldn't sleep. Whenever I closed my eyes I started running, and there was a darkness behind me, bodiless, trying to catch up. Sweaty nights usually accompany the beginnings of a big case, particularly when the media get hold of it. The watchfulness, the expectation of a country, sometimes the world, flutters at the back of your mind, lingering behind everything—the look on the guy across the train car, the tone in the waitress's words. Desperation. *Solve this. Solve this fast.* If the murders keep happening or the rapist isn't caught or a body lies unidentified beyond a reasonable time, you're almost committing the crimes yourself. *Why didn't you stop him? Why didn't you save her? Why don't you do something? What are you? How can you sleep at night?*

The front door opened and closed just as I'd finished categorizing all the different screws and nails and things by size. Eden walked in and chucked her keys onto the floor, looked at the catastrophe I marked the center of.

"Can't sleep either?"

"What are you . . . ?" she said. She blinked at some marble countertops leaning against the wall. "Never mind. Get out of the way."

I took my beer and shuffled to the side of the room, grabbed a chair, and put it in the corner. She sat and read the instructions. When she'd perused the diagrams for a minute or so, she set them aside and started grabbing pieces from around her, fitting and locking things together with satisfying clicks. She fixed things to the wall with a wood-handled screwdriver my father had owned, her hair hanging in her face. In minutes, it seemed, a frame was assembling, the bottoms of drawers and cupboards being slotted into place. She was such a capable person. I was jealous of her. Eventually she took a break and sat with her legs crossed, sipping a fake beer, looking through diagrams of drawers.

"We've got to brief Captain James in six hours," she said after a time.

"You want to lead with similar crime analysis?"

"No. The tranquilizer," she said, setting the pamphlet aside. "It's our best lead so far. Let's face it. We've got shit-all otherwise."

Images retrieved from CCTV around Centennial Park on the evening of Ivana Roth's murder were useless. Across the 467 acres of parkland, there were cameras around the gates of the park, but few inside the park itself. Those inside were designed to capture thieves or vandals targeting the café or equine center, so were not directed toward joggers on the tracks. Crime in the park was rare. There were the odd cases of assault and robbery, but not enough to erect a $20,000 surveillance system, put together a command center, or hire security guards. The place was unpopular at night, and too populated during the day for any real drama.

Our killer hadn't brought the van into the park itself, so we couldn't get a license plate number. There were three clips of Ivana running laps, her hands raised and her lips pursed as she passed the gates. No sign of anyone watching or following her. No one was keeping pace with her—she was being passed and passing others at irregular intervals, so for long stretches she would be on her own. On the third lap, we caught a glimpse of a shadow moving along the tree line in the bottom left-hand corner of the image, but there was no telling if it was in any way related to Ivana. We didn't capture any footage of her being shot, stumbling, perhaps being helped through the brush toward a gap in the fence, to a waiting car, while she fought for consciousness.

Plenty of people had seen other people getting into vans around the time Ivana was taken. After-work traffic clogged Anzac Parade, Oxford Street, and Alison Road. The Athletics Field and Queens Park were being flooded by corporate soccer and running teams as kids were being picked up from Little Athletics groups, cars whizzing in and out of the same spots, horns blasting as people squeezed into tiny gaps or waited for young ones dashing across the grass. The killer had used the cover of crowds and noise to snatch Ivana Roth away from the pack. Nobody saw anything. This was how kids like Jamie Bulger got walked right out of a crowded shopping center without anyone batting an eyelid. Crowd blindness.

Eden and I sat with our empty beer bottles, looking at the floor of my half-finished kitchen.

"The Domain footage might be better," I said.

"Hmm," Eden said.

"Where does a person get a tranquilizer gun?"

"It's not the gun we're concerned with," she said. "You could get that anywhere."

"I doubt you'd get one just anywhere."

"Well, you might get one in a black-market import. Go to a big-game company. I mean, we might spend the next three weeks going through stolen gun reports. Any farm from here to Kalgoorlie's got the right to have one. We don't want to end up doing background checks on every big-game worker from Taronga Zoo to Alice Springs. If it was me, I'd make the thing myself. Cheaper and easier to do it that way."

"And how, exactly, would you set about doing that?"

"Well I don't know *exactly*. I haven't really thought it through. But it doesn't sound hard. It's probably just some sort of gas compression job. You could take apart a .50 caliber paintball gun and—"

"Never mind." I forgot, more frequently than was probably safe, what Eden did in her spare time, what she had been responsible for in her life. It was easy to think of her as harmless when she was sitting on my kitchen floor braiding her hair. A news report I'd seen that morning on the TV in the kitchen at Imogen's house returned to me—the same one I'd heard on the radio on the day Ivana was found. *Four dead in mystery slaying south of Byron Bay. Police hunting "expert assassin."*

"So the gun's probably a dead end."

"The drugs aren't, though. There are only three families of drugs that would suit an uptake like that—through the muscle tissue, into the bloodstream," Eden said. "Sedatives, anesthetics, and paralytics. Each family's got its own characteristics. Some are faster than others, last longer, work on different parts of the body. If toxicology can tell us what type of drug we're looking for, that'd be great. But I suspect it'll be difficult—the elevated heart rate of the victims, the tiny amount that would have been delivered. We might need to try to find CCTV footage to understand how the thing worked on the victim. How long the take-down took."

"The take-down, huh?" I licked my bottom lip. "Is that what you guys would call it? You and Eric?"

I hadn't meant the question to sound nasty, particularly as she was just about finished putting my kitchen together for me. I was genuinely interested. Had she and her brother developed a language for what they did? Did they have rituals, a routine, a trophy collection, like most serial killers? But the way the question registered across her face, I could see that the effect of my words had been malignant. She went back to her work, turning the screwdriver in her skilled fingers as she fitted rails to the side of a drawer. Whatever it was between us, the unspoken understanding that we would leave her killer nature undisturbed, seemed to be thinning. The knowledge was like a black dog that followed us everywhere. I knew it wasn't going to stay quiet forever.

Had Eden killed those four people up in Byron Bay on the weekend? Had she made a day trip of it—bought a pie at a roadside 7-Eleven and sipped iced coffee as she drove, her gun on the seat beside her? What was making me think this way? Maybe I was being paranoid.

When I asked myself if I really wanted to know if Eden was still killing, I found the answer was no.

Tara thought about killing for the first time when she was sixteen. She was standing on the sports field at the edge of the cricket match, the sun blazing on her classmates' uniforms, making them blur in her vision. To her right, a group of girls had given up coverage of their section of the field and sat in a group stringing pieces of grass, some lying with their heads in the laps of others, having their hair braided.

Tara watched their easy physical intimacy and wondered about them, the popular girls, why they felt the need to constantly touch, what message that was supposed to convey. Because everything that came from them had a message. Nothing was explicitly said. Looks pierced her, words jabbed at her, turned backs left her cast out. The popular girls were always hugging and holding hands. They shamelessly caressed and groomed each other, rubbed lipstick smears from the corners of gaping mouths. Now and then they would fall on a boy, all of them brushing his hair and massaging his shoulders, gripping the hard muscle through the fabric. Peter Anderson was always among them, whenever the teacher's back was turned, guiding their hands toward the hardness of his thighs, laughing when they squealed.

No one ever touched Tara. In the second grade, the girls and boys in her class had developed a terror of her "germs." If one of them touched Tara, they would have "Tara germs." Anyone who touched the newly infected child would also have them. Tara was infectious. The game made the boys and girls squeal and run and slap at each other with their dirty, infected hands. Touching Tara meant social rejection, so when it came to grabbing a partner, getting in a group, forming a circle, Tara always found herself separated by plenty of space. The game had ended finally, worn off, over the summer holidays. But the symbolic infectiousness seemed to linger, even now that all of them were older. No one came near her.

They seemed to touch each other all the more when they knew she was near.

She watched the ball bounce nearby, walked after it as the class howled, and it was then the thought came to her.

Kill all of them.

The words in her head shocked her. She was almost tempted to look around, to see if they'd been whispered from a body outside her own. But she was alone, of course. Always alone. She squinted in the sun and heard the voice again as the bell rang and the popular girls sprang to their feet.

Kill all of them, she thought. *Make them touch each other, if that's what they want. Make the boys force their fingers into the girls until they scream. Make the girls strangle each other. Make them beg. Make them grip at each other. Make them writhe together like worms, naked, flushed with blood.*

By the pile of equipment, Mr. Willoughby was teaching a group of boys about the seam on the ball while Steven Korin wanked a cricket stump, holding it against his crotch, jerking the sanded wood. His eyes rolled up in his head. The boy directed the stump at Mr.

Willoughby's back, then turned on Tara as she got close and jabbed the dirt-clotted tip of the stump into her thigh.

"Oh baby," the boy groaned. "Gimme some a' dat sweaty lurve!"

The boys howled with laughter. Tara jammed her hands into the wet patches beneath her arms, started to run. They called after her, loud enough so that she could hear them as she ducked into the girls' bathroom. The second bell rang for the younger kids, and a crowd swelled under the awning, tiny seven-year-olds with their immaculate hats and backpacks bursting with books. Tara watched them pass beyond the door. She thought about their necks in her fingers, their knobby knees struggling and bumping on the ground as she took them.

One day, every week, Imogen took time away from her commitments at the clinic to work on her superhero life, her pursuit of Eden Archer—or Morgan Tanner, as Imogen was now sure was her real name. Imogen knew increases to the reward money for missing children nationwide would be generous, especially for a double tragedy like the Tanner children. She was confident she would have enough on Eden to scoop up the reward money almost immediately after it was announced.

With the bump to the reward for any information on the disappearance of Morgan and Marcus Tanner rumored at a hundred thousand dollars, she had to make sure she kept her investigation quiet. There would be other armchair detectives and cybersleuths out there, with search engine traps, who would happily hack her once they realized she was picking around the case. She'd run into some hard-core players, professionals who traveled the globe picking up reward money for missing kids, rich dead husbands and wives. Some handed out business cards at candlelight vigils and hounded victims' families on their doorsteps, shoulder-to-shoulder with the press.

Imogen couldn't dream of that sort of commitment, not yet. Her clinic in the city kept her obsession with police officers under control, while allowing time for her side games with the missing children. Imogen needed

multiple forms of entertainment. She'd always been a
restless girl.

There was a future growing in her mind of herself
and Frank as a partnership, using his police skills and
her investigative drive to make a real living out of
"armchairing," as it was called. She twirled the bracelet
he had given her, a guilt token he'd come home with
after the scene at Malabar. He could be controlled.
That was the first check mark in Imogen's list. He had
access to things she usually had to seduce her way
into—criminal records, driving records, family medical records, cop shoptalk, and lawyer buzz.

If Imogen could bring down Eden Archer, right in
front of Frank, it would show him how clever she was,
how blind he'd been to the possibilities of using his
skill outside his job, with its dismal salary. She could
train him up, show him the ropes, and give him a taste
of investigative work beyond the badge. Open his eyes
to his true potential. What she was doing was sometimes rougher, sometimes harder, than being a boy in
blue—but she would show him he was capable; let him
be her sidekick.

Imogen ordered a latte from the young waitress and
spread her things over the table, brought her glasses up
from her nose, and prepared to make a summary of
what she had on Eden. As soon as she had spotted the
birthmark on Eden's side in the newspaper, Imogen's
information had grown. Sunlight filtered through the
trees lining Macleay Street, making patterns across her
papers. The barista, a Brazilian girl, juggled the orders
of the men and women around her, designers and ar-
chitects and the bored housewives of Potts Point be-

ginning their day with organic biscotti served on earthenware saucers.

Her first assumption was that Eden Archer was an adult Morgan Tanner. The birthmarks looked the same—she'd tried for a photograph of the mark on Eden's side, but hadn't managed one yet. Eden was the right age, according to her service record. She looked very much like the child in the missing posters—the same sharp features, Daddy's black hair and iceberg-blue eyes. If Eden Archer was Morgan Tanner, that meant there was a good chance that her deceased brother, Eric Archer, had been the other missing Tanner child—Marcus. He was the right age, according to his service record.

The first thing Imogen had done was investigate Eden's supposed parents. The mother, Sue Harold, had been a junkie and a dropout—a wild woman who, it was reasonable to believe, had left the earth with only a box of odds and ends at her mother Maggie's house, her children long passed over to her ex-boyfriend and her bank accounts empty. Imogen had visited Maggie Harold, asked to see the box of worldly possessions Sue had bequested to her, and found not a single sentimental trace of the woman's supposed two children in it. Not a photograph. Not a card, a drawing, a teddy bear, not a child's blankie or a pair of old knitted booties—the kind of keepsake every mother kept. There was a report card from Eric's first year at school, and copies of their birth certificates. These were folded neatly and sitting in a single envelope, together, pristine.

Imogen had inferred two things. One, that Sue Harold did not own any mementos of Eden and Eric's early life because she had not, in fact, been there to experience it. Two, the records Maggie had on hand were pristine and contained in the same envelope because they were fakes, provided and then tucked away without ever being used. There was no proving either of these things beyond a reasonable doubt, however.

Why didn't Maggie have any mementos of her grandchildren? she'd asked. Any photographs? Any children's books she'd read to them before Sue handed them off to their father? They'd not been close, the woman had said. Her daughter had always been unstable. Flighty. All over the country chasing men. Her eyes had wandered the walls, evasive. Imogen had thanked her and left.

Imogen spread out the photographs she had of Eden Archer—one leaving her apartment and studio in Balmain, one of the beautiful detective getting her nails done at a local salon, one of her standing outside the Parramatta headquarters, smoking a cigarette. Eden hadn't been a smoker when Imogen had begun tailing her. Had something rattled her? Did she feel herself being watched? Eden had slipped away over the weekend, out from under Imogen's watchful eye. Did something happen? Did Eden know who her stalker was?

As the story went, Suzie Harold had dumped Eden and Eric off on their biological father, Heinrich "Hades" Archer, when the girl was seven and the boy was nine—the exact ages that Morgan and Marcus Tanner were when they were abducted. The two had grown up in the care of the decidedly older parent at the Utulla Landfill, surrounded by mountains of the city's discarded household waste—and, it was rumored, the city's discarded souls. Eden's father was an interesting character, an underworld figure seemingly retired when the two children arrived, living the quiet life in his garbage wonderland. If he had been the one responsible for organizing the Tanner murders, why did he keep the children?

Imogen unfolded all the news reports she had on the Tanner case and spread them out on top of the photographs of Eden. The joyous faces of the Tanner parents on their wedding day, his hand on the belly of her pristine satin dress, lips by her ear. The faces of the children in close-cropped pictures beneath the heavy headlines.

BROKEN GLASS, SHATTERED LIVES—INSIDE THE TANNER FAMILY MURDERS

Theories swirled through the papers, of Dr. Tanner's academic rivals worldwide, of Mrs. Tanner's questionable friends during her youth. Some were sure the two children had been snatched up to be sold into international sex rings—they'd appeared beside their father in *Scientist Weekly*, beautiful, vulnerable porcelain dolls.

Four to six men had been involved in the incident at the Long Jetty house, at which the Tanner couple had been slain and the children disappeared off the face of the earth. Bikers, the police insinuated, had been the ones to do it—smash-and-grab kidnappings were their style. But how did this connect to Hades Archer? He had never been involved with bikers. Using hired muscle to do his dirty work wasn't him, either. He'd always been a sort of overlord, a fixer of problems and mediator of disputes, too high up to hire people, to go after the petty cash of a civilian couple vacationing with their kidlets. The whole thing made no sense.

WHERE ARE THE CHILDREN? the headlines roared.

Bikers were the scapegoats, Imogen decided. An international sex ring was a long shot. But so was Imogen's growing sense that the two had been adopted by Hades Archer, raised as his own to be police officers, unaware of—or perhaps tight-lipped about—the lives they had lived before. The Tanner family fortune had remained untouched. If it was an unsuccessful, murderous kidnapping, why would Eden and Eric remain quiet about it? Was that why Eric had been killed? Had he been on the cusp of revealing everything?

Imogen stared at her untouched coffee, the foam atop it becoming stale, adhering to the edge of her cup. The whole thing was senseless—but she had faith that the right clue would fit all the pieces together. Imogen had always been a lover of puzzles. She never let one defeat her.

No matter how little you have to present in a crime report to the captain, you always present it passionately. That's the rule.

If all you've got going from a twenty-person train-car massacre is a toothpick that was maybe, maybe not, chewed by the guy sitting next to the alleged killer, you present that toothpick not only like it contains the secrets to the crime you're trying to solve, but like it's possibly the missing link in evolution, the solution to the world food shortage, and a revelation of next week's lotto numbers. If you come up bare, you're asking to be removed from the case, hurled headfirst into drug squad or something equally thankless, and usurped by someone younger, with more hunger for that mystical cup of justice. You've got to look mean and keen or they're going to throw the bone to another dog.

Eden seemed to forget this, and sat beside me in Captain James's office staring at the floor while I talked about stuff I knew nothing about—barbiturates and gas-powered guns and running apps.

We had four seconds of footage of the Domain victim, Minerva Hall. She was stumbling and falling, righting herself just as she left the frame. There was no indication if she'd simply tripped or if this was the second she'd been hit with the dart. We had a witness saying she might have seen a white van at the Ashfield crime scene, possibly with some yelling or screaming coming from inside, but she wasn't sure it hadn't been a blue van with music coming from inside it—she'd only ventured into the area in the first place because it was a nice secluded spot to shoot up.

I nipped at Eden for assistance during the briefing, but she didn't react. Just sat there thinking. I grabbed her in the corridor outside the captain's office when he let us leave.

"What the hell is wrong with you?"

"Nothing," she shrugged. "I'm tired. Jesus. Lay off."

"No, you're not right." I held on when she tried to wrestle her bicep free of my grip. "You haven't been right since you got out of the hospital. You're limping around without your crutches and you're staring at walls. Is there something we need to talk about?"

"No."

"Are you hooked on something?"

"No."

"You know I got hooked on oxy. It was easy."

"I know. I was there." She peeled my fingers off her. "I don't need you mothering me." She walked away. I followed her, keeping close to shut our words out of the ears of the beat cops strolling by on either side of us. Beat cops love rumors. They feed off them, like parasites.

"I remember saying the very same thing to you when I got hooked and you tried to mother me."

"I wasn't mothering you, Frank. I was trying to get you in touch with reality. It still hasn't worked."

"This isn't a reflection on you. On your . . . I don't know, the whole *ice queen* thing you carry on with."

"Frank, if you don't—"

"Eden—"

"If you don't drop this I'm going to hurt you." She whirled around and shoved a finger in my face, her back teeth locked. "I'm going to punch you, hard, right in your fucking head. I'm not hooked on anything. I'm not hiding anything, and I don't need your help. Back. Off. Frank."

I let her walk on a couple of steps ahead of me. Felt better. The flashing in her eyes had been the old Eden. The deadly Eden I knew. Well, sort of knew. Was familiar with. I was pleased to know she was still in there, inside the strange storm-cloudy exterior. She went to her desk and pushed things around. I perched on the edge of the desk, out of range of her swing.

"Let's run with the tranquilizer thing, then," I said.

"I'm waiting to hear back from my source."

"You've got a tranquilizer source?"

Eden ignored me, did some things on her computer. I looked up and saw Hooky walking toward us with a manila folder in her hand. She dragged a chair toward Eden from an adjacent desk and sat beside her—funny little lizard sidling up next to a lion. Her outfit was right in line with her strange rock-punk-Japanese-goth thing: leather pants I'd never have let my sixteen-year-old walk out the door in, a floppy waist-length shimmering green shirt covered in beads and spangles and little pieces of mirror. A bone through one ear and a cross on a chain. Black fingerless gloves. Her nail polish was chipped where she'd chewed.

"Want some pictures?" Hooky said.

"How did you get in here?" Eden asked, typing.

"I've got connections."

"Eden, this is Amy Hoo—"

"I know who she is." Eden gave me a warning glance.

"What pictures?" I asked, trying to defuse something I was sure was about to erupt. Women and their little seismic trembles and twitches. I didn't know what might go wrong here, but I didn't need Eden and Imogen both going after Amy. Hooky opened the folder on the desk and drew Eden's attention.

They were screenshots from Hooky's personal computer. I recognized the minimized windows at the bottom of the screen. Chat rooms for under-sixteens. *Teddies for Dolls* and *Bad Daddies*. I hadn't known the department was letting Hooky fish for predators on her *personal* computer. That seemed a bit much. Was she going out on her own? Was she freelancing? I opened my mouth to ask, but she cut me off.

"I crowdsourced photos from around Centennial Park the evening Ivana Roth was grabbed," Hooky said, spreading pages over the desk. "There were forty-seven pictures uploaded to various social media sites in the hour before she was taken. Mostly selfies, but some shots of kids on the field at Queens Park."

Eden examined the picture nearest to her, and I did the same. It was a self-taken shot of two Brazilian girls in matching white running shirts with WEWILL! printed on the chest.

"WeWill! is a cancer research foundation. They raise money and awareness training people to be competitive runners," Hooky said. "They were having a training run there that evening. Lots of photos for the promo page."

"How did you get all these?" I asked.

"I did a geographical and time-based search of image files in the Deep Web."

I stared.

Eden said to me, "The web behind the Web. It's like the backstage of a theater production. Where the code that drives the surface Internet lives."

"Never mind." Hooky grabbed the page from me. "Look here. See?"

A white van was parked behind a bush near the girls in the picture. The edges of the image were dark. I could see a slim figure dressed in black, blurred as it moved toward the front of the van. I picked up another image from the pile. Runners in the matching white shirts coming down the footpath beneath the trees. A shape crouching in the brush near them, murky and pixilated, barely more than a smudge.

"This is the best one," Hooky said. She showed me another selfie, taken by a couple sitting on a park bench. The photo had been edited, lots of little love hearts spattered around their heads, the image tone cast in sepia. But behind them, between the trees, a figure walked. A black tracksuit. A hood pulled up over a bent head. The figure was beside a "Do not feed the wildlife" sign. If we could find the sign, the techs could use the photograph to calculate things about the hooded figure: height, stride distance, even gender, maybe. In a single move, Hooky had doubled what we had on the killer.

"Good work, Hookleberry Hound." I grabbed her by the neck, rattled her skull. "Oh, she's ruthless. Nothing slips by her."

Hooky shoved me. I wrestled with her a little. I know that Hooky hates being treated like a sixteen-year-old, but sometimes I can't help myself. She's exactly as I'd have liked my own daughter to be. Feisty. Smart. If you play with Hooky long enough she gives in and wrestles you back, puts an elbow into your stomach and a foot in your hip. There's still a kid in there. I take a sort of pride in being able to get it out.

"Stop fucking around, the both of you." Eden gathered up the photographs and gave them back to Hooky, who was breathless, her clothes askew. "Get these to the tech department. See if you can get an original of the couple on the park bench. Frank and I will be out all day today, but you've got his number, haven't you?"

"I have." Hooky tucked the folder under her arm and left us, knocking my arm with hers as she went.

"Where are we going?" I asked Eden, gathering up my stuff. I patted my backside and found my phone was missing. I wondered if I'd left it in the coffee room.

"To see a friend," she said.

"You've got a *friend*?"

She didn't answer, turned her back to me, and left. Some animalistic alert made the hairs on the back of my neck stand up. Eden had never mentioned having a girlfriend, a boyfriend, an acquaintance, a confidante—anything. I assumed that her brother and her father and I were the only human beings she'd ever consensually interacted with. I jogged back to the coffee room to get my phone and felt light-headed. The sensation carried on as I followed Eden out through the foyer's huge double doors.

It was a shock to run into Caroline Eckhart on the steps. She was dressed in immaculate running gear. I wondered if she owned anything else. Eden passed her without a glance.

"Mr. Bennett," Caroline said. I offered my hand and she crushed it in hers so hard I was sure she meant to tell me something about my manhood. "I was hoping we could have a chat. I'm Caroline Eckhart."

"It's Detective Inspector Bennett," I said, watching journalists jogging up the stairs behind her. "I can't imagine what we have to chat about."

"You men and your titles, huh?" she quipped before the cameras arrived. I licked my teeth, made a sort of click sound. It was as close to a "fuck you" as I had time for.

"I was at the Minerva Hall crime scene yesterday in the Domain."

"I know."

"I want to assist in any way I can in your investigation." Caroline glanced at the cameras as they arrived, flipped her ponytail through her fingers, and did a little headshake to assert herself. *Shoulders back, chest out, chin up, ladies.* "I believe the Sydney Parks Strangler is targeting women interested in fitness. Women with *agency*. I've got a broad influence with these women. I like to think of myself as their spokeswoman, their voice. I want to make sure they have a say in the hunt for—"

"Ms. Eckhart." I struggled for words, looked around for Eden but could find only the black eyes of cameras. "You're a fitness professional. I don't know why you see yourself as having the . . . the need, or the right, or the training, to interfere in an active police investigation."

Caroline drew a breath. I saw the bones in her chest flex beneath the muscle.

"Women have been scorned for *interfering* where they are not wanted for centuries, Mr. Bennett, and only the strongest of them have ignored the command."

"Uh huh." I started down the steps. The journalists around me gasped. Cameras clicked. I couldn't comprehend the drama that they saw in the incredibly annoying Caroline Eckhart being incredibly annoying to someone. I was sure it happened all the time. She was still carrying on when I stepped onto the street.

"This guy, whoever he is, is targeting—"

"That's where we stop." I put a finger up. The cameras whizzed and flashed. "You're perpetuating unfounded rumors about the crime in the media. I don't know why. I wouldn't have thought women's fitness and murder had anything to do with each other. But when you want publicity, I guess you'll jump on any wagon."

Caroline gasped now.

"What you're doing is irresponsible. It's fearmongering. There's nothing at this stage to suggest that a man is responsible for these murders, or that the cases themselves are even related. This *man*, and his *targeting*, are your inventions, Ms. Eckhart. Not mine." I pointed my finger at her again. The journalists around me shuffled, forcing their tiny microphones at my chest. "Now look, honey, I've got to go."

I heard her fire her defense at her cameraman cronies as I walked away.

The radio was filled with speculation about the park murders. Eden hardly listened, nor did she respond with more than the necessary nods and noises to Frank's complaining about the fitness woman. She thought about the girl, Hooky, who had texted Frank to tell him that she'd found a better image of the lovers on the park bench and sent the file on to be analyzed by the forensics department.

A strange creature, that one. There was something faintly predatory about her, like a newborn crocodile, all cute except for the teeth. Losing her parents had changed Eden, darkened something inside her. Perhaps it had done the same to this young woman. What was she now, this gifted little liar? A threat? Or just a curious natural-born police officer following her instincts? Plenty of police officers Eden knew had joined the crime war because of loss, violence. The mother beaten to death by the cheating stepfather. The brother killed by a gang hit in the Cross. The favorite teacher stabbed after a mugging gone wrong. Tragedy changed lots of people, inspired them to be cops, nurses, firemen, lawyers.

Frank fell asleep beside her as she wound the car out of the city and into the western suburbs, clapboard houses whizzing unnoticed past his eyes, his arms folded and tucked into the gray woolen sweater. Given a spare minute anywhere, anytime, Frank would sleep. He slept in the locker rooms, in the coffee room, in the car while she grabbed coffee at a service station. It was as though his body went on standby when he couldn't do anything, like a computer left unattended.

She entered the Vulcan State Park. The eucalyptus trees towered here, reaching blackened fingertips toward the sky, burnt mouths gaping, shoulder to shoulder, crowding out any view of their shadowed depths. Something large and reptilian streaked into the undergrowth as she rolled through the unmanned boom gates and onto the dirt road. From here, it was an upward climb through the mountains toward Bood's house.

Morris Alexander Bood had been one of Eden's first solitary hunts, when Eric had been away two months on a murder case up north. The itch had become unbearable, and with her brother uncertain about when he'd return, she'd gathered up all the information she had on the freelance assassin, caught a plane to Hobart, and gone after him. She'd been twenty-three, violent and lusting for blood, much less controlled in her pursuits than she was now. She'd hunted down police surveillance photographs of Bood and shuffled them in her fingers on the plane, thought about his body, about the fight he'd probably put up when he discovered she planned to end him.

Six foot five, broad and thick-limbed like a draft horse on its hind legs, he made an unlikely assassin. Most Dial-a-Death guys she'd encountered had been small wiry types, the kind who could flit up stairwells and peek over roofs with their scopes for congressmen or husbands, the kind who could disappear among crowds, sail through airport checkpoints unnoticed. Bood was distinctive for his sheer size. He would draw eyes when cramming into passenger seats and holding cups of tea in his huge fingers, ducking under signs in airports and blocking out windows as he tracked his targets.

Despite his bulk, he was very good. Efficient, and so cold, so callous, he was said to be the man to hire no matter the morality of the situation. He'd take out wives for insurance money, knock off grandparents for inheritances. Morris Bood was a killer without a compass, they said. He took or passed up jobs as randomly as the results of a coin toss. Sometimes he backed out of jobs for no apparent reason. Sometimes he turned and killed his client. He was unpredictable, and very accurate.

Eden had looked forward to killing him.

Unlike most assassins she'd known, Bood hadn't stuck around to fight when she cornered him in his car on the outskirts of wet, sleepy Orford one night in June. She'd waited in the backseat for him, felt the whole vehicle rock as he swung his legs into the cavity beneath the wheel. She'd slipped the wire over his head and yanked it tight, put her lips right beside his ear, warm and soft, just as she'd imagined.

"Don't move," she'd said.

"Forget that!" he'd answered, reaching up and grabbing the wire with one hand, tugging it right out of her fingers as though it were dental floss. He'd turned, quick as a snake, and shoved her hard in the chest, the blow turning from a balled-fist punch to a flat-palm push at the last second, when he recognized her silhouette against the orange lights as that of a woman. Eden was just recovering from the surprise of the blow when Bood took off across the parking lot, running upright,

confident, like a competition sprinter. He was at the
tree line before Eden could scramble out of the backseat. She sprinted after him.

This is wrong, she'd thought as she entered the dark
forest. *You're on his game board now.*

She barreled headlong into his territory, telling herself
to turn back, remembering the crime scene photographs
she'd seen of men and women on the ground, heads
blown off, arms and legs splayed. He liked to catch
and release them, let them get ahead of him, walk
through the valleys like deer, crying and calling out.

The night air was painful in Eden's lungs as she ran.
She wove and ducked between the eucalyptus, tiny
slices of moonlight through the forest canopy her only
guide. She stopped, whirled, ran again at the faintest
movement, a shimmer of black ahead, the grind of a
leather boot. A line of white dotted against the undergrowth slowly emerged, widened, a frozen lake lit by
the moon, a mile wide. She saw the big man run out
onto the ice and followed in a direct line behind him,
sure the ice that could take his weight would also take
hers. She felt the ice give and heard a gut-deep yelp escape her lips. A popping noise, like a gunshot, the
squeaks of ice rubbing against itself. She put a foot
into slush, then another into water, and she plunged.
Eden screamed as the pain rushed into her ears and
mouth and eyes, not water but raw, red hurt.

She rose up, scrambled and grabbed at the slush and
chunks, her fingers and now hands and now wrists
numb. Eden heard her own cries and gasps and coughs
as though through cotton-stuffed ears. The edge. She
found it, climbed up it, felt it crack and tip and slide

beneath her. She found another edge and gripped at it with her fingernails. Her coat dragged her down into the darkness. Her boots kicked at nothing.

In the chaos, she saw him out there on the ice, watching her. Between sinking, drowning, hauling herself up, and sliding back, he approached her, crouched just out of reach. He was watching her die. She wouldn't beg. Eden kicked and grabbed the surface, dug in, watched the ice curl and powder as her nails scratched lines back toward the sucking depths.

Nine or ten times she hauled herself up and slid back. Each time, it took longer. Bood watched. The moon glowed above.

Eden kicked, one last time, groped at the ice, and felt his hand on her wrist. He was lying on his belly on the surface of the lake. He pulled her, and she gripped his coat, let him drag her onto the surface, drag her to the edge of the lake and dump her in the wet grass. Sounds came out of her she could not control, gasps and howls of agony. Everything was limp, useless, pulsing with her thundering heartbeat. She lay on her stomach like a doll while he pulled her coat off her arms, replaced it with his own, lifted and rolled her so that the wool brushed her numb face and her eyes took in the black sky.

"What a fighter," she'd heard him say with a laugh.

She'd lain there on the edge of the lake, listening to the sound of ambulance officers coming down the embankment, watching the sweeping flashlight beams. Bood was long gone. She hadn't seen him again for years.

And then one night, coming to the end of her glass of merlot at a bar in Wynyard, another glass had arrived before she could catch the waiter's attention. Sent from the man sitting at the bar with his back to her. The blond giant had turned, and she had seen his cheek lift with a smile.

Here she was now in the driveway of his Vulcan Park home. She parked beside the spotless Toyota HiLux under the second-floor veranda. Frank snuffled and stretched awake, took in his surroundings. A strong wind gusted up the hill and shook glass panels in the veranda above. Eden sent a text informing Bood of their arrival. There was no telling where on the property he might be.

"So this guy's our tranquilizer expert," Frank said, popping his door and sliding out. He looked at the tree line, shielded his eyes against the bright, overcast sky. "Man's got a hell of a view."

Eden led her partner up the stairs to the great sweeping porch, the huge redwood doors pierced with glass panes. The big house was open, as she expected. Frank stood in the foyer and gaped at the massive black buffalo head hanging above the table across from the door. It reached out and seemed to want to touch the nose of a glassy-eyed fox mounted on a slab of polished oak down by the buffalo's right shoulder. The foyer was themed like a log cabin sitting room, with wooly tapestries hanging among the mounted heads of deer, bison, big cats, and a variety of small, handsome forest creatures.

"Did you say you knew this guy, or . . ." Frank trailed off, spying the billiard table in the sitting room off to the left of the foyer. The bar.

"I've known him for some years, yes."

"And you've never once considered that I might

like to know him? That we might in fact make excellent best friends?" Frank wandered to the sitting room door, noted the gigantic flat-screen television above the fireplace, the sprawling cashmere lounges. "He's got a bar."

"You're a recovering alcoholic."

"A *bar!*"

"He's not your kind of guy, Frank."

"Oh Eden, really," Bood said from across the dining room to their right. His boots clunked on the polished floorboards. "I'm everyone's kind of guy."

She'd forgotten Bood's almost supernatural sense of hearing. He could hear a sugar glider taking flight from five hundred meters. The huge man looked fitting in his oversize surroundings, traversing the twelve-seater dining room table in a couple of strides, thrusting his callused palm in Frank's direction. For once, Frank seemed happy to be the less impressive specimen of masculinity in the room. He shook Bood's hand.

"Morris. Or Bood, as my friends call me."

"Frank. Great place, mate."

"Well, thank you." The big hunter smiled, folded his sheep's-leg arms over his chest. "When you've been a bachelor as long as I have, you can afford to dress your castle as a real man should. I'd love to take you on a tour."

"We don't have time for tours," Eden said. "We're here on business."

"Ever the pragmatist. My dear, dear Detective Archer." Bood put an arm out and Eden leaned into it, her arms still crossed, and let him kiss her cheek. He swept her into an unexpected squeeze, and Frank laughed as she wriggled free. "I insist, though. Frank, here, seems like a guy who really appreciates a homeowner's efforts. Come on."

Eden broke away, having seen it all before. The hot tub. The study, with its chart tables and battered maps on the walls, the cabinets full of shimmering butterflies, horned grass-dwellers, beetles of impossible colors and patterns. The wine cellar, and the door down there, chipped and blue as she recalled, salvaged from some crumbling church or some ancient library. She'd seen what lay beyond the door, where Bood kept his real trophies, the ones he would not be including in Frank's tour. Eden went into the kitchen, took a beer from the double stainless-steel fridge, and leaned against the kitchen counter, sipping it. She looked at the mountains through the glass wall to the balcony. A change was coming through. Rain. She could see its slanted gray fingers on the distant white horizon.

Frank's voice could be heard all over the house. Bood's booming laughter. When Frank returned, his eyes were wide.

"Did you see the moose?"

"I've seen the moose, yes," Eden replied.

"There's a *bear* in the back living room."

"Now, my love," Bood laughed, touching her shoulder. "We'll get to the business end of things in time. You've had a long journey. Can I get you a beer, Frank? A snack?"

Frank balked. Masculinity in peril.

"One of us has got to be sober. Cop thing. No beer for you, shithead." She jabbed Frank in the ribs. He gave her a relieved look. "He'll take the snacks, though."

Frank followed her into the huge eastern room, stopped only to take in its high ceilings, the windows darkening with the coming rain above shelves crammed with books.

"What does this guy do that he can live like this? What is it? Old money?"

"Probably something like that." Eden flipped her laptop open on a coffee table set between two red, oily leather wingback chairs. "Don't get distracted. We're here to get information, and then we're leaving."

"Look at the guns, Eden." He pointed to a rack of twelve ornate rifles wedged between two pillars of books. "There are weapons all over the goddamn house. There's a cabinet of semiautomatics near the laundry chute. We don't have this many guns in our armory at HQ."

"Mmm."

Bood entered with a plate of hors d'oeuvres and set them beside the laptop, pulled one of the wingback chairs into the V shape made by Eden and Frank's chairs. Frank set upon the crackers and cheese as if he hadn't eaten in days, collecting crumbs on his knees and the floor between his feet.

"So, Frank, you'll have caught on by now, I'm sure, that Bood here's an enthusiastic game hunter," Eden began. She drew up her email account and extracted images, sent through from the mortician, of Ivana Roth's and Minerva Hall's puncture wounds. She displayed these beside each other on the screen. She turned to Bood. "I hoped maybe you could tell us something about the tranquilizer used in capturing these two victims. I've got a toxicity report from the coroner, but we're not even close to being able to identify the chemical."

Eden let Bood take charge of the laptop. His brow

was heavy, dusted with strawberry-blond eyebrows that met over a long, wide nose. There was gray creeping into the sides of his short beard and spotted through the fur at the back of his neck. His hands came together and he rested his chin upon them, understanding, it seemed, how crucial his part in the investigation might be.

"Well, it's a smaller dart," Bood began. "This I can tell from the wounds. Darts of around 1.5 cc won't break the skin when they're extracted. Most tranquilizer darts have a rubber stopper on the needle so the animal can't pull or knock the dart out when it falls. It goes in, and the rubber stopper stops it coming back out before all the chemical can be released into the animal's system. This dart didn't have a stopper. So, it was a small, quick-acting dart, rather than a large, slow-release dart."

Frank took a notepad from his pocket and wrote.

"Whoever's using the darts must have some idea of what they're doing," Eden said, "or they would have gone over the top. Shot for an overdose, rather than have their victim limp away on an underdose. Am I right?"

"Right," Bood said. "It's a tricky thing to calculate. You've got to understand the nature of the animal itself. How its blood flows. Its epidermis. You can't hit a crocodile and a human with the same dart. Some darts will penetrate tough skin, like reptile skin. Some darts will penetrate softer skin. Some darts are good for animals with fur, feathers—some are better for hairless creatures. Something delicate was needed for human skin, and it was a delicate dart used here. If you're going to do this, you've also got to consider dosage. How fast does the heart beat? Was the animal resting or running? Was it frightened or calm? The condition of the animal will affect how quickly the chemical is absorbed into the bloodstream. You don't want to hit a resting tiger with a slow-uptake tranquilizer, or the thing will come around and have you for dinner."

"It sounds as though, if you're wanting the thing to survive, you've almost got to have the level of knowledge of an anesthesiologist," Frank said.

"Even if you don't want the animal to survive, using the right tranquilizers is fairly standard practice." Bood leaned back in his chair. "Despite what you might think, most professional hunters aren't big on animals suffering unnecessarily. Or on wasting expensive chemicals with overkill."

"Can you speculate about a weapon?"

"Probably something gun-fired. If your victim was on the move, a jab stick or a blowpipe would have been out of the question, particularly for a beginner. With the gun, you've got the scope and the possibility, with some models, of a quick refire. Have you got the toxicology report here?"

Eden handed over a wad of papers she'd wrestled from the depths of her laptop bag. Bood sat back and perused them. In time, he stood and went to one of the pillars of books beside the fireplace and pulled a shelf toward him to reveal a small, neat cabinet of handguns. Frank and Eden followed. Frank nestled in beside the bigger man, looked at the lit shelves of colorful syringes, the bottles and screw-on feather stabilizers that attached to each individual dart.

With both men blocking the cabinet, Eden had time to think about that night in Tasmania, the moment she rose from the water for what was certainly the last time and saw Bood's hand reaching out. She'd thought for a long time afterward about why he saved her, and decided, in the end, it was because there was no sport in letting her die that way. Most psychopaths Eden had known were forever in some state of consideration over how best to maximize their own pleasure.

Bood had watched her until her death failed to entertain him, and then had drawn her out of her predicament, seduced by the idea of a future playmate, perhaps. Maybe even a lover. Bood had to know now that Frank admired him. The thoughtful hand to his chin and theatrical snap of his fingers as a decision was made were all part of the show. He turned, and in his hands he had a number of tiny capped syringes. Frank watched him select a gun from the upper shelves, a narrow long-nosed pistol with a wooden handle.

"So," Bood said, "I know what it *isn't*. It isn't anything else I've got here, and I've got a fair sampler of the Australian market in this cabinet. There's a good chance that the dart you're looking for is one of these."

The group returned to the chairs by the laptop, Frank and Bood beside each other this time. Bood laid the syringes out neatly, twelve in all. Each was some shade of either pink or yellow.

"These are all paralyzers," Bood said. "They're low caliber, and they're low dose. From the levels in the report and the wounds in the photos, I think we're getting close to the mark here."

"Great," Frank said, picking up the syringe closest to him and examining it in the light of the upper windows. "Can we get any closer?"

"You said you had footage of the strike?"

"Maybe," Eden said, going back to her email. "We've got this."

She opened the file from the Domain security team and selected the video of Minerva Hall stumbling, almost falling, righting herself, and running on across the field of the camera, focused on a path that led to the back of the Art Gallery. Bood reached over and ran the video again, then twice more, intent on the screen. Eden brushed his fingers as she took over the laptop keyboard, accessed the video settings, and slowed the video. Bood watched the woman on the screen running, seeming to trip, stumbling, pushing herself off the wet asphalt with her right hand, her fingertips, then settling back into her run. Just at the very edge of the frame, Eden saw the same hand that had righted the runner reach down toward the back of her right thigh. Then she was gone.

"We don't even know if this is the moment."

"Oh, it's the moment," Bood said. He sat, considering the syringes before him. Then he selected one of the fainter pink vials, uncapped it, and stuck it into the side of Frank's neck.

"Morris!" Eden grabbed at the big man as he and Frank rose together, but it was too late. Frank stumbled backward, grabbed at the dart in his neck, his eyes moving frantically from Bood to Eden.

"Shit!" Frank pulled out the dart. Looked at the thing in his fingers. He swayed. "Shiiiit."

Then he fell.

"You fucking asshole, Morris!" Eden snarled. She pushed Bood out of the way and pulled back the coffee table. Frank had flopped onto a Persian rug before the fireplace, his top button popped and ankles crossed from twisting sideways to try to stop his fall. Eden put her hands on his chest, and as she did, his left leg gave four sharp twitches, rocking his whole body. Then he was still. Her partner's eyes were locked on the ceiling.

"He's fine," Bood said. He stood over Frank, his hands in the pockets of his trousers. "It'll be two, three minutes maximum."

"That was completely inappropriate."

"Did you want answers, or guesses?"

"Tell me, then, for Christ's sake."

"You saw those three or four little jolts of the leg there?"

"Yes."

"That's what you call a *tell*," Bood said. "It's like a signature. It makes the brand distinct. There are complex chemical reasons why some drugs have signatures, but I couldn't begin to explain what they are. Some brands of morphine make people nauseated. Some influenza medicines make people drowsy. Maduline makes your legs twitch."

"Maduline?"

"I'm almost certain," Bood said. He lowered himself back into the chair, pushed the cursor of the video back to its original place. "Her heart rate is elevated, because she's running. So absorption, and therefore side effects, is much faster. You see here? Her right leg. Twitch, twitch. She doesn't reach down to feel what hit her—so the dart probably had an anesthetic tip. It's Maduline. I'm sure of it."

Eden watched the video. Watched Minerva Hall's right leg give two tiny kicks as she shifted to her left, pushed off, righted herself. Like she was shaking water from her shoe. Trying to kick off fingers gripping at her heel. Frank gave a groan beside Eden. She uncrossed his legs for him.

"Maduline is a fast-acting, fast-absorbing tranquilizer," Bood said. "It is burned out and gone in minutes. Animal handlers use it when they want to subdue an animal instantly but not have that animal lying around anesthetized for hours afterward. The occasions for use of this drug are limited, so you'll only find a couple of suppliers in Australia. You might use Maduline if you had a deer tangled in a wire fence, for example. You subdue the animal, free it, and it moves on. If you were to use something else, the animal might become prey. It's also good for health checks for migrating stock."

Frank rolled onto his side, clawed his way into a sitting position. There was drool on his lip. He wiped it off and shook his head.

"Christ. Fuck me."

"You'll feel fine in a minute, my friend." Bood grinned at Frank, who could return only a tired stare. "What you've had is like an oversized jellyfish sting. You'll be up and moving before I finish this beer."

"I'd have liked a bit of warning," Frank slurred. "Jee-sus. That was terrifying."

Eden watched her partner reach for the back of the chair nearest to him, unsure about his new friend and his propensity to unexpectedly hit people with paralyzing drugs. He gripped his way around the chair and sat down, rubbing the sides of his skull.

"It was like my whole body dropped from underneath me."

"My sincerest apologies." Bood reached over and patted Frank's hand a couple of times, the way a man might reassure his elderly father. "But given the choice, I thought it more gentlemanly to let you take the hit than to impose such an experience on our dear Eden."

"Those girls," Frank said. He covered his eyes. Eden and Bood waited in silence. Frank ran his fingers through his short, shaggy hair. "The killer wanted to stun them. Wanted them mobile in a few minutes so they could . . . so they could experience it."

"It sounds like you're after a very nasty kind of hunter," Bood said. He glanced at Eden.

"A real prick," Frank said with a laugh.

Eden felt grateful for Frank's ever-trusting spirit. Frank was like that. Forgiving. Easily led into the darkness, into pacts he never knew were forming around him until it was too late, until he had bad choices to make and only the better of which to choose. It was why, she knew, Imogen would use him. Because he bore the kind of basic good-heartedness that begged to be used. The two men were talking again, the homicide detective and the killer. Frank explaining the horrifying yet thrilling sensation of being tranquilized like it was a skydiving adventure he'd signed up and paid for. A once-in-a-lifetime plunge. Almost proud that he'd survived it.

They enjoyed a light lunch, and Bood shepherded them to the car, holding an umbrella for Eden as the light rain fell. Frank shook the hunter's hand as they found the shelter of the veranda and stood by the car. Again, Bood opened his arm and Eden let herself be enveloped, submitted to his hairy kiss on her cheek. As

Bood spoke, she saw the words register on her partner's face.

"So, shall I expect a visit in *another* fortnight?"

Eden patted the big man on the shoulder and got into the car, as an uncomfortable silence permeated the air. She backed the vehicle around and drove. Frank sat frowning at the dashboard.

"You visited Bood two weeks ago," he said.

"I did."

Eden knew what had darkened him. His fingers pressed against the dart wound in his neck, a tiny blue bruise. She could almost see the news headlines of the last few days flickering across her partner's eyes.

FOUR DEAD IN MYSTERY SLAYING SOUTH OF BYRON

POLICE LIKELY HUNTING "EXPERT ASSASSIN"

"We need to talk about this one day," Frank said. "About you. About your people, your friends. About all of it, Eden. Sometime we're going to have to do something about us. About what I know."

She opened her mouth to give him one of her usual nasty responses. But she said nothing this time.

She was beginning to wonder if something might have to be done about Frank.

Unlike her classmates, Tara did not count the days until the senior prom. Now and then she would notice signs and markings hanging about the school like the cave paintings of a colorful and violent tribe, explosions of stars and hearts on the chalkboards swiped away when teachers arrived. Twenty-eight days. Twenty-six days. Twenty-one. The numbers meant nothing to her.

Every night was the same for Tara. Joanie came for her at sunset. Tara was hunted.

Tara thought of it very much as a hunting. A long, excruciating pursuit, a surrender, a devouring. She would run, her hips and knees springing into pain, and her mother would shuffle behind her, prodding three fingers into the tender flesh beneath her right shoulder blade like a lion's claw swiping at a zebra's back. When the prodding stopped, the yelling began. Joanie was never out of breath. She sometimes ran sideways, like a strange, lanky crab, her sneakers scraping on the wet asphalt. *Come on. Come on. Come on, Tara. Come on.*

Sometimes it was begging. Sometimes it was snarling. But the *come on, come on* never stopped. When Tara slowed, as she always did, and submitted to walking, the "come ons" rose in pitch. *You fucking failure. You selfish failure of a girl. You're not stopping, Tara. Get moving. Come on.*

Rocks in Tara's abdomen, sharp and heavy, just beneath the lowest of her ribs. The pathetic sounds that came out of her. People stared as they passed, or refused to look at all at the wounded animal being nipped at in the dark. Tara crawled and vomited in the grass, once wet her pants, dissolved into panicked, breathless tears. Nothing worked. The humiliation of one session bled into the next, until the nights flowed together in one long sunless fortnight in hell.

She would crawl into her bed afterward and unwrap treats she had snuck home from the school canteen, hold the wrapper beside her ear as she pulled it open, listen to the crinkle of the plastic. Sucking like an infant on a chocolate breast, her teeth coated, she would gorge until she felt sick and couldn't breathe, the voice of her mother still pounding in her head.

Those photos, Tara. Embarrass me in those photos and I'll fucking kill you.

Why didn't Tara think of her mother? Think of those final-year photographs framed and sitting on mantelpieces of governors and their wives, sitting in the family libraries of the Prices and the Bucklands and the Lancasters. Jesus Christ, the Lancasters. They'd put it in the paper. Saint Ellis High Class of 2011 and their charming killer-whale mascot, Tara. *Save the Whales, Harpoon a Harper!*

Joanie brought a dress home, slimming black silk, sparkling, heavy with jewels. It reminded Tara of the bats that squabbled and squeaked above them in the park. The dress was a size twelve. Tara had lifted the long skirt, watched it drip from her white fingers like ink sliding through water.

You'll fit into this or you'll go naked. I will drop you there myself, in front of everyone.

Tara had sat in the hairdresser's chair on the windy,

rainy afternoon of the prom and looked at the thing that she was, as the old Greek woman crimped and curled her hair above the black silken smock jutting beneath her double chin, Velcro pulled tight at the top of her curved spine. It was the first time her mother had called her a "thing." Before that, for a long time, there had been human tones to the words. Idiot. Bitch. But Tara was more struck with "thing"; with what it did to the way she saw her own face.

If Tara was a "thing," she was not like the others. Never had been, never had the potential of being. She'd watched the stylist circling her, brutally stripping foils from pins, from rolls of curls, dumping them in a canister. Knowing that whatever was done, Tara wouldn't look good. Wouldn't look human. The stylist was like a frustrated painter, dabbing and stabbing at lifeless eyes. Tara would never be alive. She had been born a thing.

But "things" had purpose. Every thing. She'd reached out beneath the smock and pulled a brush from the shelf beside her, turned it in her fingers. Things were created to serve. To perform.

What kind of thing was she? Her natural desire seemed to be to destroy, to consume, to stifle. Was she a killing thing?

It was kind of a relief, seeing herself as an object. She felt almost free. Free of the guilt of all her little ill-fitting parts, all the invitations refused and withheld, and all the sideways glances. She felt free of the hatred of the other boys and girls. They were only doing what was natural to them—recognizing the imposter in their midst. Tara had never been a girl. She'd never been a student, a friend, a teammate.

At the event hall, she'd stood in the corner at the back as the teachers gave their speeches and the awards were handed out. She listened, her slippered feet just beyond the reach of the gold downlights, as Rachael Jennings gave an acoustic rendition of Green Day's "Good Riddance (Time of Your Life)" and a group of boys that included Peter Anderson howled a joyful "Graduation (Friends Forever)" by Vitamin C.

The boys had all come in suit jackets and bow ties over colorful board shorts and flip-flops, a defiant mismatch that caused the teachers some concern, as the drinks began and the first glass was shattered on the floorboards by the stage. Awkward dancing, and an interlude for a PowerPoint montage: the same five or six popular boys and girls appearing between group shots of the goths and the nerds and the ugly girls, then the popular girls in primary school, high school, at the cinema, mouths full of partly chewed popcorn, boys sneaking arms along backs.

Tara did not appear in the montage.

As she stood by the restroom doors, Mrs. Foy had come and spoken to her in the colorful light. Tara liked Mrs. Foy, and the devoted biology teacher liked her. Biology had been the only class Tara had thrived in, the only time she was allowed to work alone no matter the task. The class was split on day one into five "research teams," each a pair, with one leftover—Tara. If a member of a research team was ever absent, Tara was not forced to make up the gap in the pair, because their workbooks would not match. Entering the sterile biology classroom was one of the only times in the day that Tara felt invisible, safe from those unexpected and devastating words, "All right everyone, form a group."

She sat at the back of the classroom, in her little bubble of security, and read. She dissected frogs and mice, toyed with their rubbery blue-and-red organs with her scalpel. Sometimes she ignored the class if it was too basic, and simply read the textbook.

Mrs. Foy told her at the prom that she'd be a great scientist, if she just "got out of herself." With her performance in their study of animals, her extraordinary precision and skill, she could make a very accomplished vet. She just needed confidence. Didn't she know that? Tara had stared at the floor, unanswering, until the woman gave up.

She had left the prom at eleven, when it was revealed someone had brought a couple of cases of Cruisers to the back of the building, and teens were sneaking out there to smoke and drink while others distracted the teachers on the dance floor. Tara had headed to the parking lot to seek out her limo driver, when she'd run into Louise Macken and Sam Cruitt making out against a car.

"Oh my God!" Louise had broken away from Sam, brushed down her hair. "Hey, sorry! We didn't see you there."

"Sorry," Tara had said, backing up to find another way between the cars.

"Hey, wait."

"Louise!" Sam whined.

"No wait, Tara." Louise—nimble and spritely and pretty Louise. Perfect Louise, who always did the right thing but never ratted on anyone for being bad. All the boys loved Louise. She had the seductive naïveté of all virgins written on her face. Inexperience and freshness, never tested. Unviolated lips. "Sam, I'll meet you back at the door."

Sam trundled off toward the group behind the hall. Tara kept walking, found herself in the familiar situation of animal being pursued, tried to keep her breathing regular as she headed toward the limo. Greg the driver in the distance, reading a newspaper in the yellow light of the car. She liked Greg. He never spoke.

"Tara," Louise said. "I wanted to tell you how pretty you look tonight."

Tara was surprised at how small Louise's neck was in her fingers. She could encircle the whole thing with two hands despite the stubbiness and shortness of her fingers, the thumbs overlapping over the ribbed windpipe slippery with glittery foundation. Tara squeezed, squeezed, squeezed, in long hard pulses, each bringing Louise a little closer to the ground, until the two struggled, twisted, Louise falling back into Tara's embrace as Tara's arm wound around the girl's neck. Tara put her hand into the complicated mess of curls and pins and sparkles at the back of Louise's head and pushed, pulled, felt bones grind in the girl's neck.

This was what it was like to wring the life out of a bird. Tara had always wondered about it. Kind of hoped, one day, to find herself in the position of being responsible for the mercy killing of a bird, how pretty and swift and alive they were. Tara felt Louise's feet kicking. Didn't even notice as Greg the driver stepped over them, clawed at her bare arms, his shouts like a siren in the night.

Eden and I had our feet on the boardroom table when Captain James walked in, CCTV images and reports spread around us, little evidence bags of cigarette butts and coins and hair elastics and other park debris making a mountain at the end of the table. We'd become so comfortable that when our boss arrived, I acknowledged him only when he nudged my chair.

"Morning, Cap."

"Captain" wasn't Captain James's actual police rank, but more of a nickname, an endearing nod to the inspirational and fatherly figure he represented to us. There's little you can do to make "Chief Superintendent" sound friendly and loving, so we'd abandoned it altogether for Captain. Like most police traditions, it made little sense to outsiders.

"What do you know, Bennett?"

"Tranquilizers," Eden answered for me, shifting the papers she was reading. "We're after tranquilizers. A source confirmed a brand for me, so we're hunting down a sales list from a distributor. Should be here within the hour."

"I got tranquilized," I boasted, looking at the captain. "In the neck. I went down like a bag of shit. Bit my tongue. It was great."

"We've also got clean CCTV shots, of both the killer and the van, on their way to news outlets," Eden continued. "We think the van's a Mitsubishi Express, 2008 or roundabout. We're going back now and looking for the van in the CCTV and some social media shots we've been given. I'm getting a team out on vans of that type in the area shortly."

"We've got two bloody prints on the Roth body," I said. "No matches. We're running them international."

"And this, Bennett," Captain James said. "What do you know about this?"

He slapped a newspaper onto the paperwork in front of me. I stared, unrecognizing for a few seconds, at the side of my own head. My open mouth and pointing finger. I appeared to be chastising a very indignant-looking Caroline Eckhart on the steps of the Parramatta headquarters. I read the caption and my voice broke over the words.

"'Get off my wagon, honey . . .'"

"Get off my wagon, honey?" Captain James raised his eyebrows at me.

Eden reached over and snatched the paper from me. I snatched it back.

"This is not what I said!" My voice came out higher than I'd anticipated. I cleared my throat. "Jesus Christ, these people will print anything."

"Well, I don't know about *anything*. You must have said something about a wagon," Captain James said.

"I said . . . I don't know. Shit. I said she'd jumped on the bandwagon."

"What bandwagon?"

"'Homicide Detective Francis Bennett joined lifestyle coach Caroline Eckhart in a heated row on the steps of Parramatta Police Headquarters yesterday morning,'" Eden read. She'd taken the paper back again. "'Bennett, who is known for spearheading both the Jason Beck and Camden Runaway murder investigations, accused Eckhart of interfering in an official police investigation when the respected public health champion offered her assistance in the Sydney Parks murders.'"

"Public health champion?" I scoffed.

"You didn't spearhead either of those investigations, before you get ahead of yourself," Eden sniffed, ruffling the paper. "You had your head in your ass for at least eighty percent of the Camden Runaways."

"This doesn't look good for us, Frank."

"I know that, Cap. I'm being set up here. This is not me. I didn't say it like that. I just brushed her off, the same way I would brush off any creep who tried to get their name in the true-crime book that'll come out of this. Caroline Eckhart is a fucking . . . She's standing on a soapbox."

"'Caroline Eckhart released a statement saying she is troubled by the Sydney Metro Homicide Department's unwillingness to accept public assistance in the case,'" Eden read. "'Eckhart, a renowned feminist spokesperson, called on the women of Sydney to unite in a—'"

"Oh, for the love of God!" I wailed. "A lifestyle coach, public health champion, and feminist spokesperson? What else is she? A fucking brain surgeon?"

"Typical of you," Eden said. "Demanding that she only be one thing. Mother or career woman. Lifestyle coach or feminist. Passive or aggressive. That's a very 1950s attitude you've got there, Francis."

"Don't fuck with me, Eden. Just don't."

"Did she offer you help?" Captain James asked.

"Her idea of help and mine are not the same."

"Well look, Frank," James sighed, "we can't have the people of Sydney thinking we're chauvinists."

"I am not a chauvinist! I have a girlfriend!"

"Chauvinists have girlfriends." Eden flipped down

a corner of the paper to frown at me. "Why wouldn't they have girlfriends?"

"Eden, I'm not a chauvinist. Back me up."

Eden flipped the corner of the newspaper up again.

"Frank, have Eden deal with any communication you get from this Eckhart woman or her office from now on." Captain James pointed at me. "Got it?"

"She doesn't have an office," I sneered. "She'll have a closet in a gym somewhere that reeks of rubber and ball sweat."

"She probably just works from her kitchen," Eden said. "Where she belongs."

I tried to answer, but Gina from reception was rushing past and stopped to swing in the doorway.

"Bennett, phone."

She tossed me a cordless receiver, which I barely caught.

"Female Oppression Enterprises. Frank speaking."

"It's Anthony."

"Hey, Tone. What can we do you for?"

"I wondered if you'd like to come over and pick up your murderer," he said. The smugness in his tone was dripping, even over the phone. "We don't have the space for him here."

I didn't realize that Eden's reputation for being terrifying for no obvious reason had reached all the way across the bridge to the North Sydney Metro Homicide Department, but from the look on Anthony's face as we entered, I realized it had. People had always been more scared of Eric than of Eden herself, but since her brother's death, Eden seemed able to command that wary, cornered-dog look from people, the quick scooting into empty offices away from her, the clearing of the coffee room whenever she entered. No one knows but me what it is about Eden that's so frightening. Anthony shook my hand as we entered the bull pen. His palm was clammy.

"Frank."

"Anthony, Eden Archer, my partner. Eden, Anthony Charters."

"Hi," Eden said. Shook hands. Anthony grunted in return, stuffed his hands in his pockets like a kid reluctant to concede an apology.

"Those were some big words on the phone, young man." I followed Tony as he turned across the loud, sunny bull pen toward Interrogation Row. "You're pretty confident you've got my guy?"

"It's him," Tony said, rubbing his bald head. "But I didn't get him. Come in here and meet the mother. She'll tell you what happened."

Tony opened the door on a woman in the largest of the interrogation rooms, the ones we used for scumbags with multiple lawyers or juvenile offenders with parents in tow. She was sitting at the steel table with her hands around a Styrofoam cup of coffee, a curvy woman with a golden tan, lines from smiles and ocean glare, a mother who'd spent decades chasing children in the sun. Long brown hair in a high ponytail fell shiny and light over one shoulder, combed back from a deep widow's peak. I knew the face: Ivana's mother.

Beside her, a stocky pit bull–looking thing, chocolate brown and black-snouted. A studded collar with a big name tag: NITRO. The dog sniffed as I entered, got up on its back legs and pawed at the air in my general direction as though inviting me to dance, revealing a smooth pink belly with nubby nipples. On the table before Ivana's mother lay a shining Callaway 5-iron golf club, slightly bent. Eden picked up the club and gripped either end, looked at me for explanation. I sat down.

"Charmaine, here, nabbed the killer." Anthony smiled, puffed his chest out.

"I'm Charmaine Lyon." The woman by the dog reached out and took my hand. Her skin was warm and soft. I squeezed it. "Ivana's stepmum."

"I know." I licked my lips. "Charmaine, I'm sorry we haven't met. I'm Detective Inspector Frank Bennett and this is Detective Inspector Eden Archer. We were scheduled to meet you the morning Minerva was found. You've met our secondary—"

"You don't have to apologize." She held up a hand. "I would have preferred you were out there finding the killer, rather than sitting around talking to the families."

I breathed out. "I'm very sorry for your loss."

"So am I."

"We all are," Eden said. "So let's add the mother, the dog, and the golf club together and get this story moving, shall we?"

"I found my daughter's killer," Charmaine said, giving a loud, high sniff. "And I whacked him."

"How do you know you've got our killer?" I asked.

"I've been at Sydney Harbour National Park two nights now. All night," Charmaine said. "I knew it was where he'd strike next. It's Sydney's next park up in size after Centennial and the Domain. See?" She unfolded a large battered map and spread it out before us on the table. Eden was tapping the 5-iron against my chair.

Charmaine pointed out Sydney Harbour National Park, a big solid patch of green curving like gnarled fingers around the mouth of Sydney Harbour, some of it in Mosman, some in Balgowlah Heights, and the biggest chunk in Manly. The park was probably frequented by cool, beachy business types, weekend dads, and trophy wives with blogs they ran from home. Joggers, hundreds of them, for hunting between the tall pines.

"I started by wandering around after Ivana was found," Charmaine said. "I just—I couldn't stand by at home with everyone crying and consoling each other and making fucking phone calls . . . the journalists . . . Fuck. I wanted to do something. So, I took a shot at it and I went out there. Walking around the paths was too obvious. I started taking cover. Watching. Watching. Watching. I saw some pretty sick stuff up there. Especially in the early morning."

"You lay out there all night?" I asked. I couldn't believe this woman. She looked like she ought to be running a bake sale. When I looked at the club in Eden's hands, I saw blood in the grooves of the titanium. Her daughter's body was barely even cold, and here Charmaine was, stalking possible suspects in a national park in the dead of the night.

"What'd you see?"

"Oh, there were guys going at it in the public toilets." Charmaine curled her lip. "People dumping rubbish. Drug deals. One guy trapping possums and taking them away in his truck—I don't know why. You name it, mate, they were doing it out there. Place is a friggin' circus at night."

"You were by yourself?"

"I had the dog." Charmaine nudged the animal with

her knee and it jumped up again, barked at me, wet eyes searching mine.

"All right . . ." I released a chestful of air. "So you get the idea you might lie in wait for the killer. You decide you'll do it at Sydney Harbour National Park. You go trekking around in the middle of the night spying on creepy-crawlies in the bushes. And then . . . what? You reckon you found our killer?"

"Not just found him, mate," Charmaine smiled. "I fuckin' whacked him."

"This is incredible," Eden said, sitting back in her chair. I think she meant "incredible" in the true sense of the word: not to be believed.

"George Hacker is in custody on his way here. He's been treated and released to us," Anthony said.

"And it looks good?" I said.

"From what we found on the video camera, it looks pretty good."

"He had a camera?"

"The suspect was found videotaping joggers. Women only. Navy blue hoodie, black tracksuit pants, crouching in the bushes taping women coming up the path and back down again. Lots of close-ups. From a raid on his apartment, there are plenty of tapes. Edited tapes. Compilations of women's breasts, asses, their . . . their front . . . parts," Tony coughed.

"Navy blue hoodie, was it?" I asked.

"Yep."

"And no weapons? No guns or anything?" Eden asked.

"No, nothing like that."

"And this occurred just now?"

"Four o'clock this morning," Charmaine said. "On the dot. I never believed people got up that bloody early. But the place was full of people doing yoga and running and stretching and doing that . . . what's that one they do?" She waved her arms, hands flat.

"Tai chi."

"Right," she confirmed.

Eden and I looked at each other. She turned the golf club over and over on the tabletop.

"Okay. Well, look, Charmaine," I sighed, "I'm sure my colleagues here will agree with me in saying that, speaking for the New South Wales state police force, we never encourage vigilantism. What you did was reckless and dangerous. You acted without authority, without sufficient evidence, and you might have gotten yourself killed or worse out there. I mean, that was mad, lady. It was a mad, mad thing you did, and I hope you never do anything like it ever again."

Charmaine sat and looked at me. The dog beside her panted, its tongue slicked with foamy saliva.

"Speaking as myself, though," I shrugged, "I think you're pretty fucking awesome."

Eden sighed.

"I agree," Tony laughed. "What a tiger. Pow!" He gave an imaginary golf swing, shielded his eyes as he followed an imaginary decapitated head across an imaginary skyline. "Do you even play golf?"

"I'm going to try to maintain the integrity in the room and bid you farewell," Eden said as Tony and I continued miming golf-themed assaults. "Frank and I will keep you up to date with the case as it progresses, Ms. Lyon. Thank you for your assistance."

Eden shook Charmaine's hand and left.

"You two better punish this fucking guy." Charmaine pointed at me, chewing her lips. "I'm serious."

We had the paramedic team turn around and deliver George Hacker to his apartment on the upper level of a colorful row house in Redfern. The street smelled of beer and rotting vegetables, and trash cans stood sentry in all positions—behind buildings, on the curb, in bushes, on landings. Everything smelled pissed on, both by stray dogs and drunks. The light rain that had recently passed seemed to enliven the smell. This was a place where people knew cops, uniformed or not.

There was blood on the yellow front door of George's place and an army of ants trailing under the rubber liner at its bottom, fat-bellied insects grown lazy on a gluttony of leftover pizza boxes within. The government had allotted George the upper floor and given the ground floor to a family of five headed by a single mother who used the back door of the building, minded her own business, and didn't seem to know George had been living above her at all, let alone whether he drove a van. She didn't know when she'd seen George last or what her birth date was or whether or not she'd been arrested in the last six months. She slammed the door in my face in a mixture of disdain and relief when I bid her good-bye. Her kids had been milling around her skirt as we spoke, grubby-faced and gray-toothed, like little trolls under a tree, kids who spent their whole day with a baby bottle of Coke or chin-staining strawberry soda between their teeth.

We hadn't let Anthony know how far from likely it

was that George Hacker was our man. Anthony had been so excited about Charmaine Lyon's find that I couldn't let him down by telling him that the hoodie was the wrong color, the guy had been stalking joggers at the wrong time of day, no weaponry or abduction material was found on or near him, and he'd taken a little red Hyundai, rather than a van, to the park that morning.

George Hacker, who'd dropped out of school in ninth grade to take up an apprenticeship as a mechanic, a qualification he proved incapable of completing due to poor literacy skills, was likely too dumb to know what tranquilizers were, let alone their different chemical nuances. He had one sexual assault charge dating back to age seventeen, when he'd groped a teenage girl in the surf at the beach, acting like he was trying to break his fall from a large wave. He'd been warned to keep his hands to himself before, but didn't heed the caution. He'd only served a month, being a teen. He'd mainly steered clear of trouble after that.

Like most degenerates, George was an emaciated character, short with a big forehead, like something in his skull had swelled and stretched the cranium out, pushed the parietal bone back so that it shadowed the nape of his neck. Collarbones like external plumbing popped out almost on top of the skin. He emerged handcuffed from the cab of the ambulance and stood squinting on the street. The back of his head was bandaged, two spots of dark red blood seeping through the gauze like eyes.

"This here is harassment." George spat on the ground, barely missing Eden's brown leather boot. "You cops've had it out for me since I was farkin' born. This is the third time I been picked up this month. I ain't done nothin'. You been watchin'. You been waitin'. But I wasn't doin' nothin' but—"

"This is a Redfern street, not the State Theatre," I said. "Let's save the dramatics for the official statement."

He continued unabated, spat again. "I ain't done noth—"

"No one's listening," I said. "No one cares. And you spit near my partner again and I'll put your head through that fucking mail slot."

That really set him off. Eden unlocked his cuffs and glanced at me, weary. She knew I was going to be the antagonizer, which made her the empathizer. Good cop, bad cop. The system was traditional because it worked, but I knew from experience Eden liked being the bad cop. She got bored being nice to crims. Was hardly convincing at it. That's why I liked to snatch it off her early. I didn't like good cop, either.

I'd told George Hacker that no one cared for a reason. It's as effective as a sucker punch, without all the police-brutality charges. Telling members of the lower socioeconomic rungs of Australia that no one cares about them really gives them the shits, and I'll admit, I find that amusing. I'm always entertained by how shocked they are about it. They never expect it.

If you listen to them in police station waiting rooms, on the corners, and in the shopping-center parking lots of Redfern, Kings Cross, Punchbowl, Campbelltown, all they talk about is how no one cares about them. The government. The police. The child welfare people. So, when you tell them that, right, you don't care about them, it confirms for them everything they've been telling their friends and colleagues and drug dealers all their adult years. I took George by the back of his neck and pushed him into the house. Eden followed us, half-heartedly trying to talk me down from being too rough.

I tossed George onto his sagging gray sofa and looked around the little flat in disgust. There was a half inch of brown city dust on everything, blown in from a dozen construction sites between his apartment and the central business district. The place felt damp and cramped. I brushed crumbs off a plastic outdoor chair that was waiting in the entrance to the kitchen like a neglected child. Sat down, looked at George.

"I want all of the tapes. Everything you've got," I said. "And I don't want to have to get it by rummaging through your filthy drawers."

"I'm not . . ." George sniveled, already looking to Eden for help. "This ain't something I *do*, all right? I was just out there, this one time, just trying out me new camera. I don't keep—"

"People like you always keep tapes, George."

"The fuck you mean, people like me?"

"George," I sighed. "The tapes."

"Tell us where the tapes are, George," Eden said.

"I don't—"

"Tell us where you keep them."

"I ain't got no farkin' tapes!" George screamed, and bounced once on the couch like something had bitten him. A frustrated half leap. "Jesus farkin' Christ, you coppers, you don't listen. You—"

I stood and went into the kitchen. Grabbed a tall water glass from the sink, cloudy with fingerprints. Eden watched me walk to a small rectangular fish tank on a wooden stand beside the television set, a sad little orange-and-white goldfish bobbing around the surface of the water, hunting for rainbow flakes. I looked at George, waited, but he didn't speak. I lifted my arm and swung my elbow into the front of the fish tank. The glass popped, and with a satisfying glubbing sound, the contents began to empty onto the carpet at my feet, splashing up against the glass front of the television stand.

"Fark!" George screamed, rising up off the couch. Eden pushed him down, one-handed, bored. "You stupid prick! Look what you've done!"

"Detective Bennett," Eden said. "Is that really necessary?"

I waited as the tank emptied, the water slapping on the carpet, making a large dark blue stain that reached almost to the couch. The goldfish, strangely serene, circled the tank until the flow of the water took him through the hole in the tank and into the glass in my hand. I set the full glass, goldfish bobbing on its surface, on top of the television set.

Now the room smelled of algae and fish turds. I tried to decide if it was an improvement.

"Listen, you piece of shit! I don't have anything to give you!" George's bottom lip quivered. "I'm not some crazy sicko out filming women. This whole thing—this is a fucking . . . misunderstanding. It's a mistake. Don't break any more of my shit, or I swear to God, I'll farkin' kill you!"

"Oh! Is that a threat?"

"Detective Bennett."

I pushed over a CD rack. It crashed to the kitchen floor.

"Detective Bennett!"

"Let's see where a casual search takes us," I said. I

walked to the bookshelf under the window and selected a DVD from the extensive collection there. Scumbags always have huge collections of DVDs, displayed on shelves like books. I wondered if they emulated the bookshelves of more learned environments, the offices of lawyers who handled their compensation claims, the libraries where they conducted their rental searches. This was an idiot's depository of knowledge. *Wild Wild West. Die Hard 2. The 40-Year-Old Virgin.* I popped open the plastic case in my hands. *Titanic.* I looked at the disc. It looked legitimately made, but I doubted it had been legitimately paid for.

"Nope," I said. I closed the case and flung it out the open window, over the balcony, and onto the street.

"No! Stop! Stop!"

I popped open *Terminator 2*. Clipped it closed, sent it spinning into the air.

"Not here, either."

"Please, please, tell him to stop!"

"I'd suggest if you want him to stop, you give him what he wants, George." Eden was sitting on the back of the couch, her arms folded over her chest. I flipped *The Godfather* and *Alien* off the balcony.

"Please!"

"Not here. Not here. Not here."

I flipped DVDs, put a good spin on them as they flew through the air like playing cards.

"George, give Detective Inspector Bennett what he wants. Right now we can sting you for 'public nuisance' at best," Eden said. "Tell us where we can find your collection, or we'll get more creative. Detective Bennett will start pulling apart your furniture, and I'll start thinking of interesting ways to fuck up your

world. I'm thinking 'use of surveillance devices to
record a private activity without consent.' I'm thinking
'filming for indecent purposes,' or maybe 'committing
indecent or offensive acts in a public place.' I mean,
are you absolutely certain all the runners you were
filming were adults, George? I'm wondering if 'making indecent visual images of a child under the age of
sixteen' might be in the cards."

I broke three plates, kicked over a potted plant, and
spilled a bag of rice all over the countertops and the
floor before George submitted. Eden bargained and
begged and bribed him as much as her black heart
would allow for a good hour and a half, but I think it
was the rice that did it. No matter how much you try,
you'll never get all the grains of rice up after a major
spill.

Rice. It's a bastard.

Underneath the sink, behind a row of greasy cleaning-
liquid bottles, a plastic Tupperware container of George's
homemade DVDs lay waiting for us. We left George crying on the couch and complaining of a migraine, and
took the discs back to the station for analysis. Five
officers on ten computers gave the recordings a quick
play, so we could get a feel for George's tastes,
whether they were violent or not. Eden and I stood at
the front of the computer room, allowing the others
some distance.

There was no overtly violent material present on
any of the discs.

Now, some people would say that, in a way, the
tapes *were* violent, that George's predatory gaze had
symbolically assaulted the women he filmed for his
own gratification while they frolicked freely, as they

rightly should be able to, in the assumed privacy of what should be an ungendered, "equal" public environment. That the penetrative lens of the camera had reduced these women to sexual objects with the same type of aggressive and oppressive sentiment that a rapist might express with his body, and that the nonconsensual filming, or "upskirting," of women, should in no way be considered harmless sexually themed play.

Frank Bennett: not a chauvinist.

But there was no physical violence present here, and that was what Eden and I were interested in. George had collected shots of female runners, particularly the more curvy variety, their breasts and backsides. He seemed interested in the motion of these women, the way their bodies reacted to the impact of their gait as they ran, the rise and fall of flesh. All my feminist teachings aside, I understood George's fetish.

George Hacker had created his own personal *Best of Baywatch* compilation out of female runners. It wasn't right. But that didn't mean I didn't *get* it. It was only when I noticed Eden staring at me that I realized I was humming.

"Is that the *Baywatch* theme song?" she asked.

"It is."

She gave me that look.

"I note your revulsion. And yet," I raised a finger, "it would have been impossible for you to recognize my humming as the *Baywatch* theme song without yourself having watched *Baywatch* enough times to memorize the tune."

"Can we do some police work?"

"Am I wrong?"

"Pull any and all images of suspicious characters," she told the tech nearest to us. "Email them straight through to me."

We left. I was disappointed. The day felt long already. We'd left ten men sitting in a computer room watching some Redfern idiot's soft-core porn. There was nothing except the minor sparkle of hope that George Hacker, while he had been stalking Sydney's parks fueling his erotic interests, might have caught something with his camera that would assist us.

Ruben sat in the kitchen of the house near the park and read over his translations of the newspaper stories he'd found in the upstairs bedroom. Phillipe had been uninterested in the stories Ruben pored over, texting beneath the table and sighing at the ceiling as the teacher took them through sentence structure and résumé writing in English. Phillipe put Ruben's interest in the attic room and the strange, dark presence throughout the house down to childish fantasy, but Ruben saw it differently. He felt in his gut that he was close to something he *needed* to unravel, something he had been charged to put to rest. Ruben didn't shy away from adventure. He let his curiosity lead him. It had taken him to wonderful and terrifying places.

It had been some time since he had heard any noise from the attic room. The television behind the door was silent, and when he looked up at the window from the street, he saw that the curtain over the window facing out across the park was drawn. He had a feeling that whoever was up there had sated whatever restless desire drove them, that the pacing and whispering he'd sometimes heard before had come to a peak.

Ruben also had the idea that whoever was in the attic left the attic when he wasn't around. He found food missing from what meager rations a mysterious someone stocked the kitchen with, and a white van parked in the garage at the back of the property showed signs of being driven—there were spiderwebs on everything in the garage but it, and the tires weren't deflated the way his little Hyundai's had been when he had left it outside his girlfriend's place to tour Germany the summer before. Whoever it was, they left his envelope of cash under the coffeepot for him to pick up every Tuesday. It was possible that whoever was up there had been the one to answer his emails about the job in the first place.

Ruben hadn't seen another staff member on the property, but he assumed someone other than the person in the attic trimmed the tiny garden beneath the sitting room windows, kept the dust off the porch and the vines off the side of the house. He wondered sometimes about trying to track down the gardener, whoever he or she was. Ruben had even gone so far as to drive by on Thursdays and Fridays to see if he might catch them in action, ask them about the house's owner. But he wasn't sure he could make himself understood in English yet.

Ruben had put the articles he found in chronological order. He smoothed out the first, a page from the social section of the newspaper, which mainly dealt with the married lives of American celebrities. There was a small column on the right side of one page that was devoted to Sydney socialites and their divorces, parties, and drug habits. At the top of the column was a photograph of a broad-shouldered man with a beautiful but fierce-looking blond woman on his arm, both dressed in party finery.

Australia's corporate elite gathered today to pay tribute to Michael Harper, celebrated CEO of Vota Media and chairman for TrueCare Research

Foundation, who passed away last Sunday after a long battle with pancreatic cancer.

Harper is survived by his wife, Joan, and daughter, Tara, who was unable to return from studies abroad to attend the ceremony. "It'll be lonely in the house without him," Mrs. Harper commented, before a family representative asked the press for privacy.

There was another article, this one from a cheaply printed glossy magazine, the pages littered with yellow stars and other graphics, collages with images of Australian celebrities pouring themselves out of limousines and cheering in the front rows of sporting events. A panel at the bottom of the page featured a shot of Joan Harper with her head in one hand, sitting with a girlfriend at a golden-lit restaurant.

Paparazzi in Sydney are chomping at the bit to get a look inside the Casa de Harper after the death of globe-trotting Vota Media CEO and all-round philanthropist Michael Harper, who passed away in November. Sources tell TheTalk that Harper's daughter was conspicuously absent from his funeral, and it was not because the millionaire heiress was living it up in Amsterdam, as some would suggest. A very public row at this year's Melbourne Cup between Joan Harper and Marcey Sage, mother of prima ballerina assoluta in the making Violet Sage, has bolstered claims all is not right with the mysterious Tara Harper. Oh my!

"The Harper kid is a psycho. She was an ugly, violent kid in high school and she's out of control now," says a source. "She's basically a recluse. Mummy Harper keeps her locked away from prying eyes." Principal of the prestigious Saint Ellis High School in Mosman, Richard Morris, would not confirm or deny rumors Harper Junior had engaged in self-harm throughout her troubled childhood years, or if she had launched a Carrie-style attack on another student on the evening of their senior prom. Court documents are sealed, but whispers on the grapevine tell us that the Harpers settled out of court with a Saint Ellis student in 2002 after their daughter was involved in a "serious assault"! Meow!

Is there any truth to these tall tales? It's unlikely we'll find out soon. Joanie Harper has canceled upcoming social commitments and battened down the hatches at Harper Manor. If there's more to know, *TheTalk* will know it first! Stay tuned!

The final piece was a small news report wedged between two articles, one about the drowning of a young surf competitor and one, Ruben guessed, about the opening of a new hospital. There were no pictures to accompany the article. The headline read NEW LAWS SOUGHT AFTER HIGH-PROFILE SURGERY MISHAP.

The state government has called upon federal leaders to impose regulations to curb the growing number of young Australians seeking cheap cosmetic surgery overseas. The move comes as reports arise that Tara Harper, daughter of the late philanthropist and socialite Michael Harper, was medivaced to a hospital in Darwin last week suffering from a grievously botched surgical procedure in Bangkok.

While details of the case are yet to emerge, police allege Ms. Harper, 21, traveled to Thailand to seek multiple elective surgeries and may have fallen victim to the many unqualified, or underqualified, cost-effective surgeons operating in the foreign city. "They call Bangkok the 'Butcher Shop' for a reason. Young people without the financial backing to seek the services of qualified dentists and plastic surgeons here in Australia go overseas thinking they've found the cheap way out," Deputy Police Commissioner Ryan Hennah commented. "It seems in this case, a great number of procedures were elected at once—a number and type our experts have told us would never have been approved here. Ms. Harper has also had the misfortune of choosing a facility with a terrible history of major surgical complications. She's lucky to be alive, if you ask me."

In 2014, more than seven hundred young Australians traveled to Southeast Asia to seek elective surgery and dental procedures. Of those figures, it's understood at least 25 percent were for breast augmentation. Dr. Elliot Taket of the UNSW Medical Research Department revealed the growing popularity of "surgical tourism." "You can get stuff done over there that you can't get done here," he said. "These guys will go ahead and give you breast augmentation without taking the time to decide whether or not your body can support the size and weight you're asking for. Their work is popular with models and porn stars who want to stand out in an already overcrowded industry. There are places you can go over there to get novelty work done that no one in this country would touch—facial implants and bone grafts. You'd be surprised what people want. Most of my work here is spent dealing with the cleanup—the physical and psychological fallout of bad choices and bad practices."

Member for Windsor Rooney Dennis will address the Senate this week with proposed restrictions on travel for surgical purposes.

As the sun began to set, Ruben took his articles up the stairs and crept to the door of the attic room. All was silent within. Holding his breath, he closed his eyes and knocked on the door three times, the third soft enough not to be heard, his courage already failing him. No answer came from within, not a whisper or a footstep. Ruben slid down against the door and knelt beside it, looked at the crumpled and sun-dried papers in his hands, felt sad somehow for whatever being was beyond the door, what part they had in the terrible history he held in his fingers. After some time, he cleared his throat.

"Are you Tara Harper?" he asked. There was a silence, and then a terrible thundering came against the door, so sudden and so loud Ruben fell back against the stair banister, his heart in his throat. The person behind the door was bashing on it, kicking on it, and when the noise diminished, he heard a low whisper on the other side of the wood.

"Stay away."

Ruben struggled to breathe.

He ran down the stairs and out of the house.

There were two things Ian Buvette didn't see a lot of in or anywhere near Skytree Industries; swearing, and beautiful women. But on an average Thursday night, Kent Street crowded with late-night shoppers on their way to cool their heels down by the harbor, Ian stepped out of his office building and found a beautiful young woman standing on the street, swearing. Ian hitched his shoulder bag and paused, watched her rummage through her expensive-looking leather briefcase-style handbag, then stare up at the windows above him, her hands falling at her sides. Ian was so puzzled he turned and looked at the windows himself.

"Shit," she said, seemed to consider her predicament and find that it was in fact even worse than she'd first realized, and then seethed again, "*Shit!*"

The woman stepped into the light of the sign beneath the windows, a gigantic *103*, for 103 Kent Street. She was a strange-looking woman, now that Ian could see her clearly. Smooth caramel skin, Vietnamese he guessed, but with hair cropped short—almost buzz-cut, and peroxide blond. Heavy-framed red glasses rimmed her eyes. The dress was expensive-looking, but Ian didn't know anything much about fashion. The woman set her briefcase bag down on the ground and rummaged through it in the light of the sign. Ian swallowed twice before he spoke.

"Can I help you?"

The girl glanced up at him. She looked like a beautiful, helpless child.

"Oh God, I'm sorry." She laughed, brushed hair off her forehead. "I didn't see you. I'm just . . . *Urgh!* I can't believe it. I've left my pass up there."

She gestured toward the windows. Ian looked up.

"Where?"

"Wilkins and Company. Seventh floor."

"You work here?" Ian hadn't seen anyone under the age of seventy exit the elevators at the Wilkins and Company law firm. Ever.

"As of today, and maybe only for today." The girl gave a tired little sigh-laugh, an uneasy noise. "I've left my pass *and* the new client reports I'm supposed to have done tonight up there on my desk. It's all right. It's fine. I'll just . . . I can call security. Maybe."

The girl flipped out her phone. Ian felt his stomach shift.

"Oh, um. I'm the last man out. They have private security here. First round isn't until midnight. I know, because I'm always the last man out. And often it's at midnight."

Ian thought that was a pretty good line; stuffed his hands in his pockets and leaned back on his heels to prove it. Made him sound like a hard worker—and knowledgeable, too, about the building and its security, the nuances of his workplace. Her new workplace.

"You couldn't . . ." She pressed her painted lips together until they disappeared, a humble inside-out smile. Ian felt himself smiling. He wasn't a man who'd ever held power. So, when the tiniest tastes and whispers of it entered his life, he felt them as keenly as sexual release.

"I couldn't lend you my pass?"

"You couldn't, could you?"

"Well," he said, "I don't know, lady. I've never seen you before."

"Oh please." She was really laughing now. He'd made her laugh. "Do I look like a thief?"

"A cat burglar, maybe." Where was this incredible charm and wit coming from? This was not Ian. Pudgy, video-game obsessed, mother-worshipping Ian. Something about her inspired him. It was like he was roleplaying on a stage on which he'd been performing for years. He knew the lines. They were just . . . natural.

"I'll be three minutes." She held up three manicured fingers. Her palm looked soft but firm, like satin over brick. "Three."

"I'll make you a deal," Ian said. He had no idea where this confidence was coming from. She seemed to draw it out of him on a string. "You're three minutes, or less, or you have to buy me a drink down the road at the Stanton."

She cringed. "I'll have to rush, then."

She swiped the pass out of his hands and beeped herself through the foyer doors with all the familiarity of someone who had worked at 103 Kent Street for a decade. Ian glanced at his watch once every five seconds, uncertain somehow, in the wake of the funny little firecracker who'd turned up in his life. His face felt hot, but a chill was growing in his spine. He hoped he wasn't sweating through his shirt. At two minutes and fifty-one seconds, she burst through the doors to the elevator and ran across the dark foyer, pushing the large green exit button.

"Ha!" she grinned. "Made it."

"Aww, too bad for me," Ian said, without an inch of false sentiment. The girl was laughing, tucking a manila folder into her briefcase bag.

"Maybe I'll lock myself out tomorrow." The girl winked, and Ian felt the gesture stab him right in the sternum. The sincerity in her words. The joke that Ian knew, somehow, was not a joke. "See ya, man."

"See ya," Ian said.

He stood in the street and watched her walking away. His heart aching, Ian turned toward the Stanton, glancing at his watch. There was no need to be disappointed, he told himself. A drink on the first night of meeting would have ruined it. Yes, they'd meet again. She'd deliberately lock herself out. It was perfect. It was a little Jane Austen, if he was honest with himself. It was *very* Jane Austen. Ian looked at the starless sky between the buildings above him, marveled at the world and its symmetry.

Amy walked up the block to Town Hall, stood looking at the huge ornate building lit electric-pink and yellow from floodlights in its filthy gardens. The traffic lights changed and a hundred people flooded the great intersection, passed each other like trained soldiers on the march, eyes averted.

She counted off some minutes on her sensible little gold-and-leather-band watch, her "office girl" watch, as she called it, and then walked back down the hill and turned right into the lane behind Kent Street. She kept her head bowed against the security cameras hanging above the loading zone adjacent to the fire escape belonging to 103 Kent Street. It was not likely her presence would be noted or the cameras searched for images of her, as she intended to take nothing from the building that would arouse suspicion. But Amy never shied away from extra precautions. The proactive con artist was a successful con artist. She opened the door she had left propped open when she dashed through the building with Ian's ID card, and entered the stairwell.

Being overly cautious was only one of the many natural behaviors that made a successful con artist. Amy had discovered each in turn the hard way, on her own, because people like her—liars, cheats, shadow people—were impossible to find, and were solo operators when they did reveal themselves.

Amy was in no way ignorant of the fact that Ian,

master dead-ender of Skytree Industries, would stay up all night thinking about her. That he'd dress dangerously tomorrow, that he'd think the encounter on the street had meant something, had been zingy pesto he'd been waiting for in the iceberg lettuce of his life. Amy didn't feel anything about this, other than satisfaction, now that she'd gained access to Imogen's building. Checkpoint: passed.

There are plenty of things on a personal laptop that can ruin a person—even the most measured of people. For women it's erotic photographs, letters to the ex-boyfriend, secret bank accounts, fake dating profiles. For men it's unconventional porn, party photos, gambling accounts. Amy headed straight for the laptop and brought up Imogen's email account, flipped through the recent correspondence. A lot of it was client mail about appointments and referrals, mental health care plans. Some reports back to the department about police officers who had completed therapy or still had outstanding sessions keeping them off duty.

Amy wondered if Imogen had ever been Frank's psychologist—if in fact that's where the two had met. It made sense. She glanced at the darkened door to the hall and then searched the computer for documents with "Bennett" in the title. She came upon a file named "BennettArcher.doc."

Monday, 17th September: Frank stonewalling but clearly in trouble. Oxycodone? Check prescription frequency.

There was no porn on Imogen's computer. No dating profiles in her Internet history. Amy wandered through the cookie files in Imogen's browser and settled on one that piqued her curiosity—Sandersinvestigations.com.au. Amy glanced at the contact email address, then went back to Imogen's email account and found the correspondence stream in the "Sent" folder.

imogenstonepsych@gmail.com: Brent, long time no see! Can I call on that favor you owe me for the Harrowe case?

info@sandersinvestigations.com: Nothing slips by you, Imo. Tell me what you need and we'll call it square.

imogenstonepsych@gmail.com: Really need registry files on Archer, Eden. No middle name, apparently. Weird! Particularly interested in daddy, if you can make it happen.

info@sandersinvestigations.com: You know I love a challenge. See attached.

Amy sat back in Imogen's chair, rapped the tabletop with her fingernails. There were five files attached; birth certificates belonging to Eden, her brother Eric, her father Heinrich, and her mother Sue, and a conviction report for Heinrich Archer, no middle name either, beginning with thefts, assaults, and loitering charges in 1970. In the pale white light of the laptop, Amy drew her legs up beneath her on the chair and leaned forward, digging deeper into Imogen's search history.

I got home at about nine. I'd started calling Imogen's place "home" about a month after we started dating, about the time I got my own drawer in her bedroom closet and started keeping a toothbrush in her bathroom. Imogen-home wasn't the favorite of my two homes—that would always be where Greycat was, and right now that was at my burned-out row house. Greycat was a complete asshole, but he had that quiet kind of stability a cop needed in his permanent dwelling. Every now and then I would return to my Imogen-home and find her in a bad mood and her hair all crazy or the place smelling of bleach and her clothes all stained with it and all my stuff in a pile on the laundry room floor. Greycat was never frazzled. If he had been a person, he'd have been a total stoner.

There are rough days on homicide, of course there are. But they're not the kind of rough days people imagine. Hollywood misinterprets things, or reinterprets them in more socially acceptable ways. On television, a bad day in homicide is finding a woman hanging by her neck in her apartment with her guts on the floor and her mother crying in the hall. As a matter of fact, the finding of a body is a good day in homicide. Things are fresh. Exciting. Hopeful. You've got a case. You haven't interviewed anyone yet. The scene is laid out in all its intricacies and curiosities.

You'll get to know this gutted woman better than you've known some of your family members. You'll have beers with her brother and listen to her father's war stories. You'll play with her dog. You'll watch her be buried, mourned, forgotten. The first day is the best day. It's like a very successful date. You've got it locked in. You haven't fucked it up yet. Missed something. Underestimated the importance of something. It's all downhill after the first day, until the day you land the killer. That's the second-best day.

The bad days are the days when nothing happens. There's nothing to look at. No one to talk to. Everyone with something to say about the case has said it. All the photographs and CCTV of the area have been reviewed and set aside. All the witnesses have been interviewed, all the ex-boyfriends leaned on, all the photographs and fingerprints and mouth swabs collected and sent off. The measurements taken and the powder spread and wiped back up. The case falls from the news and journalists stop calling you. It's day four. Five. Fifty-seven. The parents stop calling you, except at Christmas and the girl's birthday. A new case comes along.

It was only day four of Ivana Roth's murder, but I had that feeling of dread that starts when more leads are dismissed than present themselves in a day. I'd spent the afternoon going back over the autopsy reports on Ivana and Minerva, looking for inconsistencies and trying to understand what they meant. Eden and I had argued with each other for forty minutes over knuckle size and spread. We could measure the size of the perpetrator's hand from knuckle-print bruises on Ivana's collarbone. The hands were small. I thought there was a ring indentation on one. Eden disagreed, said it was a scratch. I'd yelled at her that she needed to get her eyes checked, she was going blind as well as deaf.

That had been the catalyst for me going home. It had been a cheap shot. Eden had come away from the last case with gunshot damage to the hearing in her left ear, and I knew she was supposed to wear a hearing aid but didn't, probably out of pride. We'd gotten nothing done on the case and I'd been mean to my partner. I wondered how early I could get through the daily pleasantries with Imogen and then get into bed.

When I walked in the door, I found all the apartment lights on and the hall smelling of grilled halloumi cheese. Ed Sheeran was playing. Female laughter erupted somewhere to the left of the hall. I froze with my hand on the knob and one foot in the stairwell.

"Baby!" Imogen said. She walked down the hall toward me. I closed the door.

"Have you got friends over?"

"I have," she said. "Sorry. I forgot to tell you. Come in—there's plenty of food."

She ran her fingernails over my scalp and ruffled my hair. I was being pulled in two directions by a magnetic force right in the center of my chest, one beckoning me back out into the stairwell, whispering warnings embedded in the male psyche about the age-old danger of Women with Wine, the other pulling me forward with promises of food. I was biologically befuddled for a second. When a tall woman passed the hall with a bag of Smith's Original potato chips in her hands, it was settled. I can spot Smith's from a mile away.

I bypassed the living room and went straight for the kitchen, the fridge. Plucked a cold fake beer from the box on the top shelf.

"Oh baby," I said, and took the first cold sip. Imogen was standing behind me. I turned and drank at the same time, peered at her with one eye, surveyed her temperature.

"Something amiss?"

"I'm just waiting for you to come and say hello," she said. I sucked air between my teeth, tasted imitation beer on the vapor of my breath. A performance was in order. I kissed her forehead.

"I just need a minute," I said. I rolled my shoulders, cracked my neck. "I've had a really rough—"

"Frank!" a woman in the doorway chirped. She was a beautiful Indian woman in a bright yellow dress, a red necklace of polished wooden beads, and red pleather heels. A bit dressy for wine and snacks with the girls. The others would talk about it while she was out of the room. Her colors. Her eagerness. "You must be Frank. We've heard so much about you."

"Frank, this is Deepa."

"Hello." I grabbed her hand and pumped it.

"We're all so interested to hear about your job. Imogen's given us a taste, but there's so much she can't answer."

Suddenly, the kitchen was full of women. I looked down and found my beer was empty.

"Frank, this is Shauna. This is Erica. This is Kim."

I was turning to get another beer at the exact moment Kim was plunging in for a kiss on my cheek. The fridge door got trapped between us and she planted her kiss right on the corner of my mouth. Her breath tasted of wine.

"Oh, hi." I laughed, put an arm around her narrow shoulders, hugged her into the fridge door.

The place swelled with chatter. I found myself holding my beer bottle against my temple.

"She did say he was handsome."

"Very."

"He's got that Joel Edgerton, outback Australian flavor to him."

"Joel Edgerton! Oh God. Now that's a flavor I wouldn't mind getting a taste of."

"Oh Jesus. Save it, Shauna."

"Don't mind them, Frank. They're drunk." Kim stroked my arm.

"What are you doing?" Imogen pulled my beer down from my head. "Stop being weird."

"Let's go back to the living room," someone announced. "I'll be the first interrogator. Are you ready for your interrogation, Frank?"

"I'm really not," I murmured to Imogen. "I'm not. At all."

"Don't be difficult." Imogen glanced at the hall, the women retreating. "It's just a bit of fun. Give us five minutes."

"I've had a really rough day," I said again.

"I would have told you about the dinner." She smoothed my hair back from my temple. "I just forgot. Ok? Just come and say hello for five minutes and then you can make an excuse and leave."

"I don't want to be interrogated. I've spent my week thus far *actually* interrogating people. I don't want to be the center of attention. Keep them off me, Imogen."

"Or what?" she laughed.

"Frank! Come on!"

"Immy, please," I said.

"Frankie, please," she imitated me, slipping into my

arms, rubbing my chest. "Come on. I've got plenty of treats. Bring a couple of beers with you."

She pulled my arm, never giving me a chance to grab the beers. I was led into the living room. There was a platter of antipasto on the coffee table, barely touched. The olives glistened black and wet like droplets of mercury. I gathered up six olives and a handful of salami and sunk into the couch. Pulled a bowl of chips toward me. If I was going to do this, I was going to do it surrounded by my faithful brothers: meat, salt, and alcohol. The lights were hot.

"So, Imogen tells us you're on the Sydney Parks Stalker case, Frank?"

"I'm one of the members of a task force charged with that, yes."

"How intriguing." Kim sat back in the armchair nearest to me, adjusted her stockings at the knee. "You've got to give us the low-down. What are the major leads?"

"I read in the paper you don't think it's a man. Is that right?"

"Well, there's no evidence thus far to suggest—"

"I don't think it's a man, either," Deepa said, barely managing to swallow her wine before the words were out of her mouth. "The faces. It's very personal. Identity-driven, not bodily driven. Sociopathic, rather than psychosexual, if you ask me."

"Oh, here we go. She'll be quoting Wilhelm Reich in a minute. It's always Reich with her."

"You're a psychologist, too?" I asked. I glanced at Imogen but she ignored me.

"We're all psychologists." Deepa smiled.

"Oh. Excellent."

"Imogen's the only law enforcement specialist among

us," Kim said, letting one of her navy blue cashmere slip-ons slide off one heel. "The only one with *murderous interests*."

"When we heard she'd snagged you off the client list we were so excited," Deepa grinned.

"Yes, off the client list," Shauna tutted at Imogen. "Naughty-naughty!"

"We'd love to hear about some of your cases."

"Yeah!" Erica gasped. "The really bad ones."

"Tell 'em about the chainsaw guy," Imogen said. A low moan of excitement rose around me. I felt Imogen's hands on my shoulders, trying to massage them but only succeeding in making them tighter. "I love that one."

Everyone was staring at me.

"Uh," I scratched my head, "the chainsaw one?"

"These twenty-year-olds are holding a work party at Palmer and Co. You know Palmer and Co.?" Imogen spread her hands.

"Oh, I know that one."

"I love that place."

"Well, these kids are having a party there in the event room. A costume party. There's, like, fifteen of them, all went to college together, all work for the same company. They're mostly film buffs, so they decide they'll have a theme to the costumes. Favorite horror flick."

I looked around. All eyes were on Imogen. I wondered if I could slip away to get a beer. I looked past Kim into the kitchen. The lovely beers. She caught my eye and slow-winked.

"This idiot kid turns up with a *real chainsaw*."

"Oh Jesus! No way!"

"What horror film is that?"

"Texas Chainsaw Massacre. God you're slow, Deepa."

"When was this?"

"Last year."

"Oh man, I think I read about this!"

I squeezed out from between the couch cushions, almost tripped on Kim's legs. Grabbed a handful of chips on my way to the kitchen. Imogen's voice was everywhere, inescapable.

"The bar staff doesn't even notice it's the real thing. They just think it's a convincing prop. Next thing you know, half the guys at the party are on ecstasy and someone grabs hold of the chainsaw and fires it up, like it's a joke, and swings it around. He's high as a kite, doesn't know what he's doing, and some kid gets his fucking arm lopped off. Chainsaw goes in at the armpit, comes out at the neck, hacks the whole thing off like a chicken wing. Kid bleeds to death on the floor before anyone's even called it in."

There were collective squeals of horror and delight. I went to the fridge and stood in the cool, looked at the beers. The fingers of my right hand were twitching. Something had awakened the old gunshot wound in my shoulder, got it toying with the nerves down my arm. I reached for the beer, then didn't feel like it. I closed my eyes and just stood there, bathed in the gentle hum of the machine. Things had quieted down in the other room.

"I mean, how do you say conclusively if that's murder or not?"

"Sounds like an accident to me."

"Ah, but the plot thickens! Sounds like an accident—

until you take into account the guy's long-standing
grudge against the victim. His history of mental ill-
ness. Rumors around the office that he'd said he was
going to 'get' the victim. That his 'days were num-
bered.'"

More sighs and groans of intrigue.

I left quietly through the front door.

When I arrived home, all the lights in my house were
on. I stood in the street and asked myself whether I
could be bothered going into defensive mode, whether I
had the strength to round the back of the house, come
through the gate to the small yard, make sure I knew
who was in my place when I wasn't home before whoever it was knew that I knew, in case some harm was
being planned for me. Then I realized that I was standing crookedly, the weight of the day heavy on my
shoulders, and that if someone meant harm to me, they
were probably going to achieve it whether I surprised
them or not. I spotted Greycat on the roof at the same
time that he spotted me, and watched him trundle
down the railings and gutters and sills that marked his
path to the second floor, then the ground floor. He did-
n't seem concerned with the state of the house. I decided the builders had left the lights on.

The front door was unlocked, and Rachmaninoff
was playing somewhere. I only knew it was Rachmaninoff because my father had been a big fan. The
hall walls were a rich English mustard yellow. I stood
looking at them, at the cream trim and baseboards. A
great hole someone had punched in the wall directly

opposite the front bedroom door had been patched and filled. The ceiling wasn't painted, but holes in it had also been filled.

"Eden?" I called.

"Yuh," she said.

I found her on the living room floor, following the ornate baseboard with that glossy cream paint from the hall. She'd done the walls here mustard, too. Though she was wearing old jeans and a man's shirt, there wasn't a fleck of paint on her. Not one. I hadn't ever met anyone who could paint like that. When I painted, I was still picking it out of my hair three weeks later.

"This was all supposed to be blue," I said.

"I know," she said. I sat down near her and watched her paint. She'd been right about the colors. The room was warmer now than it had been. It was homey, but it felt somehow expensive—seemed to fit the period architecture. The ceiling moldings popped out of the yellow like well-kept teeth. They were walls that wanted art now. Yearned for classy oils. Greycat slipped through the front door and brushed against Eden's side, flopped down on the bare, hard boards and groomed himself.

I didn't know what Eden was doing in my house, painting the walls while I wasn't there, making sure I didn't choose the wrong colors. I didn't know why she'd come that first day and helped me put my kitchen cupboards together. She might be genuinely worried that I'd wire something wrong, burn the place down and kill myself, thereby leaving her to catch the Sydney Parks Stalker by herself. Then again, she might just have been bored, lonely, unable to sleep, her own apartment already perfect and crammed with art she'd never sell.

She might have been drawn to broken things, things in need of rescue, the way her father was.

It was also possible she was trying to be close to me. Not sexually, or even emotionally, just proximity-wise. Because she couldn't ignore the fact that we needed to talk about her being a monster, about how long I was expected to sit by with the knowledge that she took lives, had taken lives, had taken one right in front of me, exchanging it for mine. I wasn't over that.

But watching her paint, so serene, so detached, I felt reluctant to ruin things. She shifted along the floor, painted the trim to the corner, sat stroking the brush along, with her back to me, tendrils of her hair falling from a knot at the top of her head down and around her slender neck.

When I couldn't stay awake any longer, I followed the cat to my bed.

The wake was the first time Tara thought about killing her mother. She'd realized one night, lying on her side in the bed, her hands slippery around the marshmallow rice bar in its wrapper, that mothers were things other things came out of. The pod that released seeds into the wind. The vessel that carried small, warm, wet, circular balls of life. But Joanie wasn't a vessel or a pod—she wasn't hollow.

Tara had examined her on one of their hellish treks through the darkened park as Joanie waited in the light of a streetlamp, her hard ribs and flat stomach, the belly button stretched taut over the abdominal muscles into a horizontal line. Nothing but thin layers of skin between her surface and the sinew beneath. When she breathed, nothing moved—the skin didn't slide up and down the ribs like it did on other skeleton people Tara had observed. There was no reservoir of fluid inside her to tap. Joanie was a stone woman. Tara didn't know where she herself had come from, but she was sure she hadn't come from inside Joanie. There was no inside Joanie.

The wake was an uproarious affair, as far as she could tell. She'd lain on the floor and listened to the noise beyond the stairwell, the shrill laughter and occasional singing, the low bubbly hum like the noises of a busy kitchen, clattering and hissing. At some point, the household was called together and a silence fell.

Tara strained to hear what was said about her father.

It was mostly men who spoke about him. Tara lay down on the carpet and put her ear to the crack beneath the wooden door and listened. She only heard snippets, but snippets were all she had ever known of her own father. Glimpses of him around doorways, flashes of him at the bottom of the stairs as he headed out to the radio station at night, as he wheeled his bags to the airport taxi in the pale blue of early dawn. His voice, low and heavy, on the phone in the yard. Tara closed her eyes and collected the words of the men downstairs.

Quiet. Heart. Big. Shadow. Drifting. Drifting man.

A drifting man. He had been to them what he had been to Tara, a dark half-captured specter forever on the way to somewhere or from somewhere but never here, never settled.

Joanie had always talked to Tara about her father in terms of time, and it always seemed somehow that it was Tara's fault: she had taken the time from her father. When he came home he would take off his huge watch and put it somewhere, on the edge of the dining room table or next to the bed, so that the time was never far away.

He doesn't have time for . . .
He can't waste his time with . . .
Every time he looks at you.
Every time.

She'd gone down into the kitchen when darkness had descended over the house, crept to the back windows, and gazed at the yard, the paper cups lying in the bushes and the possums dancing in the trees. The kitchen island was cluttered with platters half-heartedly covered with aluminum foil to trap heat long dissipated: pancetta-wrapped prawns spotted with pieces of black char, dripping oil; wedges of fruit on wilted fingers of arugula.

Tara peeled back the foil on one of the platters and found a group of cold meat pies sitting in a corner like magic stones. She had put one in her mouth without realizing it, until the salty taste of it was at the back of her teeth, mush on her gums. Daddy's wake pies. This was what a dead father tasted like, salty and slightly warm, like a bed only recently left and then returned to. Safe. Yes, there was a safety in his death. The haunting shadow was now gone. Tara put another pie into her mouth and closed her lips around it, closed her eyes.

She didn't know him, but she could taste him. His ashes.

Tara didn't notice the woman in the doorway until she spoke. Tara opened her eyes and took in the lanky figure leaning there, the nimble folded arms swathed in black satin, the dramatically painted eyes. She was an unfamiliar but beautiful creature, a ginger cat-woman wandered in from the lightly falling rain.

"Come here," the mystery woman said, smiling. Tara did as she was told, following the cat-woman into the hall. The woman put a hand on Tara's shoulder, and the girl shivered with pleasure. Touch me. Touch me again, she thought.

"I used to work with your mother," the woman said. "Before Michael. Before the money."

"Work?" Tara trembled. "What do you mean? She's never . . ."

"Yeah," the woman laughed. "Never. That's where all the details of Joanie's life before Michael live. In the never-never. You've got it exactly right, my love."

Tara followed the woman to the sideboard, where the collection of photographs lived. Twenty frames of different shapes and sizes. Joanie and Michael in Barcelona. Joanie and Michael in Nigeria. Joanie and Michael in Paris. His family. His mother. His grandmother. His father, staring out the windows of his first office building.

The mystery woman smiled at Tara and then rearranged the photographs. She collected them all up into her arms and then set them on the table in a single line.

Gregory Harper. Tall. Thin. Blond.

Marylin Harper. Short. Thin. Blond.

Jessica and Steven Harper. Tall. Thin. Blond.

Joanie Harper. Tall. Thin. Blond.

Michael Harper. Tall. Thin. Blond.

Tara Harper. Short. Fat. Raven-haired.

The girl in the hallway trembled, looked at the woman with the dark eyes whose name she would never learn.

"It's not about your body, baby girl," the woman said. "It's about your blood."

The girl and the woman turned as they heard an exhalation from the door to the sitting room. Beyond where Joanie stood seething, the wake raged on, people laughing and singing and glasses breaking, the occasional wail of surprise at a story told or a secret shared. But Joanie marked the door to a bubble of hatred that encapsulated Tara and the woman with the photographs. Tara watched the woman set the rest of the photographs down, smiling as she headed toward the huge front doors.

When she got there, she turned back and winked.

When I woke, Eden was gone and Hooky was there, standing on my porch in a long black T-shirt with JUMPING CROC TOURS emblazoned on it and the right shoulder poetically ripped. There was a black-and-white croc on her chest reaching for a slab of chicken dangled off the side of a crowded boat. I realized that I was standing there dumbly holding the door open and looking at her chest and that I was shirtless. I felt uncomfortable, strange and weird and out of sorts with a teenage girl with whom I'd never had anything but a healthy and wholesome sibling-like relationship. I hated Imogen for a second for causing that, for threatening to ruin what Hooky and I had. Luckily, Hooky didn't catch on to any of it.

"Want to go to the morgue with me?" she asked, like a kid asking a pal if he'd like to go down to the river and play.

"What do I want to go to the morgue for?"

"Uh, because it's awesome there?" Hooky frowned, as though I'd asked where the sky was.

"I've got homework," I said.

"This'll help with the homework." She winked.

I went back into the house to get my shirt.

I drove Hooky to the Glebe morgue, past the huge cheese-grater-shaped University of Technology and its towering sister apartment building dripping with greenery and hanging vines. The two buildings hugging Broadway made for strange partners, one lush and alive, one lethal-looking. As we stopped at the lights, the intersections were flooded with students dressed in touches of the absurd—fluffy penguin hats and bell-bottoms, the occasional sequined dress. One or two of those who crossed before us were barefoot. Hooky's peers.

She looked at them in a bemused way. It seemed to me that Hooky stood apart from them, as she had her high school mates, apart and above, bored by assessment tasks and exams and apparent social pressures—stuck between the nerdy kids in suits and the dope smokers on the verge of dropping out. I hoped they didn't bully her, the way she'd been bullied as a kid. After her sister did what she did, Hooky ceased to be the Hooky she'd been to her classmates. All the joy and irresponsibility was dead. I'd seen it happen to kids before, seen them become ghosts in young bodies. The others don't like it. They start pecking at the strange bird in their nest, instinctively, trying to weed out the different.

"Does Imogen know Eden?" Hooky asked. I was fiddling with the radio station. I'd just missed the news.

"Ah, yes. Eden and I were in tandem therapy with Imogen. I know. It's weird."

"They call that transference."

"What?"

"Psychology patients falling in love with their doctors," Hooky said. "The patient redirects their feelings from what they're dealing with to the psychologist during psychotherapy. The patient gets all wrapped up in the care and consideration they get from their psychologist, and they emotionally attach. Try to take it beyond the professional setting. Psychologists are supposed to keep an eye out for it. Make sure they don't take advantage of their patients while they're vulnerable."

"I quite enjoy being taken advantage of."

"So the two of them only know each other through therapy."

"Yes, Eden and Imogen are certainly not friends," I said. I remembered the evening at Malabar and cringed, turning off Broadway and onto Glebe Point Road. "Why?"

"I was just wondering how it all fit together," Hooky said.

People assume morgues are gloomy places, full of the reservation and reflection people associate with death, but they're not. Sure, the building is stuffed with dead people in various states of assembly, but being depressed about it all day long makes for a fairly unsustainable workplace for the people who work there.

The first time I ever entered a morgue as a young police officer, I was struck by the presence of a vending machine standing inside the automatic doors. A vending machine! The idea that people would casually munch a Mars bar while standing over the mangled body of a stranger, or grab a Coke before they go in to carve out semi-decayed livers and weigh them on scales, boggled my mind. But they do. People do eat Mars bars at work, even when their work is with cadavers. They also gossip, laugh, play pranks on each other, and decorate their workspaces with happy pictures and fuzzy pens. They play music. They text and take cigarette breaks. It's just like any other workplace on earth.

Just outside the automatic doors, I stopped Amy on the stairs.

"Now look. You'll probably want to make a lot of hilarious puns in here." I gestured toward the doors. "But there are tons of them, and I know them all, and they can take a long time. So, we ought to just get them out of the way before we go in, so that we don't waste time."

I rolled my shoulders. "Gee, this is the *dead center* of town, isn't it?" I said. "Well, this is anything but a *dead end* job. Oh dear, my back's feeling a bit *stiff*. This is a great place, people must be just *dying* to get in here. Care for a drink after work? Maybe some *spirits*?"

Amy looked at me.

"If you wanted to contribute," I informed her, "you could say something like, 'Oh stop, Frank, you're *killing* me!'"

She went inside.

I've known Carrie, the receptionist, for years—but I was surprised when she put the sign-in clipboard on the counter and smiled at my young partner with recognition.

"How you doing, Amy?"

"No complaints."

"Well, aren't you full of surprises?" I squinted at Hooky. "What have you been doing, hanging around my morgue?"

"Research," Amy said.

"She's *dead serious* about her research, Frank." Carrie struggled to keep a straight face.

"Oh, nice delivery on that one, Carrie. Absolutely *dead*pan."

"Excuse me, won't you?" Amy sighed. "I'm going down to lab sixteen, Carrie."

Amy turned and walked down the wide hall. I followed her, soaking up the hospital disinfectant stink. People don't like that smell, but I've never minded it. It reminds me of when my dad was dying, all the treats and attention I got, the sense of newness in the air that surrounded his passing. He wasn't a nice guy.

"How long have you been coming here?" I asked.

"I drop in and out," she said.

"And what exactly have you been telling them that has convinced them to let you in here?" I asked.

"This and that," she said.

"You're creeping farther and farther into Murder

Police territory, Hooky Bird," I said. "It's a long way from what you're approved for with the department."

"So I'm allowed to let creeps show me porn all night long, but I'm not allowed to look at stiffs? That makes sense."

"It depends on the porn."

"I'm not approved to do that, either."

"I was going to ask you about that. The chiefs know you're doing that sort of work in the offices. But was that screenshot I saw yesterday from your personal computer? It had some very questionable chat room names on the bottom of the screen."

Hooky said nothing.

"You're not going off on your own to chase these guys down, arc you?"

"So what if I am? It's the same thing I do in the office with a bunch of cops gawking at me. I still hand the guys in to the chiefs. I just don't do all the bullshit filling out of forms."

"Oh Jesus, Hooky!" I moaned. "You're too big for your own boots."

"My mother used to say that."

I bit my tongue, let a minute of silence pass, in which I tried to remember that Hooky was not my child, and if she got her privileges at the department stripped for overstepping her bounds, there was nothing I could do to stop her. She was as stubborn as an ox.

"Homicide is different. Very different. If you think you can mess around and play games with your sex crimes resources, you cannot do that here."

"You and Eden are the only ones aware of what I'm doing, Frank," she said. "No one's going to kick up a stink."

"What if I kick up a stink?" I said.

"You won't."

"Look,"—I took her arm—"I know you can get yourself anywhere you want to go. You've proven it, to everyone. No one can stop you going after what you want, and that's fine—you've earned that. You're brilliant at what you do, so people bend the rules and look the other way for you sometimes. But that doesn't mean some of us shouldn't try to stop you when you wander into dangerous territory. I'm worried about you messing around over here."

"Where? In the morgue?"

"Yes. And at crime scenes. In the evidence files. Over here, over in homicide."

She stopped walking and looked up at me. Ran a hand over her prickles and laughed, incredulous.

"You're quite happy to accept my assistance when I'm right, when it helps your case. But then I stray too far . . ."

"I'm not saying you're straying too far. I'm just saying one of these days you might. You might get in too deep, and I don't care how old you think you are. At the end of the day, you're seventeen. No amount of pretending is going to change that."

"Do you think I'm going to be traumatized, Frank?"

"I'm traumatized." I tapped my chest.

"Please." She waved her hand at me. "Don't play daddy. You're no good at it."

I couldn't control any of these women. Eden. Hooky. Imogen. None of them listened to me. I followed Amy toward Lab 16 and thought about getting angry. Sometimes getting angry with them works. Sometimes it blows up right in your face. It didn't work with Imogen. I hadn't been game to try it on Eden, in case I woke up in a hole somewhere, startled by the pattering of the first shovelful of dirt on my chest. I gathered a lungful of air and put on my most determined face.

"You—" I started, as we got to the freezer doors.

"This is Jill Noble," Hooky said, popping open one of the narrow compartments. Mist swirled around a blue tarpaulin body bag. Amy drew out the rack on which the body lay until it separated us and unzipped the thick black zipper on the side of the bag. "She came in on August fourth, thirty-six days ago."

I looked down at the passive face of Jill Noble. There was little I could tell about her from her shoulders up, other than that she'd been allowed to decompose indoors, or sheltered from the elements somewhere, for about a week before being snap-frozen in the state she was found. Her body had swelled and deflated again, the way it does in the first three days. One of her ears was black as coal from lividity, and the cheek on that side was swollen, cloudy and dark purple. I glanced into the bag at her breasts, her left arm. She'd been lying on her side for quite a while. Her tricep was pressed flat.

"Hi, Jill," I said.

"Jill Noble was the Sydney Parks Strangler's first victim," Amy said.

"Who?"

"The Sydney Parks Strangler. That's what the papers are calling him."

"Oh please. Really?"

I waited for a punchline, but there wasn't one. I took Jill's report that was lying in a slot on the freezer door, and glanced over it. Advanced ecchymosis of the left side and left hip. Lots of bruising in distinct patterns, and laceration of the right kidney. No postmortem trauma.

"Beaten to death," I said. "Probably a lump of wood. Our park girls were beaten and then strangled."

"She was severely beaten. But she was beaten too badly, so there wasn't any fight left in her for the strangling." Amy pushed Jill's matted brown hair back off her neck. There were tiny dried leaves in it. "See here? Report says this mark is from her silver necklace lying on the right side of the neck while the body lay decomposing. A postmortem weight trauma. But I don't think so. You look at the thickness of the necklace. Its weight. It was eight grams and very thin. I think this is antemortem. I think it's a light abrasion from a drawstring, a hood placed over the head."

I looked at the mark on Jill's neck. To me, it was consistent with an abrasion, rather than a weight. The first layer of skin was papery, and the mark was a light pink, rather than a deep purple or blue. It cut across her neck and disappeared around the front of the throat. I pulled Jill's hair up farther and searched for a knot mark, but there was none. If it was a drawstring, it would have been loose, hastily tied.

"See here?"

"Mmm." I ran my fingers over a dent in Jill's throat, a distinct dip in the taut skin over her jugular. "Indentation. Could suggest postmortem strangulation."

"The killer tried to strangle Jill, but Jill was already dead. Her heart had stopped beating. So, there's no bruising. She died too quickly."

"So she was kidnapped, hooded, beaten with a stick.

Maybe a bit of experimental strangling—maybe. It's a bit of a stretch, Hooky."

"Look at the date of death, though. This is the park killer's *first* victim," Amy said. "If you look at the whole picture, it fits with what we know of the killer's tactics, now that she's farther along in her training. I think she hooded Jill's face for the same reason she now beats the face beyond recognition. Because she's trying to disguise the victim from herself, allow the victim to be whoever she is fantasizing she's killing."

Again, the visualization of the killer as female. The recognition of the facial injuries as a type of revenge fantasy. Both Eden and Amy had marked the killings as the work of a woman on a woman, a living-out of some attack that, for whatever reason, could not take place in reality.

"This is what I reckon. She started with an instrument to inflict her wounds," Amy said. "But it didn't suit the fantasy. It didn't feel right, and it killed the victim before she had a chance to get really personal—to strangle her. The hood wasn't right, either. It interrupted the original fantasy. It was distracting. By the time she got to Ivana Roth, she'd dumped the weapon and the hood and she was going at it bare-handed."

It made sense. There's plenty of research into violent fantasies that become realities. As homicide detectives, it's our job to keep updated on it all. Violent fantasies can come from plenty of places, but most often they're the result of trauma. A person experiences a terrible thing, either sudden or prolonged, and they begin to relive it over and over as a symptom of post-traumatic stress disorder. The trauma goes around and around and around in their mind, becoming more tangible every time it's revisited. Kids who were sexually abused can feel their abuser's hands on them. War vets have auditory hallucinations of gunfire, mates crying for help. It takes a lot of therapy to get yourself out of it. If you recognize the potential of a trauma when it happens, and immediately treat it, you can sometimes stave off the effects of PTSD.

Very rarely, sufferers of traumatic events add on to the revisualization of the traumatic event. The child-abuse victim turns and twists the fantasy until she becomes an abuser herself. The victim of workplace bullying revisits the painful incidents and adds in the vision of himself taking an AK-47 out from under his desk, blowing his colleagues away one by one. The fantasy, an involuntary thing, becomes voluntary. Enjoyable.

Ted Bundy mused in one of his last interviews before his execution that violent pornography, viewed very young, had made him what he was. He hadn't realized it at the time, but his young, innocent mind had been violated by what he'd seen, and the reliving of the violence through the torture and killing of his victims as an adult was just the natural progression of his childhood trauma. I don't know about that. Bundy was an arrogant man, full of excuses.

What had happened to our Sydney Parks Strangler?

"Where'd we find this victim?"

"Bradfield Park, Kirribilli," Hooky said. "She was under an old blanket, up against one of the bridge walls. People thought she was just a homeless person. Curled on her side, fetal position. It was three days before the smell was enough to bother anyone. Nighttime boot-camp groups had been exercising and jogging around the park, not a hundred meters from where she lay."

"Completely covered up?"

"Yeah."

It went with the theory that this was the Parks killer's first victim. Ivana had been partly covered and hidden near bushes. Minerva had been more obvious again. The killer was getting bolder as she went along. Starting to "come out" to us. Reveal herself to her audience.

"Was she in exercise gear?"

"Tracksuit."

"Shit." I felt the muscles gather at the base of my skull, preparing for the headache of a lifetime.

The difference between three victims and two in a homicide case might not seem like much on the surface of it, but in the public eye, it's huge. The first murder stirs people. The second murder unsettles them further. At this point, people hope that there isn't a serial killer on the loose, that there's no connection between the two victims and that any link police point to could be a fluke. No one alters their behavior. Sometimes, it doesn't even make front-page news.

But whenever links can be made among three homicide victims, killed separately, that's the signal for the media firestorm. For the public panic. For the condemnation of the lead detectives and their lack of progress, no matter how well managed the case is. The fact that Jill Noble had been victim number one and we hadn't been right onto it was bad news. I zipped up Jill's body bag and closed the freezer.

"This is on the down-low until further notice, Hook." I pointed at her face so she'd know I was serious.

"Good luck keeping this under wraps," Hooky said. "You know. I know. Carrie at the desk knows. The victim's family will talk to the media, and they'll know."

"We can try," I said. I took out my phone and called Eden.

As I was putting my key into the door of my car, I heard Caroline Eckhart's voice behind me. Turning and seeing her there outside the low brown-brick building that housed the morgue was bizarre. She had no cameras in tow, but she was still wearing that running gear—the midnight-black Catwoman suit and blazing lime-green shoes. She had her hands in the front pockets of a shimmering black wind jacket, and I could see the outline of her knuckles and a phone. I wondered if she was recording me.

"Frank," she said. "Can we talk?"

"No," I said. I've had enough front pages."

I unlocked the car and gestured to Amy. She didn't get in.

"I just want to talk."

"There'll be no talking, witch. Begone!" I waved my arm. "You have no power here!"

Hooky sniggered and got into the car.

"Why has George Hacker been released from custody?"

Caroline widened her eyes, as though working up a crowd that hadn't arrived yet. "The one and only lead your people have had on the Parks killer so far."

"George Hacker is nothing but a creep. He's not the . . . Sydney Strangler, or whatever you idiots are calling the perpetrator. Hacker can barely tie his own shoelaces. Speaking of being a creep, did you know that the legal definition of stalking in New South Wales includes one or more acts of unwanted *following*, or a similar intimidatory behavior, such as the unwanted *loitering near*, *watching*, or *approaching* a person? I looked that up last night, in case this happened again." I pointed to her, to myself. "Impressive, aren't I?"

I could see Caroline's camera crew getting out of their cars on the corner. They'd struggled to find parking spaces, and she'd taken the opportunity to snag me before I drove away. I got into the car and started it up.

"Why are you visiting the morgue today, Frank?" She tapped on my window. "Are Ivana and Minerva here?"

As I drove away, I felt my stomach sinking. Ivana and Minerva were still at the police morgue. If Caroline went and started hassling Carrie at the reception desk, her journalist buddies might be able to wrangle out which lab we'd visited and who was there. I could do nothing legally to stop them. News of a third victim would be on television by the evening.

"Who *is* that chick?" Amy sneered.

"Nobody," I said. "She's a dead-set nobody."

Hades thought the dog would die.

He wasn't afraid of dogs, far from it. Dingo-dog hybrids had provided a natural alarm system for the dump for many years, and kept the stray cat and fox numbers down. But Hades didn't tempt them toward the house, as he sometimes did with the possums that clambered around his sculptures. It was better that the hounds stayed out there, in the dark.

Those night creatures were a far cry from the dog in Hades's kitchen. It was a cross also, but had some more prestigious breeds in it. It had the gray color of a Weimaraner, with the sad, delicate look of a whippet. The pink nose was a mystery. It was an expensive dog, probably had a stupid "innovation" breed name, *Whippana. Wymerippet*. The expense, the youth of the thing—the callousness had stunned the vengeful land-fill workers who discovered the creature in the bag. And then there were the bills and notes in the trash. The garbage had come from an expensive area.

Hades could understand rich people starving a dog. Rich or poor, he'd seen people do all kinds of things. Cruelty had little to nothing to do with money, and lots to do with selfishness, carelessness, irresponsibility. The dog had probably been forgotten a series of times, accidentally at first, and then half deliberately out of sheer laziness, spite, punishment for the chewed-up shoes or the pissed-on couch. The thing was probably cute as a newborn, but in time it had failed to naturally assume the behaviors of dogs that were professionally trained. Refused to sit. Didn't answer to its name. It was punished, left behind while its owners worked, took drugs, traveled, stayed over with friends. Three days turned into four. And then one day, without any real warning, the dog went from skinny to dying. Visibly, undeniably, shockingly dying—beyond what a vet could fix without having to report the animal's condition. The dog was discarded. A broken toy.

Hades sat looking at the thing in the basket at the foot of the couch, or what he could see of it, the snout jutting from the wicker rim in case any more slices of soft red roast beef came floating by, or maybe a syringe full of water or milk with honey. The dog was eating, but that meant nothing. Hades was certain that activity was a good predictor of the animal's chances, and the dog hadn't moved in two days, not so much as shifted its position in the basket. Hades hadn't seen its full body, in fact, since he'd first picked it up. That wasn't good.

Hades knew his workers had the address of the couple who owned the dog. He knew he could do nothing to stop them from enacting their vengeance. The couple, whoever they were, would probably venture out to a nightclub or a restaurant over the weekend, and a couple of big, dirty men smelling faintly of garbage would attack them. There would be no reason given. No words said.

He turned at the sound of the fire-alarm bell above the front door. A car had entered the dump. He glanced at the collection of clocks at the entrance to the hall.

There were fifteen clocks of differing sizes and styles, cuckoo clocks and stainless steel postmodern clocks, plastic clocks and an old bedside alarm clock hung by a string. Averaging their times, Hades guessed it was about seven. He hoped his visitor wasn't Eden. She only came unannounced when something was wrong.

It was a woman. Hades could hear that much from the crunch of her heels on the gravel. He didn't get up. Beside him on the tabletop, as always, lay a pistol, concealed in the glossy fold of a magazine. Hades shifted the magazine a little closer and turned his coffee cup handle toward him, sloshed the cooling brown liquid in its base.

A short silhouette appeared against the chain-link wire of the screen door. Hades took his glasses from beside his cup. The visitor rapped.

"It's open," he called.

The woman approached with a smile. This puzzled Hades. Unexpected clients were usually shaking and blood-spattered, still wired from the drug pickup gone wrong or the botched robbery or long-awaited gang hit that had brought them there. The woman came down the hall and stood behind the chair opposite Hades, her eyes half-hidden in thick chocolate-brown bangs, concealed further by black-rimmed glasses. Hades smiled. Was this Eden's hunter?

"Heinrich Archer." The woman offered her hand. "I'm Bridget Faulkner."

The name was fake. She was too heavy on the *d* in Bridget and the *l* in Faulkner to have said it a hundred thousand times over the span of a life. She wasn't a practiced liar, or if she was, she was nervous—had overthought her moves. Hades felt the first tingles of apprehension, and not a little excitement, on the nape of his leathery old neck.

Hades smiled. "How can I help you?"

He gestured to the seat across from him, and she took it.

"I'm a journalist with the *Herald*," she said. "I'm trying to round up a few sources for a feature on Kings Cross in the late seventies. I was wondering if you could help. I understand you sometimes speak to journalists . . . about your time there."

This woman was a very poor impersonator, Hades thought. He'd met enough journalists to know their ticks. Where was the notebook? Where was the recorder? Every journalist Hades had met had an elaborate title that set them apart from the other guppies in the crowded tank. Head Crime Correspondent. Assistant Lifestyle Features Editor. Government Policies Analyst. Where was all the pomp and ceremony? Hades reminded himself not to be too disarmed. It was possible Ms. Faulkner, whoever she was, was a fool, or took Hades himself for a fool. Her glance toward the folded magazine beside him suggested the latter. How long would it be before this half-baked imposter got to her real purpose?

"Oh dear, ancient history," Hades said. "Aren't you *Herald* people done with that? I thought there was a Cross piece just last year around this time."

"Well, you know. It never loses its interest. We're trying to bolster intrigue for a couple of upcoming TV series."

"Yes, I've seen snippets of some of those shows. Very dramatic. I only wish the times themselves had been so exciting. So profitable."

She laughed, and put her hands on the table. She seemed in need of something. Hades took his coffee cup.

"Can I offer you a drink, Ms. Faulkner? Coffee? Tea?"

"Oh no, thank you, no."

"Mind if I get myself one?"

"Go ahead." She had a pleasant, if crooked, smile. Her mouth was dry, the painted lips sticking to her teeth. Hades went to the counter, turned his back to the woman, almost felt her eyeing the gun before her. He took another weapon from inside a ceramic pot marked TEA. Flicked the switch on the electric kettle.

"It must have been a long road from your time as a crime lord to suburban family man," Ms. Faulkner said. Hades poured the water into his cup, watched the black coffee crystals shrink and dissolve.

"People grow. They change," Hades said.

"You're in your twilight years, if you don't mind my saying," the woman continued. "When you were the age your daughter is now, you had a stranglehold on Sydney. You had bikers and drug dealers and hitmen in terror of you. Eden, on the other hand, is a police officer. Her brother was, too. What an interesting turn of events."

"Indeed," Hades said.

"She must have been a very different child to the one you were."

"Oh, I wouldn't say that."

"What *was* Eden like as a child?" Ms. Faulkner asked.

Hades turned. Put a hand on the counter near the

gun. In the other, he held his coffee. The woman calling herself Bridget Faulkner had turned in her chair, one foot out as though ready to spring to her feet. One hand was on the table. Did she know that Hades knew who she was, *what* she was—a threat to his child, to himself, to everything he had built? Could she see in his eyes that he would never let anything destroy his accomplishments, that he was prepared to make his front door the last door this woman would ever step through alive, if it came down to it?

"It was very stupid of you to come here alone, Ms. Faulkner," he said. Out of the corner of his eye, he registered the slightest twitch in her body, a sort of electric pulse as his words coursed through her. The veils were dropped.

"What if I'm not alone?"

"Oh, you are," Hades said. "We both know you are."

"I just want answers."

"You want money."

"Why did you kill the Tanners?" Bridget said. Her jaw twitched as her back teeth ground with terror. "Why did you take their children?"

Hades licked his lower lip. Gripping the edge of the counter, he put his coffee down.

"Does Eden know who she is?" Bridget asked.

The man and the woman looked at each other across the yawning silence. The howl of one of the landfill dogs seemed to mark the abandoning of civilities. Hades reached for his gun, and as he did, Bridget's hand slipped beneath the magazine and clumsily brought the pistol's aim around to him.

Hades fired with his eyes open. The woman fired with her eyes closed, an accidental gesture, her terror at the sound of Hades's blast making her entire body flinch. Her gun blasted out the window behind him. Her sharp, squinting cower at the sound turned her head away from his aim, caused his bullet to shunt into the wall by her ear. She gathered her resolve and tried to fire again without drawing the hammer back, clicked helplessly, then dropped the gun. She tried to run and he lunged, his weapon slipping from his fingers. He heard his own yelp of agony as old wounds awakened, his body unused to panicked action. They struggled for the pistol on the counter, sent it clattering into the sink. She grabbed the coffee cup, broke it over him, splashed boiling liquid on his arms, hands, chest, her own hands. She growled. Frightened. Angry with herself.

Hades swiped at her with one arm as he went down and knocked her away from the sink. On his hands and knees, a figure shifted past him, bright and fast like a flicker of light.

He had never heard such a noise. The high, squealing bark of an animal giving itself over to the violence in its heart. The dog flew at the woman in the kitchen, frenzied, jaws snapping with rage. Hades turned and watched it back the woman into the wall, chase her into the darkness before the door.

He barely heard the door open and close, the car beyond. The woman gone, the dog gave her a few warning barks from behind the screen, then erupted into terrified squealing, skittering back to Hades, cowering with its head tucked between its front legs and tail almost invisible between its hind quarters. The dog's eyes were remorseful slits, its ears flat against its skull, bracing for a blow. *Have I done the right thing?*

"Good dog," Hades panted, trying to unlock his clenched fists. The animal licked his arm, shoulder, ear, whimpering with delight at his words. "Good dog."

Eden looked out over the water. She didn't spend a lot of time imagining herself as a victim. It wasn't in her nature. She assumed that when her parents had been murdered, that had been the time to form her childish conception of victimhood. The time to discover the benefits so many lifelong victims became addicted to: the attention, the comfort, the slow, heroic climb of recovery, little encouragements treasured along the way.

But something had gone wrong that night as she sat on the table in Hades's kitchen and let him wash the blood from her face. Something had failed to connect. Eden had picked up her life again the next day, mildly afraid of the man who had become her new guardian, concerned whether her brother would survive, whether she would have to face this strange new life alone. She wondered if, even then, there'd been too much of the natural predator in her to know how victimhood worked.

Had the night her parents died made Eden what she was? Or had the malevolent thing that made her kill always curled inside her, sleeping, until the sound of guns shook it awake? Had it been Hades who made her what she was? Or if, by some twist of fate, she and Eric had survived the night of their parents' murders but ended up in the care of a regular person—might they have ever killed? Did her parents' murders open the door on who Eden was, or close it?

Over the birthmark that connected her to the child she had been, Eden had asked for an ornate door to be

tattooed, a big oak thing with a stained-glass panel in
its top depicting birds fluttering between tree branches.
It was a door she knew well.

Her lack of victimhood made her job as a detective
interesting. Empathy was something she tried hard at.
She'd admired Frank when he'd connected so instantly
and completely with his dead girlfriend. He'd felt
moved to protect her. He'd loved her, and then he'd
grieved for her. He was probably still grieving now,
Eden imagined, but she couldn't be sure. Why else did
he bury his head so firmly in the sand in terms of his
current squeeze?

Imogen was wrong for him. He needed someone
pretty and simple and gentle, like Martina. Was he
afraid of being alone? Eden had heard it was difficult
to sleep when a partner you'd gotten used to was suddenly gone from the bed, that even washing the sheets
didn't stem the desire for their presence, their warmth,
the roll and tumble of them on the mattress as they
twisted in the night. Their snores. Was Imogen a bed-
filler to Frank?

If she was, Eden suspected she was not the first.

She sat on the bench by the water while she tightened the laces of her running shoes, drew them tight
down over her now soft, pampered feet, gone to cus-
tard through her recovery. She'd enjoyed running
once. Liked looking down at the hard yellow callouses
that formed at the tops of her toes, on her heels—runner's feet, feet that could count kilometers, swollen
and aching. Eden had not run in the street since Rye
Farm.

She stood and rolled her shoulders, looked at the
harbor of gently jostling yachts. She imagined herself

as the Sydney Parks Strangler's next victim. Anonymous female runner catching a couple of quick Ks before dinner. She opened a running app on her phone, hooked up her earphones as she watched the tennis court café writhing with people, parents with kids on the green. The evening wind was stirring. Eden stretched her calves and began to trot. Pain swelled in her hips, her abdominals. She pushed it aside. *Think victim.*

She fell into an awkward rhythm, trying not to favor her left hip, where the muscles wanted to bunch. The rhythm of her body locked her head forward, shook everything in her periphery. Running required concentration, self-focus. She listened to her breathing, her steps, her mental commentary of aches. *This hurts, this hurts, this hurts,* her ankle said. *Stop, stop, stop,* her shoulder pleaded.

She forgot about the path ahead, ducked between two walkers. She only knew when a faster runner approached a second before they passed, a sudden colorful presence, and then their calves in front pumping as they pulled away. It wouldn't be hard, she realized, to be crept up on like this. Mindlessly chugging along, slipping down a dirt path between the roadways, and feeling a dull tap in your thigh. The sudden presence of another being behind you, and the glorious exhaustion of a run almost completed, gravity turned up, legs buckling. The guiding arm of the stranger directing the drunken runner to the nearby roadside, to the open van doors.

She lifted her head and sucked in the cooling night air. Rushcutters Bay Park was not by any means a likely candidate for the killer's next hit—it was expansive and bare in parts, heavily populated by fitness groups, bordered on one side by dozens of yachts with their hundreds of gaping eyes. A few trees huddled at the roadside, the city sparkling between them, lighting hiding places between which possums crept, babies gripping at their shoulders. Eden didn't see herself running smack-bang into the Parks killer on the hunt. She just wanted to run. To get into the parklands. To try to understand the hunting grounds.

She wondered at the brazenness of the attacks. What kind of hunter risked twilight-lit parks for their playground? Eden understood parks as the wonderland of rapists. They were usually drunk or high when they committed the acts, and were half the time homeless, so the parks were where they got their food, shelter, rest—why not their sex? Eden listened to the growing evening. Children's squeals of delight echoed across the water. A truck shifted gears as it headed into the Cross City Tunnel. Lights came on in the pastel-colored apartment buildings, one by one.

She reviewed the evidence over and over, in time to her footfalls, hoping to see a pattern, a beat, like the tempo of her soles on the concrete.

Black tracksuit. CCTV. Female runners. Bludgeoned faces. Lost identities. Strangulation. Revenge. Tranquilizer. White van.

The white van might not have caught her attention had it not crossed right in front of her as Eden turned onto the long stretch of path between the water and New Beach Road, heading toward the dead end at the lip of the bay. Eden fell victim to her curiosity, lowered her head, and sprinted across the grass toward the road, knowing the van would have to turn and head back toward her before it could escape the loop. As she teetered in the uneven gravel near the roadside, she saw the van making a three-point turn in the cul-de-sac. Two joggers stopped and watched her as she leaped out onto the asphalt, speeding up to a bone-grinding pace as the van turned around a small roundabout and headed up the hill onto Yarranabbe Road.

Eden stopped, her hips screaming. She gripped at her abdomen, at the ridges of pain that throbbed and felt splintered. She closed her eyes and remembered the knife inside her, the blood running up her neck. It took her a moment to realize the pair of joggers had crossed the road and were standing near her, nibbling at her attention with their presence. They were laughing. Eden tugged the earbuds from her ears.

"Thought you spotted the Sydney Parks Strangler?" the man said. The pair was a couple. The shoes were his-and-hers versions of the same fluorescent green, scored in a two-for-one sale. The young man grinned at her, his glasses fogged with perspiration.

"Couldn't help myself," Eden said. The girl was delightfully curvy but painfully aware of it, tugging at her sweat-patched top to pull it down over the brown slit of flesh above her tights. Pixie ears and a sheepish smile. Eden licked sweat off her upper lip.

"I thought you might have been onto a winner," the girl said. "Every time I see a van around now near the park, I fucking freak. Are you a police officer?"

"A watchful citizen." Eden started walking. "Bye."

"Wasn't him." The male of the pair held up his phone. "He was just spotted ten minutes ago in Trumper. That's why we're here. We thought, 'Oh, they'll chase him away. It'll be safe.' We haven't been out since it all started. Jenny used to go alone, but no more. No more, Jenny."

Eden watched the boy shake his finger teasingly at the girl. Tried to figure out why they were still talking to her.

"He's like a shark," the girl commented. Looked to her partner for approval. "A shark going up and down the coast. Once you know which beach he's at, you can go play at one of the other ones." She giggled at her cleverness.

People liked to talk about things that scared them, Eden mused. Talk *too* much about them. She shook the fog from her head. The endorphins from the run were pumping through her, old friends missed. "Wait, did you say ten minutes ago?"

"Yeah. Trumpcr Park."

Eden snatched the man's phone, flashed her eyes over the crowdsourced news site. Her cell phone rang in her sleeve.

Frank was standing by the hood of one of the station cars, a map spread out before him, directing two uniformed officers. Eden parked in the mess of vehicles blocking Roylston Street and glanced at neighbors in the apartment buildings standing on their stairs and balconies, arms folded, skeptical. A couple with a dog had taken a seat on a bench as close to the busy police officers as they could get. They sat transfixed, listening to the radio calls.

The field was empty. On the other side, the tree line was impenetrable. Trumper Park was perfect for the killer's next hunt. Eden knew it well—the leafy tracks behind the residential buildings, dug in by the feet of hundreds of joggers; the shady ponds and wooden stairs leading into the undergrowth. She came up behind Frank and looked over his shoulder at the cordons he was trying to impose, impossible gestures, given the limited manpower in an area encompassing two dozen streets or more.

"Lock up the CCTV for Ocean Street, Craigend, Glenmore, Hervey, and Jersey," he said into his radio. "If he's gone to ground he'll be in that ring. Secondary cordon from O'Sullivan to the Eastern Distributor." Frank looked at her, hardly seeing. "Get someone down to Oxford Street in case he went that way."

"Copy that."

"What was it?" Eden asked as the officers went to work. Frank had changed his shirt since she'd seen him at the office. He'd been buried in paperwork and phone calls, now and then lifting his head to moan about how much he hated Caroline Eckhart. Eden had hardly spoken to him that day. When she'd seen him on the smoker's balcony, he'd been listening to a phone call from Imogen. She was doing most of the talking.

"Could be a false alarm," he said. "Female dog walker saw a person lingering in the trees over there. Black tracksuit, black hoodie. Doesn't know what he was looking at. When he found himself being watched, he fled to a van."

"Fled?"

"Walked quickly, head down."

"What's he doing on this side of the park?" Eden squinted at the tree line, two hundred yards away. "The hunting ground's over there."

Eden puzzled at it. Were people becoming hysterical? The stars were emerging from the burnt-orange hue above the city. It was the right time of day. A good place to hunt. The description was accurate. Was this just a reconnaissance trip? Was the killer checking out the situation on this side of the park, what threats might emerge through the tree line onto the jogging track? She realized that Frank was staring at her.

"Where have you been?"

"Me?" Eden swiped a stray hair from her brow. "Jogging."

"Where? Here?"

"No, Rushcutters Bay. I drove over."

Frank looked past her, followed her gesture to her car. He averted his eyes, cleared his throat as a uniformed officer came for more directions. Eden watched him.

His hand fluttered restlessly by his eyes, scratching at nothing.

"You're acting weird."

"Oh. Finally." He smiled. "My turn to act weird."

Eden watched him. He looked around them at the officers busy working on maps, radioing in colleagues, following the progress of checkpoints. Nearby, a woman with a dog was talking animatedly to a troupe of young female officers, pointing to a tree by the public toilets. Frank looked stressed. He tugged at his shirt. Eden only realized as he touched it how ridiculous it was on him. Too tight, salmon pink, with a visible liner on the inside collar of little crosshatches, peach, apricot, baby blue. He must have been on his way out to dinner with *her*. No idea he'd have to be seen by his colleagues in it. He kept closing it at the throat to hide the colorful lining.

"Look at what you're wearing," he finally said. Eden glanced at her tracksuit pants. Her hoodie. Black. She smirked, tried to meet his eyes, but they were locked on the trees.

"Look at what *you're* wearing."

"I'm just saying," he said.

Eden narrowed her eyes. Then she laughed.

"You think I'm the Sydney Parks Strangler."

"Well for fuck's sake, is it that much of a stretch? You're *some* kind of killer, Eden," he snapped, his gray-blue eyes at last on her. His words were low, barely audible. "I know you killed five men, at least, and that your best friend's a hunting expert." He shrugged. "What do you want me to think?"

"Whoa!"

"Yeah. Whoa."

"Frank, I want you to think *straight,* that's what I want. Think straight, and not like a fucking idiot, for once."

"I called you, what—three minutes ago? You're saying you got from Rushcutter's Bay to here in three minutes?"

"Yes, actually. I'm sorry. Should I have stopped to pick up some milk along the way?"

"You're wearing a black tracksuit . . . I hear about murders in the news and I wonder if you did them." He sounded angry. "I can't watch the news anymore. I sit there and it's like, 'kid's body found in a creek,' and I think, *Was that Eden?* 'Old man bludgeoned in an apparent home invasion.' *Was that Eden?* 'Four bodies found in a van in Byron,' looks like the killer used a souped-up sniper rifle, same kind of rifle that her hunting-enthusiast friend collects by the dozen. Was that you, Eden? Did you kill those kids in Byron?"

"Frank."

"You're the only killer I know."

"And that's the thing you're forgetting," Eden snapped. "You *know me*, you fucking asshole."

"I can't even begin . . ." He paused as one of the area chiefs walked by them, speaking into a radio. "I can't even begin to list the things I don't know about you, Eden."

"Okay, we're going to stop this now." Eden walked back to her car and got in. She put her face in her palms. Her hands were shaking. Waves of prickles rolled up and down her back. In the airless warmth of the car, she hid in her hands and flattened her tongue against the roof of her mouth and growled. She heard the door across from her open and the familiar groan and sigh of her partner as he eased himself into the car. Emotion was not her friend in any form, but this brief and paralyzing spark was not terror or rage. It was comforting, somehow. Frank sat in the passenger seat, his usual place beside her, and looked at the mess of people moving before them, a sea of blue.

"I'm trapped here," he said. Eden gripped the wheel and waited, but nothing more came. Frank stared at the dashboard.

"What do you mean?"

"I mean I'm trapped here, between Martina and her killer and what he did to her, and what I did to him, and *you*. Whenever I try to turn away from what happened, I open my eyes and there's you. Sometimes I feel like I can move on, maybe pretend she never existed. Like it never happened. But it did happen, and it happened because I left her there. I left her there because I was chasing you."

Eden watched him. He stared down at his hands, lying open in his lap.

"Martina is dead and I killed someone, because of you. And every time you've killed someone since, I've been complicit in it."

"No, you haven't," Eden said. "Most of the time you don't even know it's happened."

"Did you kill those kids in Byron Bay?"

"What did I just say?"

"There's no denying it." Frank waved his hand, dismissed her. "I'm complicit because I know what you are and I haven't stopped you. I'm not stopping you even now!" He ran his fingers through his hair. "For some fucked-up reason, I've never stopped you."

"You can't stop me," she said. "We both know that."

His restless hand fluttered at his eyes again, left a red mark on his brow when he scratched.

"Why don't you stop yourself?" Frank turned in his seat and looked at her. "Give it up. You can turn away from it, you know. You can leave it behind you. We both can."

Eden felt again that wave of familiarity. Of home.

She opened her mouth to answer. How to explain it all to him, a normal human man, someone with all his faculties, with a soul. How to explain that at the core of her being Eden killed people the way she breathed, the way she slept, that when she was hungry for blood it was as all-consuming as the need for sleep when exhausted, or the need for water to quench a thirst. Without the monsters that she hunted and caught and vanquished, she would suffocate. She ran on no other fuel. To decide not to kill was to decide to die.

I don't want to die, she thought. *I'll kill you before I let that happen, Frank. Because I'm a predator. That's the core of it. There's a beast in me, and it only knows how to kill and how to live.*

A uniformed officer tapped on Frank's window. He rolled it down, and Eden's comfort was lost.

Ruben lay in bed in the dorm past midday, which wasn't like him at all. When people came into the room to retrieve things from bags, to change, to cuddle, he turned and pretended he was sleeping. At some point Phillipe came and went, and for an hour or so Ruben heard the rhythmic smacking of his basketball on the courts outside, the rumble of the loose hoop hanging below the windows. Thursday at the big house by the park was coming. He had begun to dread the day. Terrified the night before he went, yet unable to pull away from the work, he was strangely drawn to the house, pulled within the orbit of the attic door.

As the sun set, he heard the televisions come on throughout the building, the French girls upstairs with their reality shows and the British boys catching *Neighbors* in the large living area off the bedroom in which he lay. On the edge of frightening dreams, in which an unseen presence followed him from room to room around the parkside house as he furiously cleaned dirt and grime that would not budge, he heard a familiar voice and got up.

He wandered out to the living room, wrapped in the sweat-damp comforter, his hair mussed and eyes aching. The television sat like a blazing white campfire before a semicircle of couples, some of them sipping colorful bottles of alcoholic cola, some of them passing a joint. An athletic-looking woman filled the screen, standing on the steps of a building that was out of sight, gray concrete her only backdrop. Her sunflower hair swished in a high ponytail as she talked. This was, without a doubt, the woman from the tapes in the attic room, the tapes that kept being stopped and restarted, certain words and phrases captured and replayed. The subtitles were in German, but Ruben had excelled in German in high school and could follow along as the letters flashed and flickered across the screen.

"We won't stand idly by and let our voices go unheard," the woman said. "If all goes well, this will be the biggest gathering of like-minded souls fighting for recognition in the daily struggle against domestic violence in this country. You need to escape the *you* that you've become, Sydney! It's easy!"

Hooky was distracted from the laptop on her knees by her aunt jabbering away in the kitchen, the low bubbling of her voice rising to a simmer as she walked into the large, immaculate living room, setting cutlery on the table. She was complaining about the "sickos" Hooky was chatting with on the Internet. Something about her doing it at home, rather than at the station, made her aunt Ada think Hooky did it because she enjoyed it and not because she wanted to see the men she wrote to cornered, dragged into prison cells, given back some of the pain they perpetuated on their victims.

"How can they let you do that at home, unsupervised?" Ada asked, her Vietnamese so fast and perfect Hooky had trouble following. "Who are these people? What kind of cowboys do they have running this city?"

Hooky ignored her aunt. As long as her university grades didn't slip, Ada had never made good on her promise to confront the bosses at the department about how much danger Hooky was in and how much freedom she had to hunt pedophiles online. Hooky made sure her grades were as near perfect as they could be. If the chiefs found out she was messing around with perps on her own time, she'd be kicked out of the office for good.

Her fingers flashed over the keys, her eyes following as the words pumped into the small chat box at the bottom of the screen. The chatter, StanSmiles33, had already filled the screen with text in the short time Hooky was distracted.

Hooky thought of the pedophiles she hunted as being categorized into "levels," so this was the way she reported on them when she was working alongside officers at the station. Every interaction she made, no matter how casual, had to be reported, the conversations screenshot and logged in files labeled with screen names for each individual target. Hooky had a small database of images she was allowed to use at the very end of her interactions with her prey—in the days and hours before their proposed first meeting.

More often than not, just before meeting in person, one of her chatters would ask her for a racy photograph, a "commitment," something to show that she was "real" and serious about meeting up. Hooky had naked photographs of twelve boys and twelve girls of varying ages and ethnicities, the faces cheekily hidden or obscured, as final bait for her chatters. Hooky knew these children well—the grinning twelve-year-old girl taking a selfie in the mirror, the taut-skinned, serious-looking fourteen-year-old boy posing on a bed. These were for the Level Five chatters only. She only ever used each image once.

At Level One, the target approached Hooky online, or she approached them, for casual chitchat. School, weather, parents, the latest movies at the box office. Generally, ages weren't discussed, or if they were, the men chatting to Hooky told her they were close to her age range. If she told the target that she was twelve, he pretended to be fifteen. If she was fifteen, he would say he was seventeen. Sometimes, Hooky had five Level One chatters to report on by the end of a chat session.

Level Ones often progressed to nothing. There was nothing criminal about an older man lying so that he could chat to a younger person online, as long as the chat was fairly pedestrian. An outed online predator at Level One could evoke a number of excuses—he wanted to reconnect with his own daughter, who'd become moody and detached, so he chatted to young people, tried to get a feel for their worries, their interests. He was curious about how young people interacted these days. He was living a fantasy. Having a middle-age crisis and pretending he was young. Didn't everyone think like that sometimes? *What if I could go back? Start again?* It was harmless.

For a chatter to progress to Hooky's Level Two file, chat had to be sustained for more than one conversation, and innocuous photographs were exchanged. The chatter would "add" Hooky, or the character she was pretending to be—send her a request to be her "friend," or to "link up," to "follow" each other, depending on the site. A flurry of smiley faces celebrated the newly officialized, though still completely virtual, relationship. At this point, the more experienced online child-groomer backed off a little. Tried to make Hooky comfortable— didn't want to come on too strong. Connections were sometimes encouraged between Hooky and his other online friends, which were often just the same chatter using different profiles, trying to make Hooky feel like she was part of a group instead of interacting with an individual. *If the guy had friends, he had to be all right, right?* Groups and clubs formed. The target sometimes inquired about where Hooky lived toward the end of this level.

To progress to Level Three, at which point Hooky flagged the interactions with her chief at North Sydney Police Headquarters, the talk had to turn romantic. Sometimes this was within mere hours of the chat being initiated for the first time. Sometimes it was only after months of association. It would begin with the odd love-song dedication, or a "caring" message. *I was thinking about you today*. The target would search for an opportunity to assert himself as a strong, brave, masculine hero type. If Hooky's character had a fight with his or her parents, the target would understand. The target would have experienced the same thing, or worse, from his own parents. If Hooky's character was being bullied at school, the target would reveal his evil plans for the perpetrators of the harassment. He'd reveal his real age, either in stages or all at once, confessing that while he'd lied—he was forty-one—he felt such a connection with Hooky's character that he didn't feel it mattered. *Age is just a number, right?* Often at this point, he would send money or a gift to cheer Hooky's character up. To show he cared. He would obtain Hooky's address.

At Level Four, a second "location indicator" was exchanged. The target would ask or guess where the girl or boy went to school or worked. At Level Five, plans for a real-life meeting would be discussed. At this point, Hooky would consolidate her file, print out all the information she had, tag it, and give it to her boss. That was the end of her involvement.

Chatting to the perpetrators on her own, away from the office, offered many benefits, though Hooky risked losing her job doing it. She could say what she wanted to the perps without having to get approval from the cops sitting with her. She could be more graphic. More intense. The department strictly forbade her from talking to perps on the phone or in video chat at the office. But when a target requested phone contact, and Hooky refused it, the perps usually got spooked and slipped away.

Hooky didn't like it when they got away.

When her supervisors had her reports, the department would link up with the Australian Federal Police and brief them for a joint operation. Sometimes Hooky saw her targets in the newspaper two or three months after she handed over their cases. The Feds never moved until they had everything. Computer files. Snapshots. Videos. Friends. Family. Coworkers. All picked over to within an inch of their lives.

Today, Hooky's target was ready to take it to Level Five. She drew up a picture she'd used many times before, something from the depths of the police files, something only she had access to. An image with a hundred legal documents attached to it somewhere, marking its confiscation from the girl who'd taken it and the man she'd shared it with, no idea how much trouble she was getting herself into, permission from her parents signed away for use of the image in baiting monsters like the one that had lured their baby. Hooky posted the picture and yawned, wriggled her toes, making the laptop wobble on her knees.

StanSmiles33: Dats nice baby. Really sweet ;)

HelloKitty14: U like? ;) xx

StanSmiles33: Your a beautiful girl. No . . . your a beautiful woman! No matter what your parents tell you babe I can see the incredible woman you have already become. I cant wait to see more!

HelloKitty14: You always say that lol

StanSmiles33: Stanny wantz ur fanny! :) :) :)

HelloKitty14: Oh har har har real mature

StanSmiles33: You know I'm just joking bae

HelloKitty14: lol

StanSmiles33: Meeting up 4real is my ultimate dream. I can't lie! One day well do it babe. As soon as you stop being a fraidy cat!! lol

HelloKitty14: haha maybe

StanSmiles33: Just say the word and well run away 2getha :) :) Ill treat you like the princess u really are!!!! I cant wait to hold you. Just hold you and make you feel safe. <3

Hooky noticed an icon flashing in the corner of her screen and sent smiling Stan a quick message telling him her mother had come into the room, which halted chat. She flicked over to another window and drew up a long column of boxes. The software she'd used to hack Imogen's phone told her she was texting again. Hooky stretched out on the couch and balanced the laptop on her stomach, folded her hands over her chest, and half watched the television as boxes filled the screen, one by one.

Imogen: Hey you got those bloods yet?

0447392***: Might as well go after the hope diamond than get Eden Archer's DNA.

Imogen: Any luck with the brother?

0447392***: That was easier. Managed to swipe the shirt he died in from evidence for a couple of hours. Emailing you now. I better get paid quick smart this time!

Imogen: Yeah yeah. Show me the goods!

Hooky tapped her short fingernails on the edge of the laptop, felt half thoughts zinging and crashing into each other in her mind. She drew up a quick news report on Eric Archer's accidental shooting by Eden Archer in a raid in a church in Randwick. Frank at the edge of the frame, his head in his hands, a paramedic trying to lead him away. Blood all over him. His girlfriend had been murdered only hours before. Hooky took the number from the interaction on Imogen's phone and ran it through a search engine. Peter Bryson was a low-level administration worker at Surry Hills Police Headquarters. Hooky watched an email come through to Imogen's inbox from his work email address. She opened the file and glanced at the DNA profile of Eric Archer.

"Interesting," she said aloud.

A blond woman was ranting on the television about domestic violence and a charity run in the city. Hooky looked back when the screen began flashing again.

Imogen: Any luck?

Hooky waited, knowing Imogen was waiting somewhere, probably in her office, about to leave work for the day. The text message from the new number came back promptly, like Peter's.

0415333***: Indeed. The renowned Heinrich "Hades" Archer submitted to a DNA swab over a missing drug dealer in 2011. I'll email it across when I see payment in my account.

Imogen: You're a star, Lisa. Sending payment now.

Hooky drew up her online banking surveillance on Imogen and watched $700 shift out of her savings account into the ether, heading for the account of a woman named Lisa Louise Gilbert. A quick Google search told

Hooky that Lisa Gilbert was an administrator at a Western Sydney police forensics office.

Hooky opened the DNA profiles of Eric Archer and Heinrich Archer. A mere glance, to the trained eye, told her they were not father and son. Her face felt hot. She shifted up on the couch and watched more text messages dart back and forth.

0447392***: Interesting little tidbit about that Eric Archer's profile . . . :)

Imogen: Don't leave me hangin', Peter.

0447392***: Seems it showed up unexpectedly at a crime scene. Well, not a crime scene . . . exactly. Got a weird note in the case file. Never followed up.

Imogen: Which crime scene?

0447392***: I said it WASN'T a crime scene.

Imogen: Would you get to the damn point?

0447392***: Whoops! Looks like my goodwill has run out. Anything further is going to cost you.

Imogen: Oh come on.

0447392***: $500

Imogen: Ok.

0447392***. Transferring now?

Imogen: All right all right all right all right. It's done. Now just tell me.

0447392***: Ok. Spot of Eric Archer's blood turned up at a missing person's house a week before Eric was killed. Inquiry puts it down to forensic team cross-contamination—Eric wasn't on the missing persons but one of his colleagues was. They dropped it after he was dead anyway. Never found missing guy. Might be interesting to whatever you're working on. Missing guy was Benjamin Annous. MPR 446193. Google him.

Imogen: One spot of blood?

0447392***: Yeah.

Imogen: Probably cross contamination. Nice to know, though!

0447392***: Happy to help in any way I can, babycakes haha.

Hooky waited for Imogen to give an answer, staring at the boxes on the screen. None came.

Tara remembered those frantic moments before boarding, when her excitement and terror were so tangible,
so real, they felt like a cloak of electricity brushing
against her arms, tingling at her neck, twisting down
her legs. She'd gone to the bathroom six or seven times
in the hour she'd waited in the crowded airport gate,
drawing stares every time she moved, a lumbering
force of nature. She'd never flown before. She'd almost gone on a Year Ten trip to Cairns for science
class—ninety students on the Great Barrier Reef locat-
ing, cataloging, and photographing marine life for their
end-of-year portfolios.

Photographing marine life? Joanie snorted.

Tara would need two seats, and that was just too
much for Joanie to take. Tara had looked at the skies
through the trees outside the attic windows, hoping she
would spot the plane trailing across the depthless blue.
She imagined it suddenly combusting, a bright white
spark breaking into shimmering speckles like glitter
spilled across blue icing. The screams and gasps from
below. The raw mobile-phone footage on the news.

Around this time, Tara had encountered the boy in
the park. She'd been on one of her hunting trips with
Joanie. Tara running in the dark. Gasping. Crying.
Joanie coming after her, a shadow floating between the
huge Moreton Bay figs. Tara had swerved to the right
of the long black pole emerging from the trees, sup-
pressed a scream. She stumbled to a stop, mouth open,

gasping. The pole swayed, dipped, and ducked behind a tree. A boy emerged, carrying it over his shoulder. A boy and a man. They crossed the wide path before Tara and walked into the trees.

She looked back along the road. Joanie was nowhere to be seen. She sometimes stopped and tightened her shoelaces. Tighter and tighter as the night wore on, until the cotton laces groaned.

The man and the boy were looking up at the trees. Tara followed at a distance, her heart still hammering and sweat rolling down her chin. She swallowed the sobs that had punctuated her running breaths, stuck close to a tree to observe them.

In the darkness, they spoke softly to each other, the man setting down his equipment, the small plastic animal cages, and the cloth bags. They looked into the tree canopy, pointed, murmured. The boy fiddled with the end of the pole, then turned it, aimed it into the mess of leaves above. In one swift upward thrust he jabbed at something. There was a squeal. A black bundle fell into the old man's gloved palms.

Tara gasped. The pair turned toward her.

"It's all right," the boy said. Tara emerged from the shadows, chanced a step closer. The boy had Peter Anderson's litheness and solidity about him, the sturdiness of good genes and proud parenting, a spattering of boy-next-door freckles on his nose. He took the black bundle and stepped toward her. Tara fought the urge to flee.

"We're tagging them," the boy said. "You wanna see?"

The man smiled and waited as the teenagers drew closer, Tara's pulse hammering in her neck and cheeks

as the boy opened his gloves. A small fruit bat lay
curved in his hands, the huge fingers of his glove gripping the creature by the back of its furry neck, the
leathery, bony wings crumpled and folded in the fabric. The thing was swimming somewhere between
sleep and wakefulness, glossy black eyes blinking. A
single bead of ruby-red blood emerged from the orange fur of its chest and smeared on the boy's glove.
He pulled a tiny dart from the creature's side and held
it for her to see. She took it from him and looked at it.
A tiny plastic vial, a silver spike.

"We have to knock 'em out or they panic. Get tangled in the nets. Sometimes they can hurt themselves,"
he said.

She could smell his sweet breath. Tara wondered if
she had ever stood as close to a boy as she stood now,
his arm almost touching hers. Inches from contact.
From contracting her germs. Did he know how close
he was to being infected by her, by the darkness and
terror that rippled through her? She glanced toward the
road, slipping the vial into her pocket as she turned.
Joanie was nowhere to be seen.

"Their hearts are really fragile. So, we have to be
careful with them," the boy said.

My heart is really fragile, Tara thought. *Be careful
with me*.

She followed him back to the man, tried to give the
boy space, but he seemed insistent on being near her.
She watched as they clipped the brass ring around the
animal's tiny clawed feet. The thing was waking now,
the fanged mouth opening, stretching, the pointed ears
twitching, trying to get a sense of up and down.

"Whoa," the boy said, as the black beast wriggled in

his hands. It gave a squeal and thrashed its tiny head. Tara caught the boy looking at her, and she felt the bile rise in her throat.

"Here, grab on," the boy said, thrusting his hands at her. Tara put her trembling fingers around the outside of his warm gloves, and she was, for the first time, separated from the touch of a boy by mere fabric. By choice. By strange and inexplicable choice. Her knees shook.

"One, two . . ." the boy said. Together they lifted and opened their hands, and a great flapping darkness was unleashed. The motion drew the two teenagers together. Their arms touched.

"Tara!" Joanie yelled. Tara looked back toward the road, saw shadows moving. She turned and ran.

Tara looked around the boarding gate lounge now and saw no one who reminded her of the boy in the park. There were only hollow eyes and sneering lips. She imagined her fellow passengers burning and writhing in their plane seats, blackening fingers struggling at seat belts, holes tearing down the side of the fuselage, whipping and stirring the fire. All of them shuddering in unison as the plane plummeted down levels of the atmosphere like a wayward skateboard diving and bumping down stairs. She smiled. A little girl standing by a stroller thought Tara was smiling at her and smiled back. Tara imagined the child sliding down the tipped aisle toward the pilot's cabin, fingernails gripping at the carpet.

On the plane, the usual sighs erupted as she maneuvered herself slowly toward 23B, which she discovered was in the middle of a group of three. The seat handles jutted into her hips as she wiggled down onto the cushion. A young man approached from the front of the plane, looked at Tara, looked at the numbers on the overhead locker, and hitched his bag up onto his shoulder, kept walking. Tara heard arguing at the back of the plane. She didn't pay attention to it.

When everyone was in position, Tara took the folded piece of paper from inside her bra and smoothed it out, warm and curved, against her thigh. On it, she found her own name and traced the letters with her fingernail, something she had done a number of times now, so that the letters were almost faded. *Tara Harper:*

Surgical itinerary. Because yes, the document was hers completely, had been arranged and paid for by her alone. Daddy's inheritance, finally setting her free. She followed the points and the dates on the paper with her finger, whispered the procedures to herself.

Thursday, August 5, 5:00 A.M. (GMT +7):
SAL lipectomy prep—abdomen, pubis, flanks
Thursday, August 5, 5:45 A.M. (GMT +7):
SAL lipectomy procedure—abdomen, pubis, flanks
Friday, August 6, 5:00 A.M. (GMT +7): SAL lipectomy prep—arms, breasts, submental
Friday, August 6, 5:45 A.M. (GMT +7): SAL lipectomy procedure—arms, breasts, submental

It would be a surgical marathon. Over three days, she would have sixty percent of her body fat removed. Though Tara had not been able to find another organization that would approve the procedures, Dr. Raji Benmal's "fast-track" surgical overhaul had been explained in detail on his website. Because Tara would be in a coma for the entire ordeal, and for a week afterward, her body would not go into shock between the surgery rounds—the four-to-six-week recovery between procedures wasn't necessary because she wouldn't be putting her body through the trauma of waking between lipectomy rounds.

Dr. Benmal was going to remove the weight, carve her away to the glorious muscle and sinew she knew was beneath the ragged fat, and stitch her back together like a broken doll. With unique, pioneering binding procedures, laser skin therapy, and all the care

and consideration throughout her recovery that a mother
would give a child, Tara was going to heal into a new
being, a new soul. She had laughed at that part: the
mother offering the care to the child as her body reeled
in its new form. Tara was going to return to Australia
knowing what a mother's love was really like, before
she brought all the agony she had known in her former
body down upon Joanie where she waited, unsuspect-
ing, in the parkside house.

Tara closed her eyes and imagined Joanie's face as
she walked in the door, the confusion as she tried to fit
the identity of this new, beautiful woman to the slightly
familiar face before her, the cheekbones and jawbones
she had never seen before. Tara considered changing
her name once Joanie was dead, drawing a name up
from the blood of her fallen mother as she smoothed
the warm red life liquid over her fingers, tasted it on
her tongue. A name would come as she knelt over
Joanie, triumphant. Something powerful. Something
borne of pain.

Tara realized, as she opened her eyes, that she was
laughing in an evil, snarling way, clutching the itinerary against her breasts, her tongue washing over her
bottom lip as though she was there before Joanie now,
watching the life drain from her. People around her on
the plane were staring. Tara smiled a devil's smile.

The dog had some strange behaviors. Hades didn't know much about dogs and their nighttime activities, but he'd gotten up around midnight to piss and spotted the thing in the basket dreaming. Paws twitching in sequence, running in the land of fantasy, the lips slipping upward over the shining white teeth, exposing the fleshy pink beneath. The lips came forward again and narrowed, and the thing gave a low and drawn-out howl, almost singing.

Hades had watched the dog until it fluttered out of the dream and raised its head, peered at him from beneath the hood of blanket, waiting like an old robed monk for his command. In the morning, he caught the creature standing at the doorway staring out at the workers at the bottom of the hill with the sharp, lethal stillness of a pointer. Its bony silhouette against the white dawn was like a streak of ink. When he filled its bowl, it ate so fast it choked and coughed up cubes of meat. Before the meal was finished it had been chewed and regurgitated and re-chewed a number of times.

The dog wasn't sure of Eden at all when she arrived at the door in worn jeans, black cap pulling a long ponytail up behind her head. She had dressed as she did when she hunted—androgynously, lithely, as though she would need to run at any time. The flighty Eden. She'd always been like that in times of stress: prepared to disappear, bags packed and affairs in order. Even when she was a teenager, the old man had half expected that she might one day run off on him, like a cat brought in from the wild, half listening all the time to the call of the horizon, to the seductive darkness of the road. She opened the screen door and the dog trotted to the hall entrance, looked back at Hades, ears pointed, eyes wide, and lips twitching.

"It's all right," he said. The animal's face spread into that sheepish grin, narrow eyes. The thing gave a little grateful groan and slunk to the floor beside the chair.

"Someone's put the boot into that thing," Eden said as she sat across from him. Hades gave the dog a little scratch on its hard skull.

"I wouldn't be surprised."

"Watch it doesn't turn on you. They can get confused, rescued things."

"You never did."

"No." She smiled a little. She looked at the dog. "Did you name it?"

"Yes. Jim."

Eden stared at Hades.

"Slim Jim."

"Of course." She slapped a notepad on the table. "Well, it's all over now. You've named it. It's a done deal."

"It's a dog, not a marriage."

"Still."

"So." Hades nodded at the notepad. "Where do I begin?"

"Height?"

"She was short," Hades said. He glanced at the shattered mug on the countertop, the white edges of triangle shards in lime green. Tried to imagine the woman who had attacked him sitting where Eden sat now, her nimble frame, the big eyes behind the glasses. "She was petite. Looked like she might work out."

"How was she dressed?"

"Classy. I don't remember specifically. Heels, I think. Glasses. Big tinted glasses that hid her eyes. It was very fast. We got right down to business. She must have been here less than three minutes."

"She smell like anything?"

"A woman."

"Car?"

"Didn't see it. I fell. Sounded small."

Eden kept writing. She tapped the pen on the paper and gazed at the windows. Hades pulled a folded piece of paper toward him from where it lay on top of an old newspaper to his left. Slid it across the table to Eden.

"She left this," he said. Eden unfolded the piece of paper and took the hair she found in the crease between her thumb and forefinger. She lifted the hair to her nose, smelled it, held it up against the light and examined the frayed end where the follicle should have been. She hooked the hair around both her index fingers and pulled, snapped it, squinted at the curled cross section.

"Human hair wig. Expensive."

"How can you tell?"

"It's a Caucasian hair. Cheap human hair wigs are usually made from the hair of Indian women. You can tell they've been bleached. This hasn't been bleached."

"Why is a white woman's hair more expensive than an Indian woman's hair?" Hades gave a little quizzical frown.

"Racism."

"You women with your racist wigs," the old man laughed.

"What was the style? Was it long?"

Hades put a finger up against his tricep.

"OK, so, long dark brown hair. We can assume if she's going to all the trouble of wearing a wig, she's wearing one that's as different from her normal style as possible. What's the opposite of long dark hair?"

"Short blond hair," Hades said. "You know any tricky blondes who might want to dig into your past?"

Eden wiped her eyes. It wasn't often that Hades saw her looking this tired. Her cheeks had hollowed, shadowed beneath the cap.

"None that I can think of," Eden said, squeezing the bridge of her nose. "None this cunning. It's possible Eric knew someone with a grudge. Someone he never told me about. I mean, we don't even know if it's this woman who's after us. She could easily have been someone's agent."

"I've turned the cameras on. But I don't think she'll be back."

"I don't think so, either." Eden shifted, lifted her phone out of her pocket and answered it. "Yes?"

"That's how you answer the phone to me now?" Frank said. Eden heard a television. The insistent whining of a cat.

"Darling of my heart. Sunshine of my day. How may I serve you, Vice President of the National Assholes Association?"

"There's a problem."

"What is it?"

"Turn on the TV. Channel Ten news."

Eden crossed the floor before the dog and settled on the old green couch, flipped the television on. Hades leaned over the back of his chair, his thick scarred forearm catching all the kitchen light in the gray hairs from wrist to elbow. Eden wiped dust off the television remote, found the channel she was looking for. A banner at the bottom of the screen read "Take Back the Parks launched."

"What is this bullshit?"

"Just watch," Frank said.

Caroline Eckhart was standing before a crowd of gym junkies, nylon in every color of the rainbow above a sea of uniform black tights. An army of the healthy, aluminum water bottles glimmering like guns. She raised a hand to them and they cheered. A middle-aged mother with a stroller ignored her wailing child, clapped and hooted. Caroline was yelling over gym music. There were mirrors in the background. Just stepped out of a gym class to address the masses. The glossy sweat-sheened Joan of Arc, still miked, dabbing at her impossibly flat brow with a gym towel.

"Look, Sandra, we're working on the fly here, but that's the kind of people we are at Eckhart Energy! We're pulling in favors from all sorts of wonderful organizations—Woolworth's, Kellogg's, the Cancer Council, and a whole host of other charities are on board. We need to demonstrate that violence against women just isn't okay, and we're going to do that with a dramatic show of strength. *Take Back the Parks* is going to show the people of Australia that we can change the face of this horrific social trend."

The gym class cheered. Eden felt her stomach sinking. "What exactly is *Take Back the Parks*?"

"It's a running festival. A *night* running festival," Frank said. "She's putting the whole thing together over the space of four days, and she's got the Minister for Women behind her. They run on Sunday. The marathoners start at 5pm. There are 5 km, 9 km, 21 km, and 45 km distances. Each one ends up in a different Sydney park. Did I mention the marathoners start at five fucking *pm*? Four Sydney parks are going to be absolutely flooded with people Sunday night, and there's no finish time mentioned. They could be there all night, wandering around like dumb fucking chickens just begging for the killer to come out and play."

"Jesus Christ's fucking beard." Eden covered her eyes.

"What is it?" Hades asked.

"Registration has been open for an hour. Seven thousand people have signed up for this thing already. The site's crashed twice. This is going to be huge," Frank said. "If the killer doesn't take the bait at one of the four parks mentioned, I'll eat my hat. I don't own a hat. I don't even like hats. I'll buy one specially, and I'll fucking eat it."

"Not me," Eden said. "If it was me, I'd take advantage of every police officer in Sydney being tied up in the four parks mentioned to hit one of the unattended ones."

"Well, I've been trying to get through to the bitch for an hour, but her people won't let me speak to her. She refuses to see this as a brazen act of public endangerment. She's painting it as a defiance thing. Like we're all going to get together and scare the killer off with our mighty show of fucking . . . communal spirit."

"*Urgh*," Eden sighed.

"I hate communal spirit," Frank snarled. "Communal spirit is my worst nightmare."

"I'll see you at the station," Eden said. "We'll see if we can bring this thing down."

For ten minutes, in silence, Eden and I sat on my desk and looked at a huge map of Sydney. Sometimes you've got to do that—just sit and let the thing talk to you.

I could see people drinking on balconies, cheering the hoards as they shuffled through. I could see banner-bearing teens whooping on street corners, brandishing bottles of Gatorade from on top of milk crates. Big folding tables full of paper cups of water. I'd done the City2Surf a few times, so I knew how people got into it—the way they swept, and let themselves be swept by, the momentum of the herd. Groups of businessmen in ironic lime-green tutus, faces painted, arms rocking back and forth, calves straining. Ladies with strollers powering up Heartbreak Hill.

I knew that Eden, sitting beside me with her hands resting in her lap, was thinking along the same lines, but she'd have all the lethality I lacked powering through her killer mind as she followed the neatly marked streets and lanes with her eyes, the gaping mouth of Sydney Harbour in its peaceful, monochromatic pale blue. She'd be remembering bodies we pulled out of that harbor, while I thought of my surfing days.

The four running tracks all began beside the bridge at Kirribilli, the overflow of runners stretching, exercise companies hawking merchandise, and spectators waiting to cheer on friends and family, all swirling around Bradfield Park, where Jill Noble's body had been found lying against one of the Harbour Bridge pylons. Jill had been all over the news that morning, shots of the base of the pylon buried in flowers and teddy bears beneath maps marking the run routes. The 5 km run looped around and headed over the bridge toward the city, then turned left into the Domain. The 9 km left Kirribilli and went northeast, curling around in a question-mark shape and ending up at the park surrounding Manly Dam. The 21 km runners would go northwest, finishing at Lane Cove National Park. The marathon runners looped and headed south through the city, along Anzac Parade toward La Perouse beach. They curved around the beach, ran up along the coast, taking in Coogee and Bondi Beach, before finishing in Centennial Park.

Eighty kilometers of running track had to be secured. Fifteen thousand people had registered for the run in the first four hours, and there were plenty more to come. I couldn't help wondering if there were some people running in the hopes of catching a glimpse of the killer in action, the sick fantasy of the runner ahead suddenly disappearing off the side of the darkened road in the grip of a shadow, gone in seconds. The ensuing panic of the runners nearby, the delicious heroism when the person who saw it happen is asked to give a police witness statement. "I looked up, and I saw her eyes as she was being pulled toward the roadside. I'll never forget those desperate eyes . . ." Cue interviews with the local papers.

Captain James was on a television set in the coffee room, condemning the festival and handing out warnings about personal safety. I could hear his fatherly voice above the shouting of reporters, cut off eventually by the news anchor. The government had leaped at the opportunity to support the festival—it had all the proactive feminist angles both parties liked to appear involved in (without all the fuss of actual policies and reforms). It looked good for their stance on women's health. Domestic violence. Violent crime.

Phone companies were going to surround the start and finish lines with foam mascots, and fitness companies were going to slap baseball caps on potential new members as they trotted by. High fives and big smiles. A minute's silence before the starting gun would honor the victims who had inspired the run.

Caroline Eckhart and the City of Sydney had turned three brutal killings into what would probably end up becoming an annual fitness wankfest with all the associated sweat, glory, and plastic participation medals.

This was going to be a nightmare.

Our colleagues swirled around us, distant birds fluttering, trying to stay out of Eden's orbit as they worked through the panic of police planning over the festival. She'd always frightened them. They didn't know why. Her brother had been the real terror in the hearts of the drug squad cops and beat cops and forensics experts in the office, but they still endured real nerves around Eden. They weren't sure what kind of creature Eden was, but they didn't like the look of her spikes. Only I knew how poisonous she really was.

"So," I said, gesturing to the map. Eden looked at me. "Yes?"

"How would you do it?"

"I wouldn't," she said.

"Are you still upset with me over the Trumper Park thing?"

"No," she said.

"Yes," I corrected.

"I have no emotions about the Trumper Park thing. Emotion right now would be a hindrance to our planning."

"You're upset with me about the Trumper Park thing," I nodded. "You're upset that I suggested you might be one type of killer, while really you're another."

She closed her eyes and chewed her lips. Seemed to be restraining herself from reaching over and strangling me that very second. Strangely, I didn't get the flushed cheeks and clenching stomach I usually felt when I tiptoed into dangerous territory with Eden. Maybe I was getting over my fear of her. Or more likely, I was being lulled into a false sense of security. I knew mixed into it somewhere was a real anger at her, an anger that was growing—a reaction to the physical and mental barrier she presented in my journey to wellness.

Jesus. I rubbed my eyes. I was being seduced by the support group bullshit.

"You'll get over this," Eden said, still scanning the map. "Anger is a part of grief."

"I'm not angry! You're angry!"

"You're angry. Why else would you be taking pathetic potshots at me about my nighttime activities?"

"Oh, I don't know. Because your nighttime activities are what I have devoted my life to putting a stop to?"

"Devoted your life? Please. It was cop or social worker, Frank. Let's be realistic."

"You're right. I'll get over it."

"If you had any idea what kind of killer I am, you'd be well over it," she snapped, turning her blank snake eyes on me. "It's killers like me who keep the predator count down, you absolutely clueless *fool* of a man."

I felt my cheeks flush. Ah, there it was. The old terror.

"You want to know why the Glebe morgue isn't stuffed full of more Martinas?" she asked, eyes wide. "Because of killers like me."

Eden tapped her chest, left white dots in the skin beneath her collarbone that faded before my eyes. I'd gotten to her. It was kind of cathartic, getting her all worked up. Sharing the ache and the upset.

"I don't understand what you're talking about," I said.

"That's because you're an idiot," she seethed, yanking her cap straight. "People like you see the world through a . . . a pinhole! You have no idea that there are so very many different *types* of evil. You're blind. *Blind*."

I realized that people were assembling all around us. Eden slipped off the table and walked to the map. Our colleagues were reluctant to look her in the eye. They stared at the ceiling, their shoes. Eden took a blue marker from the edge of the partition on which the map was pinned.

"People will be safe in big groups." She rolled her shoulders, shrugging off our argument and marking the four running paths on the map with savage gestures. "At the start of each run, when they're all together, there's little chance anyone will get snatched."

She took a pink marker and colored in the four paths running from the starting line, the first three kilometers north before the paths split, the bridge south.

"They'll also be under the watchful gaze of spectators at each finish line," Eden continued. "The parks will be flooded with people. They'll all be on the lookout for a white van. So, we can assume the risk there is low, too."

Eden drew a big pink circle around all four parks. I felt the tightness in my chest easing as she stood back and revealed the four paths, each now slashed by pink marks.

"Along these paths, the danger zones will be unlit areas with discreet vehicle access. The runners will spread out as they go up hills and go around corners. We can cross off these denser areas, where the killer won't want to be caught on CCTV in shop fronts and gas stations. There are also the traffic cameras, and bridges where spectators will assemble to watch the runners go underneath. So, considering all that, these are the primary zones we should man heavily."

Eden colored in eight blocks of roadway, three of them on the path belonging to the marathoners.

"The marathon runners are the bulk of our concern, obviously," she said, following the path with the butt of her pen as it looped around the beach at La Perouse. "They've got the farthest to go. There are fewer of them. They'll be under a lot more physical strain than the other runners, so they'll be easier targets for an abduction.

"A lot of these areas out here on the marathon route, especially near the prison, are bushy. There are side roads down through Port Botany where a van could easily be hidden. All this, here, behind Hillsdale—this is all industrial. Perfect place to stop and get the job done, dump the body and keep moving. The runners should be safe again by the time they head back up the coast. The backpackers in Coogee and Bondi will be out in force to cheer them on. So, we'll have to have a heavy police presence all the way from Kingsford to Chifley."

Gina from the front desk appeared in my peripheral vision, a welcome mirage in an emerald-green dress ending right above her spotless knees and immaculate calves. She stood beckoning me with a single finger beside a short, scruffy Italian-looking guy. The young man was holding sheets of photocopied paper. I went over while Eden continued directing the station staff.

"Another tip for you." Gina did a little flourish, gesturing to the Italian kid. Gina was sick of the tips—every crackpot and conspiracy theorist from Milperra to Madrid had called or visited the station to voice their thoughts, and Gina was the one cataloging them all. Some of them offered useless tidbits—overheard boasts at the local pub, neighbors acting strangely, white vans by the handful—and some of them were just the ramblings of lonely old men who spent too much time Googling in public libraries.

Gina was holding it together, but her eyes were tired and her jaw muscles twitched. I put my hand out for the Italian kid and he shuffled his papers to one hand, pumped with a callused palm. Backpacker. Fingers hardened from fruit picking, scraping scum off pots in the back of kitchens, cleaning houses. He hadn't shaved in a while, and when he had it had been a half effort. The sunglasses hanging from his neck were cheap knock-offs.

"I am Ruben Esposito."

"How you doing, Mr. Esposito?"

Gina left us, and the young man handed me a flier

for the running festival, printed from the Internet on a dodgy printer. Caroline Eckhart smiled up at me, arms folded, brandishing those carved-stone biceps. I felt flabby and angry at the sight of her.

"This . . . woman," Ruben struggled. Looked at the ceiling, licked his lips. "The festival-e. My boss is . . . ossessionato. Errr. My boss is ob-sess."

"This is your boss?" I pointed at the picture of Caroline, stabbed her face with my finger a little too hard, so that the paper crumpled.

"No. No. No. My boss," he spread his hands on his chest, "is obsess with this woman." He stabbed her face as well.

"Your boss is obsessed with Caroline Eckhart?"

"Yes."

"Well, that's nice." I looked back at the gathering around Eden, wondering what I was missing. "I've kind of got a big serial killer case going on here, though."

"I think," Ruben struggled, "my boss . . . is . . . serial killer."

I looked at the young man's eyes. Wondered if he was stoned. He looked worn. He'd snatched my words, *serial killer*, right out of the air. It didn't sound to me like he knew what they meant, but that he was parroting them back to me to hold my attention. "My boss is . . . Eh, I am afraid. The girls. The running girls?"

He pointed at Caroline. I glanced at his sheets of paper. There was a news story on the Sydney Parks Strangler, and another older clipping about a high-profile surgical bungle, something right out of the gossip columns. Plastic surgery. Caroline Eckhart. Obsessions. I didn't have time for this.

I placed the papers on top of each other and folded them.

"I'll check this out when I get a minute."

"Ehhh, she—"

"You've done great, mate." I slapped Ruben on the shoulder. "Really great. I'm going to take this information and add it to our run sheet. If you go back down to reception, Gina will give you an event number, and you'll be able to call the station and check how your information is going. *Graci. Graci*, mate."

"I—"

"Reception," I pointed. "*Recepciano*."

I went back to the desk. Eden was just wrapping up. She turned to the crowd. Eyes all around me averted again, the way they do when someone cries in public, avoiding the humiliation, ignoring the hurt. There were no questions, and the flock of frightened birds that my colleagues had become dispersed. She sat down beside me, looking at the map. I sensed again that discomfort in her, the edginess that told me that something was wrong with her lately, that it wasn't just my blossoming discontent with what she was, not just her slowly healing bones, but something much deeper disturbing her. I wavered between resenting her and wanting to help her. Found myself bumping her shoulder with my own, the way I used to, the way she'd always hated me doing, making her sway, reach out and steady herself with a hand on the desk.

"Ready for the hunt?" I asked. She gave a little quarter smile.

"Let the games begin," she said.

A target on the move is the easiest to con. Hooky knew that Ella Preston left the house every evening at half past five, leaving herself twenty minutes to grab the 989 to Bondi, four minutes to walk down the hill, another four minutes to unload her stuff in the staff common room, wash her face, apply her makeup, and get to work. Give or take a couple of minutes, she was always ready for the after-work customers to flood off the buses and in through the wide-open doors, for the surf bums to come up the hill in their bruised and warped flip-flops, spraying sand over the black rubber flooring like stars.

When Ella popped open her front door, Hooky was there in the hallway, looking at her phone, a black leather folio of printed real estate rental fliers clutched tightly against her bright red blazer. She made a delicate little noise of surprise and dropped the folio, adjusted her red glasses in embarrassment.

"Oh, excuse me!" she gushed. "You scared the life out of me."

"Oh, I'm sorry," Ella laughed, bending down and dragging the pages into a pile.

"It's my fault. I was listening very carefully," Hooky grinned. "I'm trying to get in touch with Mr. Davids? I called and I thought I heard his phone ringing inside. God, I'm so stressed! *Urgh!* Too much coffee."

Finding out who owned the apartment across from

Imogen's had been as easy as rifling through the mail-boxes.

"I'm sorry, I don't know that guy." Ella watched as Amy tried to squash the papers back into the folder with her phone pinned between her cheek and shoulder. "Did you have an appointment, or . . . ?"

"Yes, we did," Hooky sighed. "This is my day, though. This is so completely my day. I had thirteen people turn up to an auction this morning—*all* gawkers. My printer is broken, and the café next door is turning into one of those two-dollar shops with the recording playing all the time—you know the ones—"

"*Sports socks, six-packs, two dollars only*. Yeah, I know. How awful." Ella glanced at her watch.

"Well, now I'm supposed to be taking photos of Mr. Davids's apartment and he's not here." Hooky threw her hands up, or tried to, managing one full extension and one lopsided flap of her left hand, the folder pinned by an elbow into her hip. "Oh, it's hopeless. Hopeless. This apartment's got to go on the website *tonight*, for God's sake."

"Man," Ella looked at her watch again, "that sucks."

"I've got parties interested in China." Hooky rubbed her brow. "*Urgh!* If they go with the Mosman property instead of this one—"

"Um, I'm really sorry for you. I've got to go, though, so . . ." Ella started walking away.

"If only there was *some way*." Hooky turned to the door at the end of the hall, Mr. Davids's apartment, diagonally across from Ella's. She watched Ella watching the door out of the corner of her eye, as though the girl expected it to fly open at any minute and reveal Mr. Davids in all his glory, relieving the problem of the pretty real estate agent in the hall in time for Ella to catch the bus.

"Damn it." Hooky tried to keep her tone sorrowful, to not blow her cover by showing her exasperation at Ella's retreating steps. She gestured to the door across from Mr. Davids's apartment, the door next to Ella's. "Shit. I'm *so close*."

"I'm really sorry. I hope he comes back!" Ella turned and grabbed the handle of the glass door to the foyer. Hooky bit her tongue. Ella was slipping away. It was time to bring out the big guns. She sobbed, loudly, her face buried in her fist. She heard Ella pop open the door, but not the creak as the glass swung open.

Hooky sobbed again.

"Oh. Um. Are you okay?"

"I'm fine." Hooky gave a pathetic, crooked smile, and searched her pockets for a tissue. "Long day, that's all. I just wish it was over."

"I wish I could help," Ella said.

You can, you idiot, Hooky thought.

"Hang on," Ella half turned.

"Yes?" Hooky held her breath.

"Mr. Davids's apartment and Imogen's should be mirrored," Ella said. She pointed to the door next to her own. Number five. "You could take pictures of Imogen's apartment. It's just for like, a preview, right? You'll have the layout all correct. Just reverse the photos."

Ella smiled at her own genius. Hooky felt the color returning to her face.

"That's brilliant!"

"Well, you know."

"Who's Imogen?"

"She's a doctor," Ella said, walking back into the hall. "She's my neighbor, in number five there. Is she home?"

"I don't know," Hooky lied. She let hope saturate her voice. She rapped on the door to number five. There was silence. "Would she have keys to number four?"

"No. Well, I don't think so—I don't know. But I've got keys to Imogen's place. You could . . ." Ella studied Hooky. Seemed to decide she was trustworthy. "Yeah, I mean. We'll be quick."

Ella swung her backpack off her shoulder, unzipped the front pocket.

"You've got keys?" Hooky covered her mouth, maybe too dramatically. She'd have to work on that one. "That's fantastic!"

"Imogen gave me spare keys in case she ever locks herself out. All the apartments are exactly the same, so Imogen's corner apartment will be the same as Mr. Davids's. We'll go in and you can snap a few shots and then we'll be out."

"That'd be perfect!" Hooky clapped her hands, gripped the folder before it could slide again. "Oh, you're the best. You're an absolute lifesaver. You sure Imogen wouldn't mind?"

"She'd be all right with it," Ella said. "I'll go in with you and watch you. We'll be quick as a flash. She's a really nice chick. Uptight, but nice. We've got to be quick, though. I'm gonna be late in a minute."

"Quick as a flash." Hooky made a show of prancing into the apartment, knees high, a happy elf. "You're the absolute best for this. Thank you so much."

Hooky went straight into the bedroom. This was Imogen and Frank's bed. She stood wondering at its hospital corners, the expensive cream coverlet, waffle-textured, the kind she'd forbid him dragging to the sofa on movie nights. The room wasn't him at all. It was too clean, too bare, too orchestrated. The bathroom was free of stubble, no scraggy hair on the shower walls. Not even a toothbrush to symbolize that he even existed. The cat had been a resident for a short while, she knew, but it was gone too, the strange imbalance of the token Frank had taken from his dead girlfriend living and lounging in his current girlfriend's place too much—too weird.

Hooky snapped a couple of photographs. Wandered around appreciating the ceilings.

"This is perfect. Thank you again so much. You're an absolute lifesaver. Nice apartments, aren't they? My Beijing investors are going to just snap these up, I'm telling you."

"Well, I'm glad I could help." Ella was hovering by the front door, checking the time on her phone now, as though it was slower than the watch and could somehow give her more seconds before the bus pulled up. She itched to go. Hooky stalled.

"I'm just going to be a second." Hooky snapped some photos of the balcony, came inside and stood by the desk in the corner. Looked at the manila folders all in a stack, their spines labeled neatly with printed surnames and dates. "Just one sec here . . ."

Evans. Cherry. Bithway. Heildale. Smith.

She'd have the Tanner file tucked away somewhere, to prevent Frank stumbling upon it. Couldn't have him knowing she'd caught on—that his partner was possibly a fraud, a kidnap victim, the false daughter of a one-time criminal mastermind. He wouldn't believe her. Or would he? Did he already know? Hooky swiped away the camera on her phone and switched to the contacts list, pushed the dial button. Ella cocked her ear in the hallway as she heard her phone ringing inside her apartment.

"Shit. Shit! That's my landline. I'm just going to leave you for a sec . . ."

"I'm almost done!" Hooky shouted, as the door clicked closed. She threw open the drawers one at a time, found the Tanner file in the very last one, under a stack of old newspapers. She shoved the file open on the desk and spread the papers out, went back to the camera and clicked. She was just pushing the bottom drawer closed, the file replaced, when Ella threw open the door again.

"All good?"

"Yeah, hang up call." Ella shuffled her backpack higher on her shoulder, annoyance edging into her tone. "You done here?"

"All done." Hooky strode to the door, slipping the phone into the pocket of her blazer. "You've been fantastic."

If you count dreaming about work as work itself, which I do, I was on the planning for the running festival for about thirty-seven hours straight. When Imogen found me the night before *Take Back the Parks*, I was sitting at her kitchen table with a glass of milk staring at the balcony doors, my fingernails bitten down to stubs. I'd turned my phone off for an hour and was playing a mental game with myself, battling back the desire to turn it on again, when she walked into the room. I knew that when I turned it on, it would explode with messages from Eden, Hooky, Captain James, some journalists I'd known over the years. There were maps spread all over the floor of Imogen's kitchen, all over the countertops, some stuck to the fridge, all representing the structure of security for the event in different colors and patterns.

Eden and I had tracked down as many CCTV cameras on each of the run routes as possible. We'd directed a team to work through the registered runners, looking for participants with violent pasts, and we'd composed watch lists with their likenesses for the foot-patrol teams. Four security companies were covering the events. We'd briefed them all on what we were looking for, what codes to use for what kind of backup should they spot anything unusual on the night.

I'd tried about seventeen times to get through to Caroline Eckhart to cancel the event, despite being told to leave all the schmoozing to Eden. Caroline erected a wall of people to field any communication I tried to throw at her, whether it was email, call, or message. I was fairly sure if I'd attempted to send a carrier pigeon to her massive apartment on the Finger Wharf, it would have been shot down. Probably with lasers. If she didn't hear from me, she couldn't refuse my direct appeal. As far as I knew, she was doing the same to Captain James.

The tension surrounding the running festival was feverish. The journalists and the public wanted to be there when someone was killed. Everyone else wanted to prevent a killing taking place. The whole thing was like some horrific hunting expedition, the bear trap snapped open and set, teeth gaping, the trigger ready for the slightest breath of wind to whisper over it before it snapped shut. I was more afraid of what might happen if we lured and cornered the bear than of setting off the trap.

I still had no idea who the Parks killer was—what sort of creature we were dealing with. I'd stood by Jill Noble's decomposed body in Glebe morgue as Hooky waited for me outside, and tried to get a feel for the killer. All I got was a sense of malice. Pure, inhuman malice, the kind that takes over soldiers pushed too far by the intensity of war, the kind that makes them do sick things in burning villages, forgetting their humanity, forgetting their lives before. Someone out there was letting go of themselves completely with these women, and what they were surrendering to, what took hold of the steering wheel when they released their grip, was nothing less than a monster. It takes a long time to cultivate that sort of evil power in a human being. No one is born that angry—you have to be pushed that way.

Eden had said the victims were being punished by proxy, that the killer was living out revenge on them that he or she couldn't enact on the real target of their fury. The real target, it seemed, was unavailable somehow—she was dead, or out of reach. The killer couldn't strangle and beat the real target the way he or she wanted to, so it was these runners who copped the violence. The original target was a runner, then? A fitness junkie? Was her athleticism, her propensity to run, being punished? I spent three or four hours wasting time on the Internet looking into the backgrounds of famous Australian athletes, trying to find female runners who'd been issued threats, who had violent boyfriends, sons, daughters, husbands. I looked at Caroline Eckhart's ex-boyfriend for a long time, half-heartedly inspired by Mr. Esposito's weird tip. But Caroline and her bulky former beau were good friends.

I knew I was wasting my time, fishing without bait, but I couldn't stop myself. I fell into an exhausted, helpless pattern, trudging through one web page after another. Night fell. Take-out containers lay everywhere, though I didn't remember ordering or eating anything.

And then Imogen was there, with her fingers working my neck on either side beneath my ears, nails reaching up over my scalp, dragging through my hair. She bent over my chair and kissed me on the cheek, put her arms around me. I sat back and let her squeeze me. The smell of her, the warmth of her lips against my neck, was a relief as potent as a drug. I was snapped awake, electrified.

"How's the dazed detective?"

"Wide awake, now that you're home."

"I've been home for half an hour," she laughed, pressing her nose against mine. "I've had a shower and everything. You've just been sitting there staring at the windows."

"Sorry, sorry. I'm just tired. And starving, for some reason—although I think I've eaten . . ." I looked around.

"I've ordered pizza." She sat beside me. "It'll be here soon."

"Oh, you're a dollface." I reached out, squeezed her taut cheeks so that her lips poked out. "You're an absolute dollface."

Imogen was a strange creature, an odd choice for me—I knew that much without Eden having to tell me. She could be mild and gentle, as she was now, quiet in the way that suggested she'd checked off all her goals for the day and she was satisfied to pass the soft decline of the evening light curiously perusing my maps, holding my hand, now and then looking at messages from people on her phone and tapping away replies. She wanted nothing from me, not that I'd have minded if she did.

There were times, however, when I couldn't talk to her, when her mind was so tangled with clients and their problems that when she walked through the door she was ten people. She was the needy little girl with daddy issues, the OCD sufferer exhausted with worry about his health, the angry old man trying to push down the abuse he suffered as a child, which rose through the decades like bile. She could be manic with her own hidden desires and concerns—I knew the armchair detective thing was a sign of something, some ancient point she had to prove or a dream she couldn't ignore, a childhood fascination with cops that needed some outlet other than me. She needed to unravel things. Part of the attraction of the hobby was the money, which she greedily fantasized about, but part of it was the investigatory thrill that also poked its head up in her ordinary work. She dug down into people, uncovered buried traumas, brought secrets out into the light and examined them. There was power in that.

A part of me also recognized that what I liked about Imogen was what I liked about Eden. There was no wearing of the heart on the sleeve with these two. Their weaknesses, insecurities, embarrassing little joys were nowhere to be seen. Once or twice I'd seen the mask slip for both of them—I'd caught Eden once, losing herself to some tune on her headphones in the station gym locker room. When I say "losing herself," I mean she did a smooth little wiggle of her hips, frowned, and mouthed a nasty lyric or two, then went back to packing her things away in her locker, robotic. That was "losing herself" to Eden. Imogen did it, too, trying too hard to get people to like her. Doing that to me, sometimes, like when she ordered me pizzas after spending all week trying to cram carrots and hummus down my throat. When she asked hidden or sidelong questions about our future together, trying to work out how I felt about it. Whether I loved her.

Then there was her obvious, inescapable jealousy over girls she caught me looking at, over Hooky. I knew it must be a powerful kind of jealousy for it to emerge in the accusations it had over Amy—Imogen had never had a specific target for her jealousy before, so now that she did, I knew its intensity for the first time. I could see hate in her eyes at the mere mention of the girl. For some reason, she didn't feel the same way about Eden, which was strange. I spent my every working minute with Eden. It was natural, given what we'd faced together, that we might develop feelings for each other—plenty of cops did. Why was Imogen so sure Eden was no romantic threat to her? Did she know something I didn't?

I watched her scrolling through the day's news on her phone, stopping now and then to examine commentary on some high-profile sex scandal or another, an old actor and his obscenely young wife. She looked soft in the dim light from above us, gold light falling on her arms, on the curves of her collarbones, on the backs of her hands. I don't know what she'd been doing that day, as I'd commandeered the apartment and she'd gone off to entertain herself and keep out of my way, but I hoped she hadn't spent her time paying bills. I reached out and took her hand, and without looking at me, she squeezed my palm.

"You're funny," I said.

"*You're* funny." She smiled.

Of Bangkok, Tara remembered snippets. Heat. A heavy, numbing blanket of heat that made the body beg for relief outside the wall of air-conditioning that halted like held breath at the automatic doors of the airport. A throbbing in her calves as she made her way through the crowds of taxi drivers, all of them angry-looking men muttering prices as she passed, brown lips thin and dry as words too fast rippled through them. She remembered wild dogs by the highway side, slipping in and out between the long grass like snakes, tussling by the side of a brown canal. Huge wooden temples on impossibly high stands, heaped with pink and yellow flowers and bowls of rotting meat and colored rice, next to carpet shops, antique shops, supermarkets, and coconut stands. The city beyond, gray sludge in the heat haze, the gaping mouths of half-finished and abandoned apartment buildings, tattered advertising fluttering in the breeze.

Tara remembered narrow halls and darkness, the smell of incense burning. Bright red carpet everywhere, flecked with pieces of white cotton, as though someone had washed a tissue in their pocket and trailed the thing throughout the building. Thinking that there shouldn't have been carpet in the doctor's halls, that somehow the presence of carpet in a supposedly sterile, surgical environment seemed odd, out of place, the way it might in a kitchen. A bathroom.

Smiles everywhere. Excited smiles. Smiles fading

into the dark. She was signing documents in a dark room. People were whispering. Towels everywhere, stacked, different colors. Why were they different colors? There were lapses in her memory, and they were happening often. She was shivering in the cold. The lights were flickering. A machine was screaming beeps and the people around her were talking fast.

Darkness for a long time, a depth of dream Tara wasn't sure she would ever wake from, wasn't sure she wanted to wake from. She was free of her body. Weightless. That ancient ache in her hips and knees gave way and she had no hips or knees, and her chest collapsed inward, dissolved, so that she was a floating consciousness, a bee buzzing from light to light as colors flashed before her. And then her eyelids were being pulled back and someone was shoving a tube into her newly formed throat.

"Tara? Tara? Come back to us, Tara. Come back, honey. Squeeze my hand if you can hear me. Come on, girl."

Australian voices. Why were they Australian? Tara squinted, tried to wriggle away from the words. *Come on. Come on.* She was running again in the dark. Joanie was behind her. She had to run. Had to get away. She felt a rhythmic pumping on her chest, and again the squeal of machines. Darkness fell again. And then there was stillness, the crisp firmness of starched hospital sheets beneath her fingertips. Everything aching. People laughing in the busy halls.

A woman was there, wearing navy blue scrubs— one of those wrinkled, pleasant-faced people used to frowning with concern. Tara had the impression that she had seen this woman before, that in her half-drugged state the woman had been talking to her, had perhaps talked to her for days, her bony hand playing with Tara's wrist. Tara had bucked in the bed, tried to shift from a position she felt she might have been in for hours. The pain fluttered through her like a big red bird, razor-sharp feathers brushing the insides of her arms and legs, pulling on stitches. Hundreds and hundreds of stitches—she felt them tugging all at once like so many tiny spiders latched onto hunks of skin, curved teeth inserted.

People came and went, people in suits, people in police uniforms. Tara hadn't known there were so many white people in all of Bangkok. Might have said so, but she couldn't hear her own voice above the rising and falling hum of the drugs.

"You're back in Sydney," the nurse said. "You've been back in Sydney for six weeks, honey."

In time, she was sitting, and the nurse was talking gently to her, talking, talking, talking, and as the sun began to fall, Tara began to make sense of the words.

"But then," the nurse was saying, "people make bad choices. I know I have. It happens."

"What happened . . . to me?" Tara asked.

The nurse looked at her.

"You fell victim to a terrible scam, Tara," the nurse said. She reached for Tara's wrist again. "And no matter what anyone tells you, girl, you're the victim in this. You thought you were being sold a service, and . . . God, I suppose the doctor you hired thought he might have been able to provide it. Christ, I don't know. He certainly made an attempt." She seemed to want to give a laugh but swallowed it back. "Tara, your surgery in Bangkok, your weight reduction surgery, went very badly."

Tara looked at her hands. They were scarred by the savage pokes and prods of several IV tubes. She pulled back the sleeves of her gown. Bandages emerged, from wrist to forearm. From forearm to shoulder. Her arms were half the size they had been, but beneath the bandages she felt strange ripples and bulges of flesh, a seam of wide stitches that ran from the inside of her elbow to her armpit, the entire bottom half of her arm savagely cut away. Another seam ran from her armpit into her collarbone, disappearing in a mesh of grooves and dips. Tara watched the unfamiliar limbs trembling as she explored herself. She felt her ribs. Were those her ribs? Fluid moved beneath the surface of the skin, igniting with pain as she touched.

"Be gentle with yourself," the nurse advised.

"What . . . happened?"

"Your body is scarred," the nurse murmured. "We think that the doctor in Bangkok attempted the abdominal lipectomy on the first night you arrived. He performed what is commonly known as a tummy tuck. The next day—the next *day*, Tara, before your body could recover from what was, quite frankly, a *savage* procedure—he went ahead with the breasts, the arms. You've got to understand . . . this person has had little medical training. Well, little training in Western medical procedures. You've undergone an incredible physical trauma."

"Get me up," Tara said.

The nurse didn't move. Tara yanked back the blankets, felt nausea stir in her stomach. She clawed at the chrome bed frame, her new, strange form shivering violently, making the plastic bracelets on her wrists flap against the bars. The woman came to her aid, slipping under her arm, a human crutch. The floor was dust-flecked, cold linoleum, the painful trek from the bed to the bathroom traversed a thousand times before by faceless ghosts, a stumble and a half of agony before the blessed stability of the white plastic shelf before the glass. Tara stared at the unfamiliar face in the mirror. Reached up and touched the limp side, dragged the corner of her mouth up so that it aligned with the other, then let it fall. Her nose had been broken. When, in all this, had her nose been broken?

The bandaged, robed body before her was a crooked white question mark, not the round, solid hulk that she was used to. Her shoulders were high and her neck was low as she rested there, a rageful bird, both bewildered and terrified by the new world around it.

What am I? she wondered. She stared and shook. *What am I now?*

"Did you tell her?" someone whispered.

"I think she knows what's happened to her now, but not the other thing," the nurse said. Tara looked, but the voices came from beyond the bathroom door, and she couldn't travel back on her own. She leaned, saw a slice of white coat. A doctor.

"You need to tell her. Best she gets both halves at once, get it over with. Perfect timing. The shrinks can come in just in time and clean up the mess and we can all get back to what's important."

"She's still coming round," the nurse said. "I think I'm only just now getting through."

"Good," the voice said. "Well, I need you back in

the ER in an hour, so make it snappy, okay? *Sorry dear, you fucked yourself. You'll be scarred for life. Oh, and your mother's kicked the bucket. Done herself in. What a loss to the world. Right! Great! Ashes to ashes and all that! Best of luck, see you later.* Right? Then back on the ward. Got me? We can't hold their hands forever, even the rich ones."

There were footsteps. Tara gripped the ledge before her.

Eden felt happy as she wandered across the wet green grass of Bradfield Park, passing through the crooked gates and pathways that formed between the elbows and shoulders of a thousand people. She was a fox slipping between dopey hounds, her ears pricking to laughs and squeals and breathy sighs, the static excitement of a mob. A curious ripple of happiness pulsed in her. She relished the crowd—because for at least one killer tonight, these were hunting grounds, and Eden never felt more comfortable than when she walked among prey.

She could understand the appeal of them to the Parks Strangler; the runners fluttered and flapped together in gaggling groups like plump, stupid chickens. Eden thought of blood, and there was so much of it here tonight, flushing in excited cheeks and pumping through jugulars. She breathed in the scented air, pregnant with chemicals—deodorant, Tiger Balm, zinc cream, the sugary bouquets of energy drinks, chewable tablets, gels.

When the light beyond the harbor hit its deepest blue, wedged between an approaching storm and the black, still water, the orange street lamps along Alfred Street flickered and came to light, eliciting a long, low cheer from the crowd. Weighty anticipation, as real as the smell of the soil stirring in desire for the rain, another cheer as lightning pricked the distant suburbs. She picked her way up the hill toward the thick trunks of the old bridge, stopping to look at the birds high above swirling over the crowd on the bridge, ducking for moths attracted to the lights.

Hunting grounds. Was Eden being hunted?

She looked at the crowd around her. Now and then she caught a face turned toward her, eyes on her own, catching her briefly before turning away. The lanky young man in black Lyrica, stretching his gangly arms above his head. The portly middle-aged woman laughing and chewing on her water bottle nib. The old man sitting alone beneath the sprawling tree, half of his face lit by glass-front apartment buildings above Luna Park, as he tied the laces of his bulky running shoes.

Somewhere, a radio station hosting the event was commenting on the assembly of runners before the starting line, a row of stoic Kenyans and fat-free middle-aged men huffing and swaying. Was the killer here tonight? Eden stood beneath the sprawling tree and tried to guess. If she'd ever been the sort of killer to garner this sort of attention, she was sure she'd take the bait. How does one stay home from such a grandiose event, organized almost in tribute to one's nighttime games?

Eden couldn't imagine her own work ever causing such a stir. Most of her victims were old men with long-held morbid fetishes—the public-toilet child molesters and cinema masturbators of the world. When they were women, they were hard, loveless—black widows, Munchausen-by-proxy sufferers, the occasional corporate assassin. Clara McKinnie, the baby-faced beauty in Byron Bay, had been a breath of fresh air. The Parks Strangler's victims were fresh-faced girls, vulnerable to the self-esteem-crushing glimpse of love handles in shop windows, the all-too-common call of the jogger's pathway to panting redemption. They were incredibly relatable. They were daughters, colleagues, girls next door.

Eden's victims were shadows. That's what gave her the longevity she'd enjoyed as a hunter: complete lack of public outrage.

Her trail of thoughts was broken when Frank swam into view beside her, flipping the bill of her black baseball cap in the annoying manner of a teasing brother. He stood on the hill beside her and looked at the writhing crowd. He was unshaven and mussed from sleep, the Special Operations shirt ill-fitting on his lean frame, sagging at the collar. There was a police-issue leather jacket slung over one arm.

"Spotted her yet?"

"Not yet," Eden said. "Glad it's going to rain, though. Plenty of hoodies around. Very helpful."

"Are you going to jump rides?" he asked. The two hadn't discussed their own operations on the ground. It was probably good practice to have at least one of them stationed at the police command center on Macquarie Street to field calls from cops out on patrol, assess what sounded promising, and disregard the usual complaints that came with crowd control—men brawling, women falling, the inevitable midevent heart attack. Frank must have assumed it would be Eden out in the crowd jumping rides from one patrol car to another as complaints came in.

"I might run some of it," she said.

Frank looked concerned. "Be careful. You're not more than a week off that crutch."

"I'll be fine," she said. "I want to be right there if we get anything."

A low rumble of thunder over Balmain. The crowd whooped and cheered. Eden spotted Hooky coming up the hill toward them, bright green Doc Martens gripping the wet slope, making muddy tracks between the people moving toward the starting line. The girl had a computer tablet tucked under her arm.

Short blond hair, Eden thought. But no, Hooky wasn't the journalist who had turned up at Hades's home. For one, Hades had said it was a woman, and Hooky was all girl: the tiny chunks of polished wood in her earlobes, the leather straps on her wrists; that hangdog, troubled-teen look she gave everything and everyone, as if at any second she would be misunderstood, underrepresented, *oppressed*, the way so many teenagers were convinced they were.

Oh yes, the girl was brilliant. She had potential. And her upbringing—the murders. Eden didn't know much about that, hadn't bothered to look into it, but she recognized that the survival instinct was alive in Hooky. When someone close to you is murdered, it flips a switch inside. The world is no longer an inherently good place—it is full of predators, and you realize that you must become a predator in order to be immune from the same fate.

"All right," the girl said in greeting, peeling off the cover on the tablet. "Let's talk about chip timing."

"What on earth is chip timing?" Frank wrinkled his nose.

"I'm about to explain, Grandpa." Hooky drew up a map on the screen. "Just hold on to your suspenders. We've got ten minutes until the starting gun, so no stupid questions."

"No stupid questions," Frank murmured, waggling a finger in Eden's face.

"Every runner in the event has a microchip embedded in a little foam pad on the back of their bib number," Hooky continued, pointing to the crowd. Eden looked at the numbers before her, pinned to the front of tank tops and jackets. "When the runner passes over an electronic mat on the ground at the starting line, their individual chip registers and a start time is assigned. At the finish line, when the runner passes over another electronic mat, the microchip is blipped again, thereby giving an accurate digital time in which the runner ran the event. You keeping up?"

"I think so." Frank nodded. Eden nodded.

"The runner takes their registry number, the one written on the front of their bib, and looks up their results online. The chip timer also sets off an automatic camera that flashes pictures of each runner as they cross the line. The runners can punch in the number and get pictures of themselves starting and finishing the event."

"This would be really useful," Eden said, "if we knew the killer was going to register for the event. Which is about as likely as me winning the thing."

"Well, it won't be useful for that," Hooky said. "But it will be useful for discovering if anyone goes missing from the race."

"How?"

"Well." Hooky drew up the map on the tablet, tapped and highlighted the starting point, where a blue bubble flashed, indicating the location of the device. "There are electronic mats at the start line and finish line that'll tell us when runners start and when they finish.

But if, say, you were some kind of *technology whiz*, some kind of *absolute fucking genius*, you could hack the system and get access to all the runner microchips in the race. Then you could set up GPS markers, say, every five hundred meters. Like the mats, the GPS markers would give you an electronic signal, a blip, every time a runner passes over them. A runner would start the race at the start line, and then every five hundred meters—blip, blip, blip—until they're finished."

Eden took the tablet from Hooky. Looked at the little bubbles intersecting the running paths on the map, flashing as they waited for the runners.

"Why are the markers so close together? Five hundred meters isn't very far."

"I've rigged the system so that every runner in the entire event has ten minutes to complete each marker. You'd have to be going pretty damned slow to not make it five hundred meters in ten minutes. Every person who starts the race will show up on my system. If they don't get through all the markers in time, it'll send up an alert at the marker they missed. The alert will come right here, to this device. If, for some reason, a runner drops out of the race, we'll know. We'll know which five-hundred-meter block they went missing in. We'll know who they are and where they disappeared within ten minutes of the runner missing the checkpoint."

"This is . . . this is amazing!" Frank took the tablet from Eden, stared at the screen.

"Yes, I agree, I'm amazing. But it's an imperfect plan," Hooky said. "If someone sprains an ankle and stops midway through the race, you're going to get an alert. If someone stops to chat with someone on the sidelines, and doesn't make it over the next marker in time, you're going to get an alert. There are thousands of people in this event. I suspect you're going to get dozens of alerts."

"It doesn't matter," Frank said. "We'll send someone to investigate every alert we get. You never know. One of these might be someone getting snatched off the track."

"It doesn't help you if your killer doesn't nab someone in the race." Hooky looked at the crowd, distracted. "There are no rules. Anyone is fair game. They might go after one of the spectators. But fuck it. I thought it might be a useful tool."

There was howling from the starting line. Eden recognized Caroline Eckhart's voice on the speakers, fronting a techno track for the radio station covering the event, the call-and-response stirring of the crowd, the stamping of feet. "I said, Are you ready to run?"

"She's a little star, this one," Frank growled, looping an arm around Hooky's neck, crushing the girl's head against his chest. "Oh, she's a genius."

"I'll keep in contact with you on the road," Eden said, waiting for her partner to disentangle himself from the teen. She pointed to the girl. "Get her a radio. You can feed me alerts and see if I'm nearby."

"Right," Frank said. He grabbed the girl by the back of the neck, a big brother's grip. "You're comin' with me, young Einstein."

Ruben stood on the ledge beneath the attic window and looked down at the grass beneath him. He'd broken into a few places in his life when things became desperate—once into his own bedroom, after his parents had caught him out in the night and barred him from coming back in. A storm was brewing beyond the tree-lined park, just beginning to sprinkle the cars parked alongside the iron gates with rain. He'd spent the afternoon listening for sounds in the attic room, and when he was convinced no one was home, he'd begun to climb. On top of the garage, he'd remembered the white van, and peeled back a worn sheet of corrugated iron to peer into the gloomy space. The van was gone.

He was well aware now that his curiosity about the person in the attic room had crept beyond healthy interest. When he had stood on the steps outside the police headquarters with his papers in his hands, he had questioned for the last time what drove him, what sick pull was reeling him in toward the attic room. He had felt the pain and terror behind the door at the top of the stairs—but it was more than that. He had told the uninterested Australian policeman that he thought whoever was in the room was a killer. The words had rolled off his tongue, and it was only as he said them that he knew he'd believed this as soon as he read the gossip articles about the Harper girl, that this had grown and swelled in his mind when he heard the snarling beyond the door.

The Harper kid is a psycho . . . The physical and psychological fallout of bad choices . . .

Bad, bad, bad. There was no better word for what Ruben had heard there, inches from his own fingertips, a person, a thing, raging at the wood, a slave to the badness infecting its body. He couldn't see her, but Ruben could feel the black cloud swirling inside the room. He'd felt the chill of its wispy fingers slithering under the door to permeate the Harper house. There was no cleaning away that badness, no matter how hard he scrubbed.

The teen reached up, gripped the chipped ledge beneath the attic windows, and pulled. He flipped his elbows up onto the ledge, pushed up, then shoved at one of the windows. Blessedly, it gave, the brass hook resting on the edge of the eye inside the glass, not in it. He slid over the windowsill and through the curtains.

It was dark inside the attic room, and the air was thick with mold. There was no light. He scrambled to the wall and tried the light switch by the door. A bulb, long unused, snapped on above him, shuddering to life like a child shaken awake. At once, the faces pressed in on him as though they had been waiting in the dark to find him. It seemed, in the first moment of terror, that they all turned toward him. But he realized there were too many. The hundreds of faces were not real. He realized, as he crouched by the door, that they were all the same face.

Joan Harper. The sharp blond woman from the gossip column, the one he'd seen sitting at a restaurant with a friend. Pictures of her littered every surface, were tacked to every square inch of wall. Photographs from the house. Joanie in her teenage years, squeezed in between two other blond girls, her white teeth gleaming in a Cheshire cat smile. Joan Harper on the bow of a yacht, her short hair whipped across her forehead. Joan Harper on her wedding day, pulling on her snow-white heels. In a huge oil painting leaning against one corner, Joan Harper reclined in a red leather wingback chair, her fingers coiled around the stem of a wineglass.

All the pictures were eyeless. The eyes had been transformed into gaping black hollows, scribbled out so that the paper tore and black lines wound around the taut cheeks of the Joans crowding up into the corners of the room. The mouths gaped in identical black ovals, howling, hundreds of ghoul Joans screaming from the walls around him.

Ruben was trembling. He staggered to the table beside the window, put his hand down to steady himself, and gagged as a gray puff of mold swirled around a collapsed plate of what might have once been cake. Tiny flies billowed from a stack of mold-encrusted plates. Ruben pulled the window closed, felt rain on his cheeks.

As soon as I got to the command center halfway up Macquarie Street I knew I wasn't going to be there long. Before me, four folding tables sliced the little tent in two, cords running over the pavement to wide computer monitors, Eden's scribbled mess of a map pinned to the inside of the white canvas. The makeshift room was lit by a series of $24 Ikea lamps someone had run out and grabbed at the last minute, giving it the strange feel of a university dorm room. A cooler to the side of the room was packed full of cans of Coke. Every now and then, the blue arm of a beat cop slid through the wall of the tent and grabbed one before disappearing again, the hammer of boots or the ticking of a bicycle signaling their return back to the beat.

Hooky was on her iPad, tapping things, shifting things around. I watched alerts coming up on the screens in front of the cops sitting at the computers, listened to them chatter back and forth over their radios. A female officer had dropped out of the other command center, over in Kensington, and was in the process of being replaced. Officers were passing around descriptions of the killer, which to me sounded as though we were hunting a ghost. I went to the door flap of the tent, looked out at the empty road. A flash of lightning between the buildings before me on Bridge Street lit the glass side of the Museum of Sydney.

"They're almost on us," Hooky said.

I turned and looked down Macquarie toward the

Opera House and picked out a couple of runners, hovering silhouettes on the black asphalt. In seconds they were in front of me, a tight group of leaders galloping by, faces set and cheeks sucking. Behind them what was growing into a wall of humanity, the swinging arms and gaping mouths of an army of machines. The runners came up the hill and shot past me, rubber soles clopping on the oily road.

A couple of officers at the edge of the tent cheered them as they went by. One or two of the runners raised their hands in the air, pumped fists.

Someone was going to die tonight.

I could feel it in the air. It was all too jubilant. Too innocent. The runners had the look of happy sheep, enclosed in the lush, wet valley between the city buildings. But darkness was approaching. When I looked back down the street toward the harbor, I couldn't see the runners coming off the Cahill Expressway anymore. It was all shadow down there.

I went back inside and took Hooky's arm.

"Let's get outta here."

"Don't lose it," she said. "We've gotta stay level. The first alerts will come in soon."

"And I want to be there," I said. I walked out of the tent, knowing she would follow. Three Honda police motorcycles were standing in a row by the fence, helmets at the ready.

"You can't ride one of these," Hooky smirked.

"You want to make a bet?"

I chucked her a helmet. I felt a surge of delight at the flash, however brief, of admiration on her face. Her iPad blipped as she was pushing the helmet down onto her head. She grabbed it from where she'd set it on the back of the bike.

"It's an alert," she said. "One of the half-marathoners has missed a checkpoint on the Pacific Highway."

"Jump on, kid," I said. Maybe it was too much.

Eden ran. In her ears, snippets of police conversation rolled over each other, the whole of the festival police command buzzing against the steady beat of her breath.

"Lyrebird to Central Command. Shifting units four-seven-oh and four-seven-one to Domain sector four. The five-k runners are half done. Over."

"Central Command to Lyrebird. Roger the last. Over."

"Currawong to Command. Have sighted the first marathoners. Over."

"Command to Currawong. Roger that. Waterhen, let me know when you've got the first runners down where you are, mate. Should be twenty minutes or so."

"Waterhen. Gotcha, Command."

The voice of Central Command was not Frank, and as Eden ran she did not hear his voice above the murmurs and radio whistles as the marathon runners moved toward Kensington. Around her on a wide road, runners bopped along, each with their own unique shuffle, long-legged antelope men galloping ahead of her and short, plump ladies with swift, shallow steps falling behind. The storm was upon them now, but it was not as furious as it had appeared raging and flashing over the Blue Mountains. Rain fell in hard, heavy drops, pattering on her shoulders and chest. It would be gone before it could dampen her socks, dissipating out over Coogee.

As the mass of runners around her approached the University of New South Wales's sprawling front gates, a troupe of students wearing matching pink T-shirts swirled and bounced, buoyed after a gap in the crowd, their banners swaying above grinning heads.

IF YOUR PARTNER IS VIOLENT, DON'T BE SILENT!
FEAR IS NOT A SUBSTITUTE FOR RESPECT!

A young woman with electric-blue hair approached Eden with a paper cup of orange liquid. Eden shook her head and kept trotting.

She didn't need sustenance. She needed painkillers. The old wound from sternum to pelvis was burning again, the tortured muscles beneath twisting as she loped along, tearing at hardened scar tissue. She kept her eyes on the group, slowed a little to keep herself near the midpoint in the stretch of two hundred or so runners. If she turned her head, Eden could see runners a kilometer or so behind her, some the same distance ahead. It was only a selection of those who were running the marathon, but it was a good chunk. She would leave them and catch a ride with a squad car somewhere before La Perouse, to be with another group running up along the coast.

She couldn't be stationary. Not with so much prey around. Some corner of Eden's mind acknowledged that the thought of the killer being out there somewhere waiting for the perfect victim to sidle by, like a snake poised beneath a rock, would awaken the same deadly instinct in her. Because she knew someone else was hunting, Eden felt her own hunter stirring. When a couple of runners came up behind her, hooted and cheered at her side for a second, having seen the PO-LICE banner on the back of her T-shirt, it was all she could do not to reach out, grab fabric, hair, skin.

At La Perouse, she trotted past Long Bay prison and its golden-lit towers. She watched the chain-link fence bouncing with the motion of her body, saw the silhouettes of guards in the birdcage—the first intake area for new prisoners arriving in vans. Eden had put quite a lot of people into the Bay in her time. Her parents' killers had been there together. She'd visited its dark concrete halls many times, looked out from the offices at the manicured gardens inside, littered with cigarette butts. The place was so familiar she felt like waving as she passed. When she turned back to the road, she saw the face in the dark, a slice of face behind a black hood, white in the glow of a streetlamp. For just a second, the person in the jacket looked back at Eden, grinned, and turned. Eden felt the fine hairs all along her arms stand on end.

The hooded runner sped up. Eden pushed and felt her thighs respond with a bone-deep ache at her new momentum, a ripple of electricity through her chest and shoulders as her body responded to the increase in effort. She watched in breathless fury as the runner in black edged toward a female runner, drifting sideways, closer to the galloping woman in purple.

The woman didn't even glance at him. She was locked in that face-forward position, the same that had blocked all of Eden's senses as she ran through the park at Rushcutters. The hypnotic rhythm of feet, knees, hips, breath, arms, had her captured, and all it would take was one good knock from the side to send her stumbling toward the concrete gutter. Eden looked around. They were almost alone, what was previously a tight pod of runners now spread through the island in the center of Anzac Parade, sheltered by the trees. There were runners behind, but when Eden looked back at them, all she saw was blank faces, swinging arms, puckered mouths. The hooded runner grabbed the girl in purple by the back of her neck and pushed, let the momentum of the slope carry her down toward the tennis courts, her feet struggling to find traction in the wet grass.

Eden sprinted over the gutter, over the hill, launching herself down the slope toward the fence around the courts. Her fingers fumbled for the gun at the base of her spine. She had the weapon in her hands when the two runners hit the fence in a tangle of wires, tackling each other, the crash almost loud enough to drown out their laughter.

Eden skidded to a painful halt.

"We got her!" the boy laughed, dragging off the hood. He was an androgynous creature with chocolate curls and big lips, grinning at an almost identical girl. Brother and sister, Eden guessed. "We fucking got her."

"That was too easy," the girl snickered. "We're sorry, officer. We just couldn't help ourselves."

Eden licked her lips. The kids stood laughing against the fence, the boy hugging himself with a helpless kind of hilarity Eden thought had been reserved only for childhood. When she'd heard enough, she strode forward and, with one swing, cracked the boy's nose with the butt of her pistol.

The girl's laughter turned to screams, as though a

switch had been flipped. Blood gushed down the boy's face, over his lips and hands, an inky torrent.

"What did you do?" the girl screamed.

"Sorry," Eden said. She slipped her gun back into the belt holster. "Couldn't help myself."

She ran back up the hill to the road.

The first alert was on the Pacific Highway. When Hooky and I got there, we found the runner being taken care of by a few spectators. She'd sprained her ankle on one of those rubber devices that crosses the road surface to measure the frequency of passing cars. By the time we'd arrived, Hooky was dealing with two more alerts over the police radio. A runner had gone down with a dodgy knee back toward the harbor bridge, and an elderly man was being hauled off the hill over on the 5 km course with chest pains. I drove Hooky back across the bridge toward an alert in the Domain and glanced in my rearview mirror, saw her looking up at the giant ribs of the bridge passing over us faster than I could have imagined.

"Pretty good, eh?" I yelled, my words muffled by the helmet. I felt her laugh against my back. A troupe of organizers heading back toward the Domain cheered at us from the side of the bridge. It might almost have been fun, burning across the empty bridge on the hot, humming machine, had there not been half a city under threat from a being whose work I had seen firsthand. All the while, the radio crackled in our ears.

"Lyrebird, Command. We're getting reports of an assault on an individual near Little Bay Road, just after the prison there. They're saying it might have been a police officer. We'll send a unit out."

"Archer to Command. Don't bother with that one. Couple of crybabies."

Eden's voice. I listened hard.

"Command to Lyrebird, Archer. Confirmed. Let the ambos clean it up."

I swung the bike through the tollbooths and down the Cahill Expressway. The crowds in the Domain parted as I slid the bike through, the humming engine warning groups of runners of my presence. All the serious competitors had reached the finish line, mingling between the market stalls set up on the oval, sweaty brows wiped and grins spread across faces, bubbles sparkling in plastic cups. I could smell curry burning. I nosed the bike through the crowd and gunned it up a short hill behind the café, onto the road in front of the national Art Gallery. The runners were faster here—trying to give it everything they had as they came down the hill toward the finish line in the bus loop in front of the gallery. I passed sculptures of men astride horses, mouths gaping toward the moonless sky.

"What number?"

"Ends in five eight three!" Hooky yelled.

I started driving back through the runners, looking for a bib number that ended in 583. The runner had missed the last two checkpoints before the finish line. I'd told Hooky to tell me if the runner came through, but she hadn't said a word, so I had to assume the person was still stopped somewhere in the last kilometer of the race. Runners swept past me, hardly noticing the plainclothes cop on the bike, their eyes set on the finish line. Arms once swinging in parallel arcs now flailed.

Mouths gasped for air. I crept up the hill and around the corner to the top of Macquarie.

Numbers flashed past me. I looked down the hill and could see the end of the crowd, the mothers with strollers I'd seen ten minutes earlier.

"Where are they?" I asked. Hooky didn't hear me. I burned down the hill, my pulse increasing, making the helmet shift against my throbbing skull. I looked down alleyways, swept the bushes at the edge of the park with my eyes, half hoping for, half dreading, the sight of a shadowed figure bent over a fallen runner. Hooky wriggled behind me, pulled the iPad out of her jacket. I slowed the bike, listened to its rhythmic beat.

"They still haven't checked in," she said. "Must be here somewhere."

I let the bike roll, looked at the doorways of the buildings. Runners wandered past, these too unfit to finish at a jog. I scanned their numbers: 671, 332, 400.

We were parallel to the row of green-and-yellow portable toilets when the door of one crashed open. Hooky and I swung around in time to see a huge hulk of a man emerge onto the wooden crate steps beneath the doors. He tugged his sweat-damp shorts up over his hips and wiped sweat from his neck onto a hairy forearm. He spotted us and shot me a half grin. I looked at the race bib pinned to his shirt: 11583.

"Whoo!" he panted. He jogged away on spotless white sneakers, more of an exaggerated walk than a jog.

"Shit!" I seethed.

"Yes. A very time-consuming one, apparently." Hooky turned back to her iPad, which blipped the next alert.

Tara lingered in the alcove before the fire-escape door of the tunnel, watching the pretty runners go by, little pods of them bobbing away like ducks being carried along by a river current. Now and then a wave of them would come, a hundred at once, whooping and howling as they entered the concrete tube, reveling in the thrill of their own voices ballooning around the ceiling, echoing back to them. A group covered in glow-stick bands bumped past, waving their fluorescent sticks, making dim triangles of pink and green and yellow in the air above them, a little flock of fireflies.

Tara understood their rapture at the night air. The city was alive—it was crawling with humans. Every night out of the attic room was a thrill for Tara, the ritual of the kill filled with so many more things than the hunt itself. She was unused to traveling through the city streets, even when protected from its glorious wonders by the numbing encasement of a car. It was always thrilling to see the other people. To come within reach of them.

Tara felt, in their proximity, like she was one of them—she was briefly akin to them, before one of them laid eyes on her and ruined the illusion, rejected her instantly with an expression of horror. It was the way it had been before the surgery, and now after. Even when the mouth forced its way into a smile and the hands came forward, reaching, touching, soothing, the eyes always betrayed the sense that Tara was far beyond the acceptable limits of the human mold—once grossly too large for it, and now, too twisted for it. Her schoolteachers had spent years kneading and stretching and cramming Tara into that rigid "plastic fantastic" mold, Joanie beating at her fleshy edges, trying to cut away the excess with her sharp words, but there was just no fitting Tara, no fitting her anywhere. She was the elephant in every room.

A swell of runners filled the tunnel. Tara leaned out of the shadow to see them coming up over the hill, silhouettes sloshing around the rim of the tunnel mouth, hands in the air as their voices rose. *Aussie Aussie Aussie. Oi Oi Oi.* She turned a tranquilizer dart in her fingers, stroked the thin tip with her thumb. She wouldn't bother with the little dart gun she'd fashioned tonight. She wanted to get close to the runners. The sheer number of jostling people forced three runners down the side of the tunnel, between the interlocking red road barriers and the tunnel wall. Tara leaned back into the fire escape shadows as they trotted past her, unaware. She heard the voices of the cops leaning on the police car just outside the fire escape and to the left, on the other side of the barrier.

"Inside the barrier, you lot!" one yelled. "*In*side!"

Tara saw just the tips of his fingers as he flailed his arm. At the mouth of the tunnel, one runner tried to escape the press of the crowd by cutting along outside the barrier, thought again when she saw the policeman gesturing, and sunk back into the group.

"Might have to go up there and shift that last barrier," one of the cops said to the other. "Push it back against the wall so they can't squeeze through."

"Mmm," the other agreed. Neither moved.

A tight group of orange-clad runners passed, determined faces and downturned mouths. A pod of teenagers, and a father with a young son huffing away at his side. Chills rippled up Tara's spine as the cheers rose from the people passing.

Run, run, boys and girls,
Try to get away.
I won't stop, can't stop,
Gonna make you pay.

Two women ran down the outside of the barrier. Tara leaned so that one scarred eye caught the flashing blue and red of the police car at the side of the tunnel. As they passed, she slipped back into the safety of the dark, a slick sea snail snapping shut the door of its shell. One of the officers let out a dramatic sigh.

"Idiots," he grumbled, walking past the alcove. Tara watched him bumbling against the stream of runners, who ducked and weaved out of his path. One last woman slipped through the gap between the barrier and the tunnel wall, glancing at the officer as she passed.

"Sorry, sorry, sorry," she giggled. The officer waved a tired hand, heading toward the end of the barrier. He dragged the last interlocking piece diagonally against the wall, cutting off the gap. When he looked back down the aisle, it was empty. He assumed the last runner must have jumped over the barrier and rejoined the crowd. His partner was looking at the wall of the tunnel above the runners before him, the shadows of hundreds of people lit up red, then white, then blue, a strobe of pumping limbs against the flat gray curve.

It was a little cruel, Eden thought, to send the runners up Arden Street. She trotted along past the bus stations at Coogee Beach, listening to the rise and crash of waves on the pale sand, watching the runners ahead of her grinding up the massive slope toward Bronte. Out on the ocean, sheet lightning flashed pale pink. As she ran, she listened to the buzz of police activity. Her long abdominal scar was as numb now as the rest of her, her legs working like machinery, pulling tendons in her feet and ankles, making her dance over the asphalt.

Halfway up the slope, she saw the runner a few yards ahead of her waver slightly, the side of her right foot scraping the gutter. The runner dug in, head down and calves straining. The head down part wasn't a good idea, Eden thought. She watched the runner waver again and then stumble sideways into the bushes in front of one of the houses on the slope, wet orange rose petals raining on the grass.

"You all right?"

Eden bent forward over the woman, grabbed her bicep. The woman rolled, looked up, and squealed, her whole body tensing, rock-hard beneath Eden's fingers.

"Jesus!"

"Hey, what are you doing?" someone yelled. Eden straightened as two men ran toward her. When they spied the POLICE lettering on her back, they slowed.

"I'm all right, I'm all right." The woman laughed,

still panting from the run, letting Eden drag her to her feet. She was a chubby little thing with the face of a young bulldog pup. All cheeks. "The rooftop. The shadow of the rooftop made a . . . made a hood over your head . . ."

Eden looked across the road at the curved triangular roof of the postmodern monstrosity of a house. From the ground, the silhouette of the rooftop must have made a perfect hood shape over her shoulders as she bent over the woman, she surmised. It was almost laughable. A specter so close to the surface of the woman's mind, she was ready for the hard touch that picked her up to be the Sydney Parks Strangler: ghoul on the loose. More runners had gathered around them to see what drama was unfolding. Their chattering was an excited mumble, bubbling and sputtering in the dark.

"What is it? What happened?" someone asked.

"She thought the cop was the Parks Strangler," someone else said.

More runners arrived.

"Did you say Parks Strangler? Where's the Parks Strangler?"

"No, *she* thought *she* was the killer. But she's the police."

"What's wrong with her? Did the killer come after her?"

"I don't know. I don't know what's going on."

"Where is he now? Was he here? Was he around here?"

"Is she all right? Did anyone see him?"

Runners carried on past the group toward the top of the hill, catching snippets of the frightened words as they floated in the darkness. Eden watched, stunned, at how fast it was happening, the mouths jabbering all around her. She didn't like talking to groups unless it was from behind the safety of a desk, or near the protective proximity of a planning board. Still in hunting mode, she felt exposed.

"No, he wasn't here." She put her hands up. "Just calm down a second, will you all?"

Someone screamed at the top of the hill. The message had been received up there. The killer was nearby—had made an attempt on a runner farther down the hill and fled. Eden watched the group at the very top of the hill stop, gather in the center of the road. The panic was like thick smoke in the air.

We were heading to an alert in the Cross City Tunnel when the radio broadcast came through. Only seconds old, the alert popped up on Hooky's screen as we were stopped outside a hardware store on William Street, deciding where to go next. A few runners trotted here and there, but the street was mostly empty. Hooky put her iPad away, and I hummed the bike up toward the mouth of the tunnel. The entire thing was manned by two porky male beat cops who leaned, side by side, against a squad car flashing the red-and-blues up over the tunnel walls. I stopped the bike beside them and lifted my visor.

"Any dropouts?"

"Not that we've seen." One of the cops identified me as a detective. He was straight-backed, looking up and down the tunnel lined with red plastic barriers to keep people off the gutters. The other cop was picking his nails.

"No one's approached us."

"We might have a runner down in this area," I said. I turned as I heard a dull thumping start up somewhere close by, probably a car going over the top. "One of you run up top, see if you can spot anything."

The alert cop dashed off toward the mouth of the tunnel. The thumping continued. I felt a strange tension in my chest at the sound of it, like a hand was on my heart, squeezing, urging me. Urging me toward what, I didn't know.

"Heron One to Command. We're getting multiple reports of a target sighting up here on Arden Street near Queens Park."

"Archer to Command. Reject that call, please. I started a game of telephone."

Eden sounded tired. I sat listening, one hand on the bike, looking behind me at Hooky. She was listening to the muffled voices coming through my helmet, squinting as she tried to pick out the words.

"Heron Two to Command. I've got runners panicking up here. Arden and Bronte."

"Command, Heron One and Two. I've got backup on its way to you. Bronte and Tamarama units respond."

There was no response from Eden. It was possible she couldn't get through the chatter, the eastern suburbs unit radios now alive on every frequency as cars rushed to the top of Arden Street. I lifted one foot off the ground, straightened the bike, and felt Hooky wrap her arms around my waist.

I stopped. The thumping had stopped. Hooky jostled me around the ribs with her arms.

"Let's go, dickhead."

"Hang on," I said. I let her take the weight of the bike. A weird, queasy sensation had come over me, half the light-headedness that comes after too many skipped meals and half the misery of a bad hangover, the sensation that something is wrong. I was looking at the entrance to the tunnel when the thumping started again. It was so faint I hardly heard it above the rush of cars overhead.

I ripped off my helmet, ran into the dark alcove beneath the glowing green exit sign, and hit the iron crossbar with both hands. The door swung open six inches and thumped into a figure on the ground. All my muscles tensed at once. There was pure darkness before me. All the emergency lights were out.

"Amy! Amy! Amy!" I howled over my shoulder, saw her drop the bike like it was made of cardboard. She leapt over it. The cop with the nail obsession stood at the hood of the patrol car. I shoved the door open, pushing the soft, limp thing behind it sideways, and slipped into the dark. I drew my gun and peered into the murky red and blue of the stairwell. Amy slid into the stairwell with me. She fell on the body on the ground, gathering her arms and pulling the woman backward, into the light cast by the doorway. I rushed up the stairs, gun drawn, ears pricked. There was no one there. I could feel the emptiness of the space around me. No light came from the exit door above. I sprinted back down the stairs.

"She's alive." Hooky's voice in the dark was high, thin. "Help me. Help me! She's alive."

Beyond the door, I could hear the two beat cops calling for backup. I knelt in the dim light and looked at the crushed figure before me. A tiny plastic tube crunched under my knee, and I groped in the dark, felt the spike, the wetness. A dart—still full, it seemed. I looked at the victim's swollen lips moving in a bloodied face. I wiped dampness from the woman's eyes with both hands. There was no telling how old she was. One eye was already swollen shut.

"Face," she said. Her hands were on my hands, trying to touch her face. "Hard face."

"It's all right," I said. I was stammering, almost crying with terror and anger. "You're all right, baby. Your face is all right."

She passed out in my arms.

Eden didn't follow the victim to St. Vincent's with Frank. It wasn't her scene. He was the one to do the coddling and worrying—she would direct the police operation to wind down after the festival. The cordons and checkpoints she set up after the victim was found in the Cross City Tunnel proved useless, of course. By the time the sound of Frank's bike had spooked the killer, the person had run—and the kind of running the killer was doing was the most important of his or her life. Eden knew that kind of terror, the electric flight of a hunter being pursued. Bodily limitations meant nothing. It was instinctive—escape or perish.

At 3:00 A.M. she returned home, shut the door of her apartment, and breathed for the first time without obstruction, the strange tightening of her throat muscles happening whenever she was in charge. She went straight to the bath, slipped beneath the steaming water, and dragged the rack at the end of the tub toward her. For an hour or so, she clacked away at the keys of her laptop in the candlelight, sipping at a single glass of cold Moscato, now and then licking the beads of condensation from the side of the bulbous glass. When her individual officer report was finished, she moved to the bed and filled in her operations overview report, an advisory report to the media, and updated the case log on the police intranet. When the sun began to peek beneath the heavy red curtains across the balcony door, she shut the silver device and fell asleep.

It was dark beneath the curtains when she woke. Having a very expensive bed, with expensive sheets and covers, Eden always slept like the dead. But waking was always difficult, and she was often forced to throw off the sheets and let the cool of the dark room prick at her naked skin to bring her to consciousness. She took the phone from the side of the bed and read through Frank's text messages.

2:22 A.M. Victim is Fiona Ollevaris, 28. Some bad facial fracturing/broken ribs/minor strangling but no brain damage. Coma natural at this stage. Will update. FYI last thing she said to me was "hard face." Any ideas on that one?

6:47 A.M. No movement yet. Family blubbering everywhere. Media.

12:12 P.M. Family says victim is MMA fighter. What??? Picked the wrong runner! Checking hospitals for injuries in case perp comes in.

2:00 P.M. Induced coma for facial surgery.

4:14 P.M. Hard face hard face hard face hard face I'm going nuts here. Any thoughts? U there?

Eden stretched, yawned, and rolled out of the bed. She pulled on her clothes and threw open the curtains, looked at the orange-lit night. Lovers walking along the sandstone wall across the street, arm in arm. A bus roaring past almost drowned out the sound of knocking at her door. Eden padded across the cold tiles and looked at the monitor next to the intercom, a pinhole she'd installed beside the outer handle for those rare cases, like now, when someone had slipped in the front door without buzzing. The visitor waiting there made a small wave of heat sweep over her body, the instinctive sizzle of nerves rushing to their edge. She opened the door a crack.

"Hi," Amy said.

"Can I help you?"

"Yes," Amy said. Eden remembered all the times Frank had bugged her about how she greeted people. Pleasantries seemed a waste of borrowed time.

She let the teen in the dusty purple boots into the apartment and shut the door. She went to the kitchen, putting the marble island between the girl and herself. She recognized this as her first survival-mode strategy. Why had she flipped into survival mode? She found herself opening the fridge without knowing why, taking out a bottle of milk.

"Coffee? Tea?"

Eden wasn't even sure she had any tea. She heard the girl ease onto one of the stools on the other side of the island, drop her shoulder bag on the floor. There were knives in a block to the girl's right. Eden added this to the calculations hurrying through her mind.

"No, neither. Thanks."

"Did you go to the hospital with Frank?"

Keep the conversation on your terms, until you know the motive for the visit, then decide whether or not you'll allow the original reason for the visit to be addressed. Everything was about control. The conversation. The environment. The available tools. Eden opened a cupboard beneath the sink and took out a spray bottle, ran a cloth under the water as though preparing to mop up a recently noticed spill. She gave a couple of sprays, mopped at the invisible spot.

Why was she so paranoid? She paused by the sink and closed her eyes. Amy might just be trying to hold on to the Parks Strangler case while Frank was tied up, and may have gotten the message, however untruthful, however moronic, that Eden saw her as a companion until things were up and running again. Eden couldn't recall even the most subtle of indications she might have given the girl over the last few days that would inspire the idea that she was friendly. She'd mostly ignored Frank's weird little fangirl. Or so she thought.

"No. No, I hung around after the ambos got there for a little while and then I went home." The girl coughed. Eden put the kettle on. "We need to talk, though."

Eden turned, the spray bottle and cloth in hand, and looked at the girl's short blond prickles. It was an odd look. Her pale cream skin lent itself naturally to the expected striking black Asian hair framing her high cheekbones and chocolate eyes. The current style was new-recruit military, but she'd bleached it hard, so that it was almost snow-white.

Short blond hair.

The girl held Eden's eyes. Defiant.

"Out with it, then," Eden said.

The girl drew a breath and nibbled her bottom lip, just once, refusing to back away from the cliff edge she had crept to. When she spoke, the words tumbled out, one after the other, a series of gunshots.

"I know that you're Morgan Tanner."

Eden's mouth was dry, denying any verbal response. She found herself smiling, licking her dry lips. She hadn't thought it would be this easy, the solution to the problem of the woman who attacked Hades. It was terrifyingly easy. The mouse had wandered right into the cat's basket.

"Oh," Eden said. She looked at the floor. "That's interesting."

Amy opened her mouth to reply, as Eden anticipated

she would, and in those precious microseconds that she was inhaling to make her response, Eden lifted the spray bottle and pulled the trigger, saturating the girl in trichloromethane. Eden wasn't a chloroform user in any of her nighttime games—she found the practice a little unfair. But when push came to shove, a home-made cocktail of the stuff in an easy dispenser was a must for her household. She wandered around the kitchen island as the girl coughed and spluttered, wiping at her nose and eyes, the wooden stool tumbling and splitting the air as it hit the ground. A couple more puffs and the girl was on her knees.

"Wait, wait, wait!"

Eden gave the girl another good spray and watched her fall, listened to the satisfying *clunk* of the back of her head on the tiles.

Waiting for Fiona Ollevaris to wake up was like watching one of those time-lapse documentaries where a camera is set up over the carcass of a dead rabbit, and all the little creatures are captured rushing in, taking little pieces, and scuttling away quicker than the eye can follow. I sat by her in the curtained-off section of the trauma ward at St. Vincent's and observed many creatures coming and going, the doctors and nurses who monitored her vitals, poked and prodded at her, put things in her and took things out, while she lay swaddled in bandages from the neck up.

Forensics people came and photographed her injuries, took swabs from her scraped knuckles, picked and bottled skin and blood cells from beneath her fingernails, measured her abrasions and marked things down on evidence forms. Media people came and were pushed back by police officers and hospital staff like waves crashing on a breakwall.

Her family members arrived one by one and stood around—the older brother first, an awkward man who wanted to pace with his arms folded. The mother and sister came next, sobbing women, who seemed to want to smother me with affection for my role in her rescue by way of coffees and baked treats from the downstairs café. Then came the father, who took up residence at my side as a kind of silent tribute, following me like a long-faced dog when I went out to make phone calls and send texts.

When they took Fiona off to surgery, the family stood around in the empty space her bed had occupied and talked about her, as though they'd not been able to in her unconscious presence. I learned she was an amateur mixed martial arts fighter who'd had a couple of bouts with other girls her size. That probably explained the skin under the nails, the blood all over the walls of the fire escape, patterns of hands I'd glimpsed in the flashlight beams as the paramedics attended to Fiona. It explained the thumping I'd heard—the scuffle while Fiona was being strangled, a hold she knew how to get out of and was pretty close to getting out of when I arrived on my police bike with Hooky. The mother berated the father about his one-time aversion to Fiona taking up the sport, as though she'd always known somehow that the skill would come in handy one day when a serial killer struck their daughter in the middle of a public running festival. He didn't reply. I guessed they were divorced.

All the while, as I was sitting there on the stool I'd nabbed from the nurse's station, Fiona's words plagued me. *Hard face*. Was she talking about the killer's face? It was a strange message to communicate, if she meant to tell me what the killer looked like so that I could identify him or her in my suspect pool. I was looking for someone stern? Emotionless? Someone old—deeply lined and weathered? Fiona's father and brother had pretty hard faces. That didn't help. I'd have been better off knowing for sure if the killer was male or female. What color their hair was. What ethnicity, age.

Was she talking about her own face? She'd been *touching* her own face when she said it. Was she telling me the assault she'd suffered at the hands of the killer wouldn't break her, wouldn't destroy her beauty—she had a hard face? That was also a bit of a strange thing to say to your rescuing cop on the edge of impending darkness, if it was what she'd meant. From the pictures her mother had shown me, Fiona didn't have a hard face at all. She was a pretty, soft-looking girl, an oval-faced beauty with long brunette curls she kept swept up in a high ponytail when she was fighting. She had big lips and a generous smile. There was nothing hard about her, I imagined, except for her right hook. I knew that from all the skin she'd taken off her knuckles in the struggle. She'd gone right down to the bone.

The day dragged on. I drifted into a languid state. I needed something to do with my hands and people kept bringing me treats—everybody's favorite cat under the table, lolling on its side, snapping up sardines. It was not a good situation. About four in the afternoon, I was so frustrated with the "hard face" problem I was talking to myself, staring at the floor.

"Hard face," I murmured. "Hard . . . face."

"She's got the same plastic surgeon that Renee Kelly had after the bus accident," Fiona's mother was telling her father. "He did such a good job. You'd never know."

"What bus accident?"

"Bus swiped her off the side of the road while she was waiting on George Street. She was mincemeat, apparently."

"Who's Renee Kelly?"

"The singer. Renee Kelly. God, you're old."

Hard face. I turned my paper coffee cup around and around in my hands. It was stone cold. *Hard face.* *Hard face.* Fiona had had a lot of blood in her mouth.

Maybe I'd only *heard* "hard face." Maybe it was something else.

I felt my heartbeat quicken. I watched the couple beside me as they argued.

Hard race. Hard pace. Hard chase.

I needed to be systematic. Fiona's mother's sigh was like a steam train. I could almost see her breath.

Ard face. Bard face. Card face. Dard face. Eard Face. Fard face. Gard face. Hard face.

I chewed my fingernails. They tasted like butter.

Quard face. Rard face. Sard face.

Scarred face.

I stood. My coffee cup fell to the floor.

The voices came first. Eden's, and what sounded like that of an old man, but Hooky couldn't have been sure she wasn't dreaming. She opened one eye and caught a glimpse of the floor upon which she lay before her vision blurred. Tiles. Mismatched, laid in a complicated pattern that somehow accommodated them all, bathroom tiles with wave patterns and broken pieces of kitchen tile, ornate burnt gold tiles with upraised filigree. A pair of legs was near her. The voices came to her ears in bumbling tones, the words tripping over each other, sliding on top of each other, impossible to discern in order.

". . . really, really stupid."

Her hearing clarified, all at once, as though her ears had popped. She sighed through her nose, tried to moan through the duct tape on her lips. An animal came toward her—she felt the wetness of its nose in her ear, on her cheek, its hot breath against her nostrils. There were whiskers brushing her eyelashes.

"Jimmy," the old man said.

The animal disappeared. Hooky tried to move, but her fingers were numb, and strangely distant from where she expected them to be. They were at the small of her back and bunched together. She shifted her cheek against the cold tiles.

"'Asian' would have been the very first thing I said," the old man was complaining. "You'd have asked me,

'What did she look like?' and I'd have said, 'Well, she was Asian' straight up."

"I guess I don't think as racially as you do."

"Don't be smart."

"Give me a break," Eden snapped. "We're looking for a petite woman with short blond hair who knows who I am. This one turns up at my place and spills her guts. What did you expect me to do? Turn her away? You're telling me I should have expected there to be two—"

"Where are her things?" the old man asked.

"Here."

Hooky heard something slide across the floor. She was losing consciousness again. The animal, whatever it was, was near her, one golden-brown paw visible, tendons straining as the animal shifted.

"Got any spare spots?" Eden asked.

"I've always got something."

Hooky slept. The sleep was so delicious, so welcoming, that only the pain in her neck and shoulders as she was dragged along the ground drew her out of it. When she became aware of the T-shirt bunching up at her back and her arms sliding in the dirt, she was snapped into a consciousness so complete she could feel every injury she had endured in the last few hours, from bruises on her legs she must have gotten being loaded into the trunk of Eden's car, to marks on her wrists and ankles from the duct tape. Hooky twisted, tried to look around her, but all she saw were strange black mounds, some of them towering three times her height, strangely shaped silhouettes with spikes, bumps, ridges. She was in some kind of wasteland. The sour smell of rotting garbage assaulted her. She looked down and saw Eden dragging her by the left cuff of her jeans.

Hooky kicked. Eden turned and grabbed both ankles, held on as the girl struggled.

"Don't be stupid," she said.

They stopped by a hole in the earth. Hooky squirmed, caught a glimpse of the old man leaning on a cane, a squat being with scruffy gray hair. A terrifying creature hovered by his side, like the skeleton of a dog reanimated, the eyes bulbous and black. Hooky looked at the neat edge of the hole, the pile of trash lying beside it, the great yellow excavator squatting behind the pile, ready to shove the tires, bags, pieces of lumber into the black cavern dug in the earth. She felt a wave of nausea ripple through her insides and shudder in her throat. Her face was burning, damp with terror, the sweat coming from nowhere and drenching her clothes, making dirt tickle on her cheeks and neck.

"No, no, no, no, no," she moaned. She tried to twist, to look up at Eden's face. Her moaning rose to a scream. "No! No! No!"

Eden grabbed Hooky's shoulder and rolled her into the pit.

I called the Parramatta headquarters while I ran through the parking lot behind St. Vincent's hospital, huffing my way down the concrete ramps. Trying to direct Gina through my desk in the bull pen was excruciating. For a receptionist at one of the biggest law enforcement establishments in the country, she's got no ability to zero in from the big picture.

"I don't know. There's stuff everywhere!"

"It's a photocopy of a newspaper article. I would have just dropped it somewhere there on the surface."

I heard drawers opening and closing. I reached my car and got inside, my shirt clamping to my back and sides with sweat. Paper rustled on the other end of the phone.

"There's a coffee mug here with mold in it."

"It's a forensics experiment. Part of an investigation."

"Right."

"Keep looking."

"New laws sought after high-profile surgery mishap?"

"That's the one," I gasped, my heart thundering in my neck, half from the run, half from the exhilaration of the chase. "Read it to me."

"'The state government has called upon federal leaders to impose regulations to curb the growing number of young Australians seeking cheap cosmetic surgery overseas,'" Gina read. "'The move comes as reports arise that Tara Harper—'"

"Tara Harper," I said. "Did it say what kind of surgery she had?"

"It just says 'a great number at once,'" she said. "Are you onto something, Frank?"

"I'm not sure," I said. "Maybe. Get me everything you can on the Harper girl."

I had a team assembled just down the street from the Harper house by the time the sun set, eight or nine Kevlar-clad specialists, two of them women, standing around a squad car tucked behind a huge fig tree. Cars took the roundabout near us slowly, heads turning, before pulling onto Lang Road, running alongside the park itself. The yawning sandstone gated entrance to a car-lined hill was across the road from number seven. The house was a gigantic cream mansion that could easily have been divided into two profitable apartments, the ornate front garden keeping cousin with the landmark across the road by lining the property with sandstone and iron. White blackout curtains were drawn over the French doors of all four balconies, and the only thing moving on the property was a sickly-looking ginger cat who had taken up residence on the wall at the side of the house to watch the raid.

Standing on the hood of my car, I directed two of my team to the rear of the property. This involved barging through other people's houses and commandeering their back porches so we could see if there was a view into the house from there. When these two were in place, I received a report that the rear of the house was all curtained as well. A garage sat behind the property, accessed by a narrow driveway down the right-hand side of the house, but one of the agents in the back spotted a padlock and chain on the front of it.

Next I sent two agents to the front of the house, having had them don jackets over their vests. After an initial walk-by, they reported that nothing stirred. By now we'd garnered plenty of neighborly attention. A woman stood on her step with a couple of children, describing our operations into a mobile phone while the little ones pointed and gaped. It was not an uncommon reaction. People who spot a police operation in their street will invariably try to get close to it, and if they can't get any closer than they are, will report it, sharing the experience with their friends, family, sometimes the media. Almost as though she'd heard my thoughts, another housewife burst out of the house next door and jogged through the front gates, up to the porch, to join her friend for all the drama.

"All right," I told my remaining team of four, "I'm going to get those two to do a knock. You two take the sides, you two go in at the front."

They rushed off. I gave the two walkers the command to knock on the front door. When no one answered, I gave it a few seconds, then sent them in. I'd once been one of those hot-cheeked officers at the back of the raid team, wondering what was behind the closed door, bellowing down the empty halls. Now I was too important for that. My "forensically trained mind" was put to better use elsewhere, and only the "grunts" were allowed to do the front-line work, where they might brush up against danger. I missed being a grunt. It was exciting.

The two housewives on the porch had a better view of the front door than I did. When the team busted through the door, they clapped. I spotted a couple of teenagers by a tree on the other side of the park gates. One was filming the scene with her phone.

I'd learned all I could about Tara Harper while I got approval for the raid, both from what Gina phoned in over the next hour and from my own searches on my phone. There wasn't much about the girl online. She had no social media presence whatsoever, which was strange. No tried-and-failed Twitter account, blog, job-seeker profile—so far as I could tell, she'd never had a job. There wasn't a picture of the girl anywhere—not even on a memorial page dedicated to her father, set up by the company he'd worked for.

Her mother, a stunning blonde with perfect cheek-bones, was pictured frequently on society websites. Whippet-thin and eagle-eyed, she never smiled fully—she'd discovered her perfect angle for the camera and worked out a half smile that made her look both pow-erful and coy, and she stuck with it. She'd been a sports model in her later teen years, and then she'd met her sugar daddy and settled down to being a mother—which seemed to mean acting on the boards of chari-ties, drinking champagne, shopping, and going to premieres.

She ran. A lot. Half the paparazzi shots of her were snapped for "Celebrities Without Makeup," cheek-bones exaggerated as she inhaled, mouth a supple O. Even makeup-free, Joanie Harper was what I would have called a "honey." She was fantasy material. A vi-sual feast of human genes at their fittest and fairest. I didn't know what kind of surgery her daughter had sought in Thailand—all that was bottled up in media privacy laws—but I couldn't understand, if she shared even a portion of her mother's genes, why she'd sought any at all.

I was struck by the smell of the house, the shut-in stink of molds and accumulated dusts, carpets that needed airing out, and food, somewhere, that had gone off. Dead flower water, perfume reaching through stink. The place was immaculate, and gave the impression that nothing ever moved. The signs of life were missing: keys, newspapers, letters—pens that had been set where they were used. There were no magnets on the fridge and no utensils in or around the sink. When I opened the kitchen cupboards, I found no plates.

All the plates, it turned out, were in the attic room. The specialist team members called me straight there. I saw the top of Ruben's head from the stairs. He was lying as though a gust of wind from the windows had blown him right over, but the window was shut now and the curtains were drawn. I ordered the team out of the room and stood in the doorway so as not to disturb anything and looked in.

Ruben had been stabbed a bunch of times in the chest, which for a second made me wonder if I hadn't just stumbled on an isolated murder, rather than found the Parks killer. The Parks killer had never penetrated skin, which for the novice doesn't sound like a substantial advance in technique. It is, however. There's a big difference between strangling and stabbing—the bloodlessness is the main thing, but the real distinction is in effort.

It's difficult to stab someone. There are all sorts of things in the way. Clothes and ribs and, usually, the person's arms as they grab and flail and try to stop you. People make awful noises when they're stabbed. They wheeze and cough and gurgle and scream—they panic and run around. Until this murder, Tara, if she was the Parks Strangler, had been dealing with already half-subdued victims, bashing in faces close-fisted before fitting her hands around necks almost premade for the job.

Crouched at Ruben's head, I turned it with the tip of my pinkie finger. The face was barely touched—she'd knocked him down and gone for it. When I peeled his wet shirt back from his chest, I saw the wounds were many and shallow. A surprise attack, meant to be over quickly.

I didn't linger on Ruben for long. I was half listening to the specialist team commander giving an all-units alert for the suspect. We had her name, but the commander gave a pause when it came to description. We didn't know what Tara looked like. She would be flagged if she used her credit card, any transport tickets, or any cars registered in her name, but from all indications she didn't have any of those things.

While I listened to the team members trying to come up with points to look out for to broadcast to our colleagues, I walked into the attic room and beheld the display around me. The thousands of defaced faces, the mesmerizing Joanie Harper in all her stony beauty. It was a visual punch. The crowded faces all seemed to howl at once, a noise I could hear in my brain, an angry, despairing noise, the wail animals make in the final grisly seconds of being eaten alive. In this room full of moldy plates, Tara had erected an inescapable monument in which, multiplied infinitely, her mother howled at her, squealed—the hateful, accusatory pleading of a mother at a bad child.

My Googling in the car before the raid had told me that Joanie Harper had slipped peacefully away over a couple of bottles of wine and some sleeping pills. It was so gentle, so easy, that the coroner hadn't been able to determine if it was suicide or not.

I had the feeling, standing there, that Joanie's delicate exit from life hadn't been what her daughter wanted.

Hooky hit the ground with her shoulder and rolled twice. Her body took control as the terror overcame her, flattening against the bottom of the grave, a strange carpet of damp earth and rotting detritus, now and then the hard, sharp edge of a buried toothbrush, a sliver of plastic, the rim of a can. The grave had been dug neatly into the already acidic, degrading layers of waste, and as she lay panting short breaths, she felt bursts of bladder-clenching horror as Eden walked around the grave and mounted the huge backhoe. Hooky knew she should move, should make a last shot at life, but her body was paralyzed at the shuddering visions of the darkness and pressure that would come in seconds, the sickening weight of the dirt and rubbish as it piled onto her.

The machine started with a hideous roar. Hooky heard the clattering and grinding of the rubbish and soil as it moved, and the initial tumble of objects onto her legs was so gentle it made her sick. This was how her death would be. Gentle and slow and smothering, an excruciating fight against rock-solid limbs that would not struggle against the tape, that would not roll her, that would not shift toward the edge of the pit, out of sheer animal fright at what was being done to her. She was powerless to do anything but let out a long howl through her nose, her teeth biting down against her tongue as the rubbish rolled over her.

The backhoe stopped. Its engine cut, neatly and

clearly, leaving ringing silence in its wake. Somewhere beyond her grave, Hooky could hear dogs barking. She lay and shook against the dirt and listened to the night.

It took a long time for her limbs to respond. Only her legs were covered. She turned her face against the ground and saw that the pile at the side of the grave, the weight that would have smothered her, was still assembled. What had happened? Had the engine stalled? She curled in a ball and wept hard, the sobs now and then breaking into panicked snuffles that racked her entire frame, awakened what was surely cracked ribs down her side.

She was feeling pain. That was good. If she could bring herself out of shock, she could perhaps push the ordeal toward whatever end was meant for it, whether it was the starting up of the engine again and her smothering, choking death or, and she could not yet imagine it, perhaps herself climbing out of the grave. She rolled onto her good side and groped at the ground with her fingers, picked up a square of some ancient discarded thing, poked and pricked at the tape between her wrists. When the sobbing interrupted her bid for freedom, she was forced to stop. She tossed away the square when the back of her wrist brushed against something better, a sharp twist of glass. She broke the bindings and tore her wrists apart.

Hooky grabbed at the gag. The sounds, when she released them, were repetitive gasps and cries. She rolled and pulled the tape from her legs, tears pouring down her filthy cheeks.

It seemed an age getting up the slope of rubbish to the top of the eight-foot-deep grave. By the time she scrambled onto the living earth again, her crying had subsided to a tremor in all her limbs. Her teeth chattered. There, some yards away from the grave, stood Eden and the old man. The skeleton dog was there, wagging its brown tail enthusiastically. Eden looked bemused, her arms folded as she surveyed Hooky where she slumped against the ground.

"Are you sure that took long enough?" Eden drawled.

"Imogen. Imogen . . ."

"We know," Eden said. "We worked that one out by going through your things."

Hooky scrambled to a crouch and surveyed her injuries. She was sure both wrists were at least sprained, if not fractured. Her right foot was numb. The shaking would not stop. She wondered if she would vomit in front of them both.

"You stupid bitch," Hooky said. Her voice was a hellish rasp. "You stupid fucking bitch."

The old man laughed, turned his cane so it dug a hole in the ground.

"She's got you worked out," he told Eden.

"Why didn't you kill me?" Hooky howled. She looked at the hole in the ground and felt hot tears at the corners of her eyes. "Why did you—"

"You're a child," Eden said. She jerked a thumb toward the old man. "This one here's got a sort of . . . philosophy about it."

"I came to warn you."

"I realize that," Eden said. She gestured to the grave. "Now we're even."

"We're not even," Hooky snarled. "We're not done."

"Oh no, this isn't over, no. I completely agree," Eden said. "This grave will always be here waiting for you. You'll never, ever be much farther from where you were just a couple of minutes ago. No farther than a heartbeat. You should remember what it was like down there. Cement it in your mind. Because I'll be keeping it warm for you, little girl."

Hooky breathed. She didn't doubt the older woman as she stood silhouetted against the orange sodium lamps that lit the landfill, the trash mountain range behind her, an apocalyptic wasteland of discarded things.

"My parents were murdered, too," Hooky said. She scrunched her eyes against the childish sound of her own voice. Her trembling hand tapped, flat, against her own chest. "I came to you because I understand you."

Eden twitched at the words. Something in the woman looked hurt, Hooky thought, or frightened. It was only an instant of vulnerability, a flash of some past assault, the breeching of the walls by an enemy long defeated. The woman laughed to cover it, but Hooky saw a glimmer of that fear remaining in Eden's eyes. A nervous curiosity. Her lips sneered, but the rest of her beheld Hooky with the interest a lion takes in the shimmer of movement in the grass near his pride.

"Stop talking shit," Eden snapped. She jutted her chin toward the hill from where they'd come. "Get up, and get out of here."

"No," Hooky said. Even the old man laughed at that one. She tried to unlock her gritted teeth. "I said we weren't done."

Caroline Eckhart had my number from the obscene amount of times I'd tried to ring her to get her to call off the running festival. When I saw her number flash up on my cell phone at the Harper house crime scene, I was sure she was calling me to offer some bullshit apology couched in a bunch of sidelong assertions that it was all my fault.

I was holding a coffee someone had brought me in one hand, and the phone in the other, and Ruben Esposito's dead head was at my feet. All around me, forensics specialists snapped pictures, dabbed fingerprint powder, laid out little measurement stickers and exhibit numbers. I'd been waiting for Eden to get back to me, or for one of the squads to tell me they'd pulled over a white van, perhaps the one that I was hoping was missing from the empty garage. When Caroline called, I was overcome with distaste for her and couldn't imagine her helping me comb my hair, let alone helping me solve this case.

So, I canceled the call. It's possible I contributed to what ended up happening to her when I pressed that button. I was lucky, when she called a few seconds later, that curiosity overcame my prejudice against her and I answered.

"Detective Be—"

The call ended. I looked at my phone. She'd sounded out of breath, like she was on a run, though her one and a half words were in a higher octave than I was used to her speaking in. I felt a little queasy and called her back. The phone was off.

I stood thinking about the voice, running it over and over in my mind. *Detective Be—. Detective Be—.* Why would she call me in the middle of a run? Caroline Eckhart only has time to call nobodies when she's improving her blood oxygen saturation capacity and when she's on the john? Sounded about right. What hadn't sounded right was the background. She hadn't sounded like she was outside. Was she on her treadmill? Why hadn't I heard the machine, thrumming away as she plodded toward perfection?

I sucked air between my teeth, clicked my tongue against the roof of my mouth. Was I prepared to leave my current crime scene to make sure *Caroline Eckhart*, of all people, hadn't fallen down the stairs while she was on the phone to me and was not now lying in a pile of taut, cellulite-free limbs at the bottom of a fire escape somewhere? I tried calling her three more times. Then I gave the biggest sigh in human history, drawing the attention of three forensics freaks nearby.

"I'll be back," I said. Of course, I didn't let anyone know where I was going.

Caroline lived near the end of the Woolloomooloo Finger Wharf, arguably Sydney's most envied address. There was nowhere else a creature like Caroline could live—she needed to demonstrate the success, the prestige, the perfection that her public image was all about, so it was here that she took interviews with magazine journalists, doing crunches under the gaze of the cityscape. It was here that she shot "Caroline at Home" spreads for *Woman's Day*, lounging on her pristine white leather lounges, both she and the furniture hard as stone and constructed with all the care of a master sculptor. She breakfasted here on egg-white-and-kale omelets with her neighbors—the few ridiculously powerful shock jocks and Hollywood actors Australia boasted of—when they were home.

Two suited goons at the door stopped me as I tried to enter the huge open cavern of the wharf, once a wool factory and a migrant processing center for those arriving during the world wars. I flashed my badge and the goons parted. I glanced back and saw the valet scrambling for his phone. The media would be on speed dial, the apartment I accessed noted for the next edition of *TheTalk*.

It was eleven. When I pounded on the door of Caroline's fifth-floor apartment, a man in the apartment next to hers popped out of his front door, a weathered old zombie-creature with wispy white hair. He shouted some abuse. I glanced at him, still knocking.

"Caroline!" I smacked the door with an open palm, the sound echoing about the huge hall. "Yo! Car-o-line!"

I stood at the door and called her phone another three times. I tried the door and found it locked. Then I turned and started to leave, the old guy glaring at me with his sagging lizard eyes and snarling wet lips. I'd only just turned on my heel when I heard a double thump from inside Caroline's apartment.

I drew my gun, and the neighbor clambered inside his apartment.

In my policing career, I've kicked down about three doors. Two of them were very successful—dramatic knockdowns that got me plenty of cheers at the station afterward. On the third, I went crooked at the last second and sprained my ankle. I knew the old man was at least listening, so I didn't want him to hear me (a) having to take multiple shots at the door, or (b) howling in agony after I'd snapped my Achilles tendon. In the three seconds I spent preparing, I reviewed in a flash all of my academy training on doors and their tenuous relationship with feet. And then I gave it my best shot.

The door slammed open, knocking over a huge ornate vase, which shattered on the spotless cream tiles. I was overwhelmed, momentarily, with self-admiration.

All the lights were on. I stood in the doorway and dialed the Officer Assistance number, then put my phone back in my pocket. My colleagues would triangulate me via GPS and send a team, probably the same team who had crawled all over Tara Harper's house at Centennial Park. I actioned my weapon and listened. I didn't listen long before a deep, gravelly voice said "Close the door."

I did as I was told. A small hall on the left led to what was probably a bathroom door, and to the right opened onto a huge living area. The adjacent wall, all glass, looked out over the navy ships docked at Garden Island. A frigate was across from us, lit gold with a hundred yellow lights. To the left, another glass wall looked out over the black harbor. I had seconds to take in the view before I assessed the scene in front of the huge balcony.

Caroline Eckhart lay like a rag doll on the floor by a weight machine. I could see that she'd taken some good knocks to the nose and forehead. Her lip was split and her forehead was working on a huge blue egg right near her hairline. She was lying as though on a bed with her head on a pillow that was much too high, although the pillow was a set of black steel weights resting at the bottom of a pulley exercise machine. On either side of her face were two chrome bars, which kept the weights in line as they slid up and down. Above her head were suspended six weights all in a row, a solid block of steel I guessed weighed probably about sixty pounds. The cable pulling the weights ran up through a pulley, down through another pulley, and up into the hand of a woman standing by the machine.

The Sydney Parks Strangler was indeed a woman, but I only knew that because I was standing twenty feet from her and I'd heard her voice. From the shape of her in the black tracksuit, there was no telling her sex. The hood was pulled up around her face, so that I could only see two twinkling eyes in a mass of black shadow, and a widely stretched mouth. She stood with one hand by her side and one arm outstretched, fist gripping the rubber handle of the steel cable holding the weights.

"Step any closer and I'll let go," she said.

"Okay," I said.

"Put the gun down."

I did. I even kicked it away a little, out of good faith, so that the weapon slid under a side table stacked with dozens of Caroline Eckhart's ten-week weight loss program DVDs. The woman in the hood and I stood in silence, each of us carefully examining options. I was trying to recall a list of poorly written procedures I'd seen on a whiteboard more than a decade earlier in an overheated classroom in Goulburn while the crisis-negotiation specialist prattled on about hostages he'd rescued over the years.

Step one: Prolong the situation.

Step two: Ensure the safety of the hostages.

Step three: I couldn't remember. I was probably checking out the female recruits.

Step four: Foster a relationship between the hostage-taker and the negotiator, and the hostage-taker and the hostages.

"That weight's going to get heavy in a minute," I said. The wide smile in the hood remained rigid. I was beginning to notice a lopsidedness to it, a kind of menacing Joker quality to its edges that seemed to curl too high, as though the skin from the top had been folded and tucked, and now shadowed that on the bottom. A puppet smile. "Why don't you put it on the hook and we can talk without me worrying about you crushing Caroline's head like a watermelon?"

The woman in the hood laughed. "What a pretty image. The broken edges of a green skull. All that red-pink mush."

"I wouldn't rely on there being *too* much mush in there."

"Interesting tactic. Bad-mouth the victim. Try to relate to me."

"It wasn't intentional." I bit my tongue, felt sweat on my brow but didn't want to make any movements to wipe it away. "She's not my favorite person in the world, but that doesn't mean I want to see her squished."

I took a step closer. The woman took a step back. The cable twanged in the pulley, a sickening sound.

"It's been a long time since I did this," I said, "but I think we're supposed to introduce ourselves first."

"I know who you are."

"Yes, good." I opened my arms. "That saves us time, doesn't it? I'm Detective Frank Bennett—I'll be your hostage negotiator for this evening."

She didn't answer.

"And you're Ms. Harper, I presume."

"So you found Ruben."

"I found everything you left out for me," I said. I was treading in dangerous territory, so I kept my tone friendly. "I think you meant that."

I took a couple of sideways steps, then stepped back the way I'd come. I wanted her to get comfortable with the idea of me moving my feet, perhaps as a nervous gesture, so that I might try to close some of the gap between us without her noticing. I went sideways, and back again, and she didn't shift. I took half a step forward as I spoke. She didn't seem to care. The gap was now nineteen and a half feet, I guessed. Negotiations were always slow.

"Why don't you tell me what you were trying to say, Tara?"

"Why don't you tell me what I was trying to say?" she said. Her tone had changed from amused to annoyed, and I felt my chest tighten. The ability to perform such a seamless emotional change midconversation was not a good sign. Tara was not stable. "You've got me all worked out. You know me. Why don't you tell me more about myself?"

"I didn't mean—"

"'I think you meant for us to find what you left out, *Tara*. I'll be your negotiator, *Tara*. Let's not kill Caroline, *Tara*. Sweety, honey, buddy, baby! Let's be friends, Tara!'"

Her words were snarled, spittle flying off her mismatched lips, but the snarls evolved into a wet laughter so high and full of rage it made my skin tingle. My mouth was bone-dry. I tried to gather some saliva, looked at Caroline. She was really out of it. Her chest inflated and deflated in little shudders that produced soft snores through her open mouth. All she had to do was wake up and slide off the machine. But she wasn't going to. Consistent with every interaction we'd had so far, Caroline was going to be completely unhelpful to me.

"She's beautiful, isn't she?" Tara asked. She was back down to 25 percent of the 100 percent fury I'd seen in her only seconds before, sliding up and down the rage scale the way the weights above Caroline's head slid up and down as Tara adjusted her grip on the handle. I'd been put right back in my box, so I just nodded.

"Isn't it interesting, what's beautiful?" Tara said. The big dark hood probably got the disfigured girl all the way through the foyer and up to Caroline's apartment without garnering attention. But now it had slipped back a little, so that I could see the lower half of her face. Two long scars lined her jaw on either side, perfectly, as though her face was a mask that could be lifted off and set in the palm of the hand. One cheek was bigger than the other. She was looking at Caroline, and I could see that the gap between Tara's nose and mouth had an unnaturally straight slant, as if her nose was stuck on. "Why is she beautiful? Maybe that's how we're supposed to be. Pure. Strong. We're supposed to be born like that, show all those bones and edges. Built for swimming. Sprinting. Climbing. She's Mother Nature's finest work."

Tara crouched down, letting the handle of the weight go with her, the line feeding back into the bottom pulley, the top pulley, lowering the block of pure death that hung above Caroline's head. Tara stroked Caroline's temple with a single finger, found the edge of the bone in the immaculate caramel-brown flesh, and pressed down hard. I snuck a couple more steps sideways, back, and then forward. Seventeen feet.

"If you're not beautiful, you're not natural. You weren't born right."

"Is that what your mother used to tell you, Tara?"

"No," Tara smirked. "She didn't tell me anything. I had to have one of her old friends tell me, at a funeral, when I was a kid. Joanie just told me I was fat. But it wasn't that at all. Not really. All the running and the pinching and the hiding away. It wasn't about fat. It was because I wasn't born right."

She tugged back the hood. One side of her neck was lined with scars, skin bunched directly below the ear as though a seam had torn and torn again and she'd been run over back and forth with some grisly human sewing machine. She was a torn doll. Her black hair was tied back haphazardly in a ponytail, knotted and matted where the ribbon cut into the wavy locks, and I felt the desire to untangle it. To try to fix her. I had a biological longing to try to make her pretty, standing there looking at her. Perhaps I was beginning to understand.

"She met him at a stag night," Tara said quietly. "She and another girl were the entertainment. He wasn't into the whole thing—the show they were putting on. She got talking to him out on the porch. He liked her. He didn't know I was already growing inside her. I'm not sure she knew it herself."

Tara wiped at her scarred lips. Curled a hand against her cheek, a doll in thought. "I wonder what she thought when I was born. All that black hair."

"Tara," I said.

"I wonder if she knew which client it was. I wonder if he knew."

"Tara, what happened to you in Bangkok?" I asked.

"Caroline Eckhart says there's a beautiful person inside you. You've just got to reach in and pull her out," Tara said. She stood, still examining the sleeping beauty on the floor. Her voice rose to a high imitation, a child's teasing. "'Take what you've always wanted! You deserve it! You deserve it! You deserve it!'"

I tried not to shake.

"I thought maybe there was something beautiful inside me. So, I tried to fix myself. I tried to cut away the badness. I was trying to do Joanie's work, search for the beautiful thing in me, but I wanted to do it faster. I was going to be like a peach—when all that useless flesh was removed, there was going to be a seed in there that would grow a new life. A new me."

"That was never going to work," I said.

"No. Because there's no beautiful person inside me. I'm rotten. Joanie thought maybe there was a little version of her in here," she pointed to her chest. "Maybe if she beat hard enough I'd come out." Tara laughed. That crooked smile bunched the loose flesh at the corners of her eyes. "I'd planned to come out, all right. I was going to come out and show her that she couldn't hurt me anymore."

"But you didn't get that chance."

"No. She slipped away from me." Tara squeezed the handle of the weight machine. "Isn't that just perfect? I was going to show Joanie the new me, beautiful on the outside and rotten in the middle. And then . . . then I was going to show her what she looked like on the inside. I was going to give her back all the pain she had given me over the years. And before I could get to her, she slipped away and left me that pretty, pretty corpse."

"Tara."

"She was wearing the pink Chanel dress." Tara's voice dropped to a whisper. "They said she'd looked just like she was sleeping."

I heard sirens in the distance, saw flashes of red and blue between the big ships lining the distant wharf as three squad cars raced down the hill from Potts Point.

Step five: Hear the demands, and make a deal.

"Killing Caroline isn't going to give you what you missed out on with your mother, Tara," I said. "You can't deface Joanie by defacing these women. The world is full of pretty women. Joan Harper is gone, and she'll never feel what you wanted her to feel."

"It might satisfy me for a while, though." Tara let the weight slide up and down. "I might feel full."

I took a couple of steps forward. Tara took the zipper of her jacket with her spare hand and started unzipping. She let the jacket fall to the floor, then loosened her pants. Under her clothes, she was a mess of crooked seams and bubbled, puckered lines, the flesh mismatched and zigzagged as though it had caught in a sewing machine and crinkled. She had no breasts to speak of. No navel. She was a human patchwork doll. She jutted out one hip and then the other. Slid out of the black panties and kicked off her shoes. I could follow all the seams, large and small, where skin grafts had patched flesh that had been cut away, had become infected, had been replaced with fresh skin from here and there. Two great long lines down her thighs marked where a fat-reduction procedure had gone wrong, taking half the leg, leaving two uneven stilts with bulbous knees. Some parts of her were the purple of an old man's veins. I heard the telltale murmurs of the specialist raid team behind the apartment's front door and glanced that way.

"Look at me," Tara said.

"I'm looking," I said.

"This is me," she smiled. She dropped a hip, put her hands up as though modeling for a pageant, a grotesque marionette dancing on a gold lit stage. "This is what ugly looks like."

"Tara, you're not . . ." I took a step forward. I wanted to tell her she wasn't ugly, but that wasn't true. I'd seen what she had done to those runners, and it was as ugly as humanity gets. I'd been in the dark fire-escape stairwell where Tara had tried to end Fiona Ollevaris's life, the lonely parkways where Ivana, Minerva, and Jill had been dumped like trash. There was nothing but ugliness about Tara, and I realized that was what she was trying to tell me. She was an abomination. She watched me realizing this, accepting her message.

"There are plenty of ugly souls in prison," I said. "You must have thought about how well you'd fit there."

"I have thought about it," Tara said. The arm that held the weight was trembling. "I've dreamed about it. It would be just like high school, wouldn't it? But there'd be no cool kids. We'd all be rejects."

"Let me take you, then," I said. I reached out toward her, took a couple more steps. "It's over. Put the handle on the hook."

"I'd be happy there, in a safe little cage?" Tara asked.

"I'm sure you would."

"With all my ugly little friends."

"Tara, put the handle—"

"But I've never been much good at making friends."

Tara let the handle of the weight machine go.

I heard the zipping of the cable in the pulleys over my head as I dove forward on my knees, grabbed the handle as it flew toward the floor. The weights clanked. I fell on my chest, my fingers tangled in the handle and the wire. The team outside must have heard the calamity and rushed the door. There were feet all around me, three sets of hands gripping the wire and taking it from me. I glanced over in time to see them sliding an unharmed Caroline from her place on the weight guillotine. I looked across the floor, out the balcony doors, where Tara was standing with her naked back against the balcony rail.

She gave me a little wave and then curled backward over the rail, her arms and head, and then her shoulders, and then her back arching until she was a perfect curve over the edge. A backward dive into the dark night. A couple of the squad cops grabbed at her, but she'd landed three flights below before they closed their fists on air. I heard the screaming of some rich couple down there on the second-floor balcony as Tara's body crashed through their outdoor dining table.

Outside the Finger Wharf apartments, the trauma team swooped down on everyone except me. I stood in the crowd near Harry's Café Dé Wheels and watched the zombie from the apartment next door to Caroline's being wheeled out of the building on a stretcher, an oxygen mask clamped to his face. Caroline herself was on another stretcher as she was brought to the ambulance, red and blue lights bouncing off her cheekbones for the cameras. Cowper Wharf Road was blocked off, cars being redirected back through the government housing unit and up the street past the Frisco Hotel. There were water police doing laps alongside the navy boats, whose decks were busy with curious sailors.

The four people who'd been having a dinner party on their deck, before it was rudely interrupted by Tara, stood huddled in the ring of commotion, watching the police activity. Two women and two men dressed to the nines, none of them crying, one of the women wrapped about the shoulders in a little fur-lined coat. A cursory glance over the balcony rail at Tara's body told me she'd gone headfirst through a glass outdoor dining set cluttered with mid-dinner bowls and knives and glasses and plates, candles and napkins and bottles of wine. She ended up twisted into an unnatural shape, her head tilted up toward the sky and eyes closed, her naked body covered in food and glass.

I imagined Imogen would see the news report when

I didn't get home as expected, so I called her as I stood there in the night. The phone rang and then went to voicemail. When I looked up, Eden was standing beside me, watching the fray, still wearing that black baseball cap. I didn't know how long she'd been there. She hadn't said a word.

"You're like one of those people who asks if they can help just when the last plate is being dried," I said.

"I wasn't asking to help."

"She's dead," I said. I realized, now that I was talking, that shock was nibbling at me. When you've experienced it before, shock is as tangible and identifiable an experience as the onset of a cold. Usually, my teeth chattered first. Waves of goose bumps ran up and down my arms. "Olympic-grade backflip dive off the balcony."

Eden made a little half-interested noise. I rubbed my arms.

"Come on," she sighed at last. "The ants have got it."

We walked through the crowd past Harry's toward the edge of the cordon. I didn't ask where we were going or why. I was thinking about Eden's propensity to label as "ants" all the police, fire, and ambulance crews who would deconstruct the scene and drag away all the necessary samples, victims, and photographs. It was very good. She was good like that, Eden, with the metaphors. I realized my mind was wandering.

It was a relief to get into the car. Warm in there. I drew out my phone and tried to call Imogen again. She didn't answer, so I sent a text.

I'd assumed Eden was going to take us to Parramatta Headquarters, but she turned right at the end of Cowper Wharf Road and went into the tunnel. I thought she was taking me to North Sydney station—maybe we'd been called there. But before I thought about it again, we were on the Pacific Highway heading north. I wasn't too concerned. Eden was like an autopilot. You didn't have to watch her driving or question her route. She got you where you needed to go like a programmed GPS navigator. The shock wore off, and with all my adrenaline spent, I slumped in the passenger seat with my phone in my lap, only concerned about when Imogen would call me back.

"Where are we going? Are you abducting me?" I stretched and groaned. For once, she gave a little laugh.

"Something like that."

I fell asleep somewhere around Berowra, making a crack about a romantic getaway. Eden drove in the dark in silence, the headlights shining off white tiny bugs and moths that flew into the windscreen. I don't know how I rationalized it. Maybe I thought she was taking me to our next case—we were going to turn up at a parking lot in Gosford where a kid had been found stabbed, or something grisly like that. But I didn't even give it that much thought—I just trusted her, the way a little boy trusts his friend when he turns to the dense brush and beckons, "Come look at this."

I was on the come-down from a major case. All the weight and worry about Tara Harper and who her next victim would be had fallen off me. I'd shelved the case, the way I had all the others in my career, to be dragged out in flashbacks when I was sixty, when I had finally let myself be vulnerable to delayed PTSD and gone nuts, before having to be crammed into a nursing home by whoever I was shacked up with at the time. Maybe Imogen. An old and glamorous Imogen.

When I opened my eyes, we were pulling into the driveway of a large house by a lake. The moon was out, lighting water as still and flat as glass between the pine trees. Distant mountains rippled over the horizon. I guessed we were somewhere around The Entrance. I'd spent my childhood holidays here, throwing blow-up pool rafts off the shore into the tumbling, bumbling surf, being dragged with my holiday friends toward the ocean at what felt to us like breakneck speed. We used to go fishing on this very lake, and when I got out of the car, the wind whistling through the pine trees was something I remembered from that time, a sound I'd heard nowhere else, a high-pitched whisper that rose and fell like a ghoulish song.

All the lights in the house were lit. I followed Eden through the pretty garden, saw beads of dew on the blue flowers by the big oak door as she unlocked it. A stained-glass panel set at eye level in the wood, little blue birds hopping from branch to branch. She led me inside. On the wall by the door was a row of hooks. She put the keys on the only empty one. On others, there were little backpacks and little hats, a girl's pink umbrella. I looked at a family picture by the wall. Two pretty little black-haired kids and their handsome parents, the father a broad-shouldered, dark-eyed man and the mother a whippet-thin waifish type in a starched, collared white shirt. Beside the photograph was hanging a bare white canvas. I frowned at the empty canvas on the wall. Reached out and touched the unprimed material as I passed.

In the living room, more puzzles. The long dining room table was full of glasses and plates and cutlery, as if someone had just been eating there, but there was no food. A big wooden bowl was off-center, empty, where it might have held a salad. There was an empty lasagna tray on a wooden cutting board. Someone had brought their teddy bear to the make-believe dinner. It sat flopped on its side on a chair. Two of the chairs were pushed in, and two were pulled out.

Eden went to the kitchen and ran a hand over the empty counter. She looked at the couches out in the living room. I followed her eyes. The long gray couches sat in an L-shape facing huge windows looking out on the lake, and the cushions on the couches weren't arranged properly. One was on the floor by an open coloring book and pencils. There was a throw rug crumpled in one corner. From where I stood, I could see that half the page of the book was colored in, as though whoever had been working on it had just stood up and left, and was going to be back soon to finish the pink pig and the green turtle.

A family was meant to be here. But the house didn't smell like a family. That's what was missing, I realized, as I was looking at another picture on the wall, a photograph of a woman that wasn't a photograph, but printed on regular paper and framed—an imitation. But the smell—a family house smells of food and toys and damp bathrooms. It smells like laundry powder and farts and rotting fruit left too long at the bottom of school bags. It smells like plants on the kitchen windowsill and perfume and sweet toothpaste. Of chaos. Loving chaos.

This house smelled like nothing. It was a theater set. I knew, somehow, that no one had ever lived here, or if they had, that they were long gone. There was another blank canvas hanging by the entrance to the kitchen. I felt the trembling I'd experienced back in the city begin at my fingertips, but it wasn't shock this time. I'd forgotten all about Tara Harper.

"It took a long time to get it like this," Eden said. She looked at the table, at the empty glasses: two water, two wine. "I pieced it together mostly from crime scene photographs. Some of the things I had to hunt down— the toys in the bedrooms were particularly difficult. Everything went into the trash when they died. There was no one to leave it to."

"What . . ." I cleared my throat, "what is this place?"

Eden's eyes were on the distant lake. The house was secluded. I couldn't see another for miles—at least not one that was lit. Out on the water, a boat sat still as a stone on the surface. It had all the deadness of a painting.

"They came in through the French doors." Eden nodded to a doorway behind me, which led to the side of the house. "We were here, in the living room. Marcus was coloring. I was in my mother's lap. When they heard the glass breaking, they didn't move. You'd think they'd move. In the movies, they'd have got up and grabbed weapons or rushed us out the kitchen door. But my parents weren't heroes. They just sat and waited and watched, as six men came into the house."

My teeth were chattering. I clenched my jaw. Somehow, I'd lost the ability to stand straight, some powerful thing twisting in my stomach until my back started to hunch and my arms started to fold around my middle. I wasn't a hero, either. I never had been. As Eden spoke, I found myself, just like the people she was describing, rooted to the spot in the middle of the house.

"They were still in their seats when they were murdered," she said. She was looking at the couches as though she could see them there, the bodies of her parents. "They'd dragged Marcus and me out to the car by then, so we didn't see it. But we heard it. It all went wrong so quickly. It was over in seconds."

"Tan . . . Tanner," I remembered. "The Tanner family murders."

"I bought the house and I hunted down the crime scene photographs, and piece by piece, I put it all back together," Eden said. Her eyes flickered over the china cabinet against the wall, the crystal glasses inside. A wind chime hanging from the roof guttering just outside the window was still, sheltered from the wind that only seemed to touch in the trees. "I got the pictures from murder sites online. The ones that gather clues. The cutlery in the kitchen is the same. The coverlets on the beds are the same. It's all perfect. The one thing I couldn't replicate were her paintings. I didn't try. She was better than me. Far better."

"Eden," I said. "I—"

"This is the moment they entered," she continued, gesturing to the room. "Everything was just like this. Sometimes I come here and I try to be there, somehow, to stop it. It's impossible. I sit on the floor and I see them coming in, just the way they did, a group of monsters. I see myself screaming. When you're a kid, you always imagine monsters in the singular. You don't expect an army."

I'd glimpsed things about the Tanner family murders across my career, but never sat down to look at the case in detail. People talked about it when there was nothing to talk about, in elevators, in coffee rooms, at Christmas parties. It had fallen from memory into the back corner of cop conversation, and existed nowhere else. Except here. It was perfectly present here. I felt the danger in the room. Knowing what had happened here, I was being infected, drugged, with the terror of the victims. I felt in real danger of being grabbed. I was a child before her.

"You're Morgan Tanner," I said.

"Yes." She smiled a little sadly.

"Why now? Why are you telling me this?"

"Because you wanted us to address this thing between us," Eden said. She went and perched on the back of the couch, her hands between her knees. "And you were right. We needed to address it. It's been too long since you found out what I am. Part of what I am, I suppose. You're almost certain I killed Benjamin Annous. Trying to discover that cost you the woman you loved."

"Don't." My eyes began to sting.

"You deserve to know," Eden said. Her own voice sounded strange. Deeper. Threatening to crack. "I killed Benjamin Annous because he was one of the men who murdered my parents. But I'm responsible for so many more deaths. I'm a hunter. I hunt people like this."

She gestured to the French doors, as though the dead men she spoke of were standing there, frozen in her memory, hands out and reaching for her child self and her brother. Innocent at that time. About to be ruined forever. Eden wiped at her eyes. I'd never seen her like this. She seemed broken, a once perfect machine now rattled, something loose inside, ticking and scraping against its housing as it turned inside her, in need of tightening, replacement, repair. When she stood again, the thing that was broken stopped ticking, and she was that immaculate monster again, her face hardened, eyes shadowed by the cap. Lost to me.

"I like pedophiles," she said. "But I'm diverse. I like the challenge of finding and capturing other skilled hunters. I've killed drug dealers and rapists and violent husbands. I've killed mothers and wives and daughters. I look for their true nature, the predator inside, and I take them down."

I was really shaking now.

"Eden, please stop."

"It's important to me to keep the landscape thinned of monsters like the ones who took my parents. It makes me feel like I have some measure of control back from this time, this moment here, when I lost everything."

I took out my phone and dialed Imogen. I think my body knew what was happening even if my mind wasn't ready to go there yet.

"You have to understand, so one day you can accept what I've had to do."

"Just wait," I stammered. When the call went to voicemail, I fumbled with the phone to dial again. "Just wait a second."

There were tears on my face. I had to swipe at them in order to recognize the figure that emerged from the kitchen, looking behind her briefly to watch the door click closed. Hooky took her place beside Eden, and I looked at the two women before me, helpless for words.

"Imogen found out what I am," Eden said. Her words burned in my ears. "She'd been working on the Tanner case to try to get hold of the reward."

"Please, please, please, please." I ran my fingers through my sweaty hair, dialed and hung up and dialed. "Please no."

"She didn't kill her," Hooky said. I lifted my eyes to the child-woman standing before me. I didn't even ask how Hooky had been brought into this. My little friend. My damaged little genius. "She wanted to, but I said no."

"My new apprentice here has erased all the evidence Imogen gathered," Eden said, looking at Hooky. "The DNA listings have been altered. The registry files have been replaced. All the reports have been adjusted in the necessary way, so that anything Imogen has is useless now. But you know me, Frank. I let the child convince me that you wouldn't be able to handle it if I took Imogen away from you. You wouldn't be able to endure another Martina. But I need assurance. I need to show Imogen that I'm serious."

Eden reached into the back of her jeans and, from her waist belt, drew a gun. It wasn't her service weapon.

"I told Imogen I'd take everything she held dear if she whispered a word of my story to anyone," Eden said, actioning the gun. "She needs to know I mean it."

I felt the impact of the bullets before I heard the sound. Two sharp, hard punches in my midsection, the thumps of a metallic fist that doubled me slightly in the middle. I heard the sound next, two claps of thunder that made my eardrums pump. There was no pain in those first few seconds. I reached down and gripped at my torn T-shirt, not even wet yet. And then I realized I couldn't draw a breath. I'd exhaled hard with the impact. I struggled to pull in air, dropped down to my knees, and steadied myself with a hand against the floor. A sort of a pop, and the air came, and the pain was blinding, limb-crumpling, so that I folded and thumped my head on the floor.

I heard Eden say, "Go, go."

And then both the women were grabbing me, turning me over, gripping me under the arms and knees. My head fell back against Eden's chest. I was looking up at her jaw, her cold predator eyes, as they carried me through the doorway.

The fire-alarm bell sounded, and Jim began to howl. Hades remembered a time, long ago, when he'd heard the sound of a car creeping up the gravel drive as he did now, delivering a new life to him. He hadn't known it at the time, of course. He'd thought his life was in the slow and gentle roll toward stillness. He'd thought the twilight had him, and then there they were, two children for him to raise. To beautiful little killers who needed him, needed his ancient evil wisdom to guide the chaos of their minds.

Eden and Eric had been a surprise for Hades. But this child was not. He'd been expecting her. In fact, she was early.

A storm was flashing on the red horizon, glowing in the chain-link diamonds of the screen door as he wandered down the hall. He opened the door and Jim flew past him, stood on the crest of the hill before his shack, and watched the battered little Kia gripping its way onto the flat yard, parking under the tree. As she opened the car door, the objects hanging in the tree swayed and jangled in the growing winds—cogs and wheels from engines, polished and shining; bottles and chains; some tea cups and tin cans.

Hooky stepped from the car and slung a backpack shaped like a shark over one narrow shoulder. She looked tired. Gold sequined boots settled in the dust, and the skirt of her black cotton dress was lit by the distant lightning seeping through the lace.

"Old man," she said as she approached him. He looked at her fondly, remembered her swearing and snarling at Eden as the garbage dripped from her body. He remembered her spitting blood on the dirt.

Hades knew, the moment he had laid eyes upon the girl, that the same thing that had been twisted and broken away from the souls of Eden and Eric, just before they arrived on his doorstep, was indeed gone in her, too. The light that twinkled in the eyes of most children, even older children Hooky's age, had been extinguished. He didn't know yet if he could turn her off the dark path she was following, if he could somehow stop her progress toward being helplessly evil, the way that Eric had been, the way Eden sometimes was. Maybe there was something of her that could be redeemed. She was smart. She was tough. She didn't have to go bad. Maybe if he tried hard enough, he could save her.

And if he couldn't save her, he'd do the best he could to patch her up. The way he did with everything that came to him in the dump. She'd be crooked. She'd be hollow. But she'd be alive.

Hooky smiled at Hades as she walked toward the house, and he remembered seeing the same sarcastic teenage smile on Eden, many years ago. The smile that breaks through the loneliness, that gives every day new purpose.

The two walked inside. The dog followed.

EPILOGUE

It wasn't so much consciousness but a series of half-formed thoughts that whistled through my drugged brain as I lay in the bed, sometimes seeing, sometimes just watching colors and shapes. The first realization that formed with any real clarity was that I'd lost the sight in my left eye. I'd heard this mentioned a couple of times by people in the room while I slept. I didn't know for certain who was speaking, but I picked up and held little pieces of what they said, repeated them over and over in dreams.

We're seeing some minor brain damage from lack of blood flow to the brain. Nothing that'll hinder him too badly. He's been talking in his sleep. Making sense. But that left optical nerve has died. That's lifelong, that one.

There's nothing we can do to save it?

Two close-range gut shots, and twenty minutes or more to the hospital? This guy had a thirty percent chance at survival. The eye is collateral damage.

My head was turned, and the vision I now had was restricted to half the window beside my bed, the people going past, disembodied chests and shoulders and heads. Nurses in green with gentle faces. Freckles. Big smiles. Imogens, all of them, in their prettiness and simultaneous hardness, women who could care for a dying man, bring him back out of the arms of death.

I realized second that I'd been out a long time. A

good-sized beard prickled against the pillow, felt sore against my temples. Everything ached. Not a powerful or unbearable thing, but the deep ache you know is being held in check by blessed drugs, the kind of pain that will be all-consuming if the drugs so much as waiver, a feeling that makes you sick inside. Helpless.

Some story had been orchestrated about the shooting. I knew this because I had a sense that Eden had been in the room, more than once, while I floated between layers of dream. I'd heard her voice, confident and soft, commanding in the way that only pack leaders can command, with the certainty that they'll be taken seriously. No apologies. No requests. I had the feeling she had sat for some time on the end of the bed, watched me sleep.

Thirty percent chance. She had to have known those were the odds she was playing with. It had to look like she'd meant to kill me. Imogen had to think my survival had been a mistake, that if she didn't run now, Eden would come for me again when she could.

I lay and looked out the windows to the corridor with my one eye, realizing things behind the oxygen mask but not ready for anyone to realize I was awake. Imogen had never been in the room in which I lay. I couldn't remember hearing anyone talk about her as I drifted in and out, fighting for my life. That didn't mean I'd heard everything. Maybe she'd called. I doubted it. If I knew Imogen, I knew she was smart, and if she was smart she was a long way from me right now. If she loved me, she was gone. She'd have left a breakup note, packed her things, and moved to Perth, if she had any sense.

Eden had tried to kill me. And if Eden was willing

to kill me, her own partner, she was willing to go further—to kill everyone Imogen had ever loved and held dear, to make her watch, and then to come for the beautiful psychologist in the night, maybe tomorrow, maybe the next day, maybe a year from now. I was an example. If Imogen was smart, she was already changing her name, and she would never speak of Eden Archer or Morgan Tanner ever again.

No matter how far away she went, Eden would be watching. Imogen would know that.

Imogen was lost to me now, as wholly and completely as if she was dead, the way I was meant to be. She might follow my story in the paper, but she would never contact me or anyone close to me ever again. I saw her poring over newspaper reports in a sunny café in Fremantle, her hair dyed and her shoulders bronzed and those damned freckles standing out everywhere like mud spatter. I hoped that's what she was doing. I hoped she was clever and she stayed alive. I hoped I would never again lay eyes on her.

I would never bring anyone into my life like that again. Hooky had been right to turn Eden away from killing Imogen. She was right when she told the older woman that I wouldn't be able to take it. I owed Hooky so much for that. For protecting me.

I would give my life over to her now, to protect her while she lingered, however long, under the dark wing of that deathly bird she'd chosen to sidle up to. There was no way on earth Hooky knew what she had done. How completely she'd signed her soul away. I would never leave her now. I was locked to the two of them. This was what I had been destined for, from the day I walked into the Parramatta headquarters and Captain

James introduced me to my beautiful new partner. Eden had my soul now, too, and I'd never be free.

As I lay looking, a man came to the desk beyond the window ledge and stood there marking things down, a white-coated man with a thick black beard. I knew him, but I didn't recall from where. I realized who he was when I saw him lift his dark eyes to the clock on the wall behind the desk, almost instinctively, as though an alarm had gone off inside him, as it did every night. It was eight o'clock. Aamir looked at the clock, then went back to his paperwork, his jaw tightened and his brow heavy.

It's Ehan's bedtime, I saw him thinking. *I have to go say good night.*

What felt like years ago, I had told the man I was looking at that there was nothing after the cold, consuming tragedy of murder. That when you lose someone, as I had lost Martina, there was no great revelation, no meaning, no answer. I'd tried to give him realistic expectations of life after his son was lost to him.

I wasn't sure now. When Eden lost her parents, it had been just the beginning to what she was. So much would come after that. Their murders stood forever as the doorway to a life cluttered with darkness and evil and pain. She was the afterward. She was the cleanup crew, the response of nature after the event, that righted the balance of living and dead, of agony matched with agony. She was the seed that cracked free of its shell and grew, despite all odds, after the fire had ripped through the land, destroying everything else.

Eden was my fire. What was growing in me now as I lay in the bed was something so new, something so different, that I could feel its tendrils creeping up my insides, feel its curling sprouts fluttering open in my mind. Those seeds had been there a long time, but it was only the heat of the bullets Eden had put in me, and the child's heart she now held hostage, that had given them what they needed in order to sprout.

I didn't know what I was becoming. But I knew it wasn't good.

In case you missed the first exciting novel in the
ARCHER AND BENNETT *thriller series,*
keep reading to enjoy a preview excerpt from
HADES *by Candice Fox . . .*

As soon as the stranger set the bundle on the floor, Hades could tell it was the body of a child. It was curled on its side and wrapped in a worn blue sheet secured with duct tape around the neck, waist and knees. One tiny pearl-colored foot poked out from the hem, limp on his sticky linoleum. Hades leaned against the counter of his cramped, cluttered kitchen and stared at that little foot. The stranger shifted uneasily in the doorway, drew a cigarette from a packet and pulled out some matches. The man they called Hades lifted his eyes briefly to the stranger's thin angled face.

"Don't smoke in my house."

The stranger had been told how to get to Hades' place but not about its bewildering, frightening character. Beyond the iron gates of the Utulla dump, on the ragged edge of the western suburbs, lay a gravel road leading through mountains of trash to a hill that blocked out the sky, black and imposing, guarded by stars. A crown of trees and scrub on top of the hill obscured all view of the small wooden shack. The stranger had driven with painful care past piles of rubbish as high as apartment buildings crawling with every manner of night creature—owls, cats and rodents picking and sifting through old milk cartons and bags of rotting meat. Luminescent eyes peered from the cabins of burned-out car shells and from beneath sheets of twisted corrugated iron.

Farther along the gravel path, the stranger began to encounter a new breed of watchful beast. Creatures made from warped scraps of metal and pieces of discarded machinery lined the road—a broken washing machine beaten and buckled into the figure of a snarling lion, a series of bicycles woven together and curled and stretched into the body of a grazing flamingo. In the light of the moon, the animals with their kitchen-utensil feathers and Coke-bottle eyes seemed tense and ready. When the stranger entered the house he was a little relieved to be away from them and their attention. The relief evaporated when he laid eyes on the man they called the Lord of the Underworld.

Hades was standing in the corner of the kitchen when the stranger entered, as though he'd known he was coming. He had not moved from there, his furry arms folded over his barrel chest. Cold heavy-lidded eyes fixed on the bundle in the stranger's arms. There was a Walther PP handgun with a silencer on the untidy counter beside him by a half-empty glass of scotch. Hades' grey hair looked neat atop his thick skull. He was squat and bulky like an ox, power and rage barely contained in the painful closeness of the kitchen.

The air inside the little house seemed pressed tight by the trees, a dark dome licking and stroking the hot air through the windows. Hades' kitchen was adorned with things he had salvaged from the dump. Ornate bottles and jars of every conceivable color hung by fishing line from the ceiling; strange cutting and slicing implements were nailed like weapons to the walls. There were china fish and pieces of plastic fruit and a stuffed yellow ferret coiled, sleeping, in a basket by the foot of the door, jars of things there seemed no sense in keeping—colored marbles and lens-less spectacles and bottle caps in their thousands—and lines of dolls' heads along the windowsill, some with eyes and some without, gaping mouths smiling, howling, crying. Through the door to the tiny living room, a wall crammed with tattered paperbacks was visible, the books lying and standing in every position from the unpolished floorboards to the mold-spotted ceiling.

The stranger writhed in the silence. Wanted to look at everything but afraid of what he might see. Night birds moaned in the trees outside the mismatched stained-glass windows.

"Do you, uh . . ." The stranger worked the back of his neck with his fingernails. "Do you want me to go and get the other one?"

Hades said nothing for a long time. His eyes were locked on the body of the child in the worn blue sheet.

"Tell me how this happened."

The stranger felt new sweat tickle at his temples.

"Look," he sighed, "I was told there'd be no questions. I was told I could just come and drop them off and . . ."

"You were told wrong."

One of Hades' chubby fingers tapped his left bicep slowly, as though counting off time. The stranger fingered the cigarette he had failed to light, drawing it to his lips, remembered the warning. He slipped it into his pocket and stared at the bundle on the floor, at the shape of the girl's small head tucked against her chest.

"It was supposed to be the most perfect, perfect thing," the stranger said, shaking his head at the body. "It was all Benny's idea. He saw a newspaper story about this guy, Tenor I think his name was, this crazy scientist dude. He'd just copped a fat wad of cash for something he was working on with skin cancer or sunburn or some shit like that. Benny got obsessed with the guy, kept bringing us newspaper clippings. He showed us a picture of the guy and his *little wife and his two kiddies and said the family was mega-rich already and he was just adding his new cosh to a big stinking pile."*

The stranger drew a long breath that inflated his narrow chest. Hades watched, unmoving.

"We'd got word that the family was going to be alone at their holiday house in Long Jetty. So we drove up there, the six of us, to rattle their cage and take the babies—just for a bit, you know, not for long. It was going to be the easiest job, man. Bust in, bust out, keep them for a couple of days and then organize an exchange. We weren't gonna do nothing with them. I'd even borrowed some games they could play while they stayed with us."

Hades opened one of the drawers beside him and extracted a notepad and pen. From where he stood, he slapped them onto the small table by the side wall.

"These others," he said, "write down their names. And your own."

The stranger began to protest, but Hades was silent. The stranger sat on the plastic chair by the table, his fingers trembling, and began to write names on the paper. His handwriting was childlike and crooked, smeared.

"Everything just went wrong so fast," he murmured as he wrote, holding the paper steady with his long white fingers. "Benny got the idea that the dude was giving him the eye like he was gonna do something stupid. I wasn't paying attention. The woman was screaming and crying and carrying on and someone clocked her and the kids were struggling. Benny blew the parents away. He just . . . he pumped them and pumped them till his gun was flat. He was always so fucking trigger-happy. He was always so fucking ready for a fight."

The stranger seemed stirred by some emotion, letting

air out of his chest slowly through his teeth. He stared at the names he had written on the paper. Hades watched.

"One minute everything was fine. The next thing I know we're on the road with the kids in the trunk and no one to sell them to. We started talking about getting rid of them and someone said they knew you and . . ." The stranger shrugged and wiped his nose on his hand.

For the first time since the stranger had arrived, Hades left the corner of the kitchen. He seemed larger and more menacing somehow, his oversized, calloused hands godly as they cradled the tiny notepad, tearing off the page with the names. The stranger sat, defeated, in the plastic chair. He didn't raise his eyes as Hades folded the small square of paper, slipping it into his pocket. He didn't notice as the older man took up the pistol, cocked it and flicked the safety off.

"It was an accident," the stranger murmured, his bloodshot eyes brimming with tears as he stared, lips parted, at the body in the bundle. "Everything was going so well."

The man named Hades put two bullets into the stranger. The stranger's confused eyes fixed on Hades, his hands grabbing at the holes in his body. Hades put the gun back on the counter and lifted the scotch to his lips. The night birds had stopped their moaning and only the sound of the stranger dying filled the air.

Hades set the glass down with a sigh and began to trace the dump yards around the hill with his mind, searching for the best place for the body of the stranger and, somewhere separate, somewhere fitting, to bury the bodies of the little ones. There was a place he knew behind the sorting center where a tree had sprung up between the piles of garbage—the twisted and gnarled thing some-

times produced little pink flowers. He would bury the children there together and dig the stranger in somewhere, anywhere, with the dozens of rapists, killers and thieves who littered the grounds of the dump. Hades closed his eyes. Too many strangers were coming to his dump these nights with their bundles of lost lives. He would have to put the word out that no new clients were welcome. The ones he knew, his regular clients, brought him the bodies of evil ones. But these strangers. He shook his head. These strangers kept bringing innocents.

Hades set his empty glass on the counter by his gun. His eyes wandered across the cracked floor to the small pearl foot of the dead girl.

It was then that he noticed the toes were clenched.

Connect with U(s)

Visit us online at
KensingtonBooks.com
to read more from your favorite authors, see books
by series, view reading group guides, and more.

Join us on social media

for sneak peeks, chances to win books and prize packs,
and to share your thoughts with other readers.

facebook.com/kensingtonpublishing
twitter.com/kensingtonbooks

Tell us what you think!

To share your thoughts, submit a review,
or sign up for our eNewsletters, please visit:
KensingtonBooks.com/TellUs.